To T...
...

PRIYA'S WORLD

a novel by

Tara Nanayakkara

inanna poetry & fiction series

INANNA PUBLICATIONS AND EDUCATION INC.
TORONTO, CANADA

Sept 15 2012

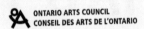

Canada Council   Conseil des Arts
for the Arts   du Canada

ONTARIO ARTS COUNCIL
CONSEIL DES ARTS DE L'ONTARIO

We gratefully acknowledge the support of the Canada Council for the Arts and the Ontario Arts Council for our publishing program.

We are also grateful for the support received from an Anonymous Fund at The Calgary Foundation.

Cover design: Val Fullard
Interior design: Luciana Ricciutelli

Library and Archives Canada Cataloguing in Publication

Nanayakkara, Tara, 1963-
        Priya's world : a novel / Tara Nanayakkara.

(Inanna poetry & fiction series)
Issued also in an electronic format.
ISBN 978-1-926708-64-5

I. Title. II. Series: Inanna poetry and fiction series

PS8577.A56P75 2012   C813'.54   C2012-903117-8

Printed and bound in Canada

Inanna Publications and Education Inc.
210 Founders College, York University
4700 Keele Street, Toronto, Ontario, Canada M3J 1P3
Telephone: (416) 736-5356 Fax: (416) 736-5765
Email: inanna@yorku.ca Website: www.yorku.ca/inanna

In memory of Geri, Ruth, and Bethany,
for being there the first time.

Chapter 1

FRIGHTENED BLUE EYES PEEKED OUT from a navy polar fleece hat, a cozy toddler number with Velcro fastenings. The owner of the hat was a little boy with wispy blonde curls spilling onto a pale forehead.

Priya De Souza, on her way back to the car after an hour of shopping, became conscious of the child trailing her through the mall parking lot only when she heard tentative baby sniffles accompanied by ragged breathing. When she turned to discover who was following so closely behind her own listless steps, she assumed that there was a child accompanied by a frazzled mom or dad. What she didn't expect was to see a child of about three or four unattached to a parental hand nor strapped into a stroller. The little boy was completely alone.

"Mama?" the boy asked plaintively, his eyes squinting at the vast parking lot. There was just a mere scattering of cars, but hardly any people, as it was 11:30 am on a weekday morning. The air felt heavy with impending rain, and the overall grayness of the day seemed a palpable reminder that fall was making way for winter. According to the electronic thermometer flashing from a billboard on the roof of the mall, it was four degrees.

Priya shivered in her black wool pea coat. Even her jeans felt heavy with cold. They were too big now anyway. She made a mental note that next time she went to the mall, she'd buy a new pair in a smaller size.

Priya looked down at the small child who barely came up to her knee. His trusting blue eyes were almost painful to observe.

"Little boy," she said tentatively. "Where's your Mama?"

The child took a long look at the woman standing in front of him and suddenly realized that she was not his mother. Thoroughly confused, he responded to the question by popping a mittened thumb into his mouth and peering at his black rain boots.

Priya had to think fast, as she had no idea how long he had been trailing her. She felt such intense compassion for him that she would have gladly picked him up and cuddled him against her coat just to keep him safe and warm, if only for a brief moment. However, she didn't dare do that, as his parents and/ or the mall authorities were bound to misinterpret her actions.

Her mind raced through her years of training to become a kindergarten teacher. She dropped to her knees so she was speaking at his level, and smiled warmly to reassure him.

"Where's your Mama?" she asked again.

He withdrew the thumb from his mouth and pointed toward the mall. "Mama's there...." He looked as though he was about to burst into tears.

"Okay, little one, don't be scared. We'll find your Mama," Priya said in her best teacher-in-training voice.

She thought she would bring him back to the Walmart, where she'd just purchased 20-lb bond paper for her next mass mailing of résumés, and turn the child over to security. Priya glanced around the parking lot hoping that his parents would appear and claim their son; but it didn't seem likely; the only people she spotted were a pair of elderly women standing next to a minivan debating where they should go for brunch.

Even though he was parked beside her late mother's green Corolla, Priya was oblivious to the middle-aged man sitting inside a metallic gray Honda, sipping coffee and unwrapping his newly purchased CD, *Irish Piano*. Priya was so preoccupied with her own predicament that she had no idea that the man had been observing her every move since she'd exited the mall.

Side-stepping the parked cars, Priya was challenged not only by a toddler weighed down by a cumbersome blue snowsuit, but also by her own encroaching weakness. She hadn't been feeling well since early that morning. It was a mistake coming out to the mall today. She should have stayed home and relaxed, but then impulse took over and here she was. She reached for the little boy's mittened hand and, trustingly, he allowed her to guide him back to the mall.

In order to keep panic at bay, she focused on the toddler's hat. It made her feel old. Priya's own childhood spanned the latter part of the seventies and early eighties. Back then it would never have occurred to anyone that a child could be strangled on the monkey bars if their hood strings got entangled in the steel structure. Parents were aware, of course, of safety issues, but now it seemed as if everyone had become paranoid about everything from hood strings to peanut butter to exercising discipline. At times it made her second guess her decision to become a kindergarten teacher. The rules were different now. When she was in school, granted it was a strict, no-nonsense Christian academy complete with green and gray checked uniforms and Bible classes, her teachers had first rights on discipline.

A cutting breeze jolted Priya back into the moment. She gripped the boy's hand more firmly as they approached the crosswalk. Another blustery gust pushed against her slim frame and the child's small body. For a moment, she felt it would take them away. Though pale and sylph-like, Priya harboured an almost obsessive smugness about her own dwindling build. She wore her size two jeans with quiet pride. She was becoming thinner and it suited her. Everyone regarded her with envy. In a world that was increasing in girth, with its supersized fries and plus-sized dresses, *she*, Priya Naomi De Souza, was bucking the trend. It was no issue to her that her hands were always cold, even in her parents' centrally heated townhouse. It didn't faze her that she needed two extra blankets when she slept at night. It was November in Ontario.

Renita, her father's older sister, who had joined them in Canada just over a year ago, was always remarking that Priya had lost a bit too much weight. Formerly, at 110 pounds, her slight, five-foot-one frame had been comfortably filled out, not heavy, not too lean. Just right, she used to think. But a deepening pre-occupation with her body, together with the grief of losing both parents at the same time, gave way to her dropping not a mere five, or even ten pounds, but fifteen and then twenty. Dr. Benson, her benevolent family doctor, declared that she was on the verge of full-blown anorexia nervosa. Priya almost laughed at the diagnosis. She'd whittled down her weight through sheer willpower. Undeniably, she'd taken some pills and supplements but she hadn't gone anywhere near Ephedra once the reports came out about it being potentially harmful if consumed in excess. She hated jogging, but she was the daughter of a track coach, so she used that knowledge as a reminder that if her father could tolerate running, so could she. Besides, running kept her in tune with her father's spirit after his death. It was almost as if he were right there with her on the track, urging her on, pushing her toward the finish line. It didn't matter that the only competition she had was with herself. And that was more important than anything. It was so simple. Why didn't people understand?

She was brought back to the present when the little boy yanked her toward the plate glass doors. Several people were filing out of the store, some with strollers, others empty-handed, a few with carts bursting with bagged merchandise.

Priya welcomed the embrace of warm air as she guided the child into the foyer. "Let's find the security people." She paused to catch her breath, feeling lightheaded for a moment. She assumed it was the rush of warm air generated by an overhead heating vent that was responsible. Once she found the child's parents, she would sit for a minute and rest. She realized she was hungry. Her last meal had been close to midnight yesterday, half of a chocolate peanut butter energy bar and four ounces of skim milk. After she'd finished eating, she'd been tempted to put on her jogging pants and beat the track outside her townhouse complex, but she managed to restrain herself. Renita was watching television in the living room. She'd drift out to the kitchen for her own snack and pester Priya about why she wanted to jog so late at night. At twenty-five, Priya knew she didn't have to justify herself to an aunt she didn't know so well, but her South Asian background demanded that she show respect for her elders. It was what her father had demanded from her.

"You might be growing up in the west, and you might have a Canadian mother," he'd thunder in his Sinhala-accented English, "but look here, you are part Sri Lankan and you will follow the values of respect and decorum as decreed by our culture and as a good Christian."

"Don't get so worked up, my son," Delaney, Priya's easy-going mother, would respond with her equally accented Newfoundland English. "It's natural to question authority. We all did it." She'd pass her husband a stern look that conveyed he'd said enough.

Priya's father, Jay De Souza, might have respected his elders, but he defied them as well. He ran away to Canada with her mother, Delaney, after they'd met in Sri Lanka. In the mid-seventies, Delaney had travelled to the country's capital, Colombo, for a three-month stint of teaching English to underprivileged children. The couple met at a beach party organized between the school where Delaney taught and the church youth group where Jay was a volunteer leader. They were immediately smitten and were married in a quiet civil ceremony within three weeks.

Delaney returned to Canada and sponsored Jay as her husband. Young and brash, their actions were a carryover from the sixties — an era Priya wished she could claim as her own. This longing to be a part of a different time and place might explain why she related more to people two or three decades older than she was. As a child of mixed heritage, Priya was still trying to figure out where she belonged.

"Code Yellow, Code Yellow," a female voice boomed over the loudspeaker. "A three-year-old boy named Zacharey Norris is missing. He has blonde hair and blue eyes, and is dressed in a blue snowsuit. His mother, Marie Norris, is waiting at the Customer Service desk."

Priya, still clutching the little boy's hand, wasted no time in rushing toward the line of cash registers, her eyes roaming ahead in search of the familiar gray customer service desk. The boy looked up at Priya with panic-stricken eyes and began to wail. Hurrying forward, she ran smack into a blue-vested Walmart employee, a middle-aged woman with graying hair stuffed into an unruly bun at the base of her neck. Her nametag indicated that she was Bev.

"Excuse me," Priya was almost hyperventilating with anxiety. "This is the little boy you're looking for."

Before the flabbergasted Bev could respond, a woman, possibly in her early twenties with long dark hair and a black wool coat almost identical to Priya's, came rushing at them. She was like an angry gale rising up from the North Atlantic bearing an untapped rage. The torrent of words and accusations she spewed at Priya was enough to put her at a category-5 hurricane status. The woman snatched the now hysterical boy from the ground and held him against her chest. "What are you doing with my child? Were you trying to kidnap him?" The level of her hysteria was enough to bring the store to a virtual standstill. Customers and employees stopped what they were doing in mid-transaction to stare.

So this was Marie Norris, the irate mother. Priya struggled to bite back her own rage at being accused and judged so unfairly. She faced the woman, her eyes flashing steel. All signs of physical weakness had vanished. Taking a deep breath, she called upon all her resources to remain as calm as possible. "You don't know what you're talking about. Your son followed me out to my car. What were *you* doing while he wandered away?" She spoke through clenched teeth.

A man wearing a yellow and black jacket with the words Mall Security splashed ominously across his chest approached her. "Ma'am, if you'll just tell us how you discovered the boy..."

"Excuse me folks," a soft male voice intoned.

Priya turned around to find a tall man standing behind her. He looked to be in his early forties. Topping the charts at well over six feet, he was lean, well-built, and dressed in a dark brown fall jacket and beige pants. He had light brown hair just starting to gray. He held a light green hat in his right hand. "Excuse me. Perhaps I can help. I know for a fact that this little boy followed the young lady into the parking lot. I was sitting in my car, unwrapping a CD and drinking a coffee, when I saw the boy wander out of the store. Someone — we won't point fingers — must have let him out of her sight. I think the little guy mistook this young lady," he touched Priya's shoulder, "for his mom because the two women are wearing similar coats, are of roughly the same height, and both have long dark hair. I think," he glared at the flustered mother who was still clasping her wailing, fidgeting son to her chest, and then spoke in a gentle but commanding tone. "Perhaps you might not only thank this young woman for bringing your child back to safety, but you could apologize for shouting at her."

His audience was spellbound. Who was this man with the distinctive Newfoundland accent that sounded just like Delaney's? Priya was intrigued, and grateful.

"I have nothing to apologize for," red-faced Marie stepped back. "My son, Zach, managed to unbuckle his stroller and get out while I was at the prescription counter getting his asthma medication. I panicked all right."

"You could apologize for accusing me of stealing your son." Priya, somewhat empowered by the tall man at her side, no longer felt the need to show her indignation.

"Oh *please*," Marie scoffed. "You turn your back for a nanosecond and your kid is gone and the next thing you know, some girl…"

"Interestingly enough," the tall stranger winked at Priya, "if you weren't wearing that coat right now, you'd probably accuse this lady of stealing that along with your child."

"Oh, man," Priya blushed as she stared down at her black Aerosoles. Enough was enough. The stranger had made his point. She wanted to forget the whole episode and vanish. Who could have ever imagined a jaunt to the mall to buy résumé paper would end in such high drama? And who was this handsome stranger who had come to her rescue?

"Whatever," Marie glared at the stranger, murmured something unintelligible to the security guard, and stalked off with her sniffling son, presumably to locate his stroller.

Bev, the Walmart employee who'd been silent all this time, now approached Priya with an apologetic smile. "I'm really sorry you had to go through that . Can I treat you to a coffee and muffin at McDonald's."

"That's not necessary," Priya said quickly as the security guard, realizing that his presence was no longer necessary, retreated into the background.

"I think it certainly is necessary," the tall stranger folded his arms across his chest. It was apparent he wasn't going anywhere.

"Excuse me?' Priya stared at him, wondering if he were a store detective.

"Now where are *my* manners?" the stranger chuckled self-consciously. "Gabe Johansen is my name. And you are?"

"Priya De Souza," she said.

"De Souza ... that name sounds so familiar. Years ago, growing up in Newfoundland, I went to school with a girl who later married a De Souza. If I recall, he was a Sri Lankan, and judging from your complexion, you're of mixed parentage, am I right?"

For a fleeting moment, Priya forgot her physical angst and became excited. "My mother, Delaney Saunders, was from St. John's. She married my father, Jay De Souza, in 1977."

"Wow!" Gabe's eyes lit up. "This is unbelievable. Would you mind if I treated you to that coffee and muffin? This has to be more than a mere coincidence."

Bev was about to protest but her name was called over the loudspeaker. She was needed in the shoe department for a price check. Apologizing profusely, she gestured toward the restaurant at the opposite end of the Walmart. "I will leave you in this gentleman's capable hands."

Priya, thrilled that this stranger might have had a connection with her late mother, readily agreed to be treated to coffee and a muffin. Yet once she was seated at a table with the taunting aroma of burgers and fries titillating her nostrils, she began to panic. Although it was well past noon, she hadn't eaten anything that morning. She was ravenous and would have given anything to eat even a small burger, but she knew she wouldn't.

"What kind of muffin would you like?" Gabe asked.

"Uh ... uh apple cinnamon..." Priya stammered. "And I take my coffee with one sweetener and one cream. Let me get some change out of my purse."

"I'll take care of it," Gabe said with a warm smile. "I'll be right back."

Priya waited politely while Gabe went to line up for the order. Yet when she caught sight of a muffin pictured on a poster, her heart started racing. That muffin was pretty big. According to her trusty old calorie counter, purchased shortly after her parents' deaths, it probably housed at least 400 calories. How could she discreetly go about appearing to eat it while not really doing so? Perhaps she could cut it in two, bag one half for later, and the other ... she thought frantically, she'd section it into tiny pieces and make it appear like crumbs. Nobody would think the less of her for leaving crumbs on her plate. She would take a few obligatory mouthfuls and sip her coffee slowly.

Even before Gabe returned with the food, the waves of light-headedness came with such unexpected force, Priya found herself lurching forward. The room was spinning before her eyes and growing steadily dimmer until ultimately her surroundings went dark, as if the power had come to a grinding halt. She collapsed in her seat, the table preventing what might have otherwise been a nasty tumble to the floor.

Chapter 2

PRIYA BLINKED IN CONSTERNATION. She had no idea what all the fuss was about. So she fainted. Strangers were hovering over her. There was talk of calling 911. Someone offered her water. Warm-cheeked with embarrassment, she struggled to pull herself back into a dignified posture.

"I'm fine, really," she insisted. Yet her voice was weak. She slouched into her chair and closed her eyes wondering if this day would ever end.

"Indeed you're not fine," her new friend and self-appointed bodyguard Gabe Johansen stated in a business-like manner. "I've snared rabbits with more strength than you."

Gradually the handful of people who'd clustered around their table began to disperse until eventually it was just Gabe and, Priya was startled to discover, the woman who'd accused her of taking her son. The little boy was soundly asleep in his stroller. It was hard to imagine that he'd been screaming less than ten minutes ago.

Seemingly contrite, Marie Norris leaned closer to Priya. "I was on my way in to get a soft drink and ... I saw ... I've got my cell phone. Want me to call anyone for you?" She regarded Priya with apparent concern.

"Oh, man," Priya buried her head in her hands. This woman felt responsible for Priya fainting. It *was* possible, but then again, fatigue and lack of food was, Priya knew, the more likely reason.

"I have a cell phone..." Priya began but stopped abruptly when she remembered that her phone was at home charging. "You know what, I'm fine."

With a nod of relief, Marie turned the stroller around and went on her way.

Determined to prove she was fine, Priya tried to stand but felt wobbly and had to sit back down again.

"You drove here in a green Corolla," Gabe, sounding very much like a detective, fired at her.

"How observant," she murmured, wondering why he had his eye on her at all. What did he really want from her?

Gabe, noting Priya's encroaching wariness, responded reassuringly. "I'm an observant kind of guy," he said lightly. "I don't think you're fit to drive anywhere. Is there a friend or relative we can call to take you to the hospital?"

"I have no intention of going to a hospital." Priya's voice was firm. She was not about to be ordered about by a man she'd known for less than half an hour. But her painfully undernourished physique told the real story. She knew she was in an extremely vulnerable position and needed whatever help she could get.

"I know your mother, remember," he said. "Is there anybody we could call — perhaps a sibling, friend or co-worker?"

"I would have called my mother, but that's impossible now as she's dead," Priya said. Her eyes rested on the tempting muffin that Gabe had placed before her. With trembling fingers, she broke it in half and then into quarters and finally eighths. This was a tricky as the muffin was warm and crumbly. Nevertheless, she managed with the deft know-how of someone comfortable with food preparation. She picked up a tiny piece of the muffin and placed it on the tip of her tongue. The cinnamon and apple tasted like home. If only eating the entire muffin would bring back her mother. Delaney had been an excellent baker. Her loaves of bread, butter tarts, and brownies alone would have put a competing bakery out of business. No wonder Priya had bulked up. If her mother hadn't died, she would still be cooking and Priya would still be eating and the pounds would keep piling on and then where would she be? "My parents died six months ago in a plane crash. I'm still dealing with it."

I'm so sorry," Gabe laid his green cap on the table and poured his large frame quietly into a chair at the opposite side of the table.

Priya barely heard him. She was off in her own world, trying to determine if she could eat another small piece of the muffin, or if she would have to pay for it on the track later in the day.

"Priya?" Gabe said her name gently. "I'd love to talk to you about your mother, but right now the goal is to get you medical attention. Do you have any relatives I can call?"

Priya pushed the balance of the muffin away. She didn't think she'd have the energy to hit the track after all. She'd sip the coffee and hope that would do for at least twelve hours. Perhaps at bedtime she could have half a cup of skim milk and another piece of that energy bar.

"I have grandparents in Newfoundland..."

"Ralph and Daisy Saunders," Gabe's blue eyes lit up with relief. "They're still alive. Thank God for you."

"They're amazing people," Priya conceded, feeling the warmth of the coffee spread throughout her body. "They were here last Christmas. It would have been our turn to fly to St. John's this year but ... anyway..."

"Do you have anyone here in Mississauga?" Gabe pressed.

"Auntie Renita, my dad's sister. There's always Serena, my mom's friend, and then there's my friend Rachel.... Maybe Serena would be the best person to call."

"Give me the number and it's done," Gabe reached into his coat pocket for a sleek, platinum-coloured cell phone and waited expectantly for Priya to furnish him with the number.

Serena Sanchez was a striking woman in her late forties. Her golden complexion and curly brown hair hinted at a fusion of races that included black, East Indian, and Portuguese. Her accent suggested a blend of South American and Caribbean that gave her a unique patois that people enjoyed hearing.

An ill-fated marriage to her former boss, Rick Diablo, brought her to Canada in 1979, a year after the Jonestown massacre. Rick had been a corporate lawyer in their native Guyana. His brains and talents won him a job in Canada. He married Serena, his secretary, just before they immigrated. Serena assumed that Rick was merely a social drinker. She didn't realize that unforeseen stress was capable of bringing out the worst of his weaknesses. Within six months of their arrival, Serena discovered that Rick was seeing a woman in the mailroom at the government office where a friend had secured employment for him.

As a new immigrant, Serena worked as a nanny while taking night courses toward certification in elder care. She had lost all interest in her former occupation of legal secretary and felt she'd be better fulfilled in a caregiving capacity. To supplement her income, she put in four hours every Saturday as a cocktail waitress at a downtown nightclub.

Despite the fact that English was Serena's first language, she enrolled in an ESL program in hopes of westernizing her accent for the job market. The class was held at the community college where she was studying to become a caregiver for the elderly. From day one, she felt a special chemistry with the warm-hearted instructor, Delaney De Souza, who was close to her in age. Their friendship developed over a series of after-class coffees at the Tim Hortons across the street from the college. Serena learned that Delaney, a Newfoundlander, was married to a Sri Lankan and that they had one child, a daughter named Priya.

Delaney, a motherly type, took Serena under her wing and nurtured her. Both women had a positive spin on life, yet were an unlikely match. Delaney was short and plump. She wore her light brown hair in a haphazard bun at the top of her head. She dressed in comfortable slacks and stretchy blouses that were often a little unkind to her ample body type. But Delaney had an open face that conveyed her sense of joy and gratitude for life.

Serena was a quieter sort who dressed well despite her economic struggles. After she left Rick, she discovered that there was no way she could afford Toronto rent, and she took up

Delaney's suggestion of looking for a place in the west end of Mississauga, close to Delaney's home. That way Delaney would be able to pick her up as she drove into downtown Toronto for her classes. However, the move to Mississauga meant she had to drop the job at the nightclub since late-night public transportation back to her Mississauga apartment would not be safe. She also had to give up her position as a nanny to the three-year-old boy she'd cared for, for nearly a year.

Serena eventually found work close to her new home as an office temp. She became a regular Sunday guest at Delaney's traditional Newfoundland-style "Jiggs dinner." Serena would occasionally bring a taste of Guyana into that kitchen and make goat curry to be eaten with dhal puri, a staple of her childhood.

Delaney admired Serena's sense of fashion. She could transform a discount store top and skirt into a stylish evening piece. "Consider yourself lucky that you are slim," Jay would laugh, casting a somewhat disparaging glance at his wife's plump figure. "It keeps you healthy, not like my girls"; he'd thump Delaney playfully on the backside while his mortified only daughter looked on self-consciously sucking in her own tummy. Even at eight or nine, Priya understood that, at least in her father's eyes, thin was desirable.

Serena would steam within herself over the continuous ridicule that Delaney tolerated. She vowed she would never be involved with a man again. "Girl," she told Delaney and Priya as recently as last Christmas, "I've taken enough garbage from one man to last me a lifetime. Since I will never find one that is good enough for me, I am imposing an indefinite moratorium on dating."

Serena's pronouncements never failed to draw amused smiles from Delaney and Priya. Jay would hover in the background, his lip curled with disapproval. He didn't have much use for Serena and made his views freely known to his wife. Yet he was polite to Serena when she came to visit and he allowed Delaney to convert his home office with the paisley futon into a guestroom whenever Serena spent the night.

Serena suspected that one of the reasons she and Delaney had become so close was because her friend was looking for a harmless escape from the doldrums of her own marriage. Delaney's cheerful disposition couldn't always hide a look of fleeting sadness that entered her eyes when she thought no one was looking. Cultural differences were there. Delaney, in the name of being agreeable, acquiesced to Jay's whims and allowed his Sri Lankan heritage to dominate the way Priya was raised. Jay didn't mind the Newfoundland cooking on Sundays. In fact, he rather liked it; but rice and curry was a staple, and Priya was to be brought up in a conservative manner.

The idea that Delaney even agreed to go on that flight with Jay was not really surprising as she would have done anything to please him. The pilot was a bit of an amateur — a friend of Jay's who had taken up flying as a weekend interest. It was a small twin-engine Cessna. A Sunday afternoon tour above Lake Ontario and the Toronto skyline ended in tragedy, leaving Priya without her parents and Serena without her best friend.

Delaney's death had brought them closer. Serena managed to keep a watchful eye on Priya, whose only remaining relative in Toronto was Jay's sister, Renita, a morose woman in her late sixties. They lived in the townhouse where the family had been residing for the past five years. Serena could see that Priya was under a lot of strain since her parents' deaths, and that she now felt responsible for her aunt. Priya hadn't allowed herself to cry — not even once. Serena couldn't understand that, but she respected Priya's manner of grieving. Now she was worried though that Priya's grief was compromising her health. Priya had lost too much weight in the months since they died.

After years of struggle and sacrifice, Serena finally had the job of her dreams. She was the personal night attendant for Ms. O'Leary, a wealthy seventy-five-year-old widow who'd been felled by a stroke five years earlier. She relied on a wheelchair and round-the-clock assistance in order to maintain her independence in her own home. Serena worked from 10:00 pm to 8:00 am four nights a week. Not a morning person by nature,

Serena had jumped at the chance to work nights and be off during the day. Priya was aware of her schedule. It was for this reason she'd asked Gabe to call her.

Serena's one bedroom unit was a comfortable place. The landlord had decorated it in red and white. This suited Serena just fine as she loved bright colours. Outwardly she was soft spoken and unassuming but inwardly she was as flamboyant as a flamenco dancer. She was luxuriating under the white duvet her cousins had given her last Christmas when the call came shortly after noon. Snug as a baby bird in its nest, she'd been more than content to listen to the rain and plan her weekend's activities and errands. She needed to get at the grout in the bathroom, and if she wasn't too tired afterward, she'd catch a flick at the Rainbow Cinema at the mall. Serena was good at being single. She could be alone and not feel lonely, most of the time.

She fumbled for the red flip phone on the oak bedside table and blinked in surprise when she heard a man's voice. Assuming a telemarketer was on the line, Serena silently cursed herself for not allowing the answering machine to do its job.

"Serena Sanchez?" The man spoke with an accent that Serena could have sworn was very similar to Delaney's.

"Yes," she said, fully alert now. "Who, may I ask, is speaking?"

"You don't know me," the man said politely, "Gabe Johansen is my name. I grew up with Delaney Saunders, who I believe was a good friend of yours."

"Oh, yes," Serena fully alert now felt her heart racing. Was this a relative of Delaney's come to Toronto? She couldn't place the name Gabe Johansen. That was strange since Delaney had shared so much about her friends and lifestyle in Newfoundland that Serena almost felt as if she knew everyone there.

"I'm at a Walmart in Meadowvale with Delaney's daughter, Priya. Now, I don't mean to alarm you, but she collapsed while shopping here. She wouldn't let us call an ambulance..."

"Here, Mr. Gabe," she said calmly, "I live just a short bus ride from that Walmart. Tell Priya I will get there as fast as I can."

"Meet us in the McDonald's," Gabe said, and then shut the phone. "Serena's coming," he added, smiling gently at Priya.

Priya was glad she'd told Gabe to call Serena to pick her up. "You don't need to wait around with me," Priya said politely. "I'm sure you have better things to do."

"I don't think so," Gabe removed his jacket and arranged it on the back of his chair as if he planned to stay awhile. He was wearing a navy wool sweater with an intricate pattern stencilled across the chest. It suited him. Priya tried not to stare. "At this moment, I am a free agent and I would very much like to get to know you. Your mom and I were good friends, remember?"

Priya gave him a self-deprecating smile. "I am a kindergarten teacher without a classroom. I graduated this May but my parents weren't alive to witness the ceremony ... anyway, such is life."

"I'm sorry," Gabe said again, his eyes sympathetic.

But Priya didn't want him to feel sorry for her, nor did she want to keep talking about herself. "Now that I've had something to eat, I'm feeling better," she said. "Let's trade memories about my mother. It will make me feel as if she is with us."

"I'll get us another round of coffee so they don't boot us out of here for taking up space," Gabe said, pushing his chair back.

"I'm fine, thanks," Priya said.

She watched as the tall man made his way back to the counter. The line-up was considerably shorter than before, as the lunch crowd had dissipated. She fidgeted with the two-tone silver and gold metal watchband that could never settle in one place on her wrist. It was loose enough to slide off. Maybe she should have the jeweller take out more links, she thought.

"Tell me about the plane crash," Gabe was back at the table. The aroma of the coffee had a comforting effect on Priya's frayed nerves.

"My Dad, Jay ... did you ever meet him?" she inquired.

"No, never," Gabe shook his head. "By the time your father

came on the scene, Delaney and I had long since lost contact."

Priya grabbed a serviette and began twisting it within tense fingers. "Ma was an ESL teacher. Dad had a Sri Lankan friend he met at church. Ashok Ratnam was a hobby pilot. He was a medical doctor back in Sri Lanka but here he worked as a ticket agent for one of the airlines while waiting for his professional qualifications to be assessed. Ashok had always dreamt of being a pilot, but his parents' expectations and his own sense of practicality saw him go into medicine instead. Here he welcomed the opportunity to take flying lessons, with the view to one day owning his own small aircraft so he could fly for pleasure. He was a quick student and passed his flying exams. When he was finally able to fly with passengers, he asked my parents to join him. What Ashok didn't know was that the small aircraft he was using had undetected mechanical problems..." Priya's voice broke. She looked away.

"Oh my," Gabe reached for her hand. "I read something in the papers about it. I was in St. John's at that time ... but that's another story. Please, go on."

"Anyway," she composed herself quickly. "They went down within the first fifteen minutes. The plane burst into flames. Ashok died too.

"It happened on April 30th of this year," she continued softly. "Two weeks after my twenty-fifth birthday."

"And you're on your own now?"

"I wish I were," Priya shuddered. "Six months before they died, Dad sponsored his sister Renita. She has been depressed since the day she landed in Canada. I don't even know why she left Sri Lanka. She had no use for Ma, barely tolerates me, though she doted on Dad."

"He sponsored her so he'd have someone to dote on him?" Gabe resorted to humour. Priya's loss, so fresh, so raw, combined with her aching thinness, was getting to him. Gabe already knew that Priya's wan face, the heavy black hair hoisted into a curly ponytail, and her pensive dark eyes would remain with him long after this afternoon became a distant memory.

"That might as well have been the case," Priya shrugged. "Dad loved to have women dote on him. He's from the school of thought that says women were created to cook, clean, and serve their men."

"Nice school. Is it too late to enrol?" Gabe grinned.

"Dad is typical of his culture," Priya fell into the present tense, as if her parents were still alive. "Anyway, Auntie Renita is much older than he is and once their parents died, Dad worried about her managing alone. And with the recurring political problems in Sri Lanka, he wanted her here. Compassionate grounds, whatever. She used to tell Ma what a wonderful cook she was and how she longed to visit Newfoundland one day. Once I overheard a phone call to one of her Sri Lankan church friends. I was at the kitchen table, reviewing a term paper, and Auntie Renita was in the next room with the cordless phone. 'Oh, that Delaney gets on my nerves. Pretending to be cheerful. And her cooking! Far too greasy and heavy. No wonder she is the size that she is. If not for Jay, I'd run back to Sri Lanka in a flash.'" Priya paused for breath, her eyes flashing fire. "To top it off, she refused to pronounce Ma's name correctly. Instead of saying De-lay-ney, she turned it into Di-lah-ni, which is a Sri Lankan name."

"Sounds like your mother put up with a lot," Gabe said, encouraging her to go on.

"Ma was a saint," Priya said. "She could get on with just about anyone. Even though she knew that Auntie didn't like her, she went out of her way to keep her happy, and you know what Gabe? I don't think Auntie appreciates it to this day. She still has nothing good to say about my mother."

"Well, that's her problem," Gabe's tone was suddenly distant, as if his thoughts had drifted.

Priya wondered if she was boring him. She had to admit that she was taken with him, and very curious about how he knew her mother. If he and Delaney were just childhood friends who'd obviously lost touch a long time ago, why would he be so interested in her family's dynamics? Whoever he was, it was strange that her mother had never mentioned him. Someone so attractive. "Sorry, I was just venting," Priya blushed, realizing that she had been staring at him intently.

But Gabe didn't hear her. His mind was so far away that he wasn't even aware that Serena was standing beside their table, preceded by the scent of Delaney's favourite perfume.

Chapter 3

SERENA GAVE PRIYA A BRIEF HUG and stepped back to take a critical look at the younger woman. She was disturbed over her weight loss and suspected that Priya couldn't be more than ninety pounds, if that. "Oh shells," she sighed. "I leave you alone for a couple of weeks and what do you do to yourself?"

This was the first time they'd seen each other since October. They'd had Thanksgiving dinner with Priya's friend, Rachel, at a restaurant in downtown Toronto. Even then Serena had been concerned about Priya's weight, but she'd looked healthy compared to how she appeared now.

"I have no answer to that," Priya inhaled the delicate scent of Serena's perfume —"Happy." It was Delaney's favourite fragrance. Priya had bought it for her last Christmas, after Serena expressed a liking for it.

"But," Priya continued, "I can introduce you to Gabe Johansen."

Gabe had emerged from his trance-like state and got to his feet. Serena was striking, smartly dressed in gray slacks and a maroon jacket that complimented her olive skin. "Pleased to meet you," he extended a hand to Serena who beamed a warm smile in his direction. "I believe your young friend needs to see a doctor but she won't listen to me."

"Well, that's tough because that's precisely what she's going to do," Serena spoke in a crisp no-nonsense tone. "Priya, honey, give me your keys. I'll drive you to Dr. Benson's walk-in clinic."

Priya knew it was pointless to argue with her. She quietly slipped her hand into the hip pocket of her jeans and extracted a set of keys from a jumble of gum wrappers and disentangled a green penlight that was on the same brass ring as the house and car keys.

"Thank you, dear," Serena jangled the keys with authoritative flair and looked Gabe in the eye. "I don't have a car but I do keep my license up."

"I see," Gabe was quietly impressed with this feisty lady. He knew she would be firm with Priya. He reached into his coat pocket for a scrap of paper and a pen. "Priya, please give me your phone number, so I can call you later to find out how you made out with the doctor."

Priya, although not in the habit of handing out her phone number to the first man that asked, readily agreed. She sensed that Gabe was a different sort all together. Besides, she quietly reasoned, he'd known her mother. She buttoned up her coat while relaying the number to him.

"Come girl, you don't look too bright. Let's go." Serena advised.

Priya was about to pick up her handbag and the resume paper but instead turned back to Gabe and impulsively threw her arms around his waist. "Thank you for looking out for me. That was an incredible thing to do."

"It's what anyone should do under the circumstances," he assured her. "I'll call you later. Take care."

He watched as the two women left the restaurant and headed toward the parking lot. As their retreating figures disappeared through the plate glass doors, he wondered when he'd get to chat with Priya again. He had a lot to talk to her about — but only when the time was right.

Dr. Mark Benson was a kindly middle-aged man from small-town Ontario. Cheerful and unassuming by nature, he favoured simple clothes and usually kept his white coat out of sight. His thinning blonde hair was turning gray, and he was starting to grow just a little thick around the middle. An avid sportsman, he ran competitively, skied in the winter, and went white-water rafting in the heat of the summer. He divided his time between a walk-in clinic at a mall and a Mississauga hospital where he had admitting privileges.

Dr. Benson met the De Souza family through Delaney when she became pregnant with Priya. He was close to the family, partly because Delaney's pregnancy was high-risk. She had suffered two miscarriages before Priya was conceived.

Priya was one of those special patients he'd watched grow from a plump, giggly infant into a bright but severely stressed-out young woman. Priya had been an occasional visitor to his office before Jay and Delaney died. She'd drop by for the routine gynecological concerns of women her age and for prescriptions for the occasional stubborn sore throat that never went away entirely on its own. Drastic changes in the weather from one day to the next and an ever-present coating of smog over the city were the usual culprits.

When Dr. Benson had seen Priya at her parents' funeral and then later that same week for grief counselling, she appeared physically healthy. Her small frame and delicate bone structure could allow her to be just a few pounds lighter if she so desired, but anything more would not be advisable. At that time, when Priya expressed a mild dissatisfaction with her appearance, he'd told her that if she felt she had to lose five pounds, he could accept it. However, further weight loss would be discouraged.

A few days later, Dr. Benson set up appointments on a bi-monthly basis for grief counselling. When her weight fell below 98 pounds, he confronted her about a possible eating disorder and asked her when she hoped to stop losing weight.

"Whenever," was her careless reply.

On this rainy Thursday afternoon, Priya huddled on the examining table of the small white office, which was softened by peach curtains and a swivel stool of the same colour. A walnut desk and two matching chairs suggested that the décor was functional but not unattractive.

Priya wrapped bony arms around herself and tucked her feet under her to retain as much warmth as possible. She focused her gaze on a poster featuring a baby in utero with long medical terms scripted over its anatomical parts. Priya wondered if she'd ever travel the path to motherhood. She knew she'd have to deal with the inevitable weight gain of pregnancy, but at this juncture in her life that seemed an impossibility.

Dr. Benson replaced the blood pressure cuff in a holder that was attached to the wall behind Priya's head.

"What's my pressure?" she asked as she slid off the table. Her bare feet trembled from the icy tile beneath them.

"It's 97/56," he responded as he moved towards the door. "A bit low, even for someone with your build. I'll be back in a moment."

Priya sensed that the doctor who was normally so warm toward her now seemed aloof. It was almost as if he was disappointed in her. This in turn disappointed *her*, as she'd nursed a mild schoolgirl crush on Dr. Benson since her late teens. She admired him and wanted to be the ultimate patient in his eyes. She figured she was a little special to him because he always managed to surreptitiously shuffle his patients to accommodate her. Ruby, Dr. Benson's secretary, was very clever at creating "cancellations" at the most opportune moments, especially after Delaney died. Every Christmas, Delaney had quietly slipped a plastic container of baked goodies over the reception desk into Ruby's eager hands. Oven fresh shortbread, brownies, and butter tarts were passed around the office, and Delaney was star for a day.

Weak with hunger and trying to ignore the persistent growling in her stomach, Priya caught a glimpse of herself in a gilt-framed mirror that was beside the poster of the baby in utero. She thought her olive-green sweater made her look bulky and large. The bagginess of the jeans seemed to magnify the girth of her legs.

"Gross," she muttered under her breath.

"Hello," there was a gentle knock on the door. "Can you join me in my office?" Dr. Benson asked.

"Sure," flushed with embarrassment, Priya hurried over to

the chair on which she had draped her black coat, pulled it around her shoulders and followed Dr. Benson into his office at the end of the hallway.

Dr. Benson sat at his paper-strewn desk across from her. Dressed in black slacks and a gray cotton shirt, he looked casual enough to pass as a counsellor, but his manner was that of a top-flight physician who cared about the well-being of his patients. "Didn't we agree that you should stop losing weight after you hit 105 pounds?" Dr. Benson kept his tone even, nonjudgmental.

Priya regarded him with silence.

"Last month you were 98 pounds and now you're down to 90. What's going on?"

"I eat," Priya entwined her fingers on her lap, "but let me tell you, it's no fun cooking for just one."

"Your aunt is living with you," Dr. Benson reminded. "Don't you have meals together?"

"She doesn't like my cooking," Priya said point blank. "Come to think of it, she's the only one I know who doesn't because I'm a pretty good cook. She likes rice and curry, but it has to be made a certain way — her way. She makes enough only for herself and eats it in front of the TV."

"And you?"

"I loved to cook when my parents were alive, but I can't be bothered to prepare nice casseroles or roasts for one person."

"What do you eat?" Dr. Benson looked at her sharply.

"TV dinners, an apple, cheese, cake. I love cake. I just don't seem to have an appetite since my parents died though." It wasn't a complete lie, but she found it hard to meet his gaze.

"I know," Dr. Benson sighed. "You're going through a heart-breaking time, but now more than ever you need the support of friends, and you need to eat." He turned his attention to her chart. "You have lost twenty percent of your weight. How are you losing the weight?"

"Don't know," Priya shook her head, "stress maybe."

"Are you taking laxatives?"

"No," she answered honestly, feeling it unnecessary to confess that she was taking metabolic enhancers that did not contain Ephedra. She also didn't feel the need to tell the doctor that she jogged five kilometres a day and went on nocturnal house-cleaning blitzes. She also didn't tell him that she bought a stash of energy bars and broke off sections to have with a quarter cup of skim milk before bed.

"In medical terms, you are considered a restrictive anorexic," Dr. Benson said at length. He'd had a few anorexic patients over the years. Most were younger than Priya, but the underlying pattern was the same. His anorexic patients came from high-achieving families, but they themselves suffered from low self-esteem. He was concerned that Priya didn't feel she was even worthy of a home-cooked meal.

"Okay, let me get this straight," Priya cut into his thoughts. "Now, if I were 200 pounds and lost 15 percent of my body weight, I would be an anorexic 170 pounder, is that right?"

"Most people wouldn't be an ideal weight at 200 pounds to begin with," Dr. Benson said patiently. "But yes, if you are very tall and large boned and are designed to be that weight, well maybe you might look a little undernourished at 170."

He closed her chart and folded his hands over it. He was in a relaxed frame of mind and wanted Priya to feel the same.

Priya began fantasizing about the hamburger she wished she'd ordered at McDonald's. If only she had the energy to run tonight, then maybe she could have allowed herself to have it but now she just didn't deserve it.

"Have you been able to cry since your parents died?" Dr. Benson asked, studying Priya's tired face. He wondered whether she'd consider taking a multivitamin. He was concerned that she had collapsed due to an abrupt drop in blood sugar. He'd sent her for a series of blood tests before examining her, but he already suspected that she was anemic and her iron was low.

"What's the point?" Priya shrugged. "Will tears bring them back? Will I have Ma at my wedding or when I have a baby? No, all that's over now. I just carry on with my life ... hopefully

I'll get a job teaching soon and then what happens, happens ... I guess..." her voice trailed off.

"Can you teach right now?" Dr. Benson asked in a business-like tone. "Do you seriously think you have the stamina to cope with a class of four- and five-year-olds?"

"I have no choice. I've done a bit of supply work since September, but it's not enough to pay the bills," she was prevaricating.

"What about the part-time job you had at Chapters? Weren't you working there on the weekends? Are you still doing that?"

"No," Priya shook her head. "I had that job throughout university, but this past summer, I just quit."

"Why?" the doctor asked kindly.

"Let's face it. Depression has become a big issue in my life. One Saturday morning, I woke up so overwhelmed with sadness, I could barely move. On impulse, I picked up the phone and said that I had to resign. The store was in downtown Toronto and suddenly the idea of driving my mother's car to the subway station, then getting on the subway and battling the thirty-degree heat and the crowds ... it was too much. Auntie Renita was disgusted with me. Oh, she didn't say anything but I didn't miss the scowls of disapproval." Priya cast her eyes to the ground because that's precisely where her self-worth lay, just below shoe level.

"That's okay," Dr. Benson said gently. "You did what you had to do at the time. Nobody should fault you for that."

Priya nodded.

"Here are the facts," he said, gazing into Priya's dark eyes, clouded over with unshed tears.

"When I left the examination room, the nurse gave me the results of your urine analysis. You are showing ketones. Blood test results won't be ready until after the weekend, but I am willing to bet you are very anemic. You are not at a healthy weight at 90 pounds. If we can get you back up to 105 and keep you there, then I will be content, but..."

"But?" Priya repeated.

"I think we've caught this early ... the anorexia," Dr. Benson said. "We can nip this in the bud before it gets out of control. If you can gain even seven to ten pounds on your own, with the help of outpatient counselling, then I'm optimistic that you can put this whole episode behind you and go on with your life. You are young, pretty, and bright. Anorexia doesn't need to hold you back if you don't let it."

"What happens if I keep on losing weight?" Priya asked.

"I'll watch the numbers and if hospitalization is called for, so be it."

Priya suddenly realized that she didn't care anymore where she spent her nights; her parents' townhouse no longer felt like home.

"Will you be my counsellor?" she asked.

"As a family physician, I can only help you to a point, but there are eating disorder specialists ... wonderful men and women who have made great strides with patients in your situation."

"Sure," she said politely.

"Priya, you collapsed because your body is crying out for food," Dr. Benson said at length. "When was your last period?"

"Even at 110 pounds, I was a bit irregular," she said truthfully. "Especially after Mom and Dad died. I've lost track ... maybe two months ago?"

"Are you involved with anyone right now?" Dr. Benson realized he had to ask the question, even though he already knew the missing periods had nothing to do with pregnancy. Priya was of childbearing age and he was obligated to ask.

"To be honest Dr. Benson, I haven't met anyone I'd care to be involved with. There were a few crushes in high school and university, and one professor..." she blushed. "Uh, that's ancient history. We won't go there."

"What did you eat today?" he picked up a pen from a ceramic mug at one end of the desk and re-opened her folder.

"I had an apple cinnamon muffin and a coffee," the half-truth rolled off her tongue with the ease of honey dripping from a spoon.

"A whole muffin?" Dr. Benson was on to her. Priya's nose was twitching and she couldn't hold his gaze.

"Uh ... yeah," she fumbled with the cuff on her sweater. "Butter on the muffin ... it was good."

"What else?" the doctor asked.

"Honestly, today not much else but that's because I woke up late. I was on the Net till 2:00 am, looking up education sites. You know what they say about job hunting. It's a full-time job in itself." This version of how she'd spent last night sounded much better than admitting that she'd been scrubbing the kitchen floor by hand to keep her from wanting to rush outside and run a good five kilometres.

Dr. Benson scribbled something on a scrap of paper and then picked up the black phone at his elbow. "Ruby, set something up with Dr. Farrel at the eating disorder clinic in Meadowvale. Thank you."

"Here," he pressed the slip of paper into Priya's hand. "While you're waiting to get in to see Dr. Farrel, I want you to start taking this multivitamin."

"There's no rush for counselling," Priya said as she glanced at her watch. It was close to 3:00. She had been with the doctor for nearly forty-five minutes.

Dr. Benson didn't acknowledge the remark because he sensed that even though Priya claimed to be receptive to the idea of treatment, she wasn't ready. He would have to keep insisting that she get the treatment.

"I'll have Ruby book you to see me in two weeks," he stood up, signaling the end of the appointment.

"Thank you for everything, Dr. Benson. I appreciate the time and trouble you take over me," Priya reached over the back of her chair and slipped on her coat which was becoming too roomy for comfort.

"Let me help you with that." With fatherly tenderness, the doctor grasped her arm, guided it into the sleeve and then snapped the top button for her. "Keep warm and stay healthy. That's all I want you to do."

"I'll try," Priya smiled weakly and slowly left the office, wondering if she should break down and eat something and then run anyway. She felt a little stronger. It was certainly something to think about.

Serena was sipping a gingerale and flipping through the pages of a fashion magazine when Priya joined her in the waiting room. "How did it go, dear?" Serena stood up, leaning forward to return the magazine to a pile scattered on a wooden coffee table.

"All I have to do is gain seven pounds and I'll be back to normal," Priya said glibly. "I'm sorry I've cut into your day. You have to work tonight and here you are stuck with me."

"Oh, shells," Serena snapped up the buttons on her jacket. "You know, Serena will always be there for you. Good health is mandatory and, girl, if you don't have that, you have nothing."

"I'm healthy, just sad, that's all."

"I know, girl," Serena nodded with sympathy. "You've had to take on a lot, but God won't give you more than you can handle."

The rain-laden sky was almost dusky when they stepped out into the parking lot. Priya wanted to drop Serena home but the older woman refused to hand over the car keys.

"Girl, you fainted today. I'm not having you drive anyone anywhere. What I'll do is take you first to that Shoppers Drug Mart across the street so you can pick up that multivitamin you said Dr. Benson wants you to take, then I'll drive you home, and then catch the bus back to my own place."

"Serena, that's not necessary..." Priya began.

"Here now, girl," Serena wagged a gloved finger at Priya, "I'm not making sport with you. If your mother were alive to see the state you're in, she'd die all over again of heartbreak. Once you're home, you'll have some soup and then rest."

"I'm not making soup for myself," Priya said as she slipped into the passenger seat of her late mother's car. She pulled the seatbelt over her shoulder and closed her eyes, quietly relieved that Serena insisted on driving.

"Your aunt could make you something," Serena slipped the key into the ignition.

"That's not going to happen," Priya yawned and closed her eyes.

"Why?" Serena sounded disappointed.

"Because we made an agreement about a month ago. She will cook for herself because according to her, my cooking is heavy like Ma's and she needs her rice and curry every day. What that translates into is, she will make enough rice and curry for herself and I am to cook whatever I want for myself."

"That seems so selfish," Serena edged the car out from between a SUV and a minivan and crossed the intersection to the Shoppers Drug Mart. "Do you want me to come in with you?" Serena asked as she searched for a new parking spot.

"No, just park by the front door and I'll run in and get the vitamins," Priya unfastened her seatbelt again.

"But that's a fire lane. What if the police come?"

"Just tell 'em you'll move," Priya was amused at Serena's nervousness. She knew it stemmed from the fact that Serena was a reluctant driver who wasn't used to getting behind the wheel very often. Priya was in and out of the drugstore within ten minutes. Though the rush hour hadn't gotten underway yet, the roads were growing thick with traffic.

"Your cooking is lovely," Serena remarked at a red light. "I used to tell your mother that you have a sweet hand when it comes to turning out those lovely dishes you make, those Thai curries, roasts and things ... I don't know what that Renita is talking about."

Priya nodded and then slipped the crinkly plastic Shoppers Drug Mart bag into the larger Walmart bag with the resume paper.

"Don't take her on," Serena advised. "The most important thing is that you eat."

"I do my best," Priya said truthfully.

"I hope so," Serena shook her head. "Does Dr. Benson think you might be anorexic?"

"Well, he said it's in the early stages, and he said this can be turned around with outpatient therapy."

"Truth," Serena nodded emphatically. "I've seen documentaries about anorexia. It's a terrible thing, this eating disorder business. I never heard of it in Guyana when I was a girl."

Priya didn't tell Serena that she secretly liked wearing the mantle of anorexia on her slender shoulders. It made her feel special. If she could keep this thing under control and hopefully not lose too much more weight, she'd be fine.

"That nice man, Gabe," Serena turned onto Winston Churchill Boulevard, a treed street dotted with low-rise apartment buildings and townhouses, "He was a friend of your mother's?"

"That's what he says," Priya tried to blink back the fatigue that was weighing down her eyelids but she was losing the battle.

"You don't believe him?" Serena queried as she turned onto Priya's street.

"I do," Priya said guardedly. "He seemed to know a lot about Ma ... but funny, how she never mentioned his name ... not to me, anyway."

"Truth," Serena agreed. "She told me so much about her life in Newfoundland, but that name never came up. Then again, from what he had to tell you, he would have been just the guy down the street ... not like a former boyfriend. I suppose, he was like one of a hundred people she knew, and you know your mother, she was friends with the whole world."

"Hmm," Priya nodded as they paused at the turn-off to her townhouse complex.

"He seemed very protective of you," Serena observed. "I was trying to understand why. True, he discovered that you are the daughter of someone he knew decades ago, but somehow ... I don't know, maybe he's just that way inclined. I guess there are some decent men around, good-looking too," her voice dissolved into a girlish giggle. "Very handsome, eh girl! You know I didn't see a ring on his finger."

"You interested?" Priya asked, feeling a bit lively now.

"You can't have too many friends, but no ... I've had my

fill of relationships," Serena said decisively as she sought out Priya's designated parking spot.

A lazy drizzle peppered their path to Priya's unit, part of a cluster of five-year-old townhouses that were a study in brick and white monotony. Each unit was fronted by a modest square of lawn, which despite the lateness of the season was green and lush. The De Souzas were one of just a handful of residents who'd made the most of their micro patch of land, adorning it with flowerbeds ringed by cobblestones and potted plants in colorful ceramic pots lining the walkway to the front door which was painted a bright white.

Through the teal-coloured blinds, Priya noticed that her aunt had turned on the lights. This was unusual as the older lady was wont to sit in the dark and brood long after dusk had settled over the neighbourhood. Priya could only assume that Renita was conducting piano lessons that evening. It was how she supplemented the modest pension she received from her teaching days in Sri Lanka and the old age pension she became eligible for upon immigrating to Canada a year earlier.

With Serena standing directly behind her, Priya turned her key in the lock and opened the door with a slight push. Jay had put weather stripping at the threshold of the front door-way last January. A small degree of force was still required to nudge the door open as the stripping tended to work a little too well and to stick.

Priya shuddered when she thought about what her father had to do to winterize their townhouse. She'd have to get some books and figure out how to do these things. Caulking on the windows had to be redone as cold air was seeping into the bedrooms at night. Salt for the driveway would have to be in ready supply for when the first snowfall hit. And then there was the shoveling! Priya was overwhelmed by the new responsibilities that lay before her.

A blast of warm air caressed her face as she entered the unit. The white ceramic tile beneath her shoes was still nice and clean as Priya had given the floors her usual frenzied scrub the previous night. When she didn't think she'd burned enough calories for what she'd eaten, she'd throw herself into a manic session of housecleaning. Even if the calories burned were minimal, every one counted in Priya's quest to stay thin.

"Will you stay for a while?" she asked Serena, knowing that her friend had to rush back home and get ready for work.

"Just long enough to see that you eat something," Serena said wearily. If she could afford to, she'd have loved to call in sick and say she wouldn't be in tonight. All she wanted was to sleep, sleep, sleep!

"Yes, Lottie," Renita's distinctly Sinhalese accent drifted in from the kitchen. She was so deeply engrossed in her phone call that she was unaware that Priya had come home. "I think that was the biggest mistake Di-lah-ni and Jay made. The girl has a right to know the truth. If not now ... then when? Why should I have to suffer in silence like this? My loss is greater than anyone else's and ... Ayo ... I don't know, Lottie, she has stopped eating ... won't look for a job properly ... I don't know what sort of people these are. In Sri Lanka, girls her age are married, holding down jobs, starting their families. I don't know what to do. I'm also not keeping too well. Yes, it's that cough. Dr. Benson wants to send me for tests, but I don't know ... right then, you'll pick me up for the Bible study tomorrow night at 6:45 ... I need the prayers. Thank you. Good night."

"Tell me what?" Priya barreled into the kitchen.

"Hello Priya," Renita's lips were poised to frown but abruptly turned up into a smile when she noticed Serena trailing behind her.

"You were talking to Auntie Lottie about me?" Priya's tone was more curious than accusing.

"Priya," Serena was chagrined.

"That's okay," Renita adjusted her blue sari smartly over her shoulder. "Jay and Di-Lah-ni, left us in quite a soup when they died. I have this wretched cough that won't allow me to sleep at night. I must lie down before my first student comes for music."

When she was out of earshot, Serena turned to Priya, a look of dismay on her face. "Oh, shells," Serena sighed. "She didn't even ask where you were today."

"That's Auntie for you," Priya shrugged out of her coat. "And to top it off, she didn't even have the courtesy to greet you."

"She smiled though. Sit down," Serena pulled out a kitchen chair from the glass-topped table and beckoned for Priya to sit. "I'll heat up a packet of soup, perhaps?"

"What do you think they were talking about, Serena?" Priya asked.

"I don't know," Serena took off her own coat and laid it over the back of a chair, "but I have a feeling she won't tell you until she's good and ready."

Chapter 4

PRIYA SPENT ANOTHER SLEEPLESS NIGHT peering out the living room window at the powdery snow that laced the front lawn in an intricate pattern. Priya hadn't exercised for more than twenty-four hours and she wasn't happy about it. She was angry with herself for letting Serena talk her into eating a bowl of pea soup. She hadn't reached the point where she felt ready to induce vomiting in order to rid her body of excess calories. She knew that once she rounded that corner, there would be no turning back. She'd read about people engaging in a steady cycle of bingeing and purging. Bulimia was receiving widespread coverage in the media. Priya prided herself on not being there yet. There had to be other ways. She made a mental note that once the malls opened in the morning, she would make a beeline for the nearest nutrition store and buy their most potent, powerful weight management product. She was hoping she wouldn't have to resort to Ephedra because that would increase the stakes of the deadly game of *fat* and mouse she was now fully involved in.

Huddled in a blue flannel blanket, Priya was on the same wooden glider that her mother had used to nurse her as a newborn. The original paisley chair pad had long since been replaced by a pale jade one that Delaney had discovered at a craft fair soon after moving into the townhouse. She had decided it was time to chuck out the old furniture and create a new beginning in a new home — the very first they'd ever owned.

Priya clasped her icy hands under her chin and peered out at the moonless gray night that was illuminated by a streetlight casting an iridescent shadow upon the front yard. The sound of a faraway ambulance and the ticking of a brass clock on the mantle were the only sounds Priya heard as she brooded over the happenings of the day. From reuniting a little boy with his mother, to collapsing, to meeting Gabe Johanson, and ultimately ending up in Dr. Benson's office, it had been a little more eventful than Priya could have imagined. Her résumé paper sat untouched in her father's den, still in its plastic bag, on the walnut workstation next to the computer.

A recently tuned black Yamaha piano was adjacent to Priya's chair. A parade of future concert pianists regularly trooped their way across the parquet floor to have their efforts heard and appraised by Renita. She had quite a coterie of students from the South Asian community in Missisauga. Most of them were the grandchildren of Renita's former classmates who were settled in Ontario. It was part of a cultural phenomenon that Priya had heard about throughout her life. Jay had gone to an exclusive boys' school in Colombo and, to the day he died, he kept in contact with his classmates. To Priya, Jay's relationship with his friends seemed like an endless class reunion. Many of them were successful professionals in Toronto. They had "school" dances and organized cricket matches and boat cruises. Priya envied their apparent closeness and knew that her own experience of going to school in North America, especially with her interracial background, was almost isolating in comparison.

Pryia, ever the outsider, knew that she came across as somewhat exotic to her peers. Even though she was born and raised in Canada, people made assumptions based on her dark complexion and South Asian features. It was only after she spoke with her Canadian accent that they realized Priya might actually have been born here. Still for many, meeting her for the first time, questions inevitably arose. "How long have you lived in Canada?" Or the prize winner, "How do you like our winters?"

In some respects she felt more Asian when it came to views on teenage dating. Her father insisted she wait until she was in university before she agreed to go out with someone on a date. While her mother didn't contradict her husband's views, she still wanted Priya to enjoy life with her friends. But Priya was very much an introvert, and even her girlfriends were few and far between. When her university friends talked about moving in with their boyfriends, Priya insisted that she would wait until marriage before she ever lived with a man.

When it came to finding a niche for herself, Priya felt as if she was in a no-man's land. Aside from her conservative outlook on life, she didn't share much in common with her father. She somehow felt more connected to Delaney's Newfoundland heritage, and was able to relate more to her mother's experiences than those of her father. Nevertheless, whenever she and her family visited St. John's, Priya still felt like an outsider. There were a handful of girls in her grandparents' neighbourhood that she had spent time with on those visits but she never quite felt that she fit in. They referred to going "round the bay" on the weekends and it seemed like they knew someone who knew someone who was connected to their family somewhere along the way. These friends were passionate about the latest hockey games and who was going "out to the cabin" on the weekend, but Delaney's family never did own a cabin on the bay. And her grandparents were city folk who didn't hunt moose or catch fish like most of the other girls' parents.

In a sense, it was almost like the island life that Jay talked about in Sri Lanka, but Priya couldn't relate to that either. Her father spoke of friends and places in Sri Lanka that were merely names to Priya. He pined for unusual fruits like *durian* and *mangostein*. And among his family and friends, they prided themselves on the higher standard they lived by, on their intellectual acheivements and business acumen. Priya always felt that she straddled the fence between two distinct island cultures.

Though Delaney hadn't enjoyed the tight-knit school experience that was Jay's, she endeared herself to her friends and had kept contact with many of them until her death. Why then, Priya wondered, didn't Gabe figure in her mother's reflections?

Priya drifted into a troubled sleep with Gabe on her mind. His showing up at Walmart just when she needed help seemed more than a little coincidental. Once Serena went home, it occurred to Priya that she had neglected to ask Gabe for *his* phone number. After locating it in the directory, she left a message on his voicemail to say that she was feeling better, and then thanked him for his concern. She hoped she would see him again soon, also because she longed for any fresh insights or memories about her mother.

The sound of the phone jolted Priya out of her sleep. It was 9:45 am. Another overcast sky was pouring silvery light through the partially opened blinds. Stretching out her cramped limbs, Priya allowed her blanket to fall to the floor as she moved across the room to the oak entertainment cabinet that housed the TV, VCR, DVD player and CD changer. She stretched her hand to the highest shelf and pulled down the white cordless phone.

"Hello," she sank to the edge of the adjacent white chesterfield.

"Priya, hi," Rachel's cheery telephone voice was just the wake-up call she needed.

"Oh, hi," Priya yawned, happy to hear the voice of her close friend.

"I know this is short notice, but are you doing anything tomorrow?" Rachel asked.

"Am I ever doing anything anymore?" Priya shrugged.

"I got lucky with some tickets for a dinner theatre tomorrow night and I want you to come with me."

"Are you sure you want me to go out with you ... to a *restaurant* of all places?" Priya asked, recalling their last fiasco of a meal together. They'd gone out for Thanksgiving and Rachel had lost her temper because Priya spent more time consulting her paperback calorie counter than she did eating.

"I thought we got past that a long time ago," Rachel said almost lightly. "I know now that you have an eating disorder and, one day, you'll know it too."

"Yeah, okay," Priya said just to be agreeable.

"So do you want to go or not?" Rachel was impatient.

"What's the production and more importantly, how much is it?" Priya's head was already spinning. Theatre she could handle, but dinner?

"The production is a Noël Coward play called *Private Lives* and it's my treat."

"You don't have to…" Priya began.

"Look, I admit I was a bit harsh during Thanksgiving," Rachel explained. "Besides, you've been so sad and lonely these past few months, I've been wanting to do something for you … but there *is* a catch."

"I knew it," Priya's gaze settled on a framed oil painting of the top of an iceberg bobbing above the surface of the Atlantic Ocean. Delaney had bought the picture on their last trip to Newfoundland the previous Christmas.

"His name is Trent Perelli," Rachel said slowly, "and that part about being a catch … I meant that literally."

"Oh, sure," Priya said. Rachel was a good friend but never in the seven years of their friendship had she been able to get Priya a decent date.

"I met him at work," Rachel explained, "and from moment one, I had a gut feeling that he was meant for you."

"Why isn't he meant for you?" Priya asked, knowing that Rachel was growing bored with her five-year relationship with her boyfriend.

"I don't think Nolan would like me two-timing him," Rachel said dryly, "and besides, Trent is not my type. He's too old-fashioned, too conservative for me. But I think he might be just what you need."

"Okay," Priya said cautiously.

"I'll take the bus out to your place tomorrow afternoon and we'll get dressed together. Trent will pick us up there."

"Why would you go to all that trouble just for me?" Priya challenged. "One subway and two buses, c'mon Rach."

"Because you've gone through a rough time since your parents' deaths. You need to get out there and have some fun.

Besides, you'll be doing me a favour taking that extra ticket off my hands. Nolan is going to a hockey game tomorrow night so he won't be joining us."

"Ah, that's where the extra ticket comes in," Priya was amused.

"The man has no culture," Rachel snorted. "He wouldn't know a good play if he woke up in one."

"What time does it start?" Priya asked.

"7:00," Rachel said. "But Trent will pick us up at 5:30. By the time we get off the 401, find parking downtown, and get our table, we'll be lucky if we're not late."

"This dinner theater is downtown and you're having Trent drive all the way into Mississauga to pick us up. Now, how thoughtless is that." Priya remarked.

"No worries," Rachel said casually. "He lives in Mississauga, close to the Erin Mills Parkway, so he doesn't have to go far out of his way."

"What are they having for the meal?" Priya asked, her mind racing.

"Roast beef and a choice of desserts after the show."

Priya wondered how she would cope with the meal without drawing negative attention to herself. She knew that she needed to spend more time out of the house, away from Renita's malevolent stares and critical comments. There were times when Priya sensed that her Auntie almost hated her. An evening with her friend would do her a world of good.

"Priya, are you there?" Rachel asked with a hint of impatience.

"Yeah, sure ... come over tomorrow and we'll get dressed together," Priya said at length.

She'd barely finished the call when she heard the familiar sound of leather flip-flops slapping against the ceramic tile in the hallway, followed by the cloying whiff of sandalwood cologne.

"Priya, are you in there?" Renita, dressed in green polyester slacks and a beige sweater approached the doorway of the living room. She was perfectly primped and put together as she normally was. Tall and fit, she could have easily passed for a decade younger than her sixty-odd years. Her long hair, a perpetual coal black, thanks to hair colouring, had been artfully arranged within the metallic clasp of a shiny green claw clip. Her delicate features and graceful movements were a ready reminder that at one time she'd been a stunning head-turner. Priya had inherited Delaney's facial features and height, but was lucky enough to share Auntie's delicate bone structure and porcelain skin.

"Good morning, Auntie," Priya put down the phone and stood up. "You had breakfast?"

"Yes, yes," the older woman nodded pleasantly. "I had an English muffin and a cup of coffee." She shifted her weight, keeping her eyes trained on Priya's face, almost as if she wanted to deliver some kind of pronouncement.

"What's wrong?" Priya inquired, picking up on her body language.

"Don't you think it's time we packed your parents' things away? It's been over six months since they died," Renita said.

Priya sighed and ran her cold hands through her tangled hair. The ends were becoming so brittle she wondered how she'd get a brush through her formerly lustrous layers.

"Are you busy now?" Renita asked.

"Okay, let's do it now and finish it off," Priya pulled her pink bathrobe around herself and led the way down the hallway toward the stairs.

"Won't you eat first?" Renita sounded concerned.

"Later," Priya shrugged.

They walked into the master bedroom, which was as pristine as a freshly made-up hotel suite. From the moment Priya accepted the fact that her parents were dead, she had treated their room with shrine-like reverence. She vacuumed it regularly, dusted the dressing table, and polished the mirror as if they were expected back after a long vacation.

The upkeep of the bedroom was accomplished on nights during which sleep eluded her. Priya would slip into the room and create a make-work project for herself. One night, it would be dusting the off white blinds, one slat at a time. On other occasions, she'd arrange and rearrange the clothes in the twin closets. She hadn't bothered to look deeply into her parents' chest of drawers because she knew all their important documents and paper work were stored in a brown accordion file in Jay's den.

Priya wasn't sure if she'd ever have the courage to open the drawers in her mother's bedside table and peer into the more intimate details of Delaney's life. She was scared that if she gave in to the floodwaters of grief, she'd have to face it alone. There would be no loving arms to embrace her, no shoulder upon which to rest her head and weep away her anguish. Those scenes took place in movies, not in real life — not Priya's, anyway. She certainly didn't expect Renita to embrace her with comforting words and a tender hug. Priya's Sri Lankan relatives were not known for open displays of affection. Jay had been different in that regard. Perhaps it was Delaney's influence that made him come out freely with terms of endearment like "darling" and "honey." When he was in a good mood, he occasionally kissed his wife and daughter, but he was the only member of the De Souza clan who engaged in such behaviour.

Priya, encouraged by Renita's apparent friendliness, felt she could inquire about that phone conversation she'd overheard her having with Lottie. "Auntie, what is it that I need to know?"

"Pardon?" Renita's face froze in a tense smile.

"Remember, yesterday afternoon when Serena and I walked in, you were on the phone…"

Renita's hollow laugh indicated she was anything but amused. "I was remarking to her that somebody needs to let you know how thin you're getting. You'll look old before your time if you continue to reduce like this."

Priya knew that this was not the kernel of conversation she'd overheard. It was something far more dire than her merely losing a couple of pounds.

"Speaking of Lottie," Auntie rushed ahead, "I thought that when she comes to pick me up for the Bible study, I can bring along some of the boxes we pack." She was referring to her church's cold weather clothing drive. She wanted to donate as much of Jay and Delaney's belongings as Priya would agree to.

"Sure," Priya nodded, realizing that it was pointless to pursue the topic of the phone call any further because it would only alienate her aunt and send her into one of her withering silences.

She perched on her mother's side of the bed. Her night table was piled high with the stack of novels and inspirational writings Delaney had planned to read over the summer. Priya opened the drawer and saw the usual assortment of photographs, pens, address books, and the other sundry keepsakes that were the essence of who Delaney was. Taking precedence above everything in the drawer was her Bible. It was bulging with photos and notes. Priya opened it on her lap and gingerly lifted out the memorabilia that spilled from its pages: photos of Priya's Confirmation at twelve, Priya's high school graduation, and then a collection of snaps of various family members in Newfoundland.

"What is that one?" Renita leaned over Priya's shoulder and pointed to a faded picture of Delaney sitting on a hospital bed, cradling a pink-cocooned bundle against her chest. Delaney's long, honey-coloured hair tumbled loosely over her shoulders and she was dressed in a powder blue silk robe.

"I guess she must have been trying to nurse me," Priya mused as she held the photograph up close to examine the details. Because her head was bent, Delaney's face was hidden from the lens of the camera.

"Hmmp," Renita scowled, "What a thing to photograph, a post-partum woman breastfeeding her child ... nothing better to take?"

"What's wrong with that?" Priya was defensive.

"Surely there are more dignified poses for mother and child," Renita's eyes flashed with a disproportionate level of anger.

Priya was stung by her aunt's insensitivity but wondered why it should come as a surprise.

"Any photos of Jay there?" With a dismissive gesture, Renita flung down the photo as if it was crawling with parasites and reached into Priya's lap for the remaining pictures. "Here's one…"

A brief smile passed over Priya's lips as she reached toward her aunt to see what she'd taken from her. "I remember that pink bathing suit. I was six or seven on that trip to Sri Lanka. We're posing by the water on Mount Lavania beach."

The photograph captured a happy family of three standing against the backdrop of the Indian Ocean with the setting sun casting an ethereal glow on their faces. Jay stood tall in navy trunks. He was good looking in an athletic kind of way, Priya decided. Delaney, plump and pretty in an aquamarine figure-flattering suit wore a broad smile on her tanned face.

"This is a lovely picture of Jay," Renita nodded, discounting her niece and sister-in-law in her usual cutting way.

However, for Priya it was the photo of Delaney on the hospital bed that tugged at her heartstrings. Her mother must have envisioned an entire lifetime with that daughter of hers, never dreaming it would end dramatically soon after Priya's twenty-fifth birthday.

"I want to keep this photo in a special place," Priya got up from the bed and moved across the beige carpeted hallway into her own room, which was adjacent to the washroom. Her bedroom had been arranged in the same way it had been when they lived in the condo on Aquitaine Avenue — Priya's only other home. She craved continuity in her life and had asked the movers to push her bed under the window and her off-white desk and chest of drawers against the wall kitty corner from the closet.

"You're twenty years old," Rachel had grumbled at the time. "Now that your parents are moving into the townhouse, why don't you get out on your own?"

"Why?" Priya had challenged. "I'll have enough of a student loan to keep me in debt for years. Why should I stress myself out over paying rent in Toronto just because I'm in my twenties?"

Rachel had shrugged. The youngest of five children, she had

left Thunder Bay in northern Ontario to live in a university dorm when she was eighteen. Two years after that, she'd met Nolan and they'd moved into a converted loft in the Bloor West Village. Rachel's parents in Thunder Bay had managed one of the town's sports facilities. As a result Rachel grew up on a diet of hockey and fries. She herself didn't play, but having four brothers on various teams made her an armchair expert on hockey and other ice sports. This is what had endeared her to Nolan. The problem with Rachel, Priya thought, was that she fancied herself an expert in all areas. Once she realized she couldn't convince Priya to "get out on her own," she thought she'd try to find a partner for her. Rachel made no secret of the fact that she thought Jay was an oppressive influence on Priya. She knew that Priya was the victim of pressure: pressure to excel at the piano, pressure to achieve academically, and, ultimately, pressure to succeed financially. Jay had wanted his only child to study medicine, but Priya's marks, though good, were not excellent. She couldn't maintain the competitive edge needed to get into medical school. Teaching was a realistic option since she liked working with children and was able to relate to the challenges and pitfalls that Delaney's students faced.

Priya was about to take her pink baby book from the top drawer of her bedside table and slip the photo in the plastic sleeve at the back but changed her mind. Instead, she tucked it into her handbag. She'd be able to look at her mother's face wherever she was, whenever she needed her strength.

Rachel thought Priya was far too thin. The cherry red silk dress flowing over her friend's delicate body looked like an oversized curtain tumbling off its supporting rod. The black tights accentuated the match-stick appearance of her legs. Only Priya's black suede pumps fit properly.

Rachel, a willowy five foot nine, felt like an Amazon next to her friend. Although she was eight months younger than Priya, she felt at least ten years older. A slender brunette with plain features that highlighted an honest face, Rachel was the ideal best friend. Her ability to keep a titillating secret rivaled her ability to plan a night on the town. Rachel prided herself on knowing a lot of people but didn't burden herself with excessive friendships. She handpicked those she got close to, and Priya was one of the closest.

They became friends in their first year modern literature class. Rachel's desk was behind Priya's. New to the big city and glowing with small town innocence, Rachel was fascinated by the girl with the *café-au-lait* skin and the curly, black-brown hair who sat in front of her. Their friendship evolved from long after-class chats that had them sharing their life stories and future plans. Priya was a shy loner, beset by insecurities about her identity and abilities. She cleaved to Rachel like a baby duckling to its mother.

After that first-year English class, the two didn't have any other courses in common. Priya went into the teaching program and Rachel studied business administration. She ended up with a basic degree in that field and was now paying her way through graduate studies as a secretary at a school of performing arts in downtown Toronto. The job was a ten-minute subway ride from her loft. She was the frequent recipient of free or discounted tickets for concerts and plays starring the alumni of the music school.

Trent Perelli, a handsome, slim Italian-Canadian was the school's most talented voice and piano teacher. In Rachel's matchmaking eyes, he was not only a romantic possibility for Priya, but also hopefully an inspiration to get her back into her music. Though Priya had been trained classically, she favoured the easy listening piano stylings of her generation. Jay's insistence on force-feeding Priya the classical composers had turned her off music all together, and her gleaming Yahama piano sat ignored by her in the family's living room.

Rachel had observed the cautious way Priya approached her iced Mochaccino during their last visit to the Second Cup. She'd become convinced that Priya was suffering from anorexia. She recognized the signs only too well. Some of the singers and dancers at the school exhibited similar signs of the disease. They looked like wraiths, but were convinced that they were too overweight to eat even a plain salad. She knew that Priya had a patchwork record of obtaining supply-teaching positions, but she suspected that Priya wasn't trying very hard to get a full-time post. Priya hadn't sent out résumés in weeks and had admitted to not even opening the bag of résumé paper that was in what used to be her father's den. Rachel felt Priya's life was going off the rails and that somebody needed to put her back on course.

At 5:15 that Saturday afternoon, a watery sun had made a furtive appearance but the flurries started as Rachel left the relative comfort of the subway to take the two buses to Priya's west Mississauga townhouse. Dressed in jeans and a green retro bomber jacket, she carried her evening wear in a purple backpack.

After Rachel arrived at the townhouse, she and Priya had sat in the kitchen with a cup of hot tea while they caught up on each other's lives. Rachel rolled her eyes in silent judgment when her underweight friend used skim milk in her tea. What Rachel couldn't pass judgement on, because she didn't know about it, was that this would be the only sustenance Priya would consume before the night's meal. Rachel also had no way of knowing that Priya had calculated and plotted her way into allowing herself a small fraction of the evening's fare. She'd logged in an hour of jogging and downed her quota of recently purchased diet pills to help mitigate the ill effects dinner would have on the scale. Priya would fool her friend into believing that she was eating normally that night. That afternoon, Priya created a stunning illusion of normalcy about her life and health in general. She didn't disclose the fact that she had collapsed at Walmart two days earlier. She did, however, refer to a "chance meeting" with one of her mother's old friends, Gabe Johansen.

Huddled over their cups, the two women whispered and

speculated about the dashing older man who'd caught Priya off guard by coming to her aid when she'd heard the Code Yellow sounding for the lost little boy in the mall.

Now, three hours later, they were sizing each other up in Priya's full-length brass mirror. Rachel was wearing a long black pencil skirt and a blue and black silk top that accentuated her figure. She projected an air of confidence that would impress anyone.

Priya looked like a delicate hospital patient. Rachel had teased Priya's hair into fluffy curls that spilled over her shoulders. The style added much needed fullness to her wan face.

Downstairs the doorbell sounded. Priya glanced at her watch. It was 5:30 sharp. "Punctual," she observed, grabbing her black sequined evening bag from the top of the dressing table.

"Your aunt is downstairs," Rachel pointed out. "She'll get the door."

"That won't happen," Priya assured her. "If she knows I'm home, she won't go near that front door. I could be in the tub and she could be reading in the living room ... she won't budge."

The doorbell sounded again.

"Priya, there is a visitor," Renita called up the stairs.

Rachel swore under her breath and grasped Priya's cold hand in hers. "Let's go."

Priya opened the front door and peered through the screen door at a tall man dressed in a black trench coat standing in the soft yellow glow of the porch light. He cast her a shy smile. She unlatched that door and in walked Trent Perelli. His understated Italian good looks took her aback. When Rachel had told her that Trent was a voice and piano teacher, she'd envisioned a nerdy looking man with short straight hair and a sharp gaze. The young man standing before her, who appeared to be in his early thirties, had warm brown eyes and curly dark hair that seemed black in the half-light of dusk.

"Hi," he said brightly. "Priya, these are for you." He extended a bouquet of red roses towards her.

"Oh ... uh," she blushed, feeling flustered and inadequate.

She'd focused on his face and hadn't bothered to look at his strong artistic hands and what they were carrying. She thought she must appear very silly in Trent's eyes.

"Sorry," she mumbled. "Come in, it's cold out there," she made a sweeping gesture with her arm toward the hallway.

"Hi, Trent," Rachel popped up from behind Priya. "You managed to find the place okay."

"You gave me excellent directions," Trent said.

"I'll find a vase for these and then we'll go," Priya said awkwardly, wondering how and where she'd find a vase that quickly.

"How fine! Not to worry," Renita floated to her side. "I'll find a vase for them. You have a wonderful evening," she said, relieving Priya of the bouquet.

"Trent, this is my aunt Renita from Sri Lanka," Priya said.

"Very nice to meet you," Trent shook her free hand.

"I'm thrilled that Priya's getting this chance to go out," Renita beamed at the stranger on her doorstep.

Priya fumbled in the closet in search of her sea green ankle-length wool coat. She was already looking forward to getting to know Trent a little better, but first she'd have to face the obstacle of a full meal — something she hadn't enjoyed in weeks, or was it months? She couldn't quite remember.

Chapter 5

PRIYA STUDIED THE PLATE OF ROAST BEEF and vegetables that sat before her. With judicious care she extricated two of the thinnest slices of moist, tender beef from one end of the plate and transferred it to the other side. She then selected one potato and a cluster of green beans, spooned a little gravy over them and shifted them next to the beef. With meticulous precision she drew an invisible line with the blade of her knife to separate the two lots of food. Then she started to eat the smaller portion. Carrots and the roll would remain untouched. She'd derive enough starch from the potato. She was willing to forego the health benefits of the beta carotene-rich carrots because of their starch content. Potatoes had starch too, but she liked them, and they would be more filling than the carrots. While she conducted her culinary operation, Priya kept Trent distracted with a lively conversation about her experiences as a supply teacher.

Trent, handsome and attentive in a long-sleeved navy shirt and gray tie, could not take his eyes off her. She knew she'd captivated him from the moment Rachel and she had climbed into his black Mercury Topaz.

Seemingly a calm man, Trent had been unfazed by the busy highway traffic as he navigated his way through the 401 and into Toronto's downtown core. Priya sat beside him and Rachel was in the back, keeping her comments to a minimum. Priya suspected Rachel was keeping a low profile so she and Trent could get to know each other. Once they arrived at the dinner theatre, a renovated music hall with shiny black floors and high ceilings, Rachel announced that she'd volunteered to help out in the coat-check room and would catch up with them later.

"I thought we were in this together," Priya hissed in a stage whisper after Trent dropped them off at the marbled foyer in search of parking.

"Who ever heard of three people on a date?" Rachel scoffed.

People drifted into the building as couples or in small groups. Most were well-dressed. A mélange of different perfumes and colognes made the air heavy.

"Don't they have regulations about not wearing perfume to these things?" Rachel grumbled after a series of sneezes had her diving into her evening bag for a tissue.

"Are you really going now? Priya asked. "Yes, I am," Rachel blew her nose. "I accompanied you tonight to break the ice between you and Trent. I'm not about to hang out with you two. I'll catch up with you a bit later."

"Oh, thanks," Priya's heart sank.

"Don't worry, you'll be fine," Rachel shrugged out of her coat. "I think Trent likes you."

"Because?" Priya queried.

"You might have been too shy to notice but his eyes lit up a birthday cake when he saw you," Rachel said.

"Yeah, okay," Priya said dismissively. "Well," she added, "you might have warned me that you were planning to do this." Rachel laughed and sauntered away. And as soon as she had vanished, Trent had appeared.

"Are you okay?" Trent asked, gently nudging her back into the moment. Rachel had already told him about the recent death of Priya's parents, and Priya herself had made reference to it in the car. He had been so empathetic, she knew he was wondering if her mind had wandered back to that earlier mention.

"I'm fine," Priya looked down at her half-eaten plate. "I had a huge lunch today so I'm not too hungry."

Trent smiled. "I saw the dessert cart when we were entering the dining room. That will make anyone hungry for sure. I can't wait until after the show to dig into that cheesecake."

Priya was impressed with Trent's perfect diction and precise enunciation. She wondered if it was a bi-product of years of voice training. "Did you go to school here in Toronto?" she asked, to get off the topic of food.

"I did," he said, "but I also spent some time at a performing arts school called Italia Conte in London, England, when I was a teenager."

"That explains your impeccable diction," Priya almost blushed, enchanted by the low timbre of Trent's voice. She imagined him to be a fine singer.

"I was told that I have talent as a vocalist," he confessed shyly, "but I was never interested in performing. I'm much happier preparing others for the stage. I like the routine of a nine-to-five job and to come home to a quiet domestic life ... one day. What about you?"

"I'm just a kindergarten teacher," Priya replied, faking a sip from her full wineglass.

"What do you mean *just* a kindergarten teacher," Trent protested. "You've got the education of the youngest learners in your hands. That's a big responsibility."

"Thank you for saying that, but ..." Priya's voice trailed off as a waiter approached their table with some water.

"Rachel tells me you're also a gifted pianist," Trent pressed.

"I like to play," Priya admitted, "but not classical music."

"That's fine," Trend said understandingly. "Priya, I might be a classical voice coach, but, believe me, I don't sit around listening only to arias on my home stereo system. I love all kinds of music."

"That's good to know," Priya said.

"I would love to hear you play," Trent went on.

"As long as you're not grading me," Priya said with a half-smile. "Now, tell me about you. Up to now, it's been me, me, and me."

"Well, that's not quite true," Trent glanced at his silver watch. "It's almost time for us to head into the auditorium for the play. Can we talk about me, me, and me over dessert?"

His playful comment drew a wide smile from Priya. Feeling

her spirits lift, Priya watched as Trent stood up, walked around their table-for-two, and pulled out her chair as she rose. "Wow," she chuckled, "I didn't think men did that anymore."

"They do when there's someone as beautiful as you sitting across from them," Trent retorted, a twinkle in his eye.

His relaxed, unassuming manner put Priya so much at ease she was convinced the rest of the evening would be a snap. She allowed Trent to take her arm and escort her toward the line that was forming in front of the doors to the auditorium. The white noise of contented chatter and canned melodies lulled Priya into a false sense of well-being.

Engulfed with shame, cheeks flaming bright red, forehead drizzling sweat, Priya slumped against the pink door of the women's washroom. Though she lacked the courage to rid herself of her wrong-doing, she knew that she'd have to do something drastic or else the urge to keep on eating would consume her like a raging forest fire.

It was all because of the double-trouble chocolate truffle cake. After the play was over, Priya and Trent had made their way back to the dining room for coffee and dessert. An oversized slice of decadence beckoned from the cloud of white chocolate sin that decorated the dessert plate. It was a beacon of disaster. She'd brought a serving to her table with the intention of eating just a quarter of it. She'd even made an indentation with her fork at the spot where her fork would take permanent retirement. Yet she was so enthralled by Trent's conversation that she kept on eating and eating and eating. Before she knew what had happened, Priya was staring at an empty plate, one that was far emptier than Trent's. He'd eaten barely half his dessert because, he'd said, it was too rich and sweet. He hadn't in speech, expression, or gesture conveyed any judgement on Priya that she should feel guilty for eating her entire slice. Priya judged herself. She knew the cake probably contained about 600 calories and fat grams in the double digits. She wanted to be like the anorexics and bulimics she'd read about in articles.

They could march themselves off to the bathroom, stick a couple of fingers down their throats, and make history out of the meal. Priya had never dared to do that. But, after hastily excusing herself from the table, she'd made a frantic retreat to the washroom. She stared at her thin face and decided it looked bloated. She saw double and triple chins where no one else would have. The image reflected back to her in the mirror was one she hated.

There was no one else in the bathroom. Priya had the privacy needed to implement this very necessary plan. She tried but the courage to follow through eluded her. Disgusted with herself, she washed her face. Every trace of foundation Rachel had patiently helped apply to her face slid down the drain in a brown stream of wasted vanity.

"You are so pathetic," she grunted at her reflection before sliding down to the white-tiled floor. She had to do something about this. She would have Trent stop at the all-night drugstore close to her townhouse so that she could buy laxatives. Better yet, she would have him take her home and then she would drive herself to the drugstore to buy the laxatives. On the other hand, she wasn't worthy of driving to the drugstore. She should walk or jog, and if she got mugged or assaulted it would be a good punishment for her gluttony. Now that she had a plan in place, she felt better equipped to face Trent.

A gentle knock on the other side of the washroom cubicle roused Priya out of her thoughts.

"Is anyone in here?" It was Rachel's familiar voice, filled with concern.

Priya struggled to her feet and unlocked the door. A startled Rachel stumbled toward her.

"What's wrong?" she demanded, taking in Priya's freshly-washed face and flushed cheeks. "Were you crying?"

"No ... why?" Priya stammered.

"Trent was very worried about you," Rachel explained. "He said you left for the washroom over fifteen minutes ago. He asked me to make sure that you're okay. Are you?"

"I'm fine," Priya, took a brush out of her handbag and made a gesture toward restyling her hair but her movements were mechanical.

"Oh, my God!" Rachel stepped back to look at her. "You didn't throw up, did you?"

"I don't know what you're talking about," Priya shrugged.

"You can lie to me, but you cannot lie to your own body. Did you…"

"No, I did not throw up," Priya said wearily. "Although any human being who could wallop a whole slice of that double-trouble chocolate truffle cheesecake should be disgusted with themselves. Even Trent didn't eat his entire slice."

Rachel sighed. "You need to eat like that a bit more often. You've lost too much weight."

Priya kept silent as she followed Rachel out the door. She had her plan and she would follow it to the letter.

Trent was waiting patiently at their table when Priya returned to her seat. "Is everything all right?" he asked kindly.

"There was a huge line-up to get into the lady's room," Priya lied effortlessly. Sensing Trent's troubled look, she ploughed on. "Now, tell me more about yourself. We were talking about your traditional Italian-style upbringing."

"I'm a second-generation Canadian but that didn't prevent my parents from indoctrinating me with the values and culture of the old country. I'm grateful for the grounding, but when you grow up here, your thinking broadens. For example, for my Dad, a meal is not a meal if it doesn't have some kind of pasta attached to it. Now, I can go for weeks without pasta if I have to, because, to tell you the truth, I love Indian food and Greek food."

"What does your father do, or is he retired now?" Priya inquired, wondering why she and Trent always steered toward food in their conversation.

"He's a child psychiatrist at Sick Kids."

"He works at Toronto's Sick Children's Hospital? That's interesting." Priya said. "And your mother?"

"When we were growing up, she was at home; but once my sister and I were in school, she began working for my Dad as his receptionist."

"You have a sister?" Priya was surprised.

"I did," Trent said thoughtfully, "but she died last Christmas Eve."

"Oh, I'm really sorry, Trent," Priya was startled.

"She was sick for a long time," his voice trailed off.

Priya wanted to ask about the nature of the illness, but she wouldn't pry. If Trent wanted her to know, he would tell her.

"Hey," he reached across the table and touched her hand. "Don't look so serious. It's over now. Tell me about what it's like being ... let's see," he furrowed his brow in mock concentration, "Half Sri Lankan, half Canadian, "

"Well, I'm kind of a neither here nor there person," Priya said.

"I don't know," Trent chuckled, " you look pretty much all there to me."

Priya smiled back at him. "What I mean is that from a cultural point of view I never knew where I stood growing up. In the Sri Lankan community, and for my father, I was considered very Canadian, yet my Canadian friends found the way we did things socially a bit different."

"In what way?" Trent asked.

"In the Sri Lankan culture, when you have a dinner party, all the children, grandparents ... everyone is a part of it. It's not child-centered but the children are around while the parents chat. It's cozy and casual and children are just part of everyday life. Whereas in Canadian culture, everything is compartmentalized. The kids are sent to bed and the parents have their dinner party with other adult couples. Unless it's specifically planned differently, adults have their time and children have theirs."

"Which style do you like?" Trent inquired

"In that way, I'm more Sri Lankan," Priya smiled. "I liked our noisy get togethers with the men arguing politics, the women sitting in clusters and the children playing around everyone."

"Sounds lively," Trent said.

"It is, but when everyone starts talking about the economic situation in Sri Lanka and the women reflect on the relatives back home, I feel at loose ends. Then again there's my mother's crowd back in St. John's. Though to them I'm just 'Laney's girl, I'm still seen as different. I can run into someone new at my Grandma's church and people who don't know me will ask me if I've been 'back home' for a visit and trust me, Trent, they don't mean Ontario!"

"And then," Trent said with a flourish, "she opens her mouth, the fluent English pours out with polish and they think hey, what's this?"

"Kind of," Priya blushed.

"Well, it's true," Trent said. "You are small and delicate but you have this air of maturity and wisdom about you. I have to say, I really like that about you."

"Thank you," Priya toyed with a serviette, then smiled. "And you seem to know really how to put me at ease. I don't usually talk this much about me."

Just then, Rachel approached their table. "I ran into some friends at the bar. We're heading out for drinks and dancing. You'll be okay with Trent?" She gave Priya a meaningful nod.

"Of course," Priya assured her, knowing that she would be more than okay with Trent. And even more okay when she got home and could go to the drugstore.

A couple of hours later, Trent kissed Priya good night at her front door, a kiss she felt to the bottom of her toes. They had agreed that on the following Friday evening he would drop by to hear her play a tune on the piano and then they go to a movie. "I'll call you before that," he placed his hands on her shoulders. "I had a wonderful time with you."

"I did too," Priya said sincerely. "I'll look forward to your call."

The lamp by the glider was still on. Priya was surprised to find her robed Auntie still up. It wasn't usual for her to wait up for Priya after a night out. Normally Renita was in bed by

10:00 pm. Her long hair was loose around her shoulders and a closed magazine lay on her lap. When Priya greeted her, she noted a faraway look in her Auntie's eyes.

"Hello, Priya, you had a nice time?" she inquired on becoming aware of the younger woman's presence. "I was coughing quite a bit ... this cold weather doesn't agree with me. Also I have an annoying pain in my rib cage," Renita grumbled. "I took some Panadol. I hope it will help."

"You still have the medicine you brought from Sri Lanka?" Priya was puzzled. "If the Panadol has passed its expiry date, I have Tylenol in the house."

"That's okay," Renita shook her head. "This is the packet I bought from the duty-free shop at the airport in London when I broke journey..."

"Auntie, that was over a year ago," Priya protested. "Where's the box?"

"These are good for two more years," she assured her.

"How bad is the pain?" Priya slipped off her shoes

"Very much better now," Renita admitted. "I didn't go to tell Jay or Delaney anything, but about a month before I got to Canada, I tripped on a curb when I was rushing to catch a bus. Fortunately there were no vehicles close by otherwise I would have been knocked down. Anyway, I bruised a couple of ribs as a result of the fall and was warded overnight at the nursing home, or what you Canadians call hospital," she'd noticed Priya's quizzical look. Then added, "it was nothing too serious, but still I have pain from time to time. As I said, this cold weather doesn't agree with me. That is why I have this cough that keeps me up at night."

"I think you should see Dr. Benson about the cough," Priya said.

"No, Priya," Renita shook her head with resignation. "It's just a nuisance, that's all. They tested me well and truly for the medical portion of my immigration interview, and besides, even for that one night in the nursing home ... my, our doctors are so thorough..." her voice drifted into a reflective silence.

"Are you sure you don't want me to take you to the hospital?" Priya asked, mentally trying to locate her car keys.

"No, that's okay. I'm feeling very much better, thank you. Your Grandma called from St. John's soon after you left. I think she wants to discuss Christmas plans with you."

"Christmas," Priya sighed. "Without Ma and Dad, I can't even imagine."

"That's the thing," Renita sighed. "Anyway, what to do? They're gone now and we have to box on."

Priya waited until her aunt went upstairs and closed her bedroom door before making a move toward the stairs herself. With heart pounding violently, she stripped off her clothes and climbed onto her white lithium weighing scale. It was past midnight and well after her full meal. There was no rationale for weighing herself when she would be invariably heavier than in the morning. That was a reality for anyone stepping on the scale in the middle of the night. Weight fluctuated throughout the day. It was a fact of physics and no amount of dieting or bingeing would change that.

"What!" Priya clapped a hand to her mouth to stifle a shriek of horror. The black number in the gray window read 93 pounds. She had gained three pounds in less than three days. She felt as if she weighed 193 pounds.

Blinded by intense rage at her gluttony, she snatched her clothes from the blue tile floor and stormed into her bedroom. Hyperventilating with emotion, she flung them onto the bed and ripped into the wooden rack on the back of the door. Fleece top, yes, but fleece pants, never! She had to suffer for her greed. She grasped a pair of white shorts from behind a handful of summer t-shirts, dressed, grabbed socks from her top drawer, slammed her feet into her white sneakers, and then glared at her tired reflection in the mirror.

She was in such a frenzied hurry to get down the stairs she was tempted to hurl herself over the wooden banister. She yanked her wallet out of her evening bag and jammed it into the hip pocket of her shorts.

"Now, see how much you can eat..." her voice faded in a litany of obscenities as she wrenched open the door.

Impervious to the frosty air that stabbed at her lungs and the frigid winds that lashed against her bare legs, she began pounding her way up the sidewalk, skillfully dodging ice patches that obstructed her path. She could hear her father's strident voice bellowing in her ear. He was goading her to perform at peak capacity.

When she was sixteen, she made the mistake of signing up for a charity run her school was sponsoring. Proceeds were to go to underprivileged kids in developing countries. Priya naively thought she would not only help those children but also help herself lose a few pounds so she could trade her size eight pants for a more flattering size four.

Jay, who coached a highly successful track team at the same school, was initially thrilled that his daughter wanted to take part in the 10K charity run. Her keenness to help children in developing countries reminded him of the young Delaney who'd captured his heart so long ago. That's why she'd been in Sri Lanka in the mid-seventies. Now their very own daughter was showing the same zeal. "You're going to win this race and get more sponsors than anyone else in the process," Priya recalled him saying.

"I'll do my best," she had agreed.

"Only if your best is good enough," Jay had said.

Priya never made it into the race. Weeks of relentless coaching by her father, weeks of browbeating, broke down her resolve. There were too many tears, too much anguish. She was never going to measure up to her father's draconian standards, so she dropped out three days before the event. She was too ashamed to tell anyone the real reason she'd withdrawn her name from the race, because she genuinely believed they would see her for the poor sport that her father already judged her to be. Instead, she fabricated an elaborate tale about a twisted ankle.

"Go, you fool!" he'd thundered to the plump sixteen-year-old meandering through the track behind their school. "Girls much slimmer than you, far more powerful ... they can run! You're overweight. Heart disease before you're thirty!" he'd bellow, running alongside her.

At the time, Priya hadn't understood that the real object of his frustration was his wife. Yet, he had enough respect and restraint not to hurl emotional abuse at her. As much as he loved Delaney, however, he didn't disguise that fact that he was turned off by the weight she'd put on. When Jay and Delaney first met in their early twenties, she was on the rounder side of slim. By her early forties, she was beyond chunky and, in his critical eyes, it just wasn't pretty. Priya was the perfect scapegoat for his misplaced rage. Jay would be damned if he was going to let his daughter turn out like her mother. As a gym teacher and sports coach he had an image to maintain. His basketball team had won trophies for being among the best in the GTA several years in a row. He pushed his athletes beyond mercy and accepted no compromises. He couldn't tolerate a sluggish, out-of-shape daughter threatening his reputation.

The browbeating and confidence-bashing had almost thrown Priya into a tailspin, but Delaney saved her before that could happen. Rather than dwelling on external assets, Delaney encouraged Priya to focus on her inner beauty and strength. Mother and daughter engaged in weekend adventures that involved going to musicals, the ballet, and exploring the newest cafés and eateries on the block. Priya saw her mother as an ally and friend.

Meanwhile, on the home front, Delaney demanded that Jay stop foisting his own insecurities and inadequacies onto his daughter. "Don't be so foolish, Jay. How can you be so abusive towards your own child," the usually mild-mannered Delaney, in a fit of maternal angst, railed at her husband when they both thought Priya was fast asleep.

"I say what I say out of love," Jay was defensive. "Your western philosophy of praising and coddling egos does nothing to shape successful minds and bodies. If I didn't care about Priya, I wouldn't demand the best from her."

"So according to you, love is shown by leveling emotional abuse at your child," Delaney was nonplussed. "If I'd known what a controlling Asian male you were I might have had second thoughts about marrying you."

"I know why you married me," Jay said teasingly. "White woman rescues native boy from the jungle or some similar scenario."

"Actually that's only part of the reason," Delaney had kidded back. "The other part was that I fell madly in love with your whip-straight black hair and bronzed skin."

The humour dissolved the tension and for several weeks Jay was almost benevolent toward Priya, encouraging her to invite her friends home more often, renting movies he thought they could watch as a family, and offering careful praise when she brought home good marks. Priya was a good student, a fine pianist, and in many ways a model teenager. She didn't run around with a hard crowd. She wasn't promiscuous. What more did Jay want? A lot, it seemed to Priya.

After a few months of peace, Jay was back to his old tricks — this time with the piano. Priya's music exams were looming. She chafed under his demands, but Priya was obedient. She played the classics that her teachers outlined for her. She brought home awards from the Kiwanis music festival and pleased her father. But she didn't enjoy any of it. Classical music made her sad. It conjured up images of a life and time that she couldn't relate to, yet she soldiered on as long as she could.

If Jay De Souza were alive now, he would be impressed with his daughter's ability to run in shorts to a drugstore in freezing temperatures exacerbated by an unforgiving wind-chill factor.

While the bath water ran, filling the tub with rich, foamy bubbles that would chase away the chill from her shivering limbs, Priya lined up the boxes of laxatives on the roll-top vanity. She'd generated more than a few strange looks from the cashiers at the all-night drugstore when she rushed in from the elements, her hands red and trembling. She'd known precisely in which aisle the laxatives were located. She picked up four packs of a generic brand and paid for them. She'd attracted some attention. It was after midnight, and here she was, a young woman in shorts on a cold November night buying laxatives.

The girl on cash appeared to be Muslim, as she wore a colourful head covering. Her English was halting, suggesting that she was a newcomer to Canada. Priya was grateful for this turn of luck. Even though the cashier might regard her with a mix of confusion and disapproval, she would not be able articulate her curiosity about what Priya was doing and why.

Breathing hard and sweating heavily, Priya peered down at the blue packages. Each contained sixteen pills. Although she was tempted to down at least one full box, good sense prevailed and she opted to follow the package instructions and use them only after meals. She'd create the illusion of eating normally when she was out with her friends and then she would find the nearest washroom and execute damage control. When she was alone, she wouldn't eat at all. This was how it would be.

The bubble bath cocooned Priya's chilled body in womb-like warmth. She felt safe and secure as she rested her head against the mint green, inflatable bath pillow. For a brief moment, life was good. Her muscles ached and her eyelids drooped. She knew that for once, sleep would come easily this night. Tender thoughts of Trent added to her sense of well-being as she toweled off and pulled on her light pink polar fleece pajamas. After taking two laxatives, she climbed into bed and tumbled into a sound sleep. The jog to the drugstore had taken twenty minutes both ways.

The house was very still when Priya woke up in the morning. Bright wintry sunshine streamed in through the blinds on her window as she luxuriated under the downy softness of her duvet. Her clock radio told her that it was 10:15 am. If her parents had been alive, Priya would have gone to church today. Instead, she climbed out of the bed and went to the washroom. The phone was ringing when she emerged a few minutes later.

She darted across the hall, back into her room, and grabbed the receiver. She lay back on her bed, her feet resting on top of the duvet. "Hello, my Duckie," Daisy Saunders said cheerfully.

"Hi, Grandma," Priya was always happy to hear her grandmother's voice. "I know you called last night but I was waiting until later to phone you. I thought you'd be at church still," Priya explained, accounting for the ninety-minute time difference between Ontario and Newfoundland. It was almost noon in St. John's. She'd assumed that her grandparents would be on the road driving home for their typical Sunday 'cooked dinner,' which actually meant lunch for Ontario-raised Priya.

"Didn't make it into church today, girl," Daisy said regretfully. "We had an awful snowfall last night and the young fella who shovels for us didn't come over yet, so we're still barred in. How are you feeling, my Duckie?"

"I'm all right," Priya said tentatively.

"Your Aunt said you're not eating properly," Daisy said.

"Well, with Christmas coming, I feel sadder than ever. How about you, Grandma?" Priya asked. "How are you and Grandpa coping?"

"Well that's just it, girl," Daisy sighed. "We cope. I keep busy with the church and my activities. I'm asked out to a bridal shower now, but sure if that old driveway isn't shovelled, I won't be going anywhere. That's a sin because I love keeping busy. It keeps my mind off Delaney. I've got a Rotary Club dinner with Grandpa on Wednesday. The whole week is blocked, but, girl, that's the only way I can face all this."

"You're doing the right thing," Priya assured her. She could imagine how hard it was for her grandparents to survive their only child. Priya admired their strength and wished they could pass some of it on to her.

"What are we doing for Christmas?" Daisy brought her back to the moment.

"If Ma and Dad were alive, you and Grandpa would have come here this year," Priya mused.

"We can still come," Daisy assured her. "I think it's very

important that we face the season together."

"I would have loved to come to St. John's," Priya admitted, "but I don't think I'm ready for that yet. I have too many memories. It would hurt too much, and besides, I can't leave Auntie Renita here by herself."

"Sure, she could come along," Daisy spoke with enthusiasm. "We have the room and there's a two-day seat sale on the go…"

"She won't come, Grandma," Priya assured her. "She's made it very clear to me that there is nothing in Canada that interests her now that Dad is gone."

"Oh, well then," Daisy sighed. "That's all we can do."

"Do you want me to go online and book the tickets for you?" Priya offered. "I might be able to get a deal."

"I don't think you'll find anything better than $99 one way," Daisy commented.

"Probably not," Priya agreed.

"Your Aunt said you'd gone to a dinner theatre with a hand-some young man last night," Daisy observed.

"Rachel introduced me to this guy, Trent Perelli. He seems really nice, but we'll wait and see."

"Perelli," Daisy mused. "Italian, is he?"

"Yes, his grandparents immigrated here from Italy."

"Perhaps you might get to know him better and we'll meet him at Christmas," Daisy suggested. 'I'd love for you to meet someone and settle down. You spend too much time alone."

"We'll see what happens," Priya said. She'd barely put down the phone when it began to ring again.

"Priya?" a friendly male voice greeted her questioningly.

"Gabe?" Priya was tentative.

"I knew your voice right away," he responded cheerfully. "You doing all right?"

"Not too bad," Priya was surprised at how happy she was to hear from him. "And you?"

"Great," Gabe said. "I called your number on Thursday evening, but the phone rang and rang. I suppose nobody was home."

"My aunt might have been on the phone," Priya said apologetically. "Even though we have call waiting, she just ignores it."

"That's too bad," Gabe said. "I was starting to worry about how you made out at the doctor's office."

"Didn't you get my message?" Priya asked.

"Definitely," Gabe assured her, "but things got pretty crazy after that. I was working right through the weekend and didn't get a chance to call you 'til just now. I was to the Ninth Line earlier today. I have a farm that I'm trying to sell. I bought it as a business investment about ten years ago, but now I think it's time to cut my losses."

Priya suddenly realized she knew virtually nothing about Gabe, other than what he'd volunteered that Thursday at McDonald's. If he was genuinely connected to her mother, Priya wanted to know all about him — and any information would be a welcome link to Delaney's past.

"How about meeting for coffee today?"

"I would like that," Priya passed a hand over her disheveled hair. She had to think fast. If she had coffee with Gabe, that would mean she could consume nothing else for the rest of the day. She'd eat and drink normally in his presence, come home, take the laxatives, rid the calories from her system, and then go for a jog at night.

"The Starbucks at Chapters is nice."

"Sounds good," Priya agreed. "I used to work at a Chapters downtown until last summer."

"Really?" Gabe was surprised. "Perhaps you might be fed up of it all, feeling like you're back at work."

"No," Priya laughed. "I love being there, no matter what. It's just that I was going through so much after my parents' deaths, I couldn't cope."

"Well, you can relax this afternoon. We'll peruse the books and have a grand old Newfoundland-style chat," Gabe suggested.

"Okay, but I could drive over and meet you there."

"Don't worry about that," he said. "Save the gas and let me pick you up. Around 2:00 pm?"

"Perfect," Priya said.

Priya called her grandmother back, wondering why it hadn't occurred to her to ask about Gabe before.

"Does the name Gabe Johanson mean anything to you?" she asked when Daisy answered the phone.

There was a lengthy pause at the other end of the line.

"Grandma?" Priya was impatient. "Are you there?"

"Imagine that now, tch ... tch ... tch," Daisy's voice had dropped to a conspiratorial low. "I haven't heard that name in years, and I mean *years*!"

"I met him here by chance the other day," Priya was not about to volunteer to her grandmother the part of the story that involved her collapsing in the middle of Walmart.

"I'll be darned..." Daisy sounded as if she were easing into a trance.

"He says he and Ma went to school together," Priya supplied.

"He's living up there now, is he?" Daisy's voice grew distant. "Honey, your Grandpa is hungry."

"Yes, but Grandma..." Priya protested. She suddenly felt like a whiny six-year-old demanding a peek at her Christmas gifts before the big day. Grandma was obviously not prepared to talk.

"Grandpa's waiting for his cooked dinner," Grandma said. "I'll call you later."

The call ended abruptly, leaving Priya not only hungry for food, but for information about Gabe.

Chapter 6

PRIYA WAS SURPRISED that Renita wasn't up yet. On a typical Sunday morning, she'd be up early preparing for church, but today there didn't seem to be much activity coming from her room. Priya went down the hall and knocked gently on the partially opened door.

"Auntie?" she called as beams of sunlight filtered through the slats of the blinds on the east window above the bed.

"Come in, come in," Renita's cheerful tone belied the sombre look on her pinched face as she waved her niece inside.

The formerly mundane guestroom had been transformed into as close a likeness to Renita's bedroom in Sri Lanka as possible. Even the lingering scent of mothballs and lilac perfume hung heavy in the air as it did in the old house in Nawala. At one end of the room was a glass-fronted wooden cupboard stacked with an array of colourful saris, cashmere, georgettes, and silks. Jay had spotted the cabinet at a yard sale the summer before Renita arrived. He claimed it was the most affordable thing he could find to replace the almara that Renita would have to leave behind in their parents' home. That was a rosewood relic with ornate carvings of tropical wildlife that went back generations in the De Souza family. A parade of teak elephants lined Renita's bedside table. It was strangely at odds with the black clock radio that screamed modernity from its plastic casing and oversized digital display.

Priya knew that Renita kept a stash of gold jewellery and precious stones in a lacquered box under her bed. Jay had pleaded with his sister to let him store her jewellery in their safety deposit box along with Delaney's and Priya's valuable pieces. He would be glad to take them out whenever Renita asked, but she had refused. As far as she was concerned, the jewellery would be far safer under her own lock and key. She was even willing to stitch them on a string to be held tight against her skin under her sari.

To Priya, the issue was moot now that Jay and Delaney were dead. Renita claimed to feel so despondent she vowed never to bother with jewellery again.

A cluster of framed family photographs hung on the wall opposite the bed. There was the requisite portrait of Renita and Jay's parents. The sepia photograph featured a conservative-looking couple with bland expressions on their faces. Their mother, a plump twenty-two-year-old at the time of her marriage, is clad in an elaborate wedding sari finished with a gold border and intricate handwork. Her upswept hair reveals a face that bears some similarity to both Renita and Priya. The father stands tall and aloof with lips that seem etched into a look of grim resignation. Only a bush of heavy black curls, which was passed through the generations to Priya, softens his angular face.

Priya had only vague recollections of her paternal grandparents. From her childhood perspective, she recalled that they were very strict and didn't talk much. The remaining pictures on the wall are of Renita and Jay at various stages in their lives. There is even one of Renita, seated in front of a grand piano, her slender wrists bobbing above the keys. There is a youthful serenity in her pretty face. Priya suspected the picture was taken when she was in her late teens or early twenties. There are no photographs of Delaney or Priya.

"How are you feeling, Auntie?" Priya inquired, noting Renita's crumpled posture on the bed, her long dark hair spilled in a knotty tangle over her drooping shoulders. Her thin body was almost nonexistent in the folds of her heavy plaid nightgown.

"Very much better, thank you," she responded agreeably.

"Are you going to church?" Priya perched on the edge of the bed, surprised by her own sense of compassion for the older woman. It must have been impossibly hard for Renita, well into her sixties, to uproot her entire life and transplant it here in Canada. Worse, she had come to Canada with the expectation that she would be living with her brother and his wife. Now what little family she could claim as her own had been wiped out in a senseless plane crash. All she was left with was Priya — a young woman who was more a stranger to her than a niece.

"No, I thought I'd stay back. With the snow and ice, I don't want to risk a fall. What about you?"

"Well," Priya sighed, "ever since Ma and Dad died, I haven't had the energy to get dressed up and go. I know I should, but I'm just not ready."

"Yes, I, too, often feel that way," Renita nodded, "but anyway we must box on because that is what Jay would have wanted." She picked up the silver brush that had been resting on her lap and began idly detangling her hair. "What's your program for the day?"

"Not too much," Priya shrugged. "I'm meeting a friend for coffee around 2:00, and in the meantime I should get to my résumés, but I'm just not motivated."

Renita ignored this. "I made quite a bit of rice and curry on Friday, so I have enough food for a few days. But if you don't mind, will you boil me an egg and prepare some tea for me?"

"Of course," Priya nodded. "Any toast, Auntie?"

"No," Renita shook her head. "My appetite has gone down these past few months ... like yours."

Priya took a long look at her father's sister and saw only pain and worry lines ingrained in her weary face. She had an intuitive feeling that there was more to her aunt's misery than the cloying grief that smothered both of their hearts.

Priya sized herself up in the oval, brass-framed mirror in the hallway by the front door. It was close to 2:00 pm and she decided she looked pretty good. Dressed in her new size zero jeans — she didn't know they made jeans that small until she went hunting for them on Friday night — and her standard black pea coat, she was pleased with her appearance. Because she was suffering from a minor headache, she had opted to wear her puffy hair down instead of confining it to its usually restrictive ponytail.

"Auntie," she called upstairs, "can I get you anything before I leave?"

"No, child," Renita called from her room. "Excuse me if I don't meet your friend, but I'm not up for company today. Perhaps later I'll come down and make myself a tea."

Renita had consumed at least five cups of loose leaf Ceylon tea since Priya brought her breakfast in bed; yet the boiled egg had barely been touched. "And they think *I'm* anorexic," she had sniffed after returning the plate to the kitchen.

"Are you sure you won't come down now?" Priya was a little surprised that Renita wasn't interested in meeting her friends, particularly a strange man who was whisking her niece away for coffee. If Jay and Delaney were here, they'd have practically demanded a police report from Gabe before allowing Priya to step out with him.

She heard a car pulling up behind hers in the driveway. She grabbed her handbag from a small marble-topped side table and proceeded to unlock the door at the sound of the bell.

Gabe, tall and imposing with a green baseball-style cap in hand, greeted Priya with a warm smile. "How's it going?" he asked.

She was about to respond when she heard Renita's footsteps descending the stairs. "Auntie," she turned toward the older woman. "This is Gabe Johanson, an old friend of Ma's."

"Hello," Renita came to stand beside her. "I can't say I've heard your name before, but it's nice to meet you."

"The pleasure is mine," Gabe shook her hand. "Yes, Delaney and I go back a long way. We grew up together in St. John's."

"Auntie, are you sure I can't get you anything before we leave?" Priya asked and then suddenly turned to Gabe. "Do you mind if Auntie joins us for coffee?"

"Not at all," Gabe said cheerfully.

"Oh no," Renita smiled, "You go and enjoy. I'll have my tea and rest a little while longer."

"Auntie hasn't been feeling too well," Priya said.

"That's too bad," Gabe nodded with understanding.

They bade good-bye to Renita and headed for the door. Once they were out in the streaming sunshine, Gabe paused to look at Priya. "Wow!" he exclaimed. "Your hair is almost bigger than you are."

"Essentially," Priya couldn't help chuckling. She rarely wore her hair down, but when she did, heads turned. "It's quite a conversation piece, wouldn't you say?"

"You're funny," Gabe said warmly, "but very, very pretty. There is one lucky guy waiting for you somewhere."

Avoiding his gaze, she stared ahead to his car that glinted silver in the sunlight.

"Starbucks still good?" he asked as he opened the passenger door for her.

"Definitely," Priya said as she slipped into her seat.

"Your Aunt doesn't seem very happy," Gabe observed as he started the car.

"She's taking the death of my father really hard, I suppose," Priya snapped her seatbelt in place.

"She seems like a nice lady, but I can see it in her eyes, she's had a lot of suffering," Gabe added thoughtfully.

"That's an interesting observation," Priya commented.

"Well, I tend to exercise my sixth sense quite a bit," Gabe admitted. "I'm pretty good at reading people."

The rest of their conversation was fairly mundane as they drove through the quiet streets of Mississauga toward the bookstore café. They discussed the weather, the Christmas decorations festooning the city, and the theatre production Priya had seen the night before. She couldn't wait to get to the café with the hope that Gabe would really open up to her.

But Priya was also in a dilemma. Gabe would be the only person with whom she would interact for the day. How would she survive on an iced mocha and a small snack for the balance of the day? She wondered if there was a way she could discreetly consume half the beverage at Starbucks and take the rest home for later.

Although seats were at a premium at the coffee shop, they managed to nab the coveted armchairs in front of the electric fireplace. A young couple had been enjoying them for some time but serendipity intervened when their cell phone rang, summoning them to a more private location. Gabe sprinted toward the chairs, gesturing for Priya to hurry. After staking their territory by arranging their coats over the chairs, Gabe asked Priya what she would like.

"I'll have a skim milk iced mocha," Priya replied.

"And to eat?" he inquired.

"Uh ... I'm not that hungry," she said evenly and then to ward off potential disapproval, she added, "Let's just go up in turn and get whatever we like."

"It was going to be my treat," Gabe seemed disappointed.

"No, thank you, that's not necessary," Priya said firmly.

"Okay, then, you go first," he suggested as he reluctantly sat down in one of the chairs.

She approached the bar, noting that there were three people and a stroller ahead of her. Lively voices, an occasional spurt of laughter, and bantering among the baristas made for a comfortable coffee-scented ambience that caused Priya's nose to swell and her taste buds to dance. What she wouldn't give for a slice of lemon poppyseed loaf paired with a rich aromatic blend. Yet a cursory glance at the people around her was a pertinent reminder that giving into temptation was sure to put her on the road to obesity. Among the university students, young parents, and retirees seated at the tables, there were hardly any that could be classified as conventionally slim. Some were very overweight, most were a little plump, though streamlined, suggesting they were doing some form of strength training to transform their fat into muscle. Only one other young woman appeared about as thin as Priya.

She looked down at her size zero jeans and frowned. She was certain it was all a gimmick. She'd read about it in a fashion magazine. Manufacturers were labeling clothes with smaller sizes to soothe the bruised egos of heavier women who liked to believe that they really weren't *that* big. Twenty years ago, the present size zero of her jeans would have easily passed for a size three. Priya remembered her mother saying that as a young woman she wore a size sixteen, yet up to the time of her death, she was wearing a size fourteen, even though she was twenty pounds heavier.

While Priya waited to be served, she studied her surroundings. The chocolate brown counter topped a chilled showcase of calorie-dense tortes and cheesecakes. Glass cookie jars exploded with a trendy assortment of biscotti and shortbread. Bundt cakes sat under glass domes, glazes oozing seductively down the sides and pooling in delicious puddles on the bottoms of their trays. The white noise of relaxed chatter was interspersed with the occasional whirring sound of coffee beans being ground and packaged to go home with caffeine-craving customers who required their half-pound fix for the week.

Before long, Priya was settled comfortably in front of the fire clasping a clear plastic cup brimming with her favourite drink of all time, complete with a dash of whipped cream and a sprinkle of chocolate on top. Who would suspect she had an eating disorder with a drink like that, she thought, smugly, to herself. She wasn't quite sure how she'd save some of the drink for later though. Gabe was sure to raise his eyebrows when he realized she wasn't capable of drinking a twelve-ounce beverage that was comprised mostly of skim milk all at once. With tremendous grit, she had managed to bypass the cakes and tortes in favour of a simple sliver of chocolate chip shortbread. After a nibble here and a bite there, her plan was to stuff the rest into her handbag and save it for dinner.

Priya closed her eyes and inhaled deeply in a vain attempt to chase away her deepening headache. Gabe returned with his order and sat down. There was a small round table between them, providing just enough room for two mugs and accompanying side plates.

"Wow, is this coffee ever good," Gabe said after a long, grateful sip.

"I agree," Priya opened her eyes and smiled. She was amused at how frequently "wow" popped into Gabe's speech. She liked it! She tried not to stare at the appealing lemon square on his plate. She would have loved one as well, but knew she wasn't worthy of such decadence.

"How are you feeling after Thursday's fainting episode?" Gabe asked, relaxing in his chair.

"Not too bad," Priya said. "Now, without meaning to be abrupt, can we talk about my mother? I'm dying to share memories here."

"You don't beat around the bush much, do you?" Gabe chuckled.

"Not really," she admitted, "I'm very direct."

"To tell you the truth," Gabe took another sip of coffee, "I had planned to tell you the whole story, right here, right now, but I'm not so sure anymore."

"Why?" Priya was startled.

"I'm not sure you can handle it … yet," Gabe took a bite of his lemon square.

"You're not so sure I can handle what?" She wrapped her hands around the cold plastic cup, clamped her lips over the straw, and drew the cool, refreshing liquid into her mouth. The combination of dairy, chocolate and espresso was soothing against her parched tongue.

"You're very vulnerable right now," Gabe said slowly. "The last thing I want to do is hurt you with startling revelations. I feel if your mother wanted you to know, she would have told you."

"Startling revelations like what?" Priya demanded.

"A lot of things…" Gabe took another sip of coffee. "I think of them as the complexities of life."

"The complexities of life," Priya cleared her throat.

"Are you going to keep on doing that?" Gabe's tone hinted at amusement.

"Doing what?" Priya demanded.

"Repeating key phrases," Gabe said.

"I'm just trying to understand." Priya tried to keep the frustration out of her voice. "Why are we here, if you're not going to tell me anything? I could be home, going for a jog — or something."

"Going for a jog or something?" Gabe's eyebrows arched with disapproval.

"Now who's repeating what!" Priya's eyes flashed with anger. "Look, Mr. Johanson, I don't know what kind of game you're playing. For all I know, you didn't even *know* my mother."

"Oh, I knew her all right," Gabe began. His words were interrupted with the ring of his cell phone. "I usually keep my phone off when I'm having coffee, but I'm on call today. Excuse me."

Priya nodded.

"No, that's fine. Call if you really need me." Gabe flipped his phone closed and laid it on the table beside his cup. "Sorry about that."

Taking a deep breath to maintain her composure, Priya fixed her eyes on Gabe's and said, "When I spoke to my grandmother on the phone this morning, I told her about meeting you at Walmart. She was really surprised."

"First of all Priya, I can assure you that I am not playing any kind of game with you. I knew your mother and your grandparents quite well." Gabe took a sip of coffee. "I think you deserve to know the whole story, and I don't know why your mother didn't share it with you. Personally, I think you have a right to know. However, you've been through a really tough year and now you're battling anorexia..."

"How would you know that?" Priya gasped. The heat rose in her face as she stumbled for something to add. "Are you a doctor? Come to think of it, I don't know anything about you."

"I'm not a doctor," Gabe said patiently, "but as I told you

a little while ago, I'm pretty good at reading people. I've been in the business-end of sales for over twenty years. Throughout my career I have interacted with hundreds of people and, as a result, I know a bit about human nature. I am also an avid reader. Books are an addiction with me."

"What kind of business have you been involved in?" Priya asked curiously, deciding that maybe knowing more about him might help her discern what he might be trying to hide about his relationship with her mother.

"I've sold everything from cars to insurance. Three years ago, however, I got bored with everything. I was single and had enough money to take early retirement, so I decided to step away from the working world to weigh my options. While I planned the second half of my life, I occupied myself with a little bit of hunting, fishing, and mountain climbing. I dabbled in some investment options that panned out nicely for me. When a new business venture brought me out of retirement to Ontario a couple of years ago, I even bought a small dairy farm, as a lark. I knew I wasn't going to make any money on it, but it was an adventure."

"Is that your main line of work here in Ontario?" Priya asked.

"Oh, no," Gabe shook his head. "In fact, I'm thinking of unloading that farm. I have a small transportation business called 'We'll Care.' It's a play on words for 'Wheel Care.' I manage a modest fleet of minivans that are used to ferry the disabled and seniors to medical and other appointments. Although I have staff running it for me, I like to take my turn driving the clients from time to time. I feel it's important to maintain that personal touch with the people you are serving."

"Hmmm," Priya mused. "My friend Rachel is in the process of getting her MBA. Did you get a degree in business before starting out."

"I don't have a university degree," Gabe said. "I have trade school — community college education, I believe they call it here in Ontario. Most of my business know-how resulted from the school of hard knocks. Now, what about yourself?"

"I'm supposed to be a kindergarten teacher, but I don't have the job to prove it," Priya admitted in her usual self-deprecating manner.

"You don't sound too happy about it," Gabe observed intuitively.

"That's life," she sighed. "You do what you must to pay the bills."

"I can see why you're not getting hired," Gabe chided gently. "You're about as enthusiastic about your chosen profession as someone facing a root canal."

Priya laughed.

"You strike me as a smart young lady who knows her own mind," Gabe continued, "so I don't understand why you would have put X number of years studying toward a career that doesn't interest you."

"My Dad would have liked me to get into medical school, but as good as my marks were, they just weren't competitive enough to get me there," Priya confessed.

"What is it *you* would really like to do?" Gabe probed.

"I don't honestly know," she shook her head. "I still feel directionless ... still overwhelmed by my parents' deaths."

"As I mentioned last Thursday," Gabe said slowly, "I knew about your parents' deaths. I was in St. John's at the time of the plane crash. It was a Cessna, right? There was a capsule account of it in the local paper. Something to the effect of 'former Newfoundlander perishes in crash.' I got more details after going online and looking at the Toronto papers."

As Priya nodded, Gabe placed both of his palms flat on the table, sliding his hands over toward her. "Years ago, Jay sent me the announcement regarding your birth," he added unexpectedly. "So, I made it a point to seek you out when I heard what happened. I thought, perhaps, I could be of help to you."

"Why would you want to help me?" Priya asked suspiciously.

"Because your mother was a very good friend of mine and I thought it was time I reached out to somebody else for a change. I've had my moments of selfishness over the years. Believe me, Priya, there is absolutely nothing I want from you. If you tell me right now, 'Gabe, stay out of my life,' I will do that for you. However, in light of what you've gone through recently, if you feel there is room for a new friend, then I'm here for you. It is as simple as that."

Priya gauged the handsome man seated in the neighbouring chair. He had a nice profile. His hands were strong and powerful. He had a gentle voice but he was nearly twice her age. Realistically speaking, what could he possibly want from her? Sex? There were far better-looking young women than herself. Gabe seemed like the type of man who could get anyone he wanted. He didn't need an overweight misfit to make his night a success. The truth was that Priya was drawn to him. If he knew, she thought, he would laugh for sure.

Placing the proverbial ball in his court, she phrased her own question. "Why didn't you tell me this on Thursday?"

"Thursday was pretty intense with you fainting and my having to call your friend Serena," Gabe reminded. "Besides, I figured there was plenty of time for us to get to know each other ... that is, if you are okay with that."

"Sure, why not," Priya shrugged.

"Do you think Serena would go out with me, as a friend?"

"As a friend?"Priya was brought up short by the question but she didn't flinch.

"I'd just like to catch up with her about Delaney's life ... if that is okay with her, and you." Gabe said.

"She misses Ma a lot. I think it'd be great if she had someone other than me to talk to about her," Priya admitted.

Priya relaxed. There was something about Gabe that inspired her trust. His face was a bit weather-worn, but his eyes were sincere, and that's what mattered. That and the fact that she was determined to discover what he was holding back from her. "Now, you know about my parents, what about yours?"

"Let me tell you now." Gabe leaned back in his chair, ever willing to share his story. He was the son of an Evangelical minister. As the youngest of three children, he experienced a traditional childhood in St. John's. He came of age in the early seventies. An independent thinker from a young age, Gabe unwittingly fashioned his own revolt against authority — the authority of his peers and contemporaries. Where his friends were into rock music and getting high on the trendiest drugs of the day, Gabe was happier spending time ice fishing with his uncles.

He told Priya how Delaney used to help him rewrite his English essays because his interpretation of the poetry assignment didn't match the narrow view of his teacher, who claimed to know the poet's mind better than her students did. Similarly, Gabe and his authoritarian father clashed more than once. Reverend Steven Johanson was a die-hard moralist who believed in pursuing life on the straight and narrow. Because Steven the Reverend felt biblical teachings were to be taken literally, Gabe was discouraged from forging his own interpretation of the Gospel. He was urged to conform to the views of his parents and their church.

Priya nodded with understanding. Gabe's father sounded a lot like Jay. Gabe prattled on good-naturedly about his various business ventures and his travels to different countries around the world. However, despite his material success, he confessed to Priya, he wasn't happy. One bright wintry day, three years earlier, he sat brooding in a fishing boat. He'd gone on a bender with a former business associate the night before. An overpowering sense of emptiness and lost opportunities had led him back to a vice that had resulted in many skirmishes with his father when he was a teenager — alcohol. When he was young and frustrated, Gabe fell under the illusion that drinking would solve all his problems. Even in his early forties, with a string of unsuccessful relationships in his wake, he naively thought he could appease his loneliness by drinking himself dumb. He realized then that if he didn't pull himself together, he'd be putting everything he had achieved at risk. That day, in the fishing boat, he decided to just stop.

The guidance he received was unexpected. It came in the form of a Buddhist monk, originally from Sri Lanka but residing and teaching in Toronto. He'd been flown to St. John's to preside at the funeral of a prominent Buddhist living in the community. While in St. John's, the monk gave a lecture at the local university. Gabe attended the lecture with the woman he was dating casually at that time. He understood then that his quest for personal truth was fueled by his remorse for mistakes that could not be undone. He was so inspired by the teachings and philosophies of Buddhism that he decided to leave behind his life as a successful entrepreneur to seek his life's purpose.

After renting out his house and selling the car dealership he'd bought and parlayed into personal profit, he took a six-month tour of India, Sri Lanka, Malaysia, and Singapore. He imbibed the cultures of his host countries. He observed Hinduism, Buddhism, and Islam by example. His spirit was touched by the generosity of people living in poverty, by the innocence of village children who didn't know much about computer games and Beyblades. He met people who smiled with sincerity because they were happy to be of service to others. He wanted to tap into that inner joy and peace he felt they manifested, and he tossed out the inspirational books he had bought to try and "find himself" and now knew were useless.

After his hiatus from "real" life, Gabe returned to Newfoundland with a refreshed and rejuvenated soul. He was no longer interested in the auto sales industry. Savvy stock trading and shrewd business investments had given Gabe a fair degree of financial independence. He vowed that whatever he did for the rest of his life, those less fortunate than himself would benefit. That was when he started his new business, which he based in Ontario, "We'll Care." Yet remaining in Ontario full-time wasn't as appealing to him as he thought. So, he also invested in a modest construction company in St. John's, which gave him an excuse to divide his time between both provinces.

He was in St. John's overseeing his construction firm at the time of Delaney's death. Back in Ontario later that summer,

he'd planned to track down Priya. He found the listing for Jay
De Souza in the phone book but decided to bide his time. He
didn't want to frighten Priya by barging into her life during
her time of grief. He thought he'd wait a few months after Jay
and Delaney's deaths before attempting to contact her. In the
meantime, Gabe searched for something about Delaney on the
Internet. And he found a brief profile of Delaney, which featured a photograph of her, Jay, and their daughter, Priya, and
which documented Delaney's academic qualifications and her
profession as an ESL teacher. Gabe had printed out the picture
and placed it in his wallet.

Gabe's motives were not purely altruistic. He felt he had a
lot to atone for, and here was a young woman whose parents
had been abruptly taken from her. Surely there was something
he could do to ease her burden *and* his guilt.

When the opportunity to meet her presented itself by accident at Walmart, he knew that fate had been at work. It was
purely by chance that both Gabe and Priya happened to visit
that particular Walmart on that Thursday morning. Gabe had
dropped by to pick up batteries for a flashlight and had stayed
long enough to purchase a new CD and a coffee at the in-store
McDonalds. He had a few minutes to kill while sipping his
coffee in the car and listening to his new CD as he was early
for a noon-hour meeting with his employees. Unbeknownst
to Priya, that meeting was postponed when Gabe recognized
her from the Internet photo.

"That's quite a story," Priya sighed when he finished. "And
here we are, connected by threads of the past."

"Threads of the past," Gabe tested the phrase on his lips as
if it were a fine new wine. "I like that. You could be a writer."

Priya laughed, unsnapped a pouch on the outside of her black
handbag and extricated a pink cell phone. She entered Serena's
number and waited for the call to be answered. "Hi, Serena,"
she greeted, when the phone was picked up on the second ring.

"How are you feeling, girl?" Serena asked warmly. "I was
going to call you this evening after setting my hair."

A self-conscious smile escaped Priya's parted lips. Listening to Serena's chatter about the routine chores of the day with Gabe almost within earshot, she felt strangely connected to these two people — one she'd known since childhood and the other whom she met just three days earlier.

"How was your date with Trent?" Serena asked.

"Oh good," she said coyly. "I'll fill you in on that later. In the meantime, do you remember Gabe Johanson?"

"Oh yes," Serena's said, sounding almost dreamy.

"Well, hmmm," Priya cleared her throat. "We're at Starbucks and he just asked me how you'd feel if he called you sometime. Can I give him your number?"

"For a date?" Serena said. "Now girl, he seems like a lovely man but I'm not interested in…"

"I think…" Priya lowered her voice, "he just wants to chat about Ma and all…" ,.,,

"I'd love to talk about Delaney," Serena said. "She was my best friend for so many years."

"Okay," Priya took a deep breath, "I'll give him your number. When is a good time for him to call you?"

"Tonight is fine," Serena responded.

"I'll tell him," Priya said, "and I'll talk to you later."

She relayed the message to Gabe. "Perfect," he nodded as he scribbled down Serena's number on a serviette.

Gabe glanced at his watch. "We have a bit of time. Would you like to browse through Chapters for a while?"

"Sounds good," Priya nodded.

"I'll be over in the history section," Gabe announced as they walked out of Starbucks into the main portion of the bookstore. "Let me know when you're ready to leave."

Once he was out of viewing range, Priya sauntered the aisles until she found what she was looking for — the shelf titled "Disorders and Ailments." She zeroed in on books with the word "anorexia" featured in the title. There were a few that piqued her interest, but the one that caught her fancy most was *Fatally Thin*, a mother's account of her teenage daughter's life-and-death struggle with anorexia nervosa. While she skimmed through the pages, she noticed a cluster of teenagers leaning against the wall peering at a fitness encyclopaedia amongst themselves. Priya noticed that all but one was slightly overweight. Casting her eyes further afield, she noted that only three other customers besides Gabe and herself were slim. The rest she felt were either plump or obese.

"What has happened to society as we know it," she lamented inwardly as she moved into the aisle containing books on diet and nutrition. All the titles seemed to beckon her attention. There was Atkins, South Beach, low-carb, high-protein, and a host of other possible fat-burning, weight-loss programs. The glut of books purporting the optimum route to a slimmer body made her shiver with excitement.

From her point of view, all the research and literature on the planet could not help people to trim down unless they were truly committed to doing so. Priya had the sinking feeling that if she ever released the tight reigns on her restrictive eating habits, she would join the legions of heavy people who routinely shuffled through the doors of diet centres and doctors' offices in pursuit of the ultimate weight loss panacea.

She selected an armload of diet books and propped them against her chest. There was a scattering of soft blue armchairs and wooden seats throughout the store. She smiled when she caught sight of a couple of giggling toddlers playing tag in the cookbook aisle while their stressed out mother hissed at them to "settle down or else."

After a near fruitless search for a comfortable place to sit, she finally found a bench fronting a floor-to-ceiling window looking out over a narrow strip of lawn bordering the parking lot. After piling some books into a small tower and draping her coat over the bench, she opted to speed-read two books. She would alternate between *Fatally Thin* and one of the diet books she'd selected. She'd just made herself comfortable, with both books splayed on her lap, their respective titles clearly visible atop every page, when she suddenly grew aware of a strong but gentle hand resting on her shoulder.

"Priya," Gabe said, "I hate to interrupt you but we need to leave now. I just got a call from one of my employees. We're having a problem with one of our vans and an eighty-year-old is at risk of missing her own birthday party. I need to get her from her senior's residence to her son's home before it starts. Hey, what are you reading there?"

Flustered because of his looming presence, Priya jumped to her feet, her face flushed with embarrassment. She tripped over her tower of books, scattering them in all directions. Dropping to the floor on one knee, she tried to gather as many books as she could, but Gabe was faster. He grasped her hands and helped her to her feet.

"I'll take care of this, sit!" he ordered.

"Oh, man!" Mortified, Priya buried her head in her hands when she saw Gabe perusing her reading list as he stacked the books into a neat pile.

"Interesting," he mused. "Are you looking to lose more weight?"

Priya didn't feel she had to justify the question with an answer. Instead, she yanked her coat off the bench and, keeping her eyes fixed on the hardwood floor, buttoned herself into it. She smouldered with suppressed rage at being intruded upon this way. As far as she was concerned, it wasn't Gabe's or anybody else's business what she chose to read. Gabe, in turn, was surprised at the defiance that flashed in her eyes.

"You know what," Priya said coolly. "I can get my own self home."

"Bus service isn't that great on Sundays," Gabe warned, "and besides, how do I know you won't attempt to walk home?"

"It's a beautiful day," Priya countered, putting on her gloves.

"It would take well over an hour to get even close to your place by walking," Gabe reasoned.

"You're very considerate but I'm not your responsibility," Priya was surprised at how close to tears she was.

"Come on now, don't be angry." Gabe placed his hands on

her shoulders and peered into her sad, watery eyes. "You *are* my responsibility," and then under his breath added, "far more than you know."

"Excuse me?" Priya quickly recovered herself.

"Coffee was my idea and I drove you here. It's my responsibility to get you home," Gabe insisted.

Priya nodded with resignation. She was tired of arguing. She was lightheaded due to a lack of sleep and food. She didn't protest when Gabe drew her close to his side with the sincere intention of guiding her to safety.

Chapter 7

SERENA WAS FEELING THE EFFECTS of middle-age creeping into her bones. She wondered if she was getting ready for "the change." Her energy was down and her iron was low. It didn't help that her job at times was exhausting. Mrs. O'Leary was a nice enough woman to work for, but when her hip bothered her, as it did more often now that the weather was cooling down, she became inpatient and testy. Serena could never fill the bath fast enough or make the soup warm enough.

Serena was relieved that Mrs. O'Leary's nieces were in town, and she could enjoy a well-deserved break. She was basking in the afterglow of a Thursday night on the town with Gabe Johanson. He'd picked her up for drinks at eight and later had taken her to a cozy Italian restaurant for pasta and wine. During the meal, Gabe asked Serena whether she'd be interested in some "real dance music."

"What do you mean, 'real?'" she'd asked, wondering if he'd heard about the hot new Latin nightspot, where the beat was lively and the tropical drinks flowed, and that Serena and her Guyanese friends hadn't yet been to.

"I'm talking about down home Newfoundland music," he'd said proudly. "A new band from St. John's is headlining in Toronto tonight."

"Sure," Serena was enthusiastic. Delaney had already given her a taste of Newfoundland music and she'd liked it. She had fond memories of Sunday afternoon jigs and reels while the dishwasher hummed. Jay, frowning, would retreat to the bedroom with his newspaper.

"What are you smiling at?" Gabe took in Serena's body-hugging black sweater, burgundy leather pants, and black ankle boots. She was stylishly slim, well made up, and her chocolate brown hair curled around her pretty face.

"Jay made no sport with Delaney when it came to having fun," Serena shuddered. "Oh, no, he was a serious chap with a chip on his shoulder."

"Tell me about them," Gabe said encouragingly.

They'd talked for hours at the restaurant. Before they knew it, the waiters were getting ready to close for the night. After they'd finally left the restaurant, Gabe took Serena to the Newfoundland club.

Serena was thankful to Gabe for livening up her night. Perhaps it was the wine or the Newfoundland Screech that caused her party girl persona to resurface after years of squashing it in order to make her marriage work. She felt utterly recharged and happy.

A razor-sharp blast of arctic air assaulted their faces as they exited the smoky warmth of the nightclub. It was on the drive home that Gabe expressed his concerns about Priya to Serena.

"The fact that she's anorexic is undeniable," he said. "We need to help her."

"I know," Serena agreed. "She's like my baby sister and, truth be told, I worry about her all the time."

"We went out for coffee on Sunday and afterward, at Chapters, she surrounded herself with diet books," Gabe said at a traffic light. "I thought: How can someone be that thin and want to read diet books? I think she believed she could hide her body under a heavy sweater, but wrists and fingers … they don't lie. I'm certain she needs medical attention."

"Yes, I've been meaning to talk to her about it," Serena said. "I wish I could get some support from that aunt of hers, but honestly, Gabe, Priya could wither away in front of her eyes and she wouldn't care. She's so wrapped up in herself. After Jay and Delaney's funeral, Renita locked herself in the bedroom for days and left Priya to cope alone. Priya's grandparents were there, trying their best to deal with their own daughter's death, and then hoping to support their granddaughter. That Daisy Saunders is an amazing woman. She was so strong. Her main concern was to help Priya manage her affairs. Priya's grandfather, Ralph, is also a nice man — very quiet, but he takes on a lot. He kept his pain to himself ... went out into the garden to smoke his cigarettes, but a gentleman if I have ever seen one. And very solicitous of Priya."

"Daisy is a wonderful person," Gabe agreed. "When we were growing up, she always opened her home to the neighbourhood kids. That house was the place to be after school. Milk, chocolate chip cookies, fresh baked bread ... wow!"

Serena, sensing that Gabe was enjoying his moment of reflection, kept silent.

"I met Renita the other day," he finally said, changing lanes to avoid getting stuck behind a slow-moving transport truck.

"And?" Serena probed.

"She's a hard lady to read," Gabe said thoughtfully. "Right away I could tell that she's preoccupied about something, but there's this coolness about her ... almost as if she defies you to get close to her."

"That's really perceptive," Serena said, nodding in agreement.

"Well," he shrugged modestly," I'm pretty good at reading people — as I keep telling Priya — although I think she didn't much appreciate it when I told her that at the Chapters. I hope I didn't offend her," he said pensively.

"Oh, shells," Serena said warmly, "you couldn't offend anyone if you tried. She's still grieving. And she's still being torn apart by unanticipated mood swings.

"Tell Priya I meant no harm and that I am, sincerely, her friend."

"You really care about her, don't you?" Serena was struck by the earnestness in his tone.

"Indeed, I do," he paused. "I didn't think the connection between us would be *this* powerful, though."

"Here Gabe," she touched his hand. "I'll do my best." She had to bite her tongue though not to press him about the nature of that connection. Something to do with Delaney, no doubt, and something that had obviously transpired between them, a long time ago. So long ago, obviously, that Delaney had never thought it important enough to share with Serena, her best friend, or her daughter, Priya.

Gabe escorted Serena up the elevator to her tenth-floor apartment where they parted with the promise to keep in touch and, together, to keep an eye Priya and try to help her out.

On Friday evening, a few minutes before 7:00 pm, Priya floated down the stairs in a happy cloud. She felt beautiful and alluring in her soft above-the-knee blue denim dress and navy tights. Trent was expected at any moment and she couldn't wait to see him. Since she had built up their date to epic proportions, she refused to believe that anything would go wrong. Her hair fell softly below her shrinking shoulders. The ends were becoming dry and brittle but she didn't care. She had managed to oil them just enough so they would curl and bob gently, and enticingly she hoped, on her shoulders and back. The scale said she was now down to 89 pounds. Life was good!

Priya's financial concerns were temporarily eased thanks to four days of supply teaching she'd accepted at a nearby public school. She'd received the call on Monday afternoon. A kindergarten teacher in a school not far from her home was out with a stomach virus, and it looked as if she wouldn't be back in the classroom until the following week. Priya had to take on her two groups of alternate-day students.

Priya had enjoyed her four days in the working world. She dressed in bulky sweaters and loose-fitting pants to hide her thinness from the other teachers who she feared would ogle her with envy. She didn't want to start on the wrong foot with the staff because one day, if she was lucky, she might actually land a full-time job at that school.

Priya's students were an interesting multicultural mix of Greek, Chinese, Indian, and Sri Lankan backgrounds. Some were children of new immigrants and others were seasoned

Canadians, wearing the latest snowsuits and TV-themed back-packs. Through her intermittent spurts of supply teaching, Priya had become well acquainted with the pop icons of the kindergarten crowd. Blue from Blue's Clues, Bob from Bob the Builder, and a host of other animated friends from TVland peppered the children's animated chatter as mothers and a handful of fathers helped their children arrange coats and backpacks on designated hooks. The mothers were in a range of costumes from the North American jeans and ski jacket to the colourful *salva kameez* of the East Indian women, and the *hijabs* of a few tradition-abiding Muslims. Priya felt a sense of kinship with these women. Being half-Sri Lankan, she related to their search for identity and sense of their place in a new and different society.

The teacher from the neighbouring class had provided Priya with the lesson plans for the week. After roll call and circle time, the children would be dispatched to their groups to work on their "journal" entries. Later, the focus of the morning would be on reading skills.

As much as she enjoyed her week in the classroom, by the end of the day Priya was exhausted and happy to go home. She ate only half an energy bar at lunch hour and survived on herbal tea for the rest of the school day. If the other teachers in the staff room observed her strange eating habits, they didn't let it show. The men seemed to have nothing but sports on their minds, and the women, when not discussing their students and extracurricular activities, chatted about their Christmas plans, diets, and the lives of their own children. Priya was detached from the casual conversations in the lunch room because she couldn't relate to the other teachers. She preferred eating her half of an energy bar in her classroom, spending the rest of the lunch hour reviewing her lesson plan.

When she came home from work that Tuesday, there were two messages on her machine. The first was from Ruby, Dr. Benson's secretary. The doctor would be away from his office for two weeks due to the death of his mother in Northern

Ontario. However, he'd left a reminder for Priya to see Dr. Farrel for counselling. Priya deleted the message. She had no intention of seeing anyone outside of Dr. Benson. If Dr. Benson wasn't available, she would cope by herself. Besides, her eating situation was under control. She was losing weight gradually and she wasn't even throwing up to achieve the results.

The second message was from Trent. He had phoned to say he was looking forward to seeing Priya on Friday evening and to hearing her play the piano, after which, he suggested they take in a movie and grab a bite to eat.

Priya had been so exhilarated by the sound of his voice that she was infused with instant energy. After a three-kilometre jog around the block, she returned home and hand-scrubbed the floors in both the first and second story washrooms. She used a toothbrush to tackle the grout developing around the ceramic tile. Somehow the swishing sound of the toothbrush coupled with her rhythmic back and forth movements had a cleansing affect on her soul. Priya visualized herself scrubbing the fat out of her cells. Ugly, disgusting, artery-clogging transfatty acids were being annihilated through her deft, swift strokes. She was purging herself of the filth that had made her stomach bulge over her belt buckle and her thighs swell under the constraint of pants that were too tight. The lemony smell of the antibacterial tile and bowl cleaner had a detoxifying effect on Priya's senses. Keeping the bathroom door firmly closed, she allowed herself to imbibe the scent of cleanliness as the room and her body became simultaneously pure. Priya was washing away the dirt of her life with panting, sweating intensity. Her hair grew damp with exertion.

While she worked, her mind began to drift. She was twenty and infatuated with her French professor, Henri. He was thirty-three and divorced. He hailed from Montreal but had studied and worked in Toronto for a few years. Once the course ended, they'd started dating. Priya introduced him to her parents, who were concerned about the age difference between them, but on the whole, seemed to think he was an acceptable suitor. It bothered Priya somewhat that she never met any of Henri's friends, but his insistence that he couldn't share her with anyone secretly delighted her. Abruptly, however, just three months after they started going out, he announced that he was returning to Montreal. He didn't encourage Priya to visit him.

Priya was heartbroken when he left but she kept in touch with him through phone calls and emails. When a seat sale was announced on a discount airliner that summer, Priya told her parents that she wanted to take advantage of the cheaper rates to take in a bit of culture in Montreal. She knew that Jay didn't approve of his single daughter chasing a man that way. Even Delaney, who was normally much more relaxed about Priya's choices, was reticent on the subject. But Priya was determined to surprise Henri for the long Canada Day weekend. When she called him from the airport, he told her that what happened in Toronto should stay in Toronto, and that she should forget about him. Besides, his wife was expecting their first baby and they were excited about it.

Wife? Baby! Priya was shattered. Biting back the hurt, she managed to get a room at a bed and breakfast and do exactly what she told her parents she would do — take in some culture, before she dragged herself back home, defeated and bewildered by this episode in her life.

She wondered why she had thrown herself at Henri and so easily believed his lies when he was in Toronto. Deep down, she knew the reason: she'd never known true love and she'd been so enamoured of this older man with his French background and sophisticated ways, she allowed herself to be swept away like a wayward fish in a tumultuous current. Now she realized that back then she'd just been too fat to really deserve to be loved. Even if he was such a cad. A harsh knock on the bathroom door brought her back to the present.

"Priya," Renita's voice cut into her thoughts with razor-edged impatience. "May I use the toilet, please?"

Priya snarled.

"Pardon?" Renita queried.

"Coming, I was just cleaning up in here," she replied hastily.

Priya hadn't interacted much with her aunt throughout the week. Their paths crossed only when Renita emerged from her bedroom to give a piano lesson to one of her students or to make herself a cup of tea. Judging from the contents in the fridge, Priya could see that Renita wasn't eating much more than she was. She wondered what was going on, but with her aunt's face dark with misery, Renita had made herself as unapproachable to Priya as she could.

On Wednesday morning, Priya had woken up with unexpected cramps. She suspected they were tied to her abuse of the laxatives and knew she wouldn't be able to remain in the classroom if she had to run to the washroom every few minutes. She decided to give her bowels a short break and restrict her eating even more. Perhaps she'd skip the half energy bar at work and merely subsist on herbal tea until she got home. Then, an hour before bed, she would have just one quarter piece of the energy bar and half a glass of skim milk. Even though she was losing weight, she felt as if she was losing control of her life. Her waking moments were being ruled by thoughts of what she should eat and when, and she was starting to feel trapped. However, Friday morning's weigh-in provided her with the welcome encouragement that she was looking for. The numbers on the scale had told her she was winning the battle against fat and that she was successfully cleansing herself of the artery-clogging filth that was destroying healthy people the world over. On Thursday, she was ecstatic to note she'd lost another pound.

While Priya was sipping her first cup of herbal tea on Friday morning, the last day of her supply teaching, Renita had come downstairs looking somewhat haggard. She'd bypassed her niece without so much as a glance and headed straight for the telephone.

"Lottie?" her tone was deceptively cheerful. "If you come for me at about 10:00 am, I can then purchase my groceries and get an early start on the cooking … ah, excellent. My, I really appreciate your coming this way for me. Right then, I'll see you." Renita hung up, retrieved a piece of paper and pen from the pocket of her bathrobe, sat down at the table, and proceeded to write.

"What's going on, Auntie?" Priya tried to sound sociable though her resentment toward the senior was becoming as dark as the wintry sky.

"Lottie is taking me to buy a few groceries," Renita's tone was conversational.

"I could take you whenever you want," Priya tried to keep the annoyance from creeping into her voice. Ever since Jay and Delaney died, Priya had willingly driven her on errands.

"That's okay," Renita nodded dismissively. "You do so much for me, I didn't want to worry you yet again."

"What do you have to buy?" Priya inquired, warming her hands around her mug. Within minutes, she'd be outside, beating the snow off the windshields and shivering while waiting for the car to warm up.

"I was going to surprise you," Renita said casually, "but now you caught me in the act. I thought with your friend Trent coming this evening, I would prepare some short eats. It's not nice, you know, when you call people to your home and not give them food."

Since when did Renita become so magnanimous? Priya wondered about this as she rinsed her empty cup at the sink and placed it on the top rack of the dishwasher.

"We're not staying here long," Priya explained. "He wants to hear me play the piano and then we're going to a movie. It's not like he's coming for dinner."

"Nevertheless, Priya," Renita's tone was haughty. "Didn't that mother of yours teach you how to treat your guests?"

"Ma was an excellent hostess," Priya said smugly. "She personified Newfoundland hospitality."

"Hmmp," Renita sniffed with open disgust. "Butter tarts and brownies!"

"Nothing wrong with that," Priya felt a steady rage building in her gut. Wanting to escape the tension in the kitchen, she went down the hall to the closet and got her coat.

"In any case, I thought I'd prepare short eats for your friend," Renita said resolutely.

"Well, thank you. I appreciate it," Priya lied. It was getting late. She had classes to teach; the best thing to do was be grateful that Renita was trying to help. It *was* possible that she was trying to turn a corner in their strained relationship. Perhaps in Renita's point of view it wasn't too late for aunt and niece to become friends. Priya had to either satisfy herself with that theory or stress over it for the rest of the day.

Renita was in the kitchen arranging trays of Sri Lankan style beef cutlets, spicy meatballs, breaded and deep-fried Indian samosas, and golden toast fingers topped with grilled sardines and chili sauce. Priya was about to comment on her hard work, but the sound of the phone prevented her from doing it.

"I hope Trent isn't calling to cancel," Renita mumbled, removing Delaney's colourful apron from around her waist and replacing it on the hook on the wall beside the microwave oven.

"Hope not," Priya gave her aunt a sidelong glance and wondered why the older lady had dressed up in one of her finer saris.

"Priya, hello," Serena was on the line.

"Hi," Priya took the white cordless phone in the living room and perched on the arm of chair. "How did it go with Gabe last night?"

"Oh, shells," Serena sighed. "I felt like a young girl again, but hear, I'm off this weekend. It's just as well, too, because I'm glad to get a chance to relax myself. Girl, all this nightlife business is fatiguing, you know ... but look, why I called is this. Gabe is very worried about you."

"Why?" Priya was puzzled. She hadn't even heard from him since they'd had coffee together last Sunday.

"He thinks he might have offended you in some way," Serena explained.

"Nonsense," Priya said brusquely. "I was only hoping that we'd have some new insights about Ma, but maybe he's bluffing."

"Oh no, Priya," Serena's voice was solemn. "He's not bluffing. He told me a few things and, girl, I must say, he's right. In your condition, you aren't able to take a lot of surprises. Trust him, he knows what he's doing."

"So now you're in on it too," Priya sighed with frustration. The doorbell rang. "I think that's Trent, I've got to go," she glanced toward the front door, knowing full well that Renita would never answer it.

"Oh yes, Trent, I forgot about that," Serena chuckled. "Well, girl, fill me in when you get a chance. I'd love to know all about this new man in your life."

Priya walked toward the entry hall, clutching the phone tightly against her ear. "Okay," Priya unlocked the front door. "Talk to you later." She hadn't meant to end her conversation with Serena on an abrupt note, but she found no matter how much in a hurry Serena claimed to be, once she got going, it was hard to get her to stop.

A beaming Trent greeted Priya with a box of Godiva chocolates and a light kiss on the cheek. She felt her heart melt as she escorted him into the living room.

"I didn't realize until just now how much I was looking forward to seeing you," Trent said as he sat down.

"I feel the same way," Priya said truthfully. "Can I get you something to drink?"

"Hello, Trent," Renita appeared almost by magic, bearing a tray of finger food which she arranged on the coffee table. "I was preparing some short eats for a church function and I thought I'd make extra for you."

"Nice!" Trent's eyes widened with admiration. "You made all of this?"

Priya's heart sank. Renita had taken one of Delaney's silver-plated trays topped with a paper doily to showcase the food she'd made. "Why, of course," Renita said cheerfully. "Priya inherited her own cooking skills from her father's side of the family. Eat, Priya. You are far too thin."

"No ... no," Priya tried to sound casual but felt she came across as stiff. "I was nibbling while we were in the kitchen. Here," she handed Trent a serviette. "Are you okay with spicy food? If so, try one of these cutlets. They *are* good."

"I love spicy food," Trent assured her. "One of my best friends in university was from Bombay ... well, Mumbai now ... and he was always inviting me to his parents' place for biriyani. I never said no, not even once. This is a real treat for me."

Trent refused an offer of wine because he'd be driving. With a glass of fruit punch in one hand and a serviette brimming with hors d'oeuvres in the other, he leaned back against the couch and eagerly awaited Priya's approach toward the gleaming black Yahama piano.

After sitting down, Priya raised the lid, removed the red velvet dust cover from the keyboard, and then opened her favourite music book. It featured movie themes from the previous four decades. She selected a page at random and launched into a haunting rendition of the main theme from the movie *Il Postino*. Her hands spanned the keyboard with a flowing grace that could have rivalled the world's best pianist. Her fingers danced an intricate ballet of tinkling arpeggios and sweeping sequences that made the music rise from the piano and envelop   the listeners in a passionate embrace.

When she finished, Trent met her gaze with silent adulation.

"Very good," Renita clapped her hands. "Here, here, an encore please."

"That was..." Trent struggled for words. "Simply put, amazing. I'm sorry, I don't mean to throw my professional weight around, but you could outperform any of my best students any day of the week."

"I don't play everything that well," Priya said shyly. "I just feel totally connected to that score. The movie was so sad.

When I watched it, I kept digging into my purse for tissues.
Did you see it?"

"I did," Trent murmured. "I loved it, too. In fact it was one
of the last movies my twin sister, Lydia, and I saw before she
died. We rented the video and for the record, she cried too."

"I'm really sorry about your sister..." Priya twisted her hands
in her lap. "Do you mind my asking how she died?"

"Not at all," Trent assured her. "She died last year, at the
age of thirty-one. She lost a fifteen-year battle with anorexia."

"Oh, I am so sorry," Priya murmured. Unable to meet his
gaze, Priya fixed her eyes on the keyboard.

"My goodness, what a thing!" Renita sighed.

A heavy silence filled the room. Priya could feel her aunt's
eyes burning into her back.

"Please," Trent, painfully aware of the discomfort he'd
unwittingly created, walked over and laid a hand on Priya's
shoulder. She flinched, wondering if he already suspected that
she was anorexic too. "Please don't feel uncomfortable. It
happened and now we move on."

Priya remained motionless on the piano stool.

Renita, attempting to bring the conversation back to neutral
territory fixed her gaze back on Trent. "I don't know if Priya
has had a chance to tell you but I, too, am a qualified music
teacher. In fact, I taught at a prestigious private school in Sri
Lanka for over thirty years."

For once Priya was grateful for Renita's intervention. She'd
saved what had become an awkward situation.

"Actually, Priya did tell me," Trent said. "Do you play much?"

"Those who can't, teach," Renita shrank into her chair with
faux humility.

"Actually, Auntie plays a lot better than I do," Priya supplied
generously.

"I'd love to hear you play," Trent said, helping himself to
another samosa. "Hmm, a woman of many talents."

Priya joined him on the chesterfield as Renita made herself
comfortable at the piano.

"Mind you, I play only the classics and songs of my girlhood."

"That's fine," Trent was enthusiastic.

Renita shifted the music books around on the stand until she found the one that appealed to her and then launched into a Chopin polonaise. Her performance was met with hearty applause from her audience of two.

While her aunt played, Priya's eyes wandered about the room. Classical music always had a way of bringing her spirits down. The years of rigid practicing with her father's critical comments piercing her eardrums had a negative effect on her perception of the great composers. She imagined crabbed old ladies in Victorian mansions enjoying their tea in draughty rooms while the music seeped in through unseen sources. Images in the old black and white movies from the thirties and forties, featuring women ravaged by mysterious illnesses and men in formal suits, with accents to match, gathered in another room to consider their options. A different time and place from Priya's reality, but still the perception was gripping.

She glanced around her family's simple living room and tried to see it through Trent's eyes. He was obviously a man who came from some means, his father being a psychiatrist. Priya imagined his parents lived in a sprawling double-garage masterpiece of a home in Don Mills. What would he have to say about the discount-store furnishings contrasting with the classy piano? Did he ever need to know that the Yahama was purchased at an end-of-year clearance sale? The longer Renita played, the lower Priya's self-image plummeted. She became aware of a scattering of dictation books on the side table next to the couch where she and Trent were seated.

Renita, pausing between selections, turned and caught Priya's eye. She quickly swooped down upon the notebooks. "One of my students left her books here. I must call her."

"Your technique is flawless," Trent said respectfully. "Just observing your fingering and posture, I can see old school discipline. Are you teaching right now?"

"I have only a handful of students," Renita tossed a smug

look at her niece. "I'd love to be in a school setting again, though. I would feel less homesick."

"Have you applied to any of the schools here?" Trent inquired.

Priya was frustrated. She thought this evening was about Trent and her getting to know each other. With an unexpected jolt, she realized why Renita had made the assortment of short eats for Trent, and had wanted to spend some time with him this evening. She was trying to wangle a job out of him!

"Trent, it's getting late. Shouldn't we get going?" Priya asked getting to her feet.

Trent might not have known what was going through Priya's mind, but he was sensitive to her overt discomfort and stood up. "Ms. De Souza, it was a real pleasure to hear you play tonight," he extended a hand to the senior.

"Call me Auntie," she said warmly. "Trent, can I possibly trouble you to take one of my résumés to your school? In Sri Lanka, it sometimes helps to know someone when it comes to getting jobs, but here it might be different."

"I'd be happy to take a résumé," Trent assured her.

That was all the encouragement Renita needed. She lifted up the lid of the piano stool and took out a manila envelope that had been conveniently stored on top of a pile of music books and papers. "I have qualifications from Sri Lanka and England. If you see here," she slid some documents out of the envelope and passed them over to Trent, who was only too happy to peruse them. "I've passed with distinction the ATCL exams and…"

Priya turned on her heel and went for her coat. If it was anyone else showing Trent their résumé, she could have understood and empathized with them, but not when that person happened to be Renita! Here was a woman who blatantly ignored Priya almost all the time. Renita never offered to share a pot of tea with Priya. She couldn't even give Priya a hug after she lost her parents, but a man who could potentially link her to a job could get the best out of the old lady.

"Are you okay?" Trent asked once they were outside.

"I'm fine," Priya tightened a bright polar fleece scarf around her neck. Frigid winter air caused her to shiver inside her coat. "I'm only sorry that Auntie put you on the spot that way. "

"No problem," Trent opened the car door for her. "She's probably missing her work, and I guess she hasn't had a chance to make too many contacts yet."

Priya wanted to tell Trent just how many times she and Delaney had urged Renita to get her qualifications assessed by a professional board. She'd refused to let go of her defeatist attitude and work toward obtaining the necessary Canadian accreditation in order to teach. She dismissed the suggestion on the grounds that she was too old to be hired. At that time, Priya thought that Renita didn't have any real incentive to earn an income because Jay had made it clear that he would support his doting sister to the best of his ability. Now that Jay was gone, perhaps the impetus to find a job had been paramount. If only Renita had been up front with Priya and told her that she wanted to speak to Trent about employment opportunities. If Renita had confided in her, Priya would have encouraged her to speak to him. However Auntie was sly. She thought she could forge ahead with little regard to how Priya would feel. For Priya, this cast a shadow over the evening.

Sensing that Priya's formerly light mood had darkened by several degrees, Trent quietly wondered if he should have even told Priya about how his sister died. The subject would never have come up if he hadn't made reference to it. He slid a CD of relaxing guitar music into the car stereo, hoping to change the mood. "It's funny you should have played "Il Postino" on the piano," he said brightly.

"Why?" she asked as she fastened her seatbelt.

"Because it happens to be on this CD, *Cinema Guitar*."

Priya's spirits brightened. "I'd love to hear it."

They talked about what movie to see while they headed into the main stream of traffic. The muffled sound of Priya's cell phone came through her handbag. She was a little unsettled by the summons, as she didn't receive many calls. This was deliberate as she didn't give out her number to many people. For her, the cell phone was only a means of communicating a basic message. It wasn't a social toy for her to discuss party plans or text message trivia with her friends. At the moment, the only people who had her number were Renita, Rachel and Serena. Instinctively an alarm bell went off in her head.

"Priya," Renita was on the line.

"Auntie, what's wrong?" Priya tried to still the pounding in her chest but she was already fearful. The last time she'd been contacted so unexpectedly on her cell phone was when the police informed her about the death of her parents. However, now there was hardly anybody else left to lose unless Renita had gotten an urgent call from St. John's. Grandma and Grandpa were in their seventies. Had something happened to one of them — or both?"

"Priya," Renita's voice was calm. "Can you come home, please?"

"What's wrong?" Priya's voice grew high-pitched with agitation.

"I'm having severe pain in my chest," she explained, her voice halting. "Please come quickly."

Chapter 8

THE EMERGENCY ROOM seemed unusually crowded that Friday night. Coughing babies and anxious parents made up the bulk of the patient load. A teenager with spiked blue hair and a sling on his right arm, an older man with crutches, and a heavily pregnant middle-aged woman were among the others in need of not-so-urgent attention. Because Renita had been brought in by ambulance and was complaining of chest pain, she was able to circumvent the tedious registration process and be taken directly to one of the many examining rooms designated for emergency patients.

After Priya received the call from Renita, things moved very quickly. While Trent sped home, dodging a few red lights along the way, Priya contacted the 24-hour health line. Once the nurse assigned to Priya's call registered Renita on their computer database, she peppered Priya with a series of questions that she wasn't sure how to answer. Where exactly was the chest discomfort? Did the senior have difficulty breathing? Was she a diabetic? It was finally determined that an ambulance should meet Priya and Trent at the townhouse. Renita would be sent to the nearest hospital.

"I'm really sorry about all of this," Priya said helplessly when Trent parked on the side of the road several yards from the house. He wanted to give the ambulance a wide berth, as the driveway was already narrow due to compacted snow on the sides.

"Sorry for what?" he asked as the flashing lights of the ambulance came into view at the opposite end of the street.

"All this!" Priya stepped out of the car and closed the door.

"We were supposed to be..."

"Look," Trent slipped his arm around her shoulder and hurried her toward the house so she'd be there to meet the paramedics. "Let's just be grateful that your aunt was able to reach us. We have a whole lifetime to go out on a date."

Priya hadn't been sure what to expect when she unlocked the door and entered. She wondered whether she'd find her aunt sprawled on the floor verging on unconsciousness. When she approached the living room, she was relieved to see that Renita was sitting comfortably on the couch, her hands in her lap, a pained expression on her face.

"What are all those flashing lights outside the window?" she asked. "Surely people haven't put their Christmas lights up yet."

As unexpected as the thought was, Priya suddenly realized that this would be Renita's second Christmas in Canada and their first without Jay and Delaney. Before she could respond to her question, the paramedic team had pushed their way inside with an orange stretcher. The two burly men assessed the situation, spoke among themselves, fired a volley of questions at Priya and her aunt, and then clamped an oxygen mask over Renita's face

"What is all this for?" a flustered Renita demanded, holding her hands up in despair. "Why are you here? Why can't Priya take me to the hospital in her car?"

"Ma'am," one of the paramedics said patiently, "the medical hotline people felt the need to get us over here, and it's a good thing too. You might be suffering from heart trouble or you might not. It's our duty to take every precaution we can."

Priya wanted to escort her aunt in the ambulance but the older woman refused. "Pointless," she waved her away with a dismissive hand. "You and Trent can meet me there."

"She can ride with you, if you like," the paramedic assured her.

"Not necessary," Renita's voice was muffled due to the mask. "She needs to lock up the house."

There was nothing to be gained by arguing so Priya merely watched as her flustered aunt was placed on the stretcher.

"I'll take you to the hospital," Trent said to her as the paramedics were preparing to leave.

That had all transpired over an hour ago. Now they were
marking time in the emergency room lobby and nobody was
coming forth with information. Priya had, however, been given
permission to enter the curtained cubicle where Renita lay.
Connected to a heart monitor and an I.V., Renita seemed lifeless and defeated. It was hard to imagine that just a few short
hours ago she'd been trying to manoeuvre a job through Trent.

"They'll take me down to X-ray soon," she said morosely.

"Can I get you anything? Water? A pillow?" Priya asked,
adjusting a flimsy blue blanket around the older woman's
shoulders.

"No ... no," she shook her head. "I just want to die. I wish it
would just happen now. I've had enough of this wretched life."

Priya was startled by the vehemence in her tone. She'd
known that Renita had been depressed for some time, but
had attributed her feelings to prolonged grief. She'd always
assumed that Renita would eventually overcome her negativity
and get on with living.

A nurse, who appeared to be in her mid-thirties, bustled
into the room with a blood pressure cuff. "Can you tell me
anything?" Priya implored.

"The doctor will be seeing your aunt soon," the nurse replied.
She fiddled with some dials on the heart monitor and adjusted
a long ribbon of paper that was printing reams of numbers.
"Everything here looks okay, but we have to wait and see."

As there were several patients in the unit connected to similar
machines as her aunt, Priya had the eerie feeling that she was
hearing the electronic beep of several heart monitors playing a
dooming symphony of multiple heartbeats in surround sound.

"Is Trent still here?" Renita asked once the nurse had finished
taking her blood pressure.

"Yes he is," Priya said.

"Send him home," Renita advised. "It's not right to let him
waste his time here."

For once Priya agreed with her aunt. There was nothing Trent could do. She knew that he had a hectic schedule preparing his students for a Christmas choral recital. He would be busy with rehearsals throughout the balance of the weekend.

Trent met Priya with a steaming cup of hot chocolate when she returned to the waiting room. "I thought you could use this," he said kindly.

Priya panicked. The soothing warmth of the paper cup and the aroma of the hot drink were almost too much to take. She wanted to drink it badly but was overwhelmed by the thought of the at least 100 unjustifiable calories flooding her body. "That's so kind of you," she said accepting the cup. She took a polite sip and made a show of blowing on it to cool it down. "It's so hot, I need to let it cool down. Don't worry about me, Trent. You don't have to stay. I know how busy you are."

"There's nowhere else I'd rather be," he showed her to a seat next to a mother rocking a newborn in a colourful infant car seat.

"Thank you for saying that," Prya felt suddenly shy.

"I really mean that," Trent gazed into her eyes. "You're different from other girls I've dated."

"Oh?"

"You're ... okay, this is going to sound corny, but you're just you, patient, down to earth. I find that really attractive."

"I don't know what I did to make you think I'm so patient," Priya smiled again.

"I kind of got the sense that your aunt was trying to take over the evening but it didn't faze you. You let her do her thing and I thought that was really gracious."

"Okay, now you're embarrassing me," Priya laughed. "I *was* irritated."

"Don't be embarrassed," he squeezed her hand. "You're very sweet."

"Thank you, Trent, and so are you by the way. Not too many guys would consider a Friday night date in a hospital a romantic prospect."

"It's about the two people, not the place," Trent said.

Shortly after midnight, Dr. John Chan, the resident caring for Renita, informed Priya that according to the battery of tests her aunt had undergone, there didn't seem to be any indication of heart trouble. The doctor was, however, concerned about shadows on some of the x-rays. He didn't elaborate, but advised that Renita be admitted once a bed was made available.

"How long do you think she'll need to stay in the hospital?" Priya inquired.

"We'd like to watch her over the weekend," he said. "On Monday, when the specialists are in, they'll study the x-rays and assess the situation."

"So, if it's not her heart, what else could it be?" Priya was puzzled.

"We aren't ruling out heart trouble completely," the doctor qualified. "But it could be any number of things. Your family doctor will be given a full report next week."

"Dr. Benson," Priya nodded. "He's out of town now."

"Well, whoever is filling in for him will get the report," the doctor's beeper went off. "Excuse me, but I should take that."

"Trent, you really don't have to stay with me," Priya said once they were alone.

"I'm not leaving till you're ready to go home and get some rest," he said resolutely.

"I'll stay here through the night," Priya decided. "Then, in the morning, if Auntie is stable, I'll go home and get a bag ready for her."

"We could do that right now," Trent suggested.

"There's no point if there's no bed available," Priya reasoned.

"Well, do you want to rest for a while now or see how your aunt is doing?"

"I'll check on her and then maybe we can hang out at the bagel shop. They're open 24 hours," Priya was pleased at how normal she sounded. If she showed him interest in spending time in a café, she reasoned, Trent would never notice how carefully she chose to eat.

"Sounds good," Trent sighed. "I could use a cup of tea. In the meantime I'll grab a table for us."

Priya threw him a warm smile and then headed through a set of swinging doors to a series of curtained examining rooms. Renita was in room four. On her way down the hall, she passed an elderly janitor pushing a mop across the floor, a metal cart stacked with blue hospital gowns and white towels, and a young woman sleeping in her wheelchair. She shuddered involuntarily. The woman in the wheelchair seemed impossibly thin, as thin as Priya wanted to be. She pulled her eyes away from the tiny woman, pushed open the orange curtain to her aunt's room, and peered inside.

"Auntie," she called softly as she approached the bed.

Renita had a thin white blanket pulled up to her chin. The red sari she'd worn earlier in the evening was folded neatly on a visitor's chair. There were three sounds Priya was acutely aware of: the ticking of the clock on the wall, the rhythmic beep of the heart monitor, and her aunt's ragged snoring.

Priya straightened the already neat bedclothes to make herself feel useful, and then quietly slipped out of the room to join Trent at the bagel shop.

"Here you are," he said as he guided her to a table in a secluded spot behind a large fern that afforded them some privacy.

Priya sat across from him at the tiny round table for two. "She was sleeping peacefully," she said.

"Good. What will you have to eat?" Trent asked glancing toward the counter.

"Oh, nothing right now," Priya said. "I had that hot chocolate earlier and it being the so late now, I don't think I want anything."

"Okay," Trent frowned. "I'll get myself a bagel and a cup of tea. You'll at least have something to drink?"

Priya glanced at the illuminated menu board on the wall behind the counter. "Well, they have green tea, orange, cranberry … sure, I'll have a cup of green tea," she reached for her purse but Trent placed a gentle hand over hers. "No way."

"But…" she began.

Ignoring her protest, he stood up and walked over to the counter. There was nobody ahead of him so he wasn't long. When he returned, he was bearing a tray with two cups of tea and a toasted poppy seed bagel with smoked salmon flavoured cream cheese that had already been cut in two.

"Have some," he urged, pushing the plate towards her. "You haven't had anything all night."

Priya, shrank into her chair in a self-effacing manner and shook her head. "No, really, I'm not hungry."

"Are you all right?" Trent asked, a frown creasing his forehead as he bit into the bagel. "There's a stomach virus doing the rounds…"

"Yes," Priya nodded, grateful for the out. "I was doing supply work at one of the elementary schools this week and lot of the kids were out with it, teachers too."

"Same story at work," Trent added.

"I'm also a bit worried about Auntie," Priya said truthfully, then added with a coy smile, "now, what were you saying earlier?"

"Well," Trent sipped his tea. "I know we've only known each other barely a week, but I am extremely attracted to you, and wonder how you'd feel about our seeing each other on a regular basis … to get to know each other better." He was smiling warmly. "I hope you don't think I am moving too fast."

"You mean, not see other people?" Priya asked.

"We could try it and see how it works," Trent seemed almost shy.

"We could," Priya agreed. "It's not as if either one of us is dating anyone else." She swirled the green tea bag around her cup, wanting to get the full strength of the leaves. She'd heard that green tea was beneficial in aiding weight loss, but wasn't sure how many cups she needed to drink. She looked up at him, and smiled back.

"You've been through a lot this year, with losing your parents, and now your aunt is sick," Trent's eyes were full of compassion as he spoke. "I just want you to know that I am here for you, night and day."

Priya noticed that the overhead florescent lighting cast a frosty glow upon his tightly curled dark hair. "You're the second man to tell me that in one week."

"I thought you said you're not dating anyone right now," there was thinly veiled disappointment in his tone as he took another bite of his bagel.

"I'm not," Priya blushed with embarrassment. "Gabe was a good friend of my mom's and he's been very helpful to me, and," she added with a mischievous grin, "he's nearly twice my age."

"Oh, well," Trent sighed. "That's different then."

"Trent, I would love to get to know you better," Priya assured him. "I'm not the only one who's gone through a hard time in terms of losing a loved one."

"Definitely, but in our case, my sister's death had more of an impact on my parents," Trent mused. "Lydia was sick for fifteen years."

"How did she die?"

"In the end, it was her heart," he said slowly. "It just stopped beating. Her body shut down gradually over a series of weeks. She had completely stopped eating a week before she died, accepting only an occasional sip of juice through a straw."

Sensing that Trent needed to talk about his sister, Priya felt it was okay to probe a little further. "That must have been hard to watch. And it must have been devastating for your parents."

"Watching someone you love slowly killing herself is not easy," he agreed. "First the eyesight, then the kidneys, and finally the heart. And yes it was. Seeing my father, a doctor, feeling so powerless to help her, was also hard."

"When did she die?" Priya asked gently.

"Christmas Eve will be the first anniversary of her death," Trent said sadly.

"Ouch," Priya shuddered. "That must be so hard for your parents."

"My parents have decided they don't want to be here for Christmas," Trent said. "They've booked their flights for Italy. They'll be gone for two weeks."

"You're going too?"

"No," Trent shook his head. "You can't run away from the pain. My dad realizes that but not my mom. She thinks a change of environment will help her through the holidays."

"So what will you do for Christmas?" Priya inquired.

"Not too much," Trent admitted. "I'll probably go to my uncle's place for the day. Your grandparents will be flying in from St. John's?"

"That's the plan," Priya said. "But in a way, we'll be in a similar situation because this will be our first Christmas without my parents."

"That is so ironic," Trent reached over the table and took Priya's hand in his. "Here is a young lady who has to face her first Christmas without her parents and here are *my* parents facing their first Christmas without their daughter."

Priya entwined her icy fingers in Trent's and sighed with contentment. "It will get better for you," he said, tenderly squeezing her hand.

"Hopefully," Priya nodded. "Tell me about your sister."

"Lydia was three minutes older than me. I don't think we were ever really much like twins, though. I was the shy, quiet one and she was the loud, flamboyant perfectionist. Interestingly, she didn't fit the profile of what the therapist *claimed* was a typical anorexic."

"They have profiles for anorexics?" Priya said innocently, trying to gauge Trent's feelings on the issue.

"Well, according to Lydia's therapist, and after what she went through, I'm not at all impressed with the treatment she received, although my father pulled all the strings he could to get her the best care possible. Anyway, according to Dr. Wexler at the eating disorder clinic where she received the bulk of her treatment the last five years of her life, anorexics are generally compliant overachievers who are always trying to please others.

Lydia was anything but that. She had been a big girl, not heavy as much as big-boned and solid. She had a powerful soprano voice that gave her a pivotal role in our church choir. I think my parents would have liked for her to go into music. But, when she was about fifteen, people started telling her that she had the right face and height to go into modelling. She took the compliments to heart and began applying to agencies all over Toronto. And that's when her troubles began."

"How?" Priya was intrigued.

"Lydia was five foot eight and 155 pounds. She went on one go-see after the other, but was always told she needed to lose at least 30 pounds to have a shot at modelling professionally. Well, she not only lost that 30 pounds, but she went on losing and losing until she became almost unrecognizable."

"How did she lose all that weight?" Priya hoped she wasn't prying too much.

"She did terrible things to her body," Trent said. "She took diuretics, spent hours working out at the gym, and, for years, she induced vomiting. She got so wrapped up in her food issues that she lost interest in modelling altogether. Once my parents caught on to her binge-and-purge cycle and her obsession with getting thinner and thinner, they had her hospitalized for a brief period of time. There was a TV hooked up in her room, and one day while channel surfing, she caught an edition of Fashion Television and decided that once she got better, she would carve out a new career for herself as a fashion designer. Of course it never happened."

"Why?" Priya asked.

"Because Lydia never gained the required amount of weight to get out of the hospital for more than a few months. She weighed 95 pounds during her first hospitalization and, you know, in fifteen years, she never came anywhere near that weight again. Eveytime she was released, we thought she would slowly get better, but she never did. At the time of her death she was 57 pounds."

"Oh, boy," Priya muttered, relieved that she was nowhere

near considering losing that much weight. She'd be happy if she could maintain her weight at 90 pounds or just less than that; a perfect weight for her.

"Lydia needed extreme emotional help because her problem had less to do with food and more to do with low self-esteem and wanting to have some degree of control over her life."

"Why wouldn't she have had control over her life?" Priya wondered out loud. "She was bright, beautiful, and had a loving, supportive family."

"I don't know," Trent shook his head. "There must have been some deep-rooted problems that she never confided in us, not even during intensive family therapy. The funny thing is, Priya, I was there for it all. In my early twenties, I moved out for a year or two, but Mom was having such a hard time coping with Lydia and her sickness that I just decided to come home for good. My Dad has a bad back and I didn't like him carrying Lydia to the car in the middle of a health crisis. I thought the best thing to do was stay with them at home for as long as they needed me."

"And you are still living with your parents?" Priya inquired.

"For now," Trent nodded. "But I put my name in for a downtown condo development and hopefully that should come together by next spring."

"Trent, I am so sorry you had to go through all of that," Priya said, suddenly realizing that they had been holding hands for a long time.

Even though the muted darkness of the hospital made it seem like the dead of night, Priya was aware that a new day was well in progress when she heard the distant sound of metal breakfast carts rattling down the hallway. The aroma of freshly brewed coffee followed close behind. The public address system crackled into life as announcements about morning rounds and staff meetings punctuated the white noise of a hospital gearing up for another busy day of challenges and triumphs. Within the following few hours, two elderly patients would die of heart failure, three babies would be born, and a teenager would be rushed into emergency surgery after sustaining severe head trauma in a two-car collision. It was all par for the course on a routine morning that didn't distinguish itself as a Saturday.

Priya blinked the sleep out of her eyes and glanced at her watch. It was almost 7:00 am. Trent, sound asleep, rested beside her, slumped in a standard waiting-room chair. They'd stayed in the bagel shop talking for hours, sharing childhood experiences and the travails of past relationships. Priya learned that Trent had been engaged once before, but had broken it off when he discovered that his girlfriend had become romantically involved with her boss.

Finally, a weary Priya and Trent made their way back to the waiting room to try and rest for a few hours. Sleep, at best, was erratic, for Priya at the best of times. Yet, she must have drowsed for a little while because she dreamt of her mother. In the dream, Priya was very sick and Delaney was standing over her bed, assuring Priya that she would be just fine, if only she could learn to trust. When Priya asked her mother whom it was she should trust, she awoke with a start. The dream had been so vivid. With a sinking heart she let her gaze wander around the waiting room, thinking that maybe the past seven months had been a nightmare and that her parents were actually still alive.

She tried to pick up the dream where she'd left off, but it wasn't meant to be. When sleep came for a second time, it was an uncomfortable and restless journey that had Priya hunched and cramped in her chair. Then it was morning and a nurse was standing over her. "We have a room for your aunt," she was saying. "It will be ready for her later this morning."

"Oh, okay," Priya stretched her legs and tried to stand up but she felt a little wobbly. "So now what?"

"She'll need her pajamas, tooth-brush, and a change of clothing," the nurse handed her a plastic grocery bag that was stuffed with Renita's belongings, including her handbag, sari, and shoes.

"How did she sleep?" Priya asked, following the nurse down the hall through the swinging doors to room four.

"As well as can be expected," the nurse explained. "It's pretty noisy in here and we have to be constantly check patients' temperatures, blood pressure, and all that, so it's hard for them to sleep undisturbed."

Renita's bed had been raised to a semi-sitting position. On her lap was a detachable table containing a breakfast tray. Priya spotted a single serving box of corn flakes, a carton of two-percent milk, a plastic container of orange juice, and a fruit cup. Renita, dishevelled and forlorn, stared vacantly at the tray.

"How are you feeling, Auntie?" Priya asked, lightly perching on the edge of the bed.

"I still have pain," she answered, "but now, it seems, it's all over my back and stomach. I don't know what this is ... must be a chill. Anyway, what to do? They want to keep me here for a few days."

"They have a room for you," Priya explained. "Do you want me to call Auntie Lottie or any of your other friends from church?"

"Yes," Renita cast her eyes toward the plastic bag that Priya was still clutching. "I have a small address book in my handbag. I'll give you two or three numbers to call. Just pass it here." She reached for the bag and sorted through it until she came found her black clutch bag. She snapped the clasp and withdrew a slim, leather address book.

"I'll go home, shower, and come back with some things for you. Is there anything you'd like me to buy ... magazines?"

"I don't want to read anything," Renita sighed. "The only thing I'd like is a new tooth-brush for this place. Can you buy me one?"

"Sure ... and anything else you think you might need?"

"No, just pack the toiletries on the vanity in the bathroom, face cream, talc ... don't you know, whatever is there that I use every day."

Priya smiled reassuringly. "Don't worry. You're in good hands here."

"Trent is still here?" Renita inquired as Priya was leaving.

"Yes, can you imagine?" Priya sighed. "The poor guy's crashed out on a chair. I didn't want him to stay the whole night, but he insisted."

"Very kind," Renita clucked approvingly.

Trent was sipping coffee when Priya returned to the waiting room."How is your aunt feeling?" he asked, standing up.

"Still in a fair bit of pain," Priya admitted. "I'll go home, shower, go by the drugstore for her, and then come back here."

"Okay," Trent frowned as he placed his hands on her shoulders. "I have only one problem with that scenario."

"What?" Priya was nonplussed.

"Nowhere on that to-do list do you mention taking a few hours off to get some sleep."

"I'll catch up on some sleep later. Right now, the priority is to get Auntie settled. And Trent, what about yourself? You have a busy schedule today. I kept you here the whole night!"

"I kept myself here the whole night," he corrected.

"You've done enough," Priya reached for her coat and put it on. "Just drop me home and then go about the rest of your day. You have things to do. I'll keep you posted. I promise."

Wordlessly, Trent led Priya out of the hospital and into the biting wind of an overcast December morning. When they arrived at the townhouse, he walked her to the door as he had done just a week earlier. "Look," he drew her into a warm and welcome embrace. "I want you to know that you are not in this alone."

"Thank you, Trent," Priya tipped her face towards his and they enjoyed a long, kiss, with a promise to be in touch throughout the day.

Priya knew that if she stopped to sit for even five minutes, she'd stumble into a deep sleep. Struggling to ignore her growling stomach, she bypassed the kitchen and living room on the main floor and went straight upstairs to shower and change. The denim dress she'd worn in anticipation of a romantic evening with Trent had acquired that nameless hospital odour — a melange of antiseptic cleansers and steam-tray gourmet. The smell had infiltrated Priya's hair, making it feel limp and greasy to the touch.

After a refreshing shower with her vanilla-scented body wash, she pulled on her favourite jeans, a tee-shirt, and a sky-blue polar fleece sweater. She twisted her freshly washed and dried hair into a French braid and then pulled a black travel bag with wheels out of Renita's bedroom closet. Priya opened the lavender-scented bottom drawer of the armoire and found two nightgowns, some underwear, and socks. She then packed a hairbrush, a claw clip, and make-up. She opened the closet and found Renita's satin bathrobe, which she neatly folded and placed in the suitcase.

Before long, she was on the road, driving toward the same drugstore she had visited after her first date with Trent. She noticed a sale on toothbrushes so she bought five, three for herself and two for Renita.

By 9:30 am, a drooping Priya was back at the hospital. She figured that she'd stay for half an hour to see that her aunt was settled. Then she would order a telephone and television for her room. Hopefully by that time, she'd be able to go home and get a few hours sleep.

Renita had already been transferred to her new room on the fifth floor when Priya arrived. The other bed in the semi-private room was unoccupied, except for Lottie perched uncomfortably on the bottom corner. Dressed in a green sari covered by a heavy, gray, winter coat, Lottie was a small woman, swimming inside her clothes, with closely cropped hair that gave the illusion of being tightly pulled back into a miniscule bun.

"Hello, Priya," she said, her voice tight.

"How are you?" Priya was polite. She usually didn't have much to say to most of Renita's friends because she sensed they were critical of her lifestyle. In their eyes, she wasn't a professional anything because she wasn't earning regularly, and for heaven's sake, why wasn't she married yet?

"Sit, Priya," Lottie beckoned her to take the armchair at the end of Renita's bed.

"Did they give you anything for the pain?" Priya asked her aunt.

"Never mind that," Renita said quietly. "I think the time has come for us to have a talk."

"Did the doctors...?" Priya began.

"Nothing to do with the doctors," Renita said impatiently. "All has to do with me and my life."

"Renita," Lottie grumbled. "This is hardly the time and place. Why do you want to worry yourself now?"

"My dear," Renita spoke with resignation. "I have been worried for the last forty years of my life ... a little respite now before I die ... that's what I want."

"What nonsense are you talking?" Now it was Lottie's turn to sound impatient. "The doctor has already said your problem might not even be connected to the heart. You had that fall by the bus stop last year, before you came, remember?"

"Yes, yes, I know," Renita leveled a warning glance at her long-time friend. To Priya, it seemed as if the two women shared an unspoken code between themselves. They spoke the same private language, which had nothing to do with their native tongue. Perhaps it was the fact that they were girlhood friends. They understood each other's body language and eye movements better than anybody else. Priya wondered if she and Rachel were that close; could they read each other so well as the years advanced?

"Would someone like to tell me what's going on?" Priya asked, smothering the sudden alarm she felt must be clearly evident in her voice.

"Right, right," Renita arranged herself more comfortably on the bed and then fixed her gaze on Priya's tired face. "I have been longing to tell you this story for years, but first Jay shut me up and then Lottie; but now I will have my say because I am not going to die with this on my chest. It is just not fair."

"What is this *die* nonsense? I don't understand," Lottie wailed, wringing her hands in disgust. She stood up and stumbled toward the window, where she stared at the parked cars below. The room was as basic and unadorned as a hospital room could be. Aside from the two beds, closet and en-suite bathroom, there wasn't a lot to make a patient, or visitor, feel at ease.

Priya wondered why Lottie didn't have the courtesy to give them some privacy. *Couldn't she go downstairs and get a coffee?* As if reading her mind, Renita spoke.

"I asked Lottie to stay because she was there when it happened, and if not for her support, I would have gone mad years ago."

Priya buried her head in her hands. She was almost afraid to ask. "What is this big secret?"

Renita was about to speak when a nurse popped into the room. "Excuse me, but we have to do another set of X-rays. The first batch didn't come out well."

"Now?" Renita was visibly flustered.

"In about ten minutes someone will take you down," she explained. "In the meantime, I need to take your temperature, blood pressure and some more blood."

Priya sighed with exasperation. It seemed as if she'd never get to the bottom of the story, any story, not with her aunt, not with Gabe, nor Serena, who it seemed knew much more than she had ever shared with Priya, even after her parents' death.

"Never mind," Renita sensing her niece's frustration extended her arm for the blood pressure cuff that the nurse held in front of her. "Once they finish all of this, I will tell you what you need to be told."

Chapter 9

THE X-RAYS WERE REPEATED, the telephone and television were on order, and Renita, with Priya's help, had washed and changed into a fresh nightgown and was reclining comfortably in bed as Priya brushed and braided her thinning black hair.

"Anyway, when the chips are down, your niece is a good girl," Lottie said approvingly from her perch on the empty bed.

"That's what I want to talk about." Renita gestured for Priya to resume her spot in the armchair.

"Okay," Priya clasped her cold hands in her lap and waited expectantly. She tried to ignore the pounding of her heart against the thin walls of her chest. "What's going on, Auntie?"

"Lottie, close the door with this," Renita turned toward a drawer in the small side table beside her, and pulled out a cardboard "Do Not Disturb" sign.

Lottie took the sign, hung it outside on the door knob before pulling the door shut, and then returned to her seat.

"Priya, I have lived for close to fifty years with this secret, but anyway, what's to be done?" Taking a deep breath, Renita fixed her gaze on the younger woman's face. "Priya Naomi De Souza, you are not my niece. You never were."

Priya gasped, jolted by the bluntness of the admission.

"What do you mean? Are you saying I'm adopted?" she asked, trying to calm the flutters in her stomach, the panic seizing her chest.

"No," Renita shook her head. "You are very much a De Souza. Your parents were Jay and Delaney. That is proven fact. But, what you need to know, is that I am not your father's sister."

"*You* were adopted?" Priya's eyes grew cloudy with confusion.

"No," Renita said abruptly. "Bluntly put, my dear, I am your grandmother."

"I don't understand," Priya clutched the armrests of the chair for support. She wondered if her sleep deprivation had caused her to misinterpret whatever it was Renita was trying to tell her.

"I had a brilliant future as a concert pianist," the older woman went on. "I could have toured the world, played in grand concert halls. I had the talent, the discipline, and the will, but *not* the circumstances."

"I always wondered why you didn't pursue..." Priya began, her voice unsteady.

"When I was twenty years old," Renita's voice shook with emotion, "I was romantically involved with a cricketer. We were actually neighbours and, don't you know? When you're young and are attracted to the opposite sex, things can happen."

Priya's thoughts flew back to Henri. She had been about the same age as Renita when she had given her heart to her French professor. Now, she wasn't sure if Renita had tossed out a rhetorical remark, or expected her to respond.

"What was his name?" Priya finally asked.

"Vincent," Renita paused before continuing. "He was a nice chap. Even my parents were fond of him. The plan was that he would go to Australia to study and, after qualifying, he would return for me and we would marry. It didn't work out that way though."

"What happened?" Priya asked.

"A week before he was to leave Sri Lanka, we got a little too amorous with each other." Renita wiped a wayward tear from her left eye. "I became pregnant. It's been said that a sari can hide a multitude of sins but I could only carry my secret for so long. Vincent was already settled in Australia when I wrote to him with the news."

"What was his reaction?" Priya demanded.

"He was furious," Renita sighed.

"Nice guy," Priya laughed wryly. "It takes two to make a

baby. He gets you pregnant and then gets mad about it."

"That's the double standard we had to tolerate," Renita said sadly. "Vincent was *wild* with anger!"

Priya stood up and began to pace. "If I were you, I'd have flown down to Australia and made his life hell until he did something about the situation."

Lottie laughed. "My, this Priya is a real character ... so incensed by all of this."

"Yes, well, I can't picture that happening here," Priya said defensively. "It does take *two* to make a baby…"

"All that is true," Renita acknowledged, smiling over the fire in Priya's eyes as she strode between the two beds, hands thrust deep into the pockets of her polar fleece.

"Anyway, don't you know our men? I miscalculated my safe days for being intimate. So, in a sense, he had every right to be angry. I gave him false information by assuring him that it was a safe time of month for relations, but as it turned out, I was wrong. That is why he blamed me."

"Ooh!" Priya shook her fist in the air.

"Sit, child, and listen to the rest of the story," Lottie admonished with a twinkle in her eye.

"Anyway," Renita cleared her throat. "He had no intention of cutting short his studies to return to Sri Lanka to marry me. As far as he was concerned, it was over between us. His plans for the future would be ruined if he married me when he wasn't ready. He had a degree to pursue, not to mention a hectic schedule of cricket matches and travel. He vanished from my life in a moment." Renita snapped her fingers to emphasize the point. "He wanted nothing to do with our baby or me. My parents felt I had shamed the family beyond redemption. You must understand, Priya, life for a young girl in the fifties was not what it is today, especially in Sri Lanka. You were judged and talked about mercilessly if you fell out of good grace. The De Souza family had a respectable place in society, and there was no room for unwed mothers and the scandal they might bring upon the home. My parents struck up a plan."

"I'm afraid to ask about this plan," Priya's eyes narrowed in fear.

"Since my mother was in her late forties, it was conceivable ... excuse the pun," Renita said lightly, "that she could still get pregnant. We put the pregnancy on her."

Priya laced her fingers together and stared at the floor.

"People were told that Mummy was having a late-in-life pregnancy, and that it was a rough one. She couldn't cope with the heat of Colombo, so arrangements were made for her to settle into the home of a second cousin ... a tea planter who had a bungalow upcountry. I was dispatched to the tea estate on the pretext of being my mother's caregiver throughout her confinement. Once the baby was born, we returned to Colombo. The only person who was aware of this outside the family and our doctor was my close friend, my Lottie. I had to confide in someone or I would go mad."

"So you were closeted in some upcountry tea estate, pregnant in real life, while your mother played a role for the benefit of society."

"Poor Renita! You don't know what she went through," Lottie sighed reflectively as she rose and placed her hand gently on her friend's shoulder.

Renita buried her head in her hands and began to weep softly.

"Okay, okay," Lottie said as she bent to embrace her friend. "Priya," she said. "The only way that Renita could keep peace in the family was to agree to have Jay raised as her younger brother. She couldn't acknowledge him as her son until he turned eighteen. By that time, everyone assumed the scandal would be stale and nobody would care anymore."

"This is unbelievable," Priya shuddered.

"Every day," Renita raised her head, tears streaming down her cheeks, "I would go to school and teach, come home, and look after the baby. I would be up with him at night when he had colic. I did all the hard work of being a mother, but could never ever acknowledge him as my son. Mummy got the credit for all his baby accomplishments. When he could read by age four, when he came first in sports, it was she who won the accolades, never me."

"And then?" Priya prodded.

"And then when I finally broke down and told Jay the truth … on his eighteenth birthday he was angry with me, really angry, for denying him as my son. He was so angry, in fact, he pulled away from the family. He despised my parents for making us all live the lie. Jay continued to live in the house with us, but he treated us like strangers. I remember his words full of rage and contempt: "One day I will get away from this house and all of you. I will never look back, liars!"

"I am convinced he married in haste just to get away from the family. Perhaps if he had been older, he wouldn't have been so wilful. He might even have married within our culture but anyway what to do? Delaney was there at the right moment and that was that. When he left Sri Lanka, I really thought he never *would* come back."

"But he *did* come back," Priya reminded. "We came to Sri Lanka as a family when I was six. Remember, the other day we were looking at those old photographs?"

"Yes, yes, all that is true," Renita agreed. "That was the one good thing Delaney did. She taught Jay to forgive."

"So where does Ma fit into all of this?" Priya inquired. She wasn't ready to ask Renita why she always seemed to have so much contempt for Delaney, her son's wife.

Renita regarded her with confusion.

"How did they really meet?" Priya pressed.

"They came together at a charity beach party for underprivileged children. Surely you know the story," Renita said, a hint of irritation in her voice.

"Yes, but I was wondering if that was the whole story," Priya explained.

"Yes, yes, all that is true," Renita assured her. "Jay and Delaney were stationed at the same barbecue pit and, according to Delaney, it was love at first sight." She cast her eyes downward.

"You're not convinced," Priya said perceptively.

"Maybe from Delaney's point of view it was love at first sight, but I know my son. He was barely *twenty* years old. What could he know about love? "

"But Auntie," Priya protested, "You were also young when you met the cricketer."

"Priya," Renita fixed her gaze on the younger woman, "Remember this my dear. A young man of twenty usually isn't as mature as a woman of twenty. Jay had been coddled all his life by my parents. Everything was done for him."

"He had to love Ma in the beginning," Priya insisted.

"I'm sure he was attracted to Delaney, but in his case it was escapism that led them to elope within two months of meeting. Delaney returned to Canada, sponsored him, and that's the story."

"Two months," Priya breathed. "Wow!"

"I think Delaney was intrigued by the idea of marrying a man from a culture so different from her own. And Jay was in an almighty hurry to leave Sri Lanka behind and start a new life with his wife." Lottie said firmly.

"So they got married while she was still in Sri Lanka," Priya mused.

"Yes," Renita nodded. "Surely you knew that."

"Yes," Priya acknowledged. "But I know that Ma's parents had a grand reception for them soon after Jay arrived in Canada. I guess in my mind, I think of that as the wedding. We have lots of pictures from that day."

"I saw them," Renita said. "Anyway, Jay only drew close to me after you were born. I supposed he realized the value of parents. Delaney somehow talked him into forgiving me for letting him believe that I was his sister. We made amends when the three of you made that trip to Sri Lanka in the early eighties. Jay never quite forgave his grandparents for the deceit, but he accepted them back into his life."

"Why didn't they tell me any of this?" Priya demanded.

"Jay never wanted you to know," Renita said slowly. "He didn't think it was relevant. It's not as if this affected your birth. You were conceived under the correct circumstances. Jay wanted to maintain the status quo for your benefit. He only prayed that you wouldn't make the same mistake that I did and that's why he pushed so hard for you to be the best at whatever you did. He didn't mind you dating once you finished your studies, but he was dead scared you'd make the same mistake."

"I'm surprised that Ma was able to keep quiet about this all these years," Priya remarked.

"She was quiet for your father's sake, Priya," Renita sighed heavily. "Your mother was a very good woman. Jay wasn't always the easiest man to live with, but she was always so … so cheerful … she tried her best to make me feel at home at your place."

"But … but," Priya sputtered.

"You're wondering why I was always so indifferent toward her," Renita began to cry again. "Don't you know, child, I was painfully jealous of your mother. She had all those wonderful years with Jay. She had the joy of giving birth to a child that she could proudly acknowledge as her own. Jay, even after coming to terms with my being his real mother, could never treat me as such. He continued to call his grandmother 'Mummy'. I was just Renita Akki … big sister, always! He said, 'how can you expect me to change after all these years?' Her words dissolved into big, gulping sobs. "Don't you know, child … when that plane crashed last April, it was my son, my one and only son who died, and until the very end, I could never call him that to his face because he didn't want you to know. He was so ashamed, so worried what others would think. That is why, Priya, I couldn't help you with your own grief after they died. That is why I retreated within myself. I couldn't cope with the loss, and still can't. I have always loved you. I would have given anything to have you call me Archi Ma, but I knew that could never be … not after everything that happened."

"Auntie…" Priya bolted toward the bed, overcome with emotion. "I am so sorry." She embraced the weeping woman.

"Maybe, you will always be 'Auntie' to me, but that's okay. I love you and I am so sorry I judged you so harshly. I didn't think I mattered to you. I thought I wasn't good enough…"

"Not good enough," Renita was puzzled. "Why?"

"Because I have never seen pictures of Ma or me on your bedroom wall."

"That was just my petty way of coping with the situation," Renita was shamefaced. "I couldn't stand that Delaney and you could enjoy a happy family life for so many years, and I was deprived of that with my own son. Circumstances turned me into a bitter, jealous woman and I am sorry about that." Renita clasped Priya against her heaving chest. "You grew up in western society, but I see a lot of the east in you. Compared to so many of these girls here, even among my piano students, you're so simple, so easy. Jay and Delaney never went through that teenage rebellion problem with you. I don't see you wearing racy clothes, too much make-up, or cheapening yourself with shallow relationships. I am so happy that Trent has entered your life. You are a beautiful young woman, but I fear for your health. When I first came to Canada, you seemed so healthy, but now … you're so thin, too thin." She turned to Lottie for confirmation, "Don't you think so, Lottie? Isn't Priya far too thin?"

Lottie nodded vigorously in agreement. "You look sick, child."

Priya smiled indulgently at both women.

Renita fumbled for a tissue and began to cry again.

"Auntie, it's okay … don't cry," Priya squeezed her hand tightly. "Now that everything is out in the open, you have nothing to worry about. The most important thing now is for you to get better."

"I want you to look at your father's birth certificate when you go home," Renita said quietly. "You will come across two versions. One is the official government document, which states that I am Jay's biological mother, and the other is the fabricated one displayed in his baby book. That is probably the birth certificate that you are familiar with."

"I've seen it in dad's baby book," Priya affirmed.

"Yes, it states that my mother was his mother."

"Hmm," Priya sighed. "Where is the real birth certificate?"

"He kept it in his confirmation Bible, and I believe it is still there."

"I know that Bible," Priya said. "It's got that worn red leather cover. King James ... he kept that in a locked drawer in his desk. Nobody was ever allowed to touch it. I used to think that it had sentimental value because it was given to him at his Confirmation."

Renita shook her head sadly.

"Anyway, now I know why the drawer was locked," Priya mused.

"Renita wiped her eyes. "You go home and sleep for a while and come back in the night. We'll talk more then, right Priya?"

Priya was more than a little relieved to be dismissed from the room. She needed time to process this information. She was deeply shaken, but had enough sensitivity to hide her emotions from her "grandmother." She would deal with the news on her terms.

Priya had no memory of how she drove herself home. She couldn't recall whether the sky was overcast or sunny. She couldn't remember stopping for gas when she realized that she was down to a quarter of a tank. All she was aware of was that her stomach was growling and protesting in a way she had never experienced before. Unbearable hunger pains lunged at her gut, forcing her to bite back the nausea that was building in her throat. She had to eat something, *now*!

Back at the townhouse, she tossed her jacket on the arm of a chair, kicked off her boots, and raced into the kitchen. Flinging open the door of the refrigerator, she searched the shelves for all vestiges of the remaining food from the night before. After scanning the contents: a carton of large brown eggs, Pyrex bowls of curry topped with colorful plastic lids, an assortment of pickles and chutneys, she finally spied her bounty neatly packed in plastic Ziploc containers behind the four-litre bag of skim milk. She shoved the milk aside, hauled out the clear blue-lidded plastic containers, and brought them to the counter. Breathing deeply, she peeled back the cover of first one and then followed through with the other two. The samosas, cutlets, and sausage rolls taunted her from their plastic nests. They were daring her to eat them. She didn't bother getting herself a plate. Instead, she opened the door of the microwave oven and pushed all three in simultaneously. It was a tight fit and two of the boxes were forced to sit pyramid style on either side of the central one. Priya entered in a time of two minutes, wondering how she could wait so long. Lacking the patience to stand there and stare, she numbly walked toward her father's den and searched for the key to the top drawer of his desk. She found it in its standard resting place, under the black gooseneck lamp with the gaping metal shade that emitted a powerful oval of light when switched on. She opened the drawer where she knew her father's King James Bible was stored. She rummaged through papers and computer disks, and then, wedged against the back of the drawer, there was the trusty old Bible. She took it out and held it up close as if she could see through the cover. The tome smelled ancient and humid. She could almost imbibe the ambience of that old house in Nawala where her grand ... no, her *great grandparents* lived. She'd only been there for two months the summer she was seven, but she remembered it like nothing else on earth. A pot-pourri of mothballs, lavender bushes, coconut oil, and LUX Beauty soap fused into an aromatic time capsule representing a different age, a different world. It seemed as if this Bible had packaged up all those sensibilities in a tidy bundle of memorabilia. Priya spied a yellowed document and gingerly eased it out of the book. This was definitely it. In a formal script that might be considered obsolete today, she saw her father's name, Jayatileke Thomas De Souza, son of Renita Hannah De Souza and Vincent Amahl Gooneratne, born November 27, 1956.

Priya was startled by the sound of the microwave beeping. Without allowing herself a moment to internalize this information, she placed the Bible on the desk and hurried back into the kitchen. The heady mix of cumin, coriander and fennel was almost too much for her. Without even checking to see how hot the leftovers were, she grabbed a samosa and rammed it full into her mouth. Within seconds, she found herself huddled against the counter plunging her fingers into the eastern delicacies. She didn't stop at just one or two samosas. She went on to eat five, and then inhaled seven cutlets and four sausage rolls. Mildly satiated but mouth burning with the aftertaste of fiery green chilies, she ran to the fridge and grabbed a bottle of calorie-reduced cranberry juice. Without stopping to reach for a glass, she wrenched off the cap and guzzled the cold liquid down her throat. She staggered around the room with the carnal pleasure of a drunk about to hit his fifth of gin after a truckload of beer. Spiritually and physically starved, she slid down to the floor, clutching the bottle of juice in her hand. After she'd taken a few hefty gulps, she decided to quell the penchant for more calories by raiding the freezer. Renita always kept a stash of strawberry ice cream in there. Priya had never been a fan of ice cream but she was one now. Gasping for breath, sweat trickling down her forehead, she sank a spoon into the open container, eyed the content with the same voracious greed as a wild animal stalking its prey, and stuffed spoonful after spoonful into her gaping mouth. After she got bored with the ice cream, she tossed it aside and pawed through the cupboards until she found crackers. She located cheddar cheese on the shelf inside the door of the fridge. She hacked off a thick wedge with a bread knife and bolted it down, alternately crunching loudly and greedily on the crisp, flaky crackers. Gasping for breath, she sought out more liquid to quench her insatiable thirst. This time it was milk, cup after cup of milk, and what about that giant slab of dark chocolate next to the cheese? Surely Renita wouldn't mind, would she? Priya tore off the wrapper and bit off a large chunk. The subtle sweetness sent a tidal wave of serotonin flooding through her brain, giving her a false self of well-being and comfort. Washing down the chocolate with cold creamy milk made her gasp with delight. Finally satiated, she backed away from the counter and surveyed the wreckage. Cracker crumbs all over the floor, bits and pieces of pastry from the samosa and sausage rolls clung stubbornly to the soles of her socks. The ice cream was starting to melt. She had the presence of mind to return it to the freezer. She wanted to sweep up the crumbs, but she could do no more. Overwhelmed with exhaustion and a sickening sensation of being stuffed, she rinsed her hands in the sink and then meandered down the hall to her bedroom. Hurling herself onto the bed, she wrapped her arms around her distended abdomen and fell into a deep, dark sleep.

Priya awoke with a jolt. Reams of afternoon sunlight spilled across her bed and fell directly into her range of vision. She glanced at her watch. It was 2:30 pm. Still feeling stuffed and uncomfortable, she roused herself from the bed and trudged into the bathroom. After stripping off her clothes, she got on the scale. She hated herself when she saw that she was back up to 93 pounds. She had gained five pounds since Friday morning. Well, that was simply not acceptable.

"You need to learn a lesson, friend," she glared at her image in the mirror and then snatched her clothes off the bathroom floor and stormed back into the bedroom where she tossed them onto the bed. She'd wear them later when it was time to return to the hospital to visit Renita. For now, she pulled on her gray jogging suit, strode into the kitchen, and summarily picked up a broom and began sweeping up the debris from her binge. Having done that, she took a good hard look at the ceramic tiled floor in the kitchen and wondered why her parents had chosen to make it white. Didn't they realize that after five years dirt was going to develop between the squares? What would Trent think if he saw the squiggly lines of dirt trapped between the tiles?

With deliberate calm, she went into the bedroom where her three toothbrushes still lay in their plastic bag. She took them out, one at a time, pink, peach and lime green, and held them up for inspection.

"You don't deserve the ease of a mop and pail, or a sponge for that matter," she hissed, shaking the brushes in the air. "You'll get down on your hands and knees and burn enough calories to undo the damage you did, or you might as well be dead!"

A deep untapped rage surged to the surface, causing Priya to charge back into the kitchen where she picked up a chair from the table and hurled it against the wall. Gritting her teeth, she went to the broom closet, retrieved a green pail and filled it with warm sudsy water. "Now you learn the price of gluttony," she snarled at herself.

With meticulous precision, she set about scrubbing in between the tiles in much the same manner she had done with the upstairs bathroom just a few days earlier. Once again, she was compelled to clean the floor and, in so doing, to brush the filth out of her body. She didn't stop until her hands were red and calluses started to form between the thumb and fore-fingers of both her hands. While she found herself growing quietly intoxicated by the odour of the cleansers, she harked back to what Renita had told her in the hospital. It all made perfect sense but why, oh, why didn't her own mother trust Priya enough to share the truth with her? What was so wrong with what Renita had done? So, she was an unwed mother. Big deal! Priya had gone to school with a few. It wasn't the end of the world. Why did her father's family have to be so harsh and narrow-minded in their judgements?

While she worked, her eyes travelled around the bright, sunny kitchen. The one thing Delaney had insisted on when they were looking for a new home was that there should be provision for a lot of natural light to filter in. The kitchen in their apartment had been a small galley-style affair, minus a window. In the townhouse, the kitchen was big enough to house a small island that Delaney had used for chopping vegetables and rolling out pastry. The white appliances still boasted their fresh-from-the-showroom gleam because Priya had become fastidious about keeping them spotless during her night-time roaming. She caught sight of the state-of-the-art electronic food scale Jay had bought Delaney on their last wedding anniversary.

"You and your friends talk about dieting but I don't see any evidence," he'd said lightly. "So I thought this would inspire you to jump-start the process."

If Delaney had been offended by her husband's choice of anniversary gift, she didn't indicate it in word, thought, or deed. Instead, she accepted the scale with equanimity and agreed to make the best use of it. However she never did. It sat untouched, unused until now, until Priya decided to pay it long-deserved attention.

Putting down a toothbrush, she straightened up, flexing the stiffness in her knees and went about assessing the damage she'd done to her body. She started with the cheddar cheese, which according to the package, weighed in at 227 grams. She didn't know how big a chunk she'd hacked off for herself but she weighed what was remaining of the package. 1t came in at less than 125 grams. She was mortified to think that she had consumed half a bar of cheese. She weighed the balance of the crackers and calculated that she had eaten at least fifteen, which weighed in at 60 grams. Milk and cranberry juice she guesstimated at about two-and-a-half cups. And the ice cream! Eight scoops of ice cream placed in a lightweight plastic bowl registered at 375 ml.

"You are truly unbelievable," she muttered venomously to herself, dropping back down on her knees hard. She'd just picked up the toothbrush when she was hit by a wave of nausea. Shaken by the intensity of the urge to vomit, she bolted to the bathroom down the hall, just barely in time.

Priya suffered for the next several hours with cramping, nausea and diarrhea. During a brief respite from symptoms, she managed to phone the hospital and leave a message with the nurses' station that she would not be in to visit her aunt for the next two days as she felt she might have contracted a stomach bug. She didn't want to risk infecting Renita, her Auntie, her grandmother. Priya could have phoned Renita directly, but didn't want to cause her undue worry; so instead, she requested that the nurse convey that she was exhausted and thought she'd stay in that evening to catch up on her rest.

Throughout the night and well into the next morning, Priya went through three sets of pyjamas. Then, finally, when her body stopped raging against her, when four straight hours passed without having to visit the bathroom, she slipped on her pink robe and crept into the kitchen for a handful of seedless grapes and a glass of iced water. Apple juice would have been a safe choice in terms of filling a weakened stomach, but it wasn't that safe where calories were concerned. She recalled an old adage about the so-called "first" foods to eat when recovering from a stomach upset: bananas, rice, applesauce and tea. But bananas had fruit sugar and, like any other sugar, they would be converted to fat. Rice was a carbo-nightmare, and applesauce ... well, she just didn't have any. The tea was the only attainable item of the four. Iced water, grapes and tea became her mantra. Until she was completely free of the bug she would focus on those three items and nothing more. She dared to weigh herself after eating three grapes and half a cup of tea. Much to her delight, the suffering she had undergone left her at 89 pounds.

"I don't believe this," she whispered to herself. "Throwing up isn't so bad after all."

Sunday afternoon was a bright and sunny reminder that not all the days of winter were gloomy and overcast. Gabe Johanson was in a great frame of mind. In a few days he would head up north for a week of fishing before settling in to enjoy the Christmas season. He and Serena were becoming good friends and he he had at last made contact with Priya De Souza, his old friend, Delaney's, charming but troubled daughter. What to do about Priya was a big question on his mind. He'd worried about her all week. He couldn't understand why there was such a powerful connection between them, but he knew that he had to help her, not only because of Delaney but because ... well, just because.

He suspected the time was right for Priya to learn the truth about her mother. He wanted to take her back to Starbucks on this glorious winter afternoon and treat her to the drink of her choice. While they sipped their fancy lattes, he would tell her the entire story. He was concerned that he'd upset her the last time they'd been there. Yet, if she knew that his motives and concern were genuine, she might be better disposed toward him.

As Gabe enjoyed his solitary lunch of leftover pot roast and root vegetables, he reflected on the past couple of weeks. In a short time, he'd met two women who intrigued him for different reasons. Gabe didn't think it strange how his mind vacillated between Serena and Priya. Aside from their mutual connection to Delaney, the two women had nothing much in common. Serena was a jazzy middle-aged woman who camouflaged her inner depth with a flashy exterior. Priya was a delicate woman-child who was writhing under the pressure of an invisible conflict. Both, for different reasons, fascinated him.

The sound of the phone jarred him from his quiet reverie at the kitchen table.

"Hello," he picked up the phone on the third ring.

"Gabe?" a tentative Serena was on the line.

"Well, well, well, I was just thinking about you," Gabe said, a wide smile on his face. "What's on the go?"

"Actually, Gabe," Serena's tone implied urgency, "I'm a little concerned about Priya. I've been trying to get a hold of her since last night, but all I get is a busy signal. I have the number of one of Delaney's neighbours who I called this morning when I still couldn't get through. I thought perhaps Priya didn't realize her phone was off the hook. Well now, Gabe, the neighbour dropped over and sure enough Priya's car was in the driveway and there were lights on. She rang the bell and nobody answered. Up to now the phone is still engaged."

"Funny you should mention that," Gabe was puzzled. "I was just about to call Priya myself and ask if she wanted to take a run up to Starbucks."

"Here, Gabe, what we'll do is this," Serena cleared her throat and continued in a voice that sounded as if she were issuing directives to an emergency task force. "You'll pick me up and we'll go over there together. Something is amiss with that girl."

"I'll be right over," Gabe promised. "I'm sure you're worrying for nothing." His manner was light, but he, too, was starting to feel there was something a little off key about the situation. If Priya was allegedly at home, why was she not answering the door? Furthermore, if she didn't want to answer the phone, all she had to do was put her voice mail on call forward and she could get her messages later. Serena wasn't the only one who felt something was amiss with Priya.

Chapter 10

THE INCESSANT RINGING of the doorbell drew Priya from a sleepy fog. Drowsily peeling back the layers of blankets, she struggled out of bed and reached for her pink robe that lay in a heap on the floor. Sliding her arms into the sleeves, she ambled down the hall and peered through the screen after unlocking the main door.

She was surprised to find Gabe and Serena standing on the front step. Pushing the limp hair off her face, she tentatively unlatched the screen. "Oh, hi," she said shyly. "If I were you guys, I wouldn't bother coming in. I'm getting over some kind of stomach bug ... I think..."

"Oh, my," Serena shielded her face as if she were dodging a physical blow. "I've used up my quota of sick days for the year. What with that awful sinus congestion thing I had in April, and then that bone density scan, the suspicious blood report in June that turned out to be nothing but a false alarm..."

"Hmm," Gabe, arms folded across his chest, gave Serena a teasing wink. "Are we going to stand on Priya's doorstep while you download your entire medical history, or we going in?"

"*Men!*" Serena huffed as she shouldered her way through the door.

Priya couldn't help smiling at her friends. They looked so good together — Gabe, tall and striking in his dark brown winter jacket, and Serena, svelte in a short faux fur black jacket, a multi-hued silk scarf sassily tossed around her shoulders. As always, she'd made up her face as if she was going to a party and, as always, it worked to her advantage. The eye shadow complimenting the sparkle of her eyes, blush that highlighted

Serena's well-defined cheekbones. Priya's fragile self-image plummeted to subterranean levels.

Gabe's light mood grew solemn when he took in Priya's frail appearance. On the two occasions that he had seen her, she was dressed in loose-fitting jeans and oversized sweaters. Wearing a short nightie and matching robe, her frailty was more than a little apparent. Pencil-thin legs, slim hands that were inexplicably red and calloused, and brittle hair that spilled out of a haphazard ponytail highlighted what he knew were the early effects of her disease. Winter clothes could artfully hide the ravages of anorexia from the public eye, but at home there was no escape.

"A wimpy little stomach bug didn't do *this* to you," he said quietly.

"Do what?" Priya asked innocently.

"Oh, shells," Serena threw off her leather gloves and took Priya's roughened, red hands in hers. "What happened here, girl?"

"Ahem," Priya cleared her throat. "It seems I have an allergy to some cleaning products. I spent a few minutes mopping the floor ... before I got sick, but I had to stop because of the irritation to my fingers."

"How?" Serena was curious. "You don't handle the water or the soap when you mop. You used a mop, am I not mistaken? You mop the floor with a mop?"

"Yes, but..." Priya began and chose to digress. "I was really sick," she took their coats and hung them up. "If you only knew..."

"Girl, I tried calling you so many times since last night, but your line was busy. And then I got worried and had one of your neighbours check on you, but you wouldn't answer the door," Serena headed straight for the living room. "Oh look, here we are," she said, noting a red light flashing on the TALK button on Priya's white cordless phone. "Oh, my guy, why did you have it off the hook?" She snapped off the TALK button and replaced the phone on the handset.

"I didn't know," Priya said. "Last night, I phoned the hospital to say that I wouldn't be in to see Auntie, and I remember cutting the call short to get to the bathroom in a hurry."

"Renita? Hospital? What is this?" Serena took Priya's arm and gently steered her to the chesterfield. "Gabe, are you coming?"

Gabe, deep in thought, lingered in the entry hall. At Serena's beckoning, he joined the women in the living room and listened while Priya told them about calling the ambulance for Renita on Friday night.

"Anyway, they don't think it's the heart," Priya toyed with the satin belt of her robe and looked down at the carpet. Her eyes suddenly filled with tears.

"Honey?" Serena touched her shoulder. "What's wrong?"

"She's not my aunt to begin with," with volcanic force, pent up tears that Priya had hoarded for too long, came rushing to the surface. "She told me the saddest story and I know it's true. I saw the birth certificate."

"What birth certificate?" Gabe asked, sitting down beside her.

"Take your time, love," said Serena, who reached for her paisley-print clutch bag on the coffee table, and pulled out perfume-scented tissues that she pressed into Priya's trembling hand.

Weeping in much the same fashion as Renita had the day before, Priya told them everything Renita had confessed about Jay and their unacknowledged relationship. "You know what I don't understand," Priya said through her tears, "why my mother didn't tell me any of this. Why did I have to find out this way?"

"Gosh, girl, I don't know," Serena shook her head in puzzlement. "Here, you relax yourself. I'll make you some tea. Gabe?"

"I'd love a cup," he called out as she strode into the kitchen.

Priya felt a little self-conscious alone with Gabe. She wanted to pull herself together but wasn't quite sure how.

"I'm overwhelmed by Renita's bombshell and I'm tired," she choked.

"I know," Gabe said, tenderly gathering her into his arms.

Priya buried her head on his shoulder and continued to sob.

"Perhaps your mother didn't have a choice in the matter," Gabe said gently, as he stroked her hair.

"We all have choices," Priya choked. "I mean, what a way to find out a family secret. In a hospital, of all places, with Auntie Lottie looking on. I must have looked like a real fool."

"You could never look like a fool," Gabe tipped her face towards him and peered into her deep dark eyes. "No matter what."

"There was no reason not to tell me all these years," Priya sniffled.

"Sometimes it's for the best," Gabe reasoned. "Your dad might have been uncomfortable with this knowledge and shame kept him quiet."

"What shame?" Priya demanded.

"You're right," Gabe agreed. "In today's world there is no shame. Things happen, but we're going back a generation or two. From what Serena's told me, I suspect your dad was steeped in the old culture, and I'm willing to bet it caused numerous conflicts between your parents."

Priya nodded. He'd summed up the scenario fairly accurately. Wiping the tears from her face, she settled back into her own comfortable spot on the couch.

"Here you go," Serena returned with a steaming mug of green tea for Priya. She set it on the coffee table. "Something to eat, love?"

"No," she shook her head. "I don't want to risk getting sick again ... you know the virus and all."

"Perhaps you're right," Serena agreed. "Well, girl, you just relax and get some rest. We're right here, if you need anything."

The phone rang. Serena grabbed the handset and placed it in Priya's outstretched hand. "It might be the hospital," Serena suggested.

"Hello," Trent was on the line. "How are you?" His voice was brimming with concern. "I thought something was wrong with your phone because I tried to call earlier..."

"It was off the hook by accident," Priya wiped her eyes and wondered whether Trent would be able to tell from the sound of her voice that she'd been crying. "I was pretty sick last night. It seems I got that awful stomach flu that's going around."

"Oh no," he sighed. "I was actually calling to find out, first of all, how your aunt was, and then to let you know that I've got rush tickets for the symphony this evening. I pictured you at the hospital all day and wanted to give you a break."

"Great," Priya groaned. "I would have loved that."

"Don't worry," Trent said reassuringly. "There'll always be other performances. We can go another time."

"You could still go," Priya reasoned.

"I'd rather go with you. Never mind, maybe my parents can make use of the tickets. How is your aunt?"

"I think she's stable for now," Priya said. "Hopefully we'll know more by tomorrow. I should be feeling well enough to get to the hospital by then."

"How are you managing by yourself now?" Trent asked.

"Actually, I'm not by myself right now," Priya said evenly. "Serena and Gabe came over to check on me."

"Can I bring anything over for you?" Trent asked.

"Thanks, but I feel bad enough that these guys dropped over. You've got that recital coming up..."

"I'll let you rest tonight and catch up with you tomorrow," Trent said reluctantly.

As she hung up, Priya realized just how much she would have loved Trent to come, but at the same time thought better of it. It was one thing to be vulnerable with Gabe and Serena. It would be quite another thing for Trent to witness the state she was in. For sure she'd scare him off and that would be the end.

"How are things going with you and Trent?" Serena asked, replacing the phone on its base.

"Pretty good," Priya said. "We're sort of officially seeing each other now."

"That's great," Gabe said. "I realize it's none of my business, but have you told Trent about your uh ... eating disorder?"

"I don't have an eating disorder, Gabe. Whatever do you mean?" Priya twisted the band of her watch around her weak fingers. The two-tone gold and silver pattern dissolved into a platinum hue whenever sunlight played upon the delicate links.

"Priya…" Gabe began.

"I'm fine. My eating is under control," she insisted. "Trent's twin sister didn't make it though," she said, finally looking up at him. "Trent lost his sister to anorexia last year. Nothing like that is going to happen to me." *And I don't want him ever to think that it might.*

"Well, girl," Serena called on her way back from the kitchen. "I'm worried about you, too. Here Gabe, here's your own," Serena said, placing a second mug of tea on the coffee table next to Priya's, which remained untouched.

"What about you? Won't you have any?" Priya asked.

"Later, girl. While you rest, I want to straighten up the place for you. Perhaps I'll remake your bed so you can get comfortable for the night before we leave."

"That's so sweet," Priya was deeply touched. "Gabe, why do you think I should say something to Trent about my…" She couldn't bring herself to admit she had an eating disorder, or to link herself to the term "anorexia." She liked being thin.

"Well," Gabe sighed thoughtfully, "I have never met the man, so I can't say. However, if he genuinely cares about you, he will try to help you rather than run away from the problem."

"But why should I say something?" Priya persisted.

"If he can't figure it out for himself or chooses not to see it, then I'd be a little concerned," Gabe responded. "See where your relationship is going and then decide. You'll want to be honest with him. Tell him when you're ready. In the meantime, why don't you get some rest?

"Do you have to leave now?" Priya was dismayed.

"Absolutely not," he assured her.

"You mean you want to stay?" Priya was surprised.

"For sure," Gabe said.

"Here look, love, cover up. I'm feeling cold just looking at you," Serena laid a knitted afghan over Priya and slid a cushion under her head. "We'll be right here if you need anything."

Serena not only had the smooth, gentle hands of a caregiver, but the soothing voice of an attentive nurse. As Priya settled in for a nap, she felt sheer gratitude that Serena had given up her afternoon to care for her. Before long, she sank into the deep restful sleep of someone who knew she was being truly looked after. For the first time in months, she felt at peace with her surroundings. She felt as though Serena and Gabe were helping her pick up the jagged slivers of her life and fuse them back in place.

Serena hadn't said anything but as soon as she entered the townhouse, she'd been overpowered by the odour of lemon scented cleaners and bleach. While making the tea, she'd spotted a pail of water, an array of household cleaners and, strangely enough, three toothbrushes scattered on the floor. There was no sign of a mop.

"Gabe," she whispered, gesturing for him to follow her into the kitchen.

"What's going on?" he asked coming behind her.

"What is this?" she asked, pointing to the toothbrushes. "Who cleans floors with toothbrushes?"

"Apparently, Priya does," his tone belied his concern. "What are you thinking?"

"Oh, Gabe," Serena's brow furrowed in concentration. "I've seen this on talk shows. Anorexics sometimes engage in obsessive compulsive behaviour. Here, look," she pointed to the garbage can under the sink. It was stuffed with an overabundance of paper towel and food scraps. A shower of cracker crumbs threatened to rain down on anyone who yanked on the top of the plastic liner the wrong way. "I could be wrong, but it looks as if she went on an eating frenzy and tried to hide the evidence. She needs help, Gabe."

"I know that," he agreed soberly." But until she can see it for herself, there's not much we can do." He caught sight of the food scale. "Do you think she bought that to weigh her food?"

"I wouldn't be surprised if she weighs her food, but that scale was actually Jay's last anniversary gift to Delaney," Serena opened the broom closet and took out the broom and dust pan.

"You're kidding," Gabe frowned.

"I wish," Serena sighed.

"But what woman would put up with that? If Dad gave Ma a food scale without her asking for it, she'd likely have thrown it at him."

"Well," Serena said, " I think, despite her cheerful personality, Delaney was deeply hurt by Jay's attitude towards her. She was so kind ... our Delaney wouldn't harm a fly, much less tell Jay where to go. She had some deep-seated compassion for him but I never understood why. Oh, don't get me wrong, he had his nice ways too and he was no wife-beater ... not in a physical sense anyway, but shells, Gabe, true love really *is* blind I guess.

"Here, Gabe, this garbage is busting at the seams. There's a large can on the back steps. Can you take this please?" With brisk efficiency, Serena rested the broom against the counter, heaved the kitchen bag out of the bin, and knotted it with a simple twitch of the finger.

"Wow, you treat this place like home, don't you," Gabe was impressed.

"Delaney made sure I did," Serena said fondly. "She helped me so much, Gabe, that whenever I was over here on a Sunday, I'd pick up the broom and put things to rights. Delaney was a lovely person, but she wasn't the greatest housekeeper. She had to do everything because Jay wouldn't help much, so it was hard to keep up what with working full-time too."

"Jay sounds like a real piece of work," Gabe said wryly as he relieved Serena of the garbage.

While he was on the back steps placing the bag into the metal trash can, Serena slipped a fresh bag into the kitchen bin and resumed her sweeping. "I'll go in and fix up Priya's room. She'd be far more comfortable in bed," Serena observed.

"I heard you telling Priya to relax," Gabe said. "Can't you

take your own advice and sit for a minute."

"Oh shells," Serena blushed, washed her hands at the sink, and plugged in the kettle for more tea. Soon they were seated across from each other at the table, steaming mugs of green tea and a plate of Ovaltine biscuits between them. "Priya has always made sure that Renita is well supplied with her special cookies," Serena said. "She goes all the way across town to the Sri Lankan shop to buy them for her. My, that girl tries so hard with Renita. I hope the old woman appreciates it."

"If she didn't before, she might now that she's admitted to Priya who she really is," Gabe commented.

"So when was the last time you saw Delaney?" Serena asked suddenly.

"Nearly twenty years ago, if you can believe that!" Gabe was pensive. "It seems like just yesterday, though."

"Why weren't you guys in contact?" Serena took a second cookie from the plate, nibbling daintily around the edges. "These are good."

"It was just one of those things," Gabe was evasive. "Although when I saw Priya in the parking lot at Walmart the other day, I was astounded at how much she resembles her mother when she was young. Mainly in terms of her mannerisms and warmth, but with respect to frame and build, Delaney was a much larger boned woman. I can't imagine that Priya was ever very big at all."

"Truth," Serena agreed. "Would you like to see some pictures of the family?"

"I'd love to, but perhaps Priya might not like that," Gabe was doubtful.

"I know that girl," Serena smiled. "If she were feeling well, she'd be showing you them herself."

"That was all the encouragement Gabe needed as he followed Serena into the den. Serena headed to the white pressboard bookcase and pulled out a pink baby book with the words "Our Baby Girl" scripted in gold lettering. A border of the same style framed a drawing of a white bassinet. "Here's

Priya's baby book," she said, handing it to Gabe, who settled down on the futon. A startled look crossed his face when he opened to the first page and saw a newborn Priya nestled in her mother's arms, with a caption featuring her birth statistics in green calligraphy.

Serena spotted Jay's birth certificate lying on the opposite end of the futon.

"Oh my guy, here," she sighed as she picked it up. "Renita Hannah De Souza, mother of Jaya ... Jayatileke Thomas. What a thing, eh, Gabe? What a thing!"

Gabe was lost in a world of his own. Oblivious to Serena and the birth certificate, his attention was firmly fixed on the photos of Priya. One shot in particular stole his heart. Priya was dressed in a pink sweater, custard yellow slacks and white shoes. A cloud of chocolate coloured curls was fastened with a pink satin bow. The caption read, "Our baby Bows at 18 months."

"Gabe," Serena peered over his shoulder at the mesmerizing photo. "What's wrong?"

"Oh, nothing," he said quietly. He closed the book abruptly as if he'd seen too much. "Show me pictures of a healthy Priya ... before the anorexia."

"Here, Gabe, look," Serena picked up a gilt-framed photo of Priya in her convocation cap and gown. The shot had been taken just weeks after Jay and Delaney died. In it, a brave-looking Priya smiled shyly at the camera. Nobody would have ever suspected the sadness that lurked behind her warm eyes. Nobody would suspect that barely a year and a half later that healthy looking school teacher would be reduced to a sickly 89-pound invalid.

"She's beautiful," Gabe was surprised. "And she thought she was *fat!*"

"Sorry to say," Serena nodded. "Priya looked good then. She was covered, if you know what I mean. When she said she wanted to throw off some weight, I thought okay, well maybe her self-esteem needs boosting and a couple of pounds won't hurt. But she didn't want to stop losing. She told me it was fun. At Thanksgiving, she was down to 95 pounds and I put my foot down, I said enough was enough."

"Apparently it wasn't," Gabe said.

"She and her close friend, Rachel, had a big fight that day," Serena reflected. "It was Priya's first Thanksgiving without her parents ... a very sad time for her. Rachel thought that we should take Priya out for dinner. Rachel's family lives in Thunder Bay, but she wasn't going home that weekend because she was busy with term papers, and besides, she had to work on Thanksgiving Monday. Anyway, we went to a nice restaurant for a turkey dinner with all the trimmings. It was our treat. Priya ate one slice of turkey, a little bit of stuffing and half a piece of pumpkin pie. Rachel and I stuffed ourselves. We'd saved up our calories for that night and we were there to eat, man! Rachel was so angry."

"Why angry?" Gabe was puzzled as he studied a series of family photos on the wall: Delaney's parents, Jay's relatives, and an assortment of friends at social gatherings.

"Rachel has a big appetite, and, like most, wouldn't mind losing a pound or two. That's quite unlike me. God gave me a speedy metabolism and I can eat a lot and I don't gain too much. Rachel ate up a storm and felt that Priya was staring at her and judging how much food she put away. What made it worse was that Priya had brought along a calorie counter and kept consulting it like a Bible every time Rachel put something in her mouth!" This last remark ended on a giggle.

"You women are something else," Gabe chuckled. "Priya judging Rachel with the calorie counter-turned-Bible? What next?"

"The way Rachel carried on about Priya's obsession with calorie counting. I think ... now I might be wrong on this score, but I think that's the reason she treated Priya to that dinner theatre. She wanted to see if Priya would eat. Things were strained between the two for several weeks after Thanksgiving."

"Interesting," Gabe observed.

"Personally, I can't understand why Priya doesn't want to get better." Serena grumbled.

"Perhaps because she's not ready to accept the fact that she has an eating disorder. She needs to be able to acknowledge she needs help and she's not there yet."

They became aware of a slight rustling from the living room.

"I wonder if Priya is up," Serena got to her feet. The speediness in her movements reflected her profession. "Let's see."

Gabe was close behind, racking his mind to find a way to do or say something that would help Priya get better. He was startled to acknowledge to himself that he had feelings for her.

For the first time in many months, Priya allowed herself to think about the day her parents died. She was comfortable enough in Gabe and Serena's presence to realize that if she dissolved into tears again, they would be there to console her. She wouldn't have to face the anguish alone, as she did at home with Renita.

Jay and Delaney died on a sunny Sunday afternoon toward the end of April, just ten days after Priya's twenty-fifth birthday. Priya accompanied her parents and Renita to church as she routinely did. They lingered briefly at the post-service coffee hour to chat with their fellow parishioners over refreshments. Delaney, the social director of the coffee committee recruited two families a week to provide cakes and cookies on a designated Sunday. On that particular day, two Guyanese families served apple-toffee coffeecake and spicy cheese sandwiches. Priya not only ate normally, she approached the food with a healthy degree of enthusiasm.

They didn't stay as long as they usually did because Delaney was going to prepare the family a quick lunch as Jay's friend was taking them on a forty-five minute flight over southwestern Ontario. There was room for Renita and Priya in the twin engine Cessna, but Renita had no interest whatsoever in travelling on another plane. She'd experienced some swelling in her legs on the long journey from Sri Lanka. She had no intention of flying anywhere for fun. Besides, there was that annoying little cough she'd developed over time. Priya didn't relish spending the afternoon with her father's friends, and had a good excuse not to accompany them on the flight. She had landed a month-long supply teaching stint and felt that she was falling behind on her lesson plans. The teacher she was replacing had left a mere outline of what she had intended to do with her class. Priya had earmarked that particular afternoon to go to the mall and purchase phonics games for her kindergarten classes.

Priya had no way of knowing that her life would change irrevocably in the time it took for her to shop and enjoy a coffee and a donut at the Tim Hortons in the food court. When her cell phone rang, she knew instantly something had happened. Was it Renita?

"Priya, the cough is not the thing," Renita had said in response to Priya's concerned query about her health.

When Priya tried to probe, Renita weeping, handed the phone to a policeman. "Ma'am, you need to get home as soon as you can..."

With a sinking feeling, Priya knew that the "something terrible" Renita had alluded to had nothing to do with her elderly grandparents in St. John's. She careened, sensing her life had taken a drastic turn. It was her parents. She couldn't say for sure that she knew that Jay and Delaney were dead, but she knew that they had met with a dire fate. Maintaining her composure, Priya tossed her empty coffee cup into a trash can and walked out to her car. Focusing on the road, her hands gripping the steering wheel, she blanked her mind to keep the heart-thumping panic at bay, managing somehow to get home safely.

Renita was seated on the chesterfield, flanked by a male and female police team. Things moved very quickly. Priya was driven to the hospital closest to the crash site where her parents had been taken. There was no issue regarding the severity of their injuries. She was told that the plane crashed only minutes after taking off. All three passengers had died on impact. Their bodies were broken almost beyond recognition.

Her grandparents took the first flight out of St. John's to be with her. Rachel came over. Friends from church and from Delaney and Jay's places of employment all gathered at the townhouse. A police investigation was carried out to determine the cause of the crash. Through the grief and confusion, a double funeral was planned. Somehow, seven days after that, the Sri Lankan tradition of an alms-giving was organized. A selected group of indigent parishioners was treated to a meal at the church hall. The menu consisted of Jay and Delaney's favourite dishes. Priya, ever the dutiful daughter, along with members of the Sri Lankan community and staff members from Delaney and Jay's schools, presided over the event. Renita stayed on the periphery. She'd been adamant about the alms-giving, but lacked the emotional wherewithal to contribute.

Priya managed to hold herself together while her grandparents were in town. She was sensitive enough to not lose sight of the fact that they had buried their one and only daughter, and if not for Priya herself, they no longer had anyone they could consider their child.

In the beginning, Priya attributed her dwindling interest in food to the raw wound of grief that seared her heart. She knew it was normal for some people to lose their appetite upon the death of a loved one. On the other hand, there were those whose appetite increased. Renita was one of them. She ate mindlessly, to numb the pain. Strangely, she didn't gain weight. In fact, it was soon after the deaths that she actually began losing weight. Priya thought the fact that she and her aunt were losing weight concurrently was a bizarre coincidence given that one was eating too much and the other, too little.

Priya justified her weight loss by claiming that she was too sad to eat. The first five pounds slipped off within a month of her parents' deaths. As spring bloomed into summer, the skimpy dresses and shorts came out, and Priya dared to be seen in low rise, body-hugging jeans, the compliments trickled in from all directions. Even Rachel was wowed by Priya's physical transformation and demanded to know her secret for losing weight. As she tried to set her life in order without her parents, Priya began to bask in the attention she was getting because of her new, slimmer body. By August, she'd dropped another five pounds and decided she'd never looked better. When Serena started expressing subtle concerns that maybe she was "throwing off a bit too much weight," Priya got excited. For her, the pull to lower the numbers on the scale became a seductive lure. She felt sexy and desirable as the pounds tumbled off, until that rainy Thursday in late November when Dr. Benson forced her confront the fact that she was a "restrictive anorexic." At the time, she had denied it vehemently. That was just a few short weeks ago.

Even now, as she lay under the afghan, her icy fingers could trace through her nightgown a map of bones that were formerly covered in fatty tissue. The slenderness of her thighs, sharp edges protruding through her knees, made her feel alluring and beautiful.

"Priya, honey," Serena's gentle voice roused her from her waking thoughts.

"I'm glad you're still here," she smiled.

"Why don't I heat up some soup for you?" Serena placed an experienced hand on Priya's forehead to determine if she had fever.

"No, no soup," Priya shook her head and slowly eased herself into a sitting position. She huddled at one end of the couch with the afghan wrapped tightly around her trembling body.

"Oh, why?" Serena pleaded. "Girl, you need the strength. Look at yourself! You're cold and shaking. Talk to her, Gabe."

"She's right, Priya," Gabe sat down beside Priya and clasped her hands in his. "You might end up sharing a room with your aunt."

"Grandmother," Priya corrected tiredly.

"Truth," Serena agreed. "Girl, you're giving me a hard time. You need to eat something ... *anything*!"

"Later," Priya said confidently. With Gabe so close to her,

Priya modestly rearranged the afghan around her legs. She rested her head against the arm of the chesterfield and took comfort from his presence. This was only the third time they'd seen each other, but she felt she could be herself with him. Delaney was the nexus that bound them together, but this profound connection between them was almost uncanny. When would he tell her the truth about his relationship to her mother? She marvelled at the fact that though Gabe and Jay were practically the same age, they were entirely different men. Priya could not remember her father holding her, not even once. His brand of occasional affection was to press a few bills into her hand and tell her to buy herself something pretty to wear or to take the money and treat a friend to a movie. She wondered what Trent would think if he walked into the room then. Would he be jealous? The thought was exciting to her.

"She still looks a bit green, Serena," Gabe said thoughtfully. "Perhaps she should have something lighter than soup."

Priya mentally rhymed off her new mantra. "Seedless grapes, iced water, and green tea are good enough for me."

"Dear, there was a pail of cold water sitting in the middle of the kitchen floor so I got rid of it," Serena said gently. "But I'm wondering why you left toothbrushes on the floor. What were you doing?"

"There was some dirt between the tiles," Priya mumbled almost inaudibly.

"Why wouldn't you use a regular scrub brush?" Serena probed.

Priya was about to confess that she was angry with herself for bingeing and needed to learn a lesson by forcing herself to do some really hard work, but she didn't think Serena would understand. "I didn't think a scrub brush would get into those crevices," Priya said.

Serena frowned.

"I'll have a few grapes," Priya said, hoping to take Serena's mind off the toothbrushes. "Maybe three."

"Excuse me!" Serena was wide-eyed.

"Okay, five then," Priya conceded.

Grumbling, under her breath, Serena stomped into the kitchen, startling Priya as she angrily slammed cupboard doors and drawers. "Maybe Serena isn't happy that you're comforting me so much," Priya smiled shyly at Gabe.

"Let's get something straight," his tone was gentle but firm. "Serena and I are only friends and as far as we are both concerned, that's as far as it's going between us. Serena is upset because you're not eating, and she's very worried about your health." He paused for a moment and then added in a matter of fact tone, "On the drive over here, I told her that you are a very important part of my life. And I am worried too."

"I'm grateful for her support," Priya said. "And yours too ... of course," she added, feeling suddenly shy.

"You have been through a very difficult time and now you're not well and you have no family support. I'm going to be here for you, no matter what. As will Serena."

Priya was too exhausted to argue.

Physically and emotionally fortified by the unexpected care she received from her friends that Sunday afternoon, Priya felt brave enough to take on the world when she drove to the hospital on Monday morning. She'd promised to inform Serena, Gabe, and Trent as soon as she got some news about Renita's condition.

As keen as she was to see Trent again, she was a little nervous about it. It would have been much easier if Trent hadn't lost his sister to anorexia.

A light snow was falling by the time she arrived at the hospital. Feeling a little weak when she woke up that morning, she'd allowed herself the privilege of eating eight grapes and a generous mug of green tea before leaving home. If she gave into temptation and ate anything else, she knew she'd be forced to take action, as she had just learned to do.

When she arrived in Renita's room, she was surprised to find it empty. The housekeeping attendant who was changing the linen said that Renita had been taken to the next floor for more tests, and she wasn't sure when Renita was expected back.

Priya went down the hall to the nurses' station. The two nurses on duty were both occupied with their respective phones. Priya leaned against the pale blue counter, resigned to a lengthy wait. One nurse was busy, flipping through charts as she spoke; the other was deftly entering information into her computer with the phone wedged between her ear and shoulder.

Priya watched the drama of real life in a suburban hospital play itself out. Elderly patients in various shapes and sizes strolled in and out of the rooms that lined the expansive corridor. A cluster of white-coated doctors sipped coffee by the water cooler while peering at clipboards. The intercom periodically crackled to life with a familiar litany of announcements about car headlights left on, doctors being paged here and there, and the day's roster of meetings and conferences. Two overweight nurses emerged from a kitchenette, nibbling on buttered croissants. Priya was almost brought to her knees with longing for those delicious pastries. One bite, just one bite!

"Priya," she turned when she felt a gentle tap on her shoulder. Dr. Benson was standing behind her, a grim look on his face. At once she assumed that he was displeased with her for not booking her appointment with the counsellor, Dr. Farrel.

Sheepishly, she turned to face her doctor. "Hi," she managed furtively. "I was really sorry to hear about your mother…"

"Thank you," he said. "She was eighty-five and in poor health, so it wasn't a huge surprise."

Priya nodded. "But I guess no matter how old you are, losing a parent is hard."

Dr. Benson's face softened. "You're right and you more than anybody would understand. We'll talk in my office later on this week. I'll have Ruby set something up and call you…" his voice trailed off.

Priya waited for him to mention Dr. Farrel. What would she say? She shifted her weight from one foot to the other and decided to change the subject to Renita — a safe topic under the circumstances. "You heard about my, uh ... aunt," she said, wondering now whether she should start calling her "grandmother."

"Yes," a shadow passed over his face. "In fact I was waiting to see her after her latest round of tests and then I was to contact you regarding her situation."

"Situation?" Priya remarked.

"Priya, come with me," the abruptness of his tone startled her.

"Why, what's wrong?" she asked, sensing that Dr. Benson had more on his mind than her missed appointment with Dr. Farrel.

"Let's go to Renita's room," he said quietly. "We need to talk."

Chapter 11

THERE WAS SOMETHING VERY POWERFUL about room 503 in the cardiac unit. For the second time in less than forty-eight hours, Priya was destined to hear startling news about Renita. While the first revelation was a family secret that would forever alter Priya's perception of the past, the second was one that would have devastating consequences for the future. Though he remained standing, Dr. Benson urged Priya to sit in the visitor's chair beside Renita's empty bed. An unfamiliar gray duffel bag was on the other bed, indicating that Renita had a new roommate.

"When did you first notice Renita's cough?" Dr. Benson asked.

"Cough?" Priya asked. She was so caught up in her own problems, she could not pinpoint when she first became aware of her aunt's cough. It seemed as if it had always been there — a part of her.

"A constant, hacking, wet cough that never seems to go away," the doctor prodded patiently.

"I don't know. I'm sorry," Priya murmured softly.

"Don't worry," Dr. Benson said gently. "Have you noticed Renita losing weight in recent months?"

"Now, *that* I have definitely noticed," Priya said, relieved that her powers of observation weren't as skewed as she thought. "I can't imagine that Auntie is anorexic. That wouldn't make sense."

"I think if Renita had the physical ability to eat, she would consume a horse," Dr. Benson smiled.

"So what's the problem?" Priya asked, fiddling with the band of her watch.

"In light of what you had to go through this year, with losing your parents, coping with anorexia ... it's a tough hand, but I'm afraid things are going to get a little tougher before they can get better," he said quietly.

"Just tell me," Priya said flatly.

"A biopsy will confirm this, but we already suspect that Renita is fighting a highly aggressive cancer in the pancreas. Over the weekend, a series of repeat X-rays revealed the same troubling dark spots in different regions of her stomach and back. Blood work shows that her counts are abnormal and a battery of other tests, including an MRI, being done right now as we speak, will give us more information. A biopsy scheduled for later this week will tell us a lot more, but it doesn't look good."

"Chemotherapy, surgery?" Priya questioned, thinking back to her first year of university when one of her classmates was diagnosed with leukemia and died six months later, despite the intervention of conventional and unconventional treatments.

"We could open her up and do some exploratory surgery, but from what the oncologist told me, Renita's tests indicate that the cancer is so advanced it wouldn't save her."

"How long has she had cancer?" Priya asked deadpan.

"It's been lurking in her body for at least a year and a half. How long has she been in Canada now?"

"Fourteen months," Priya said.

"Did she ever complain of pain to you before Friday?" Dr. Benson asked.

"Very specifically, yes ... the Saturday night before last. She put the discomfort on a fall she had in Sri Lanka."

"She tripped on a curb and fell," Dr. Benson nodded. "She told me when she came to see me about the pain a few weeks ago."

"I didn't think it was all that serious," Priya looked down at her hands, ashamed that she hadn't noticed Renita's failing health. Perhaps now Dr. Benson would see how selfish she actually was.

"She didn't want you to know." As if reading her mind, Dr. Benson touched Priya's shoulder and gave her a look that conveyed empathy. "She felt you were going through too much and didn't want to burden you. She shared her concerns with her friend, Lottie."

"Renita Auntie and I aren't very close," Priya wondered if Dr. Benson knew that Renita was actually her grandmother.

"Renita has a lot of issues..." Dr. Benson explained. "She told me that she had some family news to share with you."

Priya nodded. "It seems she's my grandmother and not my aunt."

"Are you okay with that?" Dr. Benson regarded her kindly.

"I have to be," Priya said philosophically. There was a moment of silence as doctor and patient tried to discern what direction their conversation should take.

Dr. Benson never wore a white coat, even when he did rounds at the hospital. Today he was dressed in black slacks and a light blue cotton shirt. Priya had always found him easy to talk to, especially now. As usual, he'd taken time just for her. Whether he was working at the hospital or his clinic, he was the same, caring, devoted doctor. "Priya, your aunt's injuries healed a long time ago," he said slowly. "She suffered a bruised rib in that fall and not much else."

"So if she does have cancer, is it terminal?" Priya wanted to know.

"I'm sorry to say, she'll have about three to six months to live, and that's being optimistic," Dr. Benson walked over to the window and peered out at the cloud-laden sky. "They say we're in for a storm."

Priya huddled in her chair as if hoping to shield herself from further bad news.

"Ayurvedic medicine," she said at length. "Maybe if I take her back to Sri Lanka..."

"She's too weak to travel round trip," Dr. Benson turned back to face Priya. "Renita doesn't know any of this yet. If we tell her she has only X number of weeks or months to live, she might give up all together. On the other hand, she might fight for her life and defy the odds."

"Not Auntie," Priya said with conviction. "She told me on Saturday that she not only wants to die, she thinks she already is ... dying. After my father died, Renita gave up on life."

"I know," Dr. Benson said sadly. "You need time to digest this information. After the biopsy we'll discuss what to tell Renita."

"How do I face her in the meantime?" Priya asked as footsteps approached the door.

"Just treat her as you normally would," Dr. Benson glanced at the door. A tall, white-haired woman with a metal walker approached the entrance.

"Oh my goodness, I thought I lost my way back to my room, but here I am," she chuckled to herself, tossing Dr. Benson a whimsical smile as she came in. Priya was instantly reminded of Daisy Saunders, her maternal grandmother. She even dressed like her with the navy tailored pants and bright flowered blouse stretched over a generous stomach.

"It's fairly easy to get lost here," Dr. Benson said to the cheerful senior, who parked the walker next to the closet and then walked slowly towards her duffel bag. "Cold weather never did much for my arthritis," she grumbled lightly.

"You're doing fine," the doctor assured her.

"It's crazy, you know," she shrugged. "I have a bit of angina, but the kids made my doctor admit me. I'm seventy-five years old and they don't want to take chances. What chances! I've lived a long happy life." She turned to Priya. "I'm Florence Marchand."

"Nice to meet you," Priya shook her plump hand and felt the strength in her grasp. "I'm Priya De Souza."

"You're awfully young to be in this ward," Florence clucked disapprovingly.

"She's here to visit a relative," Dr. Benson cut in firmly. "Renita De Souza ... your roommate."

"Oh yes, we met in the lounge. Sad lady, but hopefully what ails her won't keep her here too long. My, I have so much to do

before Christmas. I have no time to be in hospital, you know."
While she chatted, Florence opened the blinds, unpacked her
bag, and arranged five paperbacks on her bedside table.

Watching the senior filled Priya with an unexpected surge
of hope. In a few short weeks, her grandparents would fly in
from St. John's for Christmas and then, for a brief period, all
would be right with the world.

It was 4:30 pm. Dusk had already coloured the sky a deep
shade of gray. Priya was seated in a cozy lounge across the hall
from a newspaper stand. She was nursing a cup of green tea
and pretending to show interest in an oatmeal raisin muffin
than she actually had no intention of eating. She had purchased
it at the hospital coffee shop to make it look as if she were
taking care of herself in front of the two doctors that flanked
her on either side. Dr. Benson was on her left, sipping a cup
of coffee, and oncologist Dr. Joan Blair sat on her right with
a manila folder balanced on her knees. A middle-aged blonde
with a matronly build and warm hazel eyes, she looked as if
she might be more at home teaching a cooking course. Priya
could imagine this doctor with the prestigious title and daunting
responsibilities wearing a flour-splattered apron and running
a rolling pin over a sheet of pastry. Even her tone of voice had
a motherly quality that made it no surprise to Priya when she
learned that the doctor was indeed the mother of two universi-
ty-aged students. She had a gentle way of delivering bad news.

There was talk of withholding the biopsy because the results
of the MRI told the doctors what they didn't want to accept.
Renita had a highly invasive cancer that had already attacked
the liver, lungs and pancreas. Cancer cells were running ram-
pant through her lymphatic system and there was nothing
that could be done to stop them. Even surgery and aggressive
drug treatments were no longer viable options due to the speed
of deterioration. If the cancer had been discovered even two
months earlier, there might have been some hope of arresting
it, but not under the present circumstances.

"What we can do for your aunt is this," Dr. Blair opened the folder and spread it out as neatly as she could on her ample lap. "We can make her comfortable. Right now she is on Demerol for the pain, but that won't be enough for long…" She waited for Priya to digest this information.

"Are you okay?" Dr. Benson placed a gentle hand on her arm.

"So far," Priya nodded, somewhat unable to fully assimilate the news. She felt detached, as if she were watching people in a movie.

"Do you have any questions?" Dr. Blair asked.

"You say the Demerol won't be enough for long," Priya said slowly. "I assume, then, that things will get much worse before they get better."

"Barring a miracle," the doctor sighed, "it won't get better. Your aunt will reach a stage when she needs to be on morphine, and at that point, we will need to re-admit her to the hospital … to the palliative care unit."

"Isn't that where people go when there's no hope left?" Priya's mind flashed back to her classmate, who she'd heard had died in a palliative care unit when cancer finally claimed her life.

"Until the last breath is taken, there is always hope," Dr. Blair said cautiously. Offering useless platitudes was one part of the job description she would have gladly passed up, but she knew when she committed herself to cancer treatment that she'd have to take the good with the bad. "However hopeless things may look from a medical perspective, I gather from talking to Renita that she is a woman of prayer and she has an entire congregation to support her."

Priya nodded glumly. "You talk about re-admitting her when the pain gets really bad, so does that mean I can take her home now?"

"At some point this evening Renita will be moved into the oncology ward and in a few days she will go home with her friend Lottie. Arrangements have been made," Dr. Benson said quietly.

"What? Why!" Priya was stunned. "I'm her next of kin. Why wouldn't she go home with me?"

"We're not advising that she go home with you simply because you aren't up to it," Dr. Benson said gently.

"Why is that?" Priya felt the hard edge of anger creeping into her tone.

"Priya," Dr. Benson continued patiently, "you are a confirmed anorexic and you are making no attempts to seek treatment to halt the progress of your condition. You are not physically or emotionally capable of looking after yourself, never mind your ... grandmother. This is in no way a statement about your personality or character. This is a message about your denial of treatment for a psychiatric illness, which is precisely what anorexia nervosa is."

"Who decided all of this?" Priya glanced first at one doctor and then the other. She was aware of people passing through the lounge and felt self-conscious. Priya shrank into her chair in an attempt to be as self-effacing as possible.

"Renita suggested it to me," Dr. Benson admitted. "And when Lottie came by after lunch, she seconded it. "

"And you both agree with them." Priya felt humiliated and betrayed. She could understand Dr. Blair's position in the matter. Until that afternoon, she hadn't known Priya from Betty Crocker, but Dr. Benson! Surely he should have known better. He'd known Priya since before she was even born. They thought she was an unfit guardian. She looked away, unable to conceal the devastation she felt.

"I'm sorry, Priya," Dr. Blair said quietly, "but Dr Benson is right. You need to look after yourself before you can consider looking after anybody else. Besides, you mustn't be too hard on yourself. According to Renita, you've been through far too much this year already, with losing both your parents. Lottie has her health, a good husband, not to mention the support of her church behind her. She is far better equipped than you to help Renita at this time."

"So, that's it then," Priya shrugged. "I'm out of the picture.

I let my grandmother down and she is letting me know it."

"No, Priya,' Dr. Benson said. "You are still Renita's next of kin. Ultimately it is you who will have to decide on her treatment the day she is no longer physically or mentally competent to do so. You will have to make various arrangements, including funeral plans. Renita doesn't have much time and she told me that she wants you to come to Lottie's as often as you can to see her."

"I don't know why she didn't tell me any of this herself," Priya said slowly. "I was with her for two hours after she came back from her MRI this morning and not a word."

"Okay, let me get blunt here for a second," Dr. Benson's tone was stern. "Renita is afraid to look at you. She feels you look more the cancer patient than she does."

"She knows she has cancer!" Priya was startled.

"She does now," Dr. Benson nodded. "After lunch, she came right out and asked me if she had cancer."

Dr. Blair's pager emitted a series of staccato beeps. "I'm going to have to leave you," she stood up," as I'm already late for a meeting. Priya, here is my number if you have any questions. Please call any time." She reached into a side pocket of her white coat and took out a business card.

"Thank you," Priya accepted the card and slipped it into her handbag.

"I'll have Ruby call you later in the week," Dr. Benson said as he too stood up to leave. "I hope you will start to give some serious consideration to setting up an appointment with Dr. Farrell."

Priya nodded politely, but the reality was that she still had no intention of ever setting up that appointment with Dr. Farrell. Dr. Benson had betrayed her. She no longer needed his or anybody else's help.

"Are you staying on at the hospital?" he asked.

"I'll wait till Auntie is settled for the night," Priya decided.

"Don't stay too late," Dr. Benson warned. "It's pretty stormy out there and I hear that roads are already very slippery."

"Dr. Benson," Priya asked hesitantly, "does Auntie's medical team know that she is my grandmother?"

He nodded. "In the bigger scheme of things, that's just a detail. To us, Renita De Souza is one of a number of valued patients we have to treat. She is a special lady and she will get the best we have to offer."

"Thank you," Priya nodded, noting a large sign on the wall discouraging the use of cell phones as their frequencies might interfere with hospital equipment. Stuffing the uneaten muffin back into its recycled paper bag, she unzipped her handbag and wedged it in between her wallet and cell phone. She forced the zipper closed and excused herself, then went toward the bank of payphones by the bagel shop she and Trent had visited on Friday evening, and called him at work. Up to this point, she hadn't had a chance to give him an update on Renita's condition.

"Priya, hi," Rachel answered the phone. "How are you doing?"

"Hey, I thought this was Trent's number," Priya said.

"It is, but I happened to be in here dropping off some paperwork for him and he stepped out to the photocopier for a second.

"I suppose Trent told you about Auntie Renita being in the hospital," Priya said.

"Yeah, he did. What's happening over there? What are the doctors saying?"

"It's not good," Priya lowered her voice, assuring herself of as much privacy as she could in a busy urban hospital where the neighbouring phones were occupied by other harried visitors briefing concerned relatives about sick family members.

"What is it?" Rachel demanded.

"She has a very aggressive cancer that has invaded her liver, lungs, and pancreas."

"Oh my God!" Rachel gasped.

"That's why I was trying to get a hold of Trent. He wanted to know..." Priya began.

"I am so sorry, Priya. You know I am here for you whenever

you need me," Rachel said, the concern in her voice palpable.

"Thank you, dear friend," Priya said.

Hang on a sec, I'll get Trent," Rachel sounded as if she were almost relieved to distance herself from the phone.

Priya waited patiently for Trent to pick up the line. When he did, a surge of relief washed over her. It was so good to hear his voice!

"Priya ... Rachel just told me the news. How are you doing?"

"It hasn't really sunk in yet," she admitted.

"Tell you what," he was all business now. "I'm heading to the hospital now. Rachel wants to come with me. Priya, the roads are really bad so don't plan on driving back home tonight. I'll take you."

"Trent, that's sweet, but I can't just leave my car here..." Priya began.

"Oh, yes, you can," he said firmly. "They're expecting fifteen to twenty centimetres of snow and very high winds this evening. I'll be right there."

"Thank you, Trent," Priya said. "Auntie is being moved into the oncology ward. When you get here, have me paged to come to the lobby because I'm not sure where I'll be. Right now Auntie is still on the fifth floor, but I'm not sure when they'll move her."

"Don't worry," he assured her. "I'll find you."

Priya knew that there was no point in trying to contact Serena because she'd be getting ready to go to work for the rest of the evening. She put more coins into the phone, dialled Gabe's number, and repeated the same news to him, as well as the fact that she'd been deemed not suitable to look after Renita.

"I'll be right over," he promised her.

"Thank you," Priya was just as relieved to know that Gabe was coming as she was that Trent was on his way, but for a different reason. Gabe was the only person with whom she could share her shame of being overlooked as a caregiver for her grandmother. How was she going to explain to Trent that Renita would be staying at her friend's place instead of Priya's?

Half an hour later, Gabe shook the snow off his jacket as he walked into the hospital lobby on a blast of arctic air. Priya knew it would take Trent longer to get to the hospital from downtown Toronto. With the traffic and road reports being as bad as they were, the thirty minute drive on the 401 could take up to an hour or more.

"How is your aunt ... or, your grandmother, I should say? How are *you* coping?" Gabe peeled off his icy gloves, cupped Priya's face in his chilled hands, and peered searchingly into her eyes.

"Actually, I'm really mad," she said stepping back. "I'm insulted to think that Dr. Benson and Renita's new doctor feel that I'm not a fit caregiver for Auntie Renita."

Gabe placed his hands on Priya's shoulders and guided her over to the bagel shop. "We need to have a chat."

For the first time that day, she noticed the fibre optic Christmas tree in the middle of the lobby, its shimmering brightness dissolving into a rainbow of different colours that gave a series of foil-wrapped gift boxes a radioactive glow as the light played upon them. A medley of Christmas songs piped through the sound system tried to lend a festive atmosphere to the hospital.

"You know they're right," Gabe said gently as they sat in the same seats that Priya and Trent had occupied just three nights earlier.

"What are you talking about?" Priya struggled to maintain her patience.

"We all feel that you are not physically or emotionally capable of looking after your grandmother during this difficult time." Gabe said evenly.

"You too?" Priya placed her cold hands in her lap and looked away. She didn't trust herself to look at Gabe, worried she'd burst into tears. She felt hurt and abandoned, and she wasn't quite sure why.

"Priya, I don't know how you really perceive yourself at the moment," Gabe said tenderly, "but the rest of us see a very frail young woman who is crying out for help and refusing to take it when it's offered. Believe me, in your own way, you are as ill as your grandmother. She has terminal cancer, but if you go on like this, you'll have terminal anorexia. I'm sure your doctor has already told you what will happen if you keep restricting your food."

"What makes you the expert?" Priya muttered, fixing her gaze on the Christmas tree and wondering if the gift-wrapped parcels contained presents or were empty boxes.

"I've been reading extensively on anorexia since that Sunday we had coffee at Starbucks," Gabe admitted.

"Why?" Priya asked.

"Why?" Gabe gave his answer some thought. "Maybe because I care about what happens to you. I don't know why you're not seeking treatment. Perhaps you don't feel ready but you strike me as an extremely bright, articulate young woman. I know you are still grieving, and that part of that grieving might include anger at your parents having left you. And maybe you are punishing yourself by depriving yourself of food. But this is not the answer and you need to find another way to deal with your grief. For me, writing has always been cathartic. Have you thought about writing away your anger?"

"Not really," Priya was honest. "Writing my thoughts will not bring my parents back..."

"No, but it might help you understand why you have this eating disorder. I've kept a journal for many years, and it has always helped me understand what I was feeling or going through during particular periods of my life. I think if you did the same, it might help you work through your grief, and even your eating disorder. Besides, something tells me that you would be really good at it."

"And then what?" Priya listened with only half interest. A cluster of young carollers made their way around the corner, singing "White Christmas" as they passed a window display of a winter village, complete with Santa and his reindeer.

"You write your heart out," Gabe said thoughtfully. "Perhaps you could help other women ... young women and girls who are coping with eating disorders. According to what I have read so far, most victims of anorexia are adolescent girls. You're bright, mature, and trained as a teacher. You are in an ideal position to help so many."

"I can't take care of my grandmother, but I can suddenly take care of young girls with anorexia?" Priya was bewildered by Gabe's suggestion.

"Remember that little boy at Walmart? When we first met?" There was almost an urgency in Gabe's tone.

"Yes, what about him?" Priya asked.

"I was touched by your compassion for him. I saw right away that you're good with kids, Priya. If you could only get well, I feel you could do wonders ... not only in front of the classroom, but maybe in front of the podium."

"Why do you feel this way? Why is this even important to you?" Priya was curious.

"I don't know," Gabe admitted, "but I have a sense about things. I couldn't get you out of my mind yesterday. I could feel how sorry you were that you might not be able to make things right with Renita. That's what got me thinking: if Priya writes down her thoughts, keeps a journal, she might be able to find a way to help herself and others along the way."

Priya pondered his words. But, before she had a chance to respond, Trent and Rachel had made their way to the table. "You're here," she jumped to her feet, almost guiltily.

Trent, in a snow speckled trench-coat, looked more like a corporate businessman than a performing arts instructor. He struck Priya as very handsome, but conservative with his simply styled hair and Italian leather briefcase. Rachel, dressed in a puffy blue and white ski jacket and sensible navy wool mittens, gave the clear message that, for her, function ruled over fashion. She gave Priya a powerful hug. "What's happened to you!" she demanded.

Choosing to ignore the pointed reference to her appearance, Priya introduced her three friends to each other. She didn't miss the critical way Trent and Gabe sized each other up. Gabe, powerfully built and weather-worn, and Trent, tall and elegant, and much *much* closer to Priya's age.

"Your aunt will come home with you tomorrow?" Trent asked as the four sat down.

"No..." Priya began to fidget. Again the question arose in her mind, taunting her with its insistence upon an answer. How was she going to tell Trent that the doctors didn't think she was a suitable caregiver?

Gabe, sensing Priya's predicament rushed to the rescue. "Renita's doctors have decided that it's best for her to stay at her friend Lottie's house. For one thing it's closer to the hospital, and since the two women are childhood friends, they feel that it might be better for Renita to be looked after by someone from her past. For another thing, the doctors feel that Priya has been under a tremendous strain since her parents died. They want to cut her some slack and give her some guilt-free time to herself."

He sounded so convincing that Priya decided to accept his version as truth. He had packaged the facts in such a tidy little bundle, there was no room for questions.

"Renita needs all the psychological reinforcements she can get," Gabe folded his arms across his chest and sighed with satisfaction.

"Poor Renita," Trent said ruefully. "I gave her résumé to Human Resources this morning. There's actually an opening coming up next September when one of our teaching assistants retire."

"From what Priya says, I don't think Renita will be around next September," Rachel mumbled.

"Let's keep it positive," Priya said diplomatically. "We can go in pairs to visit her."

"Sounds good," Gabe nodded.

They rode the elevator to the fifth floor. The sounds and smells of dinner carts making their way through the halls made Priya's mouth water. As they proceeded down the hall toward Renita's room, she played a solitary game of guess-that-meal as the aroma of roast beef and steamed vegetables assaulted her nostrils.

"Hospital food must have come a long way over the years," Trent said, falling into step beside her, "because something smells really good."

"Tell me about it," Priya tried to sound offhand, even though hunger pangs were squeezing her stomach like an accordion. She tried not to think about the fact that all she'd eaten so far that day was a handful of grapes.

"After we see your aunt, we can grab something at the bagel place again," he suggested, taking her hand in his.

Priya was about to interject that Renita was not *actually* her aunt, but something made her keep silent. She wasn't sure what Trent would say and she wanted this particular conversation to take place in private.

"Priya?" He gave her a quizzical look.

"Actually, my appetite hasn't fully come back after my stomach bug," Priya said carefully avoiding his eyes, "but I can sit with you guys while you have something."

"That's okay," Trent said," I'm sure my mother has a nice meal waiting for me at home. That reminds me, one of these days I'm going to have to bring you by the house to meet my parents."

Priya knew she had to nip that idea in the bud as soon as possible. She was in no frame of mind to meet Trent's parents, parents who had lost a daughter with an eating disorder. She was almost certain that if they met her, they'd figure out that she, too, had an eating disorder. They might then talk Trent into dropping her. Even though they'd only been out a few times, Priya suspected that Trent wanted them to be an official couple. Why else would he be so anxious for her to meet his parents?

"Uh, Trent, I don't think I'm ready to face anybody's parents 'til after Christmas. The memory of my own parents' deaths is still so painful ... and Christmas is too much of a family time of year. Can you understand that?" She gave his hand a gentle squeeze.

Trent drew her into his arms. "Priya, I am so sorry," he kissed her cheek, "I didn't mean to sound insensitive. It's just that I care about you so much, I can't wait to share you with my family ... but only when you're ready."

"Thank you," she sighed gratefully. "What did you do with the symphony tickets?"

"I tried to give them to my parents but Dad was too tired to go, so, in the end, I took my mom," Trent explained.

"That was nice," Priya said, smiling at him warmly. "I'm sure she was really happy to spend some time with you."

While Rachel and Gabe commiserated about life in northern Ontario, Priya took Trent into Renita's room. The older woman was staring half-heartedly at a plate of steamed vegetables, rice, and what looked like beef.

"How are you feeling, Auntie?" Priya asked, dropping a kiss on her cheek.

"Don't you know..." the older woman shrugged, "they're giving me something for the pain, but I can't eat, Priya. The food looks lovely and I think I am hungry, but there is no appetite."

"Maybe if you take small bites," Priya picked up the cutlery on the tray and began cutting the beef into slivers.

"I feel nauseous just looking at it," Renita looked away and then glanced toward the doorway where Trent, somewhat unsure of himself, remained standing. "How are you, Trent?" she asked as she beckoned him closer.

"You're looking good," Trent said cheerfully as he advanced into the room. Trying to keep the conversation as normal as possible, he continued, "I gave your résumé to Human Resources this morning. I know there's an opening coming up for September..."

"That's very kind of you," Renita gave him a forced smile, "but I won't be here in September."

"What do you mean?" Priya asked, the anxiety in her voice sounding shrill.

"I'll be with Jay by then. I don't have long to live," Renita said deadpan.

"We don't know that for sure," Priya gasped. "Please don't say that."

"I asked Dr. Blair when she came by to see me about ten minutes ago. She couldn't lie, and why should she?"

"Where is Auntie Lottie?" Priya asked. " I understand you're going home with her tomorrow."

"She went back to her place to prepare the guest room for me," Renita explained. "Surely, Priya, you understand why I can't come back to the townhouse."

Priya glanced nervously at Trent. She didn't want Renita to continue. "Of course I understand," she said, and backed away from the bed. "Rachel is in the hallway waiting to say to see you, and so is my friend, Gabe."

"A short visit, if you don't mind. I'm rather tired."

"Stay here, Priya," Trent said. "I'll get them." He smiled at Renita and slipped out of the room.

"What can I do for you?" Priya asked once they were alone.

"I heard the nurses talking about a terrible storm. Go home soon. I'll be all right for the night," Renita gestured toward the window. It was well past 7:00 pm, and though night had fallen, the sky was bright with the reflection of the snow against the streetlights. "Trent suggested I leave my car here and he'll drive me home," Priya assured her.

"He's such a good boy," Renita sighed with approval. "You are, indeed, lucky to have him."

"Hi there," Rachel called brightly.

"Come, come," Renita beckoned with as much hospitality as she could muster.

First Rachel and then Gabe self-consciously ventured into the room. "How are you doing, Ma'am?" Gabe tipped his hat toward her.

"I'm not keeping too well, but then what's to be done?" Renita spoke with resignation.

"Well, look, if there is anything we can do for you, Priya knows that we're here to help," Rachel slouched into her coat. She seemed uncomfortable standing next to the bed. She smiled awkwardly at Renita and moved to stand beside Priya, giving her friend's shoulder a hardy squeeze.

Gabe merely nodded, somewhat at a loss for words.

"Yes," Renita nodded. "They are taking care of me."

Priya glanced toward the window. "We should probably get going. Auntie needs to rest."

"Thank you for dropping by," Renita said politely as Rachel and Gabe moved toward the door.

"Right, then, Auntie," Priya dropped a dutiful kiss on her cheek. "I'll see you tomorrow."

Once they rejoined Trent in the hallway, Gabe suggested that it would be more sensible for Trent to get Rachel home safely and for him to drop Priya, as it was on his way. Trent reluctantly agreed. "I guess this makes sense on a night like this."

"Priya, I'd like to grab a cup of coffee to take on the ride back into Toronto. God knows how long we'll be idling on the 401." Rachel wound her scarf tightly around her neck, and tossed her a meaningful look.

"Okay," Priya shrugged. "We'll catch up with you guys in the lobby," she threw a look over her shoulder to Trent and Gabe.

"I'm buying you something to eat," Rachel said as they entered the bagel shop.

"That's not necessary," Priya protested as they made their way to the counter.

"You're all bones. It's very necessary," Rachel countered.

"Look, I thought you got me down here so you could buy a coffee," Priya responded, trying to ignore the titillating smell of freshly baked bagels and their myriad toppings temptingly displayed in a glass-fronted showcase. The choices of toppings — smoked salmon, strawberry cream cheese, BLT — were overwhelming.

"I did," Rachel ordered a coffee and a ham and Swiss on a poppy seed bagel. "At least share this with me."

"Trent tried that trick on Friday night when we were here, but it didn't work," Priya turned away from the counter.

"You know, he already suspects something," Rachel brought her order to a nearby table. Throughout the tiny shop, hospital staff, as well as visitors, were crowded around tables, enjoying something warm and filling to eat. It was a popular spot, Priya surmised, ignoring the growls of hunger coming from her stomach.

"Did Trent say something to you?" Priya asked warily.

"Yeah, when we were coming in. You and Gabe were sitting by the Christmas tree. Trent was suddenly taken aback at how skinny you are. If he didn't see it before, he sure sees it now. His exact words were, 'either Priya is wearing spray-on jeans or she's extremely thin.'"

"And you said?" Priya prodded.

"Mmm, this is sooo good!" Rachel took a generous bite of her bagel and, with her mouth bulging with food, added, "I said 'Yeah. We think she's anorexic.'"

"Oh my God, Rachel, you had no right! How could you?" Priya almost screamed.

"Sorry, Priya, but I call a spade 'a spade.' He asked, and I wasn't about to lie," Rachel said in a matter-of-fact tone of voice. "I assume you guys are dating regularly so..."

"We won't be if he thinks there's something wrong with me," Priya wailed.

"Why?" Rachel was nonplussed.

"Because his sister was anorexic. She died at 57 pounds," Priya struggled to keep her anger under control but it was hard.

"I know about that," Rachel spoke through a mouthful. "I went to her funeral. If what happened to Lydia doesn't scare you, nothing will."

"I'm not anorexic! I'll know when to stop losing weight," Priya insisted. She couldn't help but feel as if she were driving a train that was veering off the rails, and she was completely out of control.

"I can assure you that Trent is not so shallow as to drop you just because you have the same eating disorder that his sister had. Give the man some credit," she paused for a gulp of coffee. "He thinks a lot of you. And you should tell him the truth. Given what he's been through, he has a right to know. Did it ever occur to you that he might want to help you deal with your anorexia? He might be able to empathize."

"What do you mean 'he thinks a lot of me'?" Priya asked.

"He likes your personality. He thinks you are smart, kind, down-to-earth, and beautiful ... that's what he tells me anyway."

"I think he's one of the nicest men I've ever met," Priya responded. "And Gabe? Has he said something to you?"

"He's told me he's concerned, yes," Rachel said, eyeing Priya with a quizzical look.

Priya fidgeted with the serviette dispenser on the table.

"That's unique," Rachel shook her head. "Trent is supposedly the man you're going out with and Gabe is ... *what* exactly is Gabe to you?"

"He was a friend of Ma's. You know that," Priya grew agitated.

"Okay, just wondering, that's all," Rachel frowned.

"What?" Priya stood up. She didn't want to continue the conversation.

"He seems really nice, but he acts like he owns you, that's all. Who is he to decide how you get home from the hospital?"

"He's just very concerned about me. He's almost twice my age Rachel, please!"

"Yeah, okay." Unconvinced, Rachel balled up the wax paper her bagel had been wrapped in, and shot it into the trash can across from the table "As long as Trent understands that," she added curtly as she stood up.

Priya was shaken. She didn't know what to think anymore and suddenly felt extremely tired. They found the men waiting for them beside a video game machine in the lobby.

"I'll call you later tonight," Trent embraced Priya.

"I'll look forward to that," she said quietly. "Trent, thank you for coming all the way out here and for bringing Rachel with you. It was really kind."

"It was nothing at all," he assured her. "You need a lot of support now."

"I told her the same thing," Gabe nodded.

As she and Gabe drove away from the hospital, Priya snuggled deep into her seat, settling into what would be a slow journey through icy streets and buffeting winds. Gabe didn't talk much because of the slippery roads. Priya, too, was lost in thought. When they finally made it back to the townhouse, Gabe broke their comfortable silence to remind her to think about what they had discussed earlier that evening.

"Think about what we talked about earlier, Priya. Write down your thoughts in a journal. It will help you a lot," he said as he came round to help her out of the car.

"Sure," but Priya wasn't interested. The day had been too stimulating, too stressful for her to take on new ideas. "You don't need to walk me to the front door. I'll be fine...." Her words were lost in a ferocious gust of wind.

"I don't think so," he grasped her arm firmly in his. "I'm scared if I let you go now, the wind will blow you right across the street."

Priya acquiesced gracefully.

"Call me if you need anything, anything whatsoever," he said firmly while she unlocked her front door.

"Thank you, Gabe," she said humbly. "I really *do* appreciate your support. Can I get you a coffee or anything before you head out?"

"There's nothing I'd like better than to have coffee with you, but..." he glanced at his watch, "I told Serena not to venture out by herself to get to work tonight. I said I'd give her a ride, so she's probably waiting for me now."

Priya nodded. "Drive safely and give my love to Serena. Gabe?"

"Yes, Priya?" he slipped his hand under her coat, and placed it on her shoulder, his eyes boring into hers, the warmth of his hand spreading throughout her body.

"Tell Serena about Auntie Renita," she said, shrugging the feeling of warmth off her body.

"Definitely," he gave her a quick hug and left.

Once Priya was inside, with her coat and boots put away, she walked into the kitchen to check her machine for messages. There were two. One was from Ruby reminding her she needed to make an appointment with Dr. Farrell, and the second was from Priya's grandmother in St. John's.

"How are you, my Duckie?" her grandmother said warmly. Priya sat on the edge of a chair to hear what she had to say. "I have disappointing news for you. Grandpa fell on the ice and broke his hip this morning. He's in the hospital now and it's all a big mess. I don't think we can fly up there to your place for Christmas. It's 5:30 pm. Newfoundland time. Give me a call when you get in, honey, and I'll tell you the details."

Priya buried her head in her hands and exhaled loudly. "Can things get any worse?" she cried out to the empty room. "Really, can they possibly get any worse?"

Chapter 12

THE SNOW FELL, the radio played carols, and people shopped. Priya De Souza let it all happen around her. The townhouse was a sad, empty place quite unlike it had been in previous years. Delaney and Jay were holiday enthusiasts and had gone all out to make the season as festive as finances and schedules would permit. It was the one time of year Jay relaxed his inflexible ways and joined his wife and daughter in the planning of gifts, parties and matters of spirituality. Whether the family flew out to St. John's to be with Delaney's parents or Daisy and Ralph came to Mississauga for the holidays, festive fever in the De Souza household soared off the charts. Jay was on the cutting edge when it came to the newest and trendiest light displays both in and outside the house. If rope lighting was hot, he was the first in line. If icicle lighting was in, then he knew about it. If the fashion was white only, then that's what the De Souzas had. If Jay were alive this Christmas, there would have been at least two decorative table top fibre optic trees, one for the living room and one for the den.

If Delaney were alive, she would have been directing a mass baking drive in the kitchen with Priya and Serena recruited to roll out pastry or chop fruit for one of the two Christmas cakes she made every year. As a nod to her multicultural marriage, Delaney baked up a traditional Sri Lankan-style fruitcake with its myriad fruits, aromatic brandy, hot buttered semolina, and a dozen eggs. She would also hark back into her own heritage for a typical Newfoundland-style boiled Christmas cake. Food was to be shared, not only with family and friends, but also among the parishioners at their church as well as among her students — many of whom would be spending the holiday season away from home.

This year the townhouse would remain dark and uninviting. Priya was barely home as the loneliness was too much to bear. When she wasn't spending time at Lottie's, trying to make herself as useful as possible to Renita, she was patching together an uneven string of teaching days or hiding out at Chapters, reading about how to lose even more weight. Now at a disturbing 84 pounds, Priya's diet consisted soley of grapes, green tea and the occasional energy bar washed down with a quarter cup of skim milk. When she was in the company of others, she indulged in normal eating habits, but excused herself to the washroom as quickly as possible and purged the meal out of her system. It being winter time, it was easy to hide her ongoing weight loss from Gabe and Serena and Rachel. She had an abundance of roomy sweat tops and pants that also kept her warm.

One sorry by-product of Renita's cancer was that every time she lost a pound or two, Priya secretly felt compelled to compete. In her troubled mind, Priya couldn't bear to see Renita become thinner than she was. Although she was genuinely concerned about Renita's well-being, she couldn't help inquiring after her day-to-day weight loss. Although she was being sustained with high calorie meal-replacement drinks, Renita still continued to lose and Priya continued to compete.

On days when the scale went down for Renita but not for Priya, the younger woman would drive home in a silent rage and throw herself into a marathon cleaning frenzy. On her hands and knees, scouring furiously at the ceramic with her toothbrushes, she would berate herself for not being a worthy enough guardian for her grandmother.

One night, while taking a break from her rigorous cleaning ritual, she flopped on the couch with the remote control and began channel surfing. After passing up the mélange of reality shows, documentaries, and sitcoms, she came across a talk show touting the benefits of hot red pepper as it related to weight loss. Routinely used in South Asian cooking, it was alleged to speed up the metabolism when sprinkled on a healthy meal. After the program ended, Priya filled a spice bottle with red chili powder and stored it in her purse. From that day onward, she made a point of sprinkling everything she ate and drank with the fiery red powder..

Priya felt as if she was drifting in a canoe without paddles. Her life lacked direction and more importantly, hope. She ignored Ruby's calls reminding her to make and keep appointments with Dr. Benson and Dr. Farrel. As far as Priya was concerned, Dr. Benson was no longer a part of her life. Her routine felt safe and comfortable and it didn't really interfere much with her day-to-day life, or so she tried to tell herself.

Daisy didn't know about Priya's weight loss, as Priya had been careful to shield her Newfoundland grandmother from that aspect of her life. Daisy and Ralph Saunders had suffered enough with the death of their only daughter, and now Ralph was back at home recovering from his broken hip. With all of that to contend with, Daisy was trying to make arrangements to fly up to Ontario in January to offer some badly needed support to Priya while she coped with Renita's cancer. Priya didn't know how she would explain the weight loss to Daisy, but at the same time, she longed for her motherly companionship. Priya saw Trent on the weekends and managed to eat normally when they were together. She made sure her visits to the bathroom were prompt. She didn't see much of Gabe during this time, as he was busy with his work. After taking a week off to go fishing somewhere up north, he flew back to Newfoundland on business and didn't return to Mississauga until a week before Christmas. Both he and Serena had plans to visit family and friends over the holidays, and Rachel, too, was planning to head back to Thunder Bay for a traditional family Christmas.

The Sunday afternoon before his scheduled flight to Banff, Gabe invited Priya to Starbucks. Having evolved into a ritual meeting spot for them, Priya and Gabe were wont to consider it "their place," and Sunday afternoons had morphed into "their time" to be together.

"Are you sure you'll be okay during Christmas?" Gabe asked, setting down an eggnog latte in front of Priya. As far as he was concerned, there were three major issues in her life that were leading toward an emotional breakdown: receiving the news about Renita's cancer, facing her first Christmas without her parents, and her ongoing battle with anorexia.

"I'll be all right," she assured him. "Trent invited me to his uncle's place for Christmas dinner, but I told him I can't go."

"Why not?" Gabe demanded.

"I'm not ready to meet new people," she confessed, enjoying the warmth of the mug against her chilled hands. It's too stressful, and, besides, this year my place is with Auntie Renita. I'll have Christmas dinner at Auntie Lottie's house and, later in the evening, I'll see Trent."

"Oh, well," Gabe stirred his coffee thoughtfully, "sounds like a plan come together then. I've got my Christmas gift for you in the car, but don't open it now. Save it for Christmas Day. I feel badly about not being here with you at Christmas, and I know Serena does too."

Then why are you leaving me? Priya wondered to herself.

As if reading her mind, Gabe fixed his gaze on Priya. "I hadn't really anticipated going away again after coming back from Newfoundland, but then Serena pointed out that since this is likely Renita's last Christmas, she and you might need the extra time to heal your relationship. So, when some friends invited me skiing at their chalet over the holidays, I thought it might be a good idea. Serena too thought a visit with family was in order. And besides," he smiled, " Do you really want the two of us hanging around while you and Trent get to know each other."

Priya sighed.

"What is it?" Gabe asked.

"It's just that Trent is a wonderful man but I'm not sure I

want to see him exclusively," she took a deep breath.

"Oh?" Gabe looked at her.

"He wants things to move faster than I do... That's what I sense anyway but..."

"Don't let him pressure you," Gabe suggested. "Take your relationship one day at a time, that's all."

"True," said Priya, in what she hoped was a cheerful tone of voice. "You know how much I appreciate your support and friendship. I too have a gift for you too back at the townhouse. And I'll give Serena hers before she leaves."

"Speaking for myself, the only gift I want is for you to get better," Gabe said patting her hand. "I won't give you a hard time about the eating, but I know you've lost even more weight since Renita was diagnosed with cancer. What are you doing?" He looked up sharply when he noticed Priya pour a reddish powder onto her cup.

"It's a new type of nutmeg," Priya said easily. "It goes really well with steamed milk."

"Can I try some?" Gabe peered inquisitively at the spice bottle in her hand.

"It wouldn't work with your eggnog latte," she hurriedly slipped the bottle back into her purse, took a long sip of her drink, and tried hard to bite back the heat of the chili powder as it blasted her mouth. She needed to distract him.

"Gabe," Priya lifted her mug to her lips and looked away.

"What's wrong, Priya?"

"It's just that ... well I know it's foolish, but I feel sad that you and Serena are going away. I've come to depend on you guys so much... You're like my family now."

"We feel sad, too," Gabe touched her hair. "But we're both only away for a few days ... oh," he paused briefly. "Are you're worried that maybe something will happen to both of us like with your parents?" he added thoughtfully.

Priya looked down at the table, relieved that that was what Gabe thought. She felt herself blush; she could never tell him that she had missed him more than she had anticipated while he was away, and now it would be several more days before she would see him again. "Listen to me, Priya," Gabe tipped her face towards him. "Nothing bad is going to happen to me or to Serena. We'll both be back with in a day or two of each other and life will carry on, hopefully with you making a new year's resolution to get treatment for your anorexia."

"We'll see what happens," Priya sighed despondently. At this point, she was so depressed she scarcely wanted to live, much less seek a recovery for her condition.

At 7:00 pm on Christmas Eve, Priya admired herself in front of the mirrored closet in her bedroom. She was wearing a pink jacket with black trim, a white blouse, and a black miniskirt. For once in her life, her short legs appeared long, coltish and model thin! Her hair was swept back with a tortoise-shell claw clip. At a healthier weight, her hair would have hung in soft ringlets around her shoulders, but now it felt dry and brittle against her very pronounced collarbone. She was too proud to hide her legs in sensible snow boots and decided instead to wear her black suede pumps. She felt like a million bucks. And she couldn't wait for Trent to see her when he came to pick her up.

After putting on silver hoop earrings and attaching a Christmas tree pin to her pink jacket, she reviewed the contents of her overnight bag. Trent and she would accompany Renita and Lottie's family to midnight service and then Priya would spend the night at Lottie's place. Nobody wanted to see Priya wake up alone in the townhouse on Christmas morning. A few minutes later, Trent arrived and greeted her with a kiss.

"You look beautiful," he said.

"Thanks," Priya smiled. "You look pretty good yourself."

Trent was dressed in a simple gray suit that enhanced the softness of his dark eyes. He took Priya's overnight bag and they set off to Lottie's semi-detached bungalow in the heart of Mississauga.

"I wonder if Auntie will even be well enough to go to church,"

Priya said. Even though she'd known that Renita was her grandmother for several weeks now, she hadn't shared the information with Trent and couldn't explain even to herself why she still felt insecure around him. He had done nothing to foster doubt, but, still, she was unable to fully reveal herself to him.

"Has she been able to leave the house at all since being discharged from the hospital?" Trent inquired.

"She attended one meeting of her prayer group," Priya said.

"Well that's encouraging," Trent said as he unlocked the passenger door for her.

The city of Mississauga was a wonderland of Christmas colourful lights and decorations. A soft snow was falling, but the air was relatively breezeless. They listened to a Christmas CD as they drove through the unusually peaceful streets. Aside from motorists headed to the various churches scattered throughout the city, traffic was at a minimum as most people were at home gearing up for the festivities of the following day.

"Are you sure I can't talk you into spending Christmas Day with me?" Trent asked hopefully as they paused for a red light.

"Not this year," Priya said firmly. "I need to be with my aunt."

"I know," Trent touched her knee. "I don't mean to sound selfish, it's just that I'm longing to spend more time with you. I feel that even though we've known each other for almost two months now, we really haven't had much time together alone."

Priya nodded. She didn't tell him that it was better this way. She didn't want him to be so close that he might notice something was wrong with her.

The tantalizing aroma of fried rice struck Priya when they arrived at Lottie's place. She was serving an après-service meal for her immediate family. When they returned from the service, they would eat, chat a while and then retire for the evening. In the morning, they'd have devotions and healing prayers for Renita and then commence with the day's festivities. Priya would stay at Lottie's until 8:00 pm, at which point Trent would pick her up and bring her back to his place. Priya was apprehensive, knowing that Trent had also been invited to stay for the early supper. She hated the thought of having to induce vomiting in her Christmas clothes, but the idea of having her waistband feel tight and her stomach bloat after a heavy, spicy meal was even more repugnant.

Lottie's home was almost a mirror image of Priya's town-house. Simply decorated with a mantelpiece nativity set and a number of festive candles and wreaths placed in strategic spots, the main focus of the living room was the artificial blue spruce tree, resplendent with the usual assortment of colour-ful ornaments. Renita reclined in the armchair, dressed in a green sari, her hair hanging loose down her back. Although she appeared frail and feverish, she wasn't as emaciated as might be expected.

"Hello, Priya," she greeted with a weak smile.

"Auntie?" Priya unzipped her overnight bag and withdrew a slim red package and laid it under the tree. "I'm leaving your gift here."

"What Christmas gift for me?" Renita shrugged hopelessly. "I can't take it where I'm going."

"Well, I hope you will like it," Priya said. It was a book of inspirational verses that she thought might be comforting.

"How are you feeling today?" Trent asked, edging into the room.

"I am in a lot of pain, but I am determined to get to service tonight," Renita explained.

Lottie's two daughters and their families were gathered in the kitchen, sampling an alcohol-based eggnog punch. One of Lottie's granddaughters, a stylishly-dressed teenager in low-rise jeans and a sequined black top, approached Priya with a punch glass. "Thank you, but not for me," she declined graciously.

The girl rolled her eyes "You couldn't get me away from eggnog if my life depended on it." She studied Priya for a long moment, eyeing the black miniskirt, legs elongated by thinness, and the tiny wrists. "You look really cool!"

"Thanks," Priya said, only mildly curious about the teen's sudden interest in her.

"I'm Sara, by the way. Do you like my hair? I got it done this afternoon. Like it's Christmas and all."

Priya politely admired the two-tone red and black hair and wondered why Sara, born with lustrous black curls, would want to dye it partially red. In Priya's opinion, she resembled a parrot. "You look fine," she finally said.

"Not bad, but I'm trying to lose a couple of pounds. I want to try modelling after my fifteenth birthday next year. If I could just stop overeating, I could look like you, but I'm totally unfocused." There was a hint of envy in her tone.

An alarm rang in Priya's head when she realized where the conversation was headed.

"Were you always this skinny?" Without giving Priya a chance to answer, the teenager continued to pepper her with questions. Nervous and agitated, she took a big gulp out of the punch glass she had offered Priya. "What do you do to look like that? Please tell me!"

"Listen," Priya glanced over her shoulder, relieved to find Trent deep in conversation about the political situation in the Middle East with Lottie's husband. It was unlikely he would notice Priya quickly ushering Sara to a loveseat in front of the fireplace.

"You do not want to look like me," Priya said firmly.

"But you're beautiful," Sara protested. "I've been staring at you from the minute you walked in. You've got the most gorgeous guy by your side and you have the perfect body. It's like you have everything going for you."

"I don't," Priya assured her. "In fact, everyone tells me that I have an eating disorder, that I am most likely an anorexic. Do you what that is?"

"Oh, yeah," Sara shrugged dismissively. "Big deal. I'd rather have that than be fat."

"It's not what you think," Priya said patiently. "I starve myself. I throw up after meals. I do all kinds of terrible things to my body. Do you want to go through all that trouble to be skinny, when you are already nice and slim?" Priya was stunned to hear herself finally acknowledge out loud, and to someone else, her eating disorder. It was almost a relief.

"Being anorexic isn't the worst thing that could happen to me," Sara countered. "I know girls in school who might have it, but, like I said, it's better than being fat."

"Anorexia can kill if it's allowed to progress long enough," Priya added matter-of-factly. She pointed impulsively towards Trent. "See that 'gorgeous guy' I'm with? Well, his sister died of the disease last year. She was only 57 pounds."

"No way!" Sara whistled. "That's like ... like totally unbelievable."

"It's a fact," Priya corrected.

"So, if anorexia is so bad, why do you do those things to yourself?" Sara was puzzled. "Like, I mean, if you know it's wrong and all?"

"I don't know," Priya admitted after a deep breath. She was in fact dumbfounded that she had spilled out all this information to someone she barely knew, when she had spent the last few months conspiring to hide her condition from all those around her. "Maybe because I never looked as good as you do now when I was your age. Perhaps I'm trying to make up for lost time. You are young and beautiful. You enjoy that eggnog in your hand, and if you ever feel that you're gaining weight too rapidly for your height and age, seek advice from a nutritionist. There is a healthy way to maintain your ideal body weight."

"You should follow your own advice and then maybe I'll be able to listen to you," Sara retorted sharply.

"Priya," Trent was standing over her. "I think everyone is getting ready to leave for church."

"Okay," she stood up and then turned back to Sara, who had a frown on her face. "Maybe we can talk later."

"Whatever..." Sara shrugged dismissively and walked away. Priya had the sinking feeling that, once again, she had let somebody down.

Priya had trouble sleeping that Christmas Eve. Trent had declined the invitation to dinner on the grounds that he felt tired and had decided to go home. After he left, Priya had gone to bed on an empty stomach, while Lottie's family had feasted on savoury rice and a wide selection of meat and vegetable curries. But it wasn't hunger pangs that caused her to twist and tumble on unfamiliar sheets on an uncomfortable camp cot in the guestroom. It was the image of Sara's desperate face that worried her. She suspected that the teen was on the road to an eating disorder. When Sara overheard Priya announcing that she wouldn't have dinner with the family because she wanted to help Renita prepare for bed, Sara tried to come up with her own rationale for not enjoying the meal: late-night eating gave her indigestion. She'd stuffed herself with pizza earlier on in the day. A strict father who ordered her to dine with the rest of the family ignored her excuses.

Renita would have loved to eat, but her appetite was dwindling day by day and she was often nauseous at the sight of food. The night seemed endless. There would be no joy for Priya that Christmas morning, but she knew she had to put on a brave face for the sake of the others. Lottie and her family were going out of their way to accommodate Renita. The least Priya could do was act with grace and gratitude.

Christmas morning was as dull and overcast as the day that preceded it. Priya joined Lottie's family beside the tree and opened her modest share of gifts. She received a gift certificate for Chapters from Renita, and a gold box of Belgium chocolates from Lottie and her family. Since Priya already knew that Trent's gift would be waiting for her at his place, there were only two other gifts for her to open. She reached for Serena's brightly colored gift bag and opened it slowly. Amidst layers of coloured tissue paper lay a two-piece outfit, black slacks and a ruby-red silk shirt with black trim. The accompanying note, written in Serena's precise script read: *Dearest Priya, this is a stylish size four pantsuit I spotted the other day. I thought it would be perfect for you when you're at least 100 pounds or more. Right now, it will appear too big, especially on the shoulders, so keep your eyes on the goal of wearing this cool kit when you're more or less back to yourself. Love Serena.*

After dutifully showing off the outfit to Lottie and her family, she put it aside and reached for Gabe's package. It contained two soft-cover, large-format books. The first one was a nutrition guide to reaching and maintaining your ideal weight for your height and build, and the other was an inspirational guide to believing in yourself enough to achieve your dreams, no matter how impossible or insurmountable they may seem. His Christmas card showed a picture of a man scaling a mountain to reach a beautiful tree at the summit. The words read: "To encourage your Christmas spirit." Inside the card, he wrote: *Priya, these books are intended to help you on your way to achieving all of your dreams. I know you can do it, love Gabe.*

Too touched for words, she picked up her presents and momentarily excused herself to her bedroom. Before getting dressed, she tried on Serena's pantsuit. She was right. The outfit was far too big. The top hung on Priya's shrunken shoulders like a sheet clinging to a frayed clothesline. The pants appeared baggy and loose, especially around the waist. When she surveyed herself in the full-length mirror, Priya decided that if she didn't look fat before she tried on the clothes, she certainly did now. Disgusted with herself, she took them off and stuffed them back into the gift bag. She then put on the clothes she'd worn the evening before.

Priya tried to keep memories of Christmases past at bay while she interacted with Lottie and her family. Renita and she were the obvious outsiders in an intimate family celebration that involved private jokes and stories to which only the family could relate. Yet the Gooneratnes were very gracious to Priya and loving toward Renita, who was treated like a cherished maiden aunt by the grandchildren in the household.

Lunch was an ordeal for Priya. Turkey, ham and all the trimmings, not to mention more savoury rice, and a spicy roast beef dish called beef smo' were almost too much for her malnourished stomach and diminishing will. She served herself a normal plateful and ate with the others, but she was overly conscious of the tightening effect each mouthful had on her waistband. She felt so big she was certain the top button on her size one skirt would pop, and then what? She'd look like a complete idiot, holding the skirt up with one hand while rushing pell-mell to the bathroom to fix herself up. She kept on eating because Sara was watching her. She wanted to be a good example to the young girl.

"This is so delicious," she enthused.

"Eat, Priya, there's lots to enjoy," Lottie encouraged. "Sara, child, eat some vegetables. You're getting thin."

"I'm not thin compared to Priya," Sara shot back as she grudgingly heaped a spoonful of broccoli in cheese sauce onto the edge of her plate. Her remark was met with a brief silence, broken only when Renita coughed uncontrollably and someone had to hold a glass of water to her mouth. The tension eased at that point and conversation resumed its normal pace.

As soon as she had finished eating, Priya excused herself and headed for the upstairs washroom. She glanced over her shoulder to see if Sara was following her, but the gifts under the tree had stolen her attention. Priya locked the bathroom door and then proceeded to purge the entire meal out of her system. She felt cleansed and liberated after she'd finished. She gargled with mouthwash, washed her hands and face, and then popped a breath mint into her mouth. With all evidence of her wrongdoing flushed down the toilet, she restyled her ponytail and went back into the living room to check on Renita. Lottie's daughter told her that she had gone back to bed.

Trent greeted Priya with a tender kiss when he picked her up later that evening. "Your gift is at my place," he said with a shy smile as he accepted the silver foil gift bag she pressed into his hand.

"You're my gift," she beamed as she watched him open the bag.

"Oh, nice!" he exclaimed, unwrapping the navy leather CD wallet.

"It's actually Italian leather, and when I saw it, I couldn't help thinking of you," Priya explained.

"I love it," he drew her into his arms again. "I can't go anywhere without my CDs and you probably noticed the sorry state of my present CD case."

"Actually, no" Priya said truthfully. "I'm glad you like it." Renita was still resting in her room when they went in to say goodnight to her. "Auntie, I'll come tomorrow afternoon to spend more time with you," Priya promised.

"Right, Priya," Renita nodded sleepily. "Have a good time tonight."

"Can I do anything for you before we leave?" Priya asked.

"No ... I just want to sleep..." Renita closed her eyes and drifted off before Priya had a chance to turn off the light.

It was snowing lightly when they got into Trent's car. The city was deliciously quiet, and they had the streets to themselves. They listened to carols on the radio while Priya admired the houses along the way. Some were elaborately decorated with illuminated ice sculptures on the lawn, and others had a modest string of coloured lights framing a single window. Trent's family lived on a wide street with generous lots. He parked in front of a sprawling two-garage executive house that sat on the crest of a sloping road, overlooking a ravine.

"Welcome home," Trent said brightly as he turned off the engine.

"You did a great job with the decorating," Priya said as she stepped out of the car. The structure of the house was highlighted by a multicoloured halo of light that sparkled like precious gems against the backdrop of a velvety night sky. The trees on the lawn were bathed in the same type of lighting. A host of ornamental angels sat regally on the wrought iron railings flanking the inlaid brick steps leading into the house.

With Priya close behind, Trent unlocked the door and disarmed the security system. As soon as she entered the blue marbled foyer with its brass fittings and white louvered doors, she was awash with insecurity. What were the likes of Priya

De Souza doing in a house like this? She was grateful that she didn't have to face Trent's parents yet. She was certain to be no match for any woman they might have in mind for their only son. She retreated into her coat and wondered how she could talk Trent into taking her home.

"Let me take your coat," he urged.

"Okay," she was reluctant, but slipped it off and gave it to him anyway. She then followed him into the sunken living room that was fashioned in neutral shades of cream and beige and tastefully furnished with high-end pieces. Priya's stocking feet felt slippery and cold against the varnished hardwood floor. She caught sight of a black baby grand piano under a bay window, which, during the day, would offer the player an abundance of natural light.

"Did you have dinner at Lottie's?" Trent asked kindly.

"Oh, yes," Priya said quickly. "How was dinner at your uncle's place?"

"It was all right," Trent shrugged. "I tried to make the best of it, but to tell you the truth, I was missing you and my parents."

"Well, we're together now," Priya glanced around the room. Trent had taken just as much trouble decorating the inside of the house as he had the outside. The six-foot tree opposite the piano was trimmed with care. There were a few presents scattered beneath the tree that stood on a red and green crocheted rug.

"Can I make you an espresso or tea?" Trent asked.

"Actually, I'd love an espresso," Priya said, grateful for a beverage she knew had scant calories, even if factoring in the sugar.

"My aunt gave me some homemade biscotti…" Trent began.

"No … really, I'm stuffed," she assured him, "just the espresso, please."

"First, your gifts." Trent went to the tree, picked out a gold gift bag and handed it to Priya, who was still standing in the centre of the room, taking in her surroundings.

"Sit," he slipped his arm around her waist and led her to the chesterfield.

Priya gently pulled back the tissue paper and withdrew two simply wrapped red and green packages from inside the bag. The first contained a cubic zirconia pendant on a slim gold chain, and the other was a Josh Groban CD.

"He sings 'Il Postino' on it. When I saw it ... I couldn't help thinking about you," Trent sounded almost shy.

Priya was thrilled. "*Closer* ... I wanted to buy this CD. How did you know?"

"I didn't," Trent chuckled, relieved that he had guessed right about her taste in music. "You just struck me as the type who'd go for his kind of music."

"I have his first CD ... oh, Trent, could we listen to it now, while having our espresso?" For the first time that day, she felt genuine happiness. The jewellery was a nice gift, but "Il Postino" was close to her heart; it reminded her of the two men who'd entered her life at a time when she needed support the most.

Trent threw his arms around her and gave her a whirlwind hug. "Oh my God ... I think I love you!" He peppered her face with kisses and began to laugh. "I'm being terribly impulsive, but I can't help how I feel."

Priya had feelings for Trent, but she wasn't sure if they qualified as love. After the experience with Henri, she vowed she'd be very cautious about when she uttered those words to another man. "You are being terribly wonderful," she kissed him back, then used her nails to slit the cellophane wrap on the CD.

"Here, let me put this on for you." He took the disc out of its case and brought it over to the sound system beside the chesterfield.

"Start with number three," Priya urged. "That's 'Il Postino.'" She basked in the tenderness of Josh Groban's baritone, accompanied by a haunting violin and full orchestra. "Trent, this is just too beautiful ... sad, but beautiful," Priya felt a lump building in her throat.

"Just like you," he nodded. "Sad and beautiful, all at the same time."

While he was in the kitchen making the espresso, Priya walked around the living room, allowing the music to wash over her. She spotted a series of leather-bound photo albums on the rack below the sound system.

"Do you mind if I take a look at one of your photo albums?" she asked.

"Not at all," Trent called back. "There's a whole bunch under the stereo."

"Yes, I can see that." Priya selected the one at the very end because it was easier to remove without toppling the rest out of place. Trent joined her on the chesterfield while she studied the pages. The photos were fairly recent ones of Trent and his family. "Oh, no," he groaned when Priya spotted a picture of him standing with a short, dark-haired woman over what appeared to be Rainbow Bridge on the Canadian side of Niagara Falls.

"What's wrong?" Priya asked.

"You don't need to see that," he shrugged self-consciously. "That's my ex-girlfriend."

"Big deal," Priya was amused. "You're thirty years old. If you didn't have a past, I'd worry about you."

"You're sweet," he squeezed her knee. "But Jenny was something else. We were together for four years, and for the last of those four, she was sleeping with her boss. I didn't think anything of it when she said they were meeting for lunch. I assumed it was just business. She kept telling me they were just friends, and I had believed that for a while, but I was wrong. She had fallen in love with him. It was just crazy."

"So, now you don't think men and women can be friends without the romantic bit?" Priya asked cautiously.

Trent shook his head. "I learned my lesson the hard way."

"So you would object, then, if I told you I had male friends?" Priya tensed.

"Are you talking about Gabe?" Trent stood up. "I think the espresso is ready."

"Well, yes ... Gabe."

"Gabe is nearly twice your age," Trent said casually, but for some reason he chose not to elaborate, so Priya really wasn't sure how he felt about her friendship with him. She thought it best not to push it at this juncture.

"Can you put that song on again … number eight?" Priya requested, hoping to break any tension that might have developed between them.

"'Broken Vow,' sure," Trent found the track and pressed it.

"That is heartbreaking, and yet … oh I don't know…" Priya leaned back, caressing the tiny white espresso cup in her hand. "Mmm, this smells so good!" She then abruptly put the cup down on a coaster and rummaged in her purse for her bottle of chili powder. She poured a liberal sprinkling on top of the beverage and sipped slowly. She wanted her drink to last because she was determined to have nothing else for the night. She replaced her cup on the coaster and went back to the album. A blue, vinyl envelope of pictures fell into her lap.

"Oh, what are these?" Priya was intrigued.

"You don't want to look at those," Trent sighed.

"Why?" Priya asked, even more curious as a result of his apparent reluctance to show them to her.

"I have no problem with you looking at them. It's just that they're not very nice. They're photos of Lydia before she died. My parents thought that if she could look at herself the way others saw her, it might have scared her into gaining back some weight.

"Did it?" Priya asked gently.

"Of course not," Trent looked away. "I personally can't stand to look at those pictures because it's too painful, but my mom insists on hanging on to them."

Priya's initial reaction when she saw the first of the four shots was one of shock and pity. A skeletal woman with stringy dark hair, dressed in an oversized pants-and-top set was languishing in a hospital bed. Her face was mottled and her hands were covered with a fine downy hair Priya knew to be lunago, typical for those in the last stages of anorexia.

Her fingers appeared brittle and bent, as if they'd snap at the slightest hint of pressure. Her eyes were sunken into her skull; her cheekbones hollow enough to store food on the outside. Priya hadn't seen anyone this thin even in her history books, which depicted images of concentration camp survivors. Yes, even *they* looked plump in comparison.

But the longer she studied the pictures, the less startled and the more fascinated she became with them. As she looked down at her own body, the darkest thought crept into her mind. Why was this Lydia thinner than *she* was, after all the trouble Priya took to keep food out of her body? A brooding rage started building in her gut. Priya knew that before the night was over, before Trent brought her home, she would have to steal at least one of those photos and keep it in her wallet for reference. She needed to know every detail of what Lydia had done to become so thin.

Chapter 13

PRIYA IMAGINED SHE MIGHT HAVE TO EMPLOY a little bit of chicanery to manoeuvre one of those pictures into her handbag, but in the end serendipity was on her side. The ringing of the telephone demanded Trent's attention. The rapid succession of rings was the usual way Ontario long-distance signalled an out-of-town call.

"It might be my cousin calling from BC," Trent said as he made his way to the phone. "Back in a second."

"I'll put the album away," Priya said, closing the book with a thud of finality. Once Trent left the room, she rifled through Lydia's pictures, chose one at random, and surreptitiously slid it into her purse between her wallet and cell phone. She would use the picture as an inspirational tool to help her with discipline. She put the remainder of the photos in the envelope and tucked the envelope somewhere in the middle of the album, then replaced it on the shelf beneath the sound system.

Priya tried to convince herself that nobody would even miss that picture — not Trent for sure, as he couldn't bring himself to look at the photos anyway. She hoped that Trent's mother wouldn't be able to recall how many pictures were supposed to be in the envelope. Since all of the poses were similar, it was unlikely she'd notice that one had been removed.

"That *was* my cousin with Christmas wishes," Trent rejoined her shortly.

"It's so easy when everyone is in the same country," Priya smiled faintly. "I think back to the years when Auntie Renita and her parents were in Sri Lanka and every Christmas Dad would be on the phone for hours trying to get through."

"I can just imagine," Trent gazed at Priya fondly. "Speaking of calls, when my Mom phoned this morning I told her that you were coming over today."

"What did she say?" Priya asked.

"She wishes you a merry Christmas and can't wait to meet you after they return to Toronto in January."

"That will be nice," Priya murmured. She didn't know how long she'd be able to put off meeting Trent's parents. As close as she felt to him, Priya was starting to wonder if they were rushing the relationship. Maybe she needed to come to terms with her issues first. As thin as she appeared to others, she felt like a fat failure on the inside and she was certain that Trent's parents would see through her, having witnessed the anorexic turmoil that ultimately killed their own daughter. What Priya had never told anybody was that she'd never had a problem with weighing 100 pounds. Her fear stemmed from the fact that she wouldn't be able to stop herself from gaining weight and that it could soar into the one hundred and forties or fifties. Awash with a fresh wave of doubt and insecurity, Priya stood up abruptly. "I think I should be going home," she said quietly.

"But it's not even ten," Trent protested.

"I know," she agreed, "but I promised Auntie Renita that I would come back tomorrow and I'm just feeling very tired. It's been a sad day for me."

"What exactly are you sad about?" Trent looked at her sharply. "Are you missing your parents? Or is it Gabe?"

The question assaulted Priya with the force of a slap across the face. Struggling to hide her surprise and guilt, she forced herself to meet Trent's face. "I miss my parents," she said calmly. "I am haunted by the thought that I will go through marriage and childbirth without the benefit of my parents to support me."

"You're right," Trent grasped her hand and gently eased her down beside him. "I was being insensitive."

"That's okay," Priya said. "You're going through a lot yourself this Christmas with the anniversary of your sister's death."

"So, please stay," Trent pleaded. "We can cheer each other up."

There was a part of Priya that longed to spend the night with Trent. She yearned to be held in a male embrace, comforted and loved. In fact, she'd packed the most romantic nightie she owned in anticipation of a memorable night of intimacy. Her heart and body cried out for a man's loving touch, but fear overruled. If they were together now, Trent would discover how truly thin she actually was. He would discover that her black stockings concealed the new skin folds in the back of her knees. When she had first noticed them in the shower the other day, she assumed that more fat was building up on the back of her legs. However, a quick glance at a book on eating disorders told her that what was actually happening was a situation where loose skin, no longer supported by fatty tissue, was clinging to bone and cartilage. Priya was also worried that her shrunken and concave abdomen would repulse Trent. He might even be able to count the vertebrae that branched out from the spinal column. He was sure to be reminded of his sister. Priya now had to face the fact that even intimacy had to take a backseat to anorexia.

"I'm just really tired," she pulled away from him.

"Priya," Trent laid a gentle hand on her thigh. "I know today has been very difficult for you ... the first Christmas without your parents and Renita being as sick as she is, but you need to look past the negative ... even just for one night. I love you and want to be with you."

"I'm just not ready," she whispered, standing up again.

She wished that she had the courage to tell him that they should to slow things down for a while and maybe even see other people, but she just didn't have the heart or the energy.

"I won't push you," but the sad look on Trent's face said that was exactly what he wanted to do. His words and gestures spoke of tolerance, but Priya sensed he was running out of patience.

"Trent, give me time. We've barely known each other a couple of months." As she put on her coat, she felt a heavy weight descend upon her chest. She didn't know how to continue to stall Trent's desire for more intimacy without giving sway to an honest discussion about her anorexia. She wondered why he hadn't called her on it. If Rachel had already told him about Priya's condition, why was he keeping silent? She suspected it was a matter of time before he confronted her. She knew they couldn't go on much longer with her eating disorder hanging between them like a glass wall, so painfully transparent and obvious to everybody but Trent.

Fate gave Priya an unexpected reprieve from confiding her anorexic lifestyle to Trent. Trent came down with a virulent bug before the week was out. New Year's Eve plans had to be shelved due to his soaring temperature and relentless chills. On the phone, he told Priya that he was concerned about not only passing the bug on to her, but was worried about Renita picking it up. In her compromised state, even a seasonal virus could be detrimental to her fragile health. Priya made the appropriate sounds of regret over the phone, but was quietly relieved. At the moment, Priya's most powerful relationship was with her weighing scale.

While Priya battled her inner demons, trying to function with a semblance of normalcy, Renita's condition took a steep decline throughout the rest of Christmas week. Nurses made daily visits to Lottie's house. There was talk of putting Renita on morphine as the pain grew increasingly worse with every passing day. Priya herself had practically moved into Lottie's home to care for Renita. She even brought her scale with her and stashed it under the camp cot she was sleeping on. Because all attention was focused on Renita, it was easy for Priya to stick to her diet of chili-enhanced energy bars, milk, and green tea. Nobody even noticed her. Priya would leave Lottie's house for a brisk jog when she knew that Renita was sleeping comfortably. On returning, she would busy herself with cleaning as a means of justifying her stay at this house. Lottie frowned at Priya's zealous determination to make herself as useful as possible. "Child, you should be spending your time talking

PRIYA'S WORLD   203

to Renita and keeping her company, not scrubbing floors and vacuuming."

"You're kind enough to let me stay here with Auntie Renita," Priya would reason. "So, let me make myself as useful as possible. Besides, Auntie sleeps most of the time, anyway."

Whenever she suspected she was genuinely making Lottie feel uncomfortable, she would do her cleaning in private by confining it to Renita's room. She would arrange and rearrange the contents on the dressing table, including Renita's medicine bottles, and then she'd launder and fold the clothes in Renita's suitcase. When Lottie and her husband were out of the house, no matter how brief their absence, Priya would resort to old tactics. She would take her trusty trio of toothbrushes to the main bathroom, lock the door and get to work. It was a fine way of burning off the tension in her body, not to mention a few calories.

One evening, Dr. Blair made an unexpected stop at Lottie's house. As it happened, one of her sisters lived in the neighbourhood and after leaving her sister's home, she thought she'd check in on Renita. It was almost an unheard of act of kindness from a busy specialist like Dr. Blair. When she showed up at the door and inquired about Renita, Priya invited the compassionate doctor into her Auntie's room. Though lucid, Renita was subdued by the amount of pain she was forced to endure. After checking her vital signs and evaluating the report that the day's visiting nurse had written, she determined that Renita was going down faster than earlier anticipated. The three to six month window of survival was narrowed to a scant two months.

One night in mid-January, Priya sat by Renita's bedside holding a bowl while the older woman vomited. The nausea was a reaction to the morphine. There was talk of admitting Renita to palliative care after the weekend. Priya and Lottie spelled each other throughout the night. At times Renita rallied back and wanted to talk about Jay and the recurring dreams she'd had about him within the past few days. The dreams were similar in content. Jay was always standing on one side of a riverbank, his arms outstretched. Referring to Renita as "Mummy," he was encouraging her to come over. He would help her cross the river. All she had to do was trust him. According to Renita, he wasn't communicating the message as much through words as he was through facial expressions and gestures. Renita dismissed the first dream as a classic case of wishful thinking. However, the sheer intensity and persistence of these dreams ultimately convinced her that she was receiving a message from the afterlife. After the third consecutive night of seeing Jay in her dreams, Renita prevailed upon Priya to contact the same funeral home that had handled Jay and Delaney's funerals. She wanted to plan the flowers for her grave and even the people she wanted honoured at the alms-giving to be held seven days after her death. One morning she had Priya call her parish priest to Lottie's place so they could plan the celebration of life service that Renita had outlined in her mind.

Priya was grateful for the errands because they kept her busy. There were offices to visit, people to meet, and plans to be made — not happy plans, but plans just the same. During this period, Priya kept a low profile and saw virtually no one outside of Lottie's family. She communicated by phone to Serena, Gabe, and Trent, but that was it.

Toward the end of January, Renita was too weak to leave her bed unassisted. She was on the highest dosage of morphine medically permitted, but it wasn't enough. She rarely complained about the pain and, despite her reluctance to fight the cancer, she clung to life. Her voice grew soft and husky as if she was trying to conserve the last of her energy.

Renita's beloved collection of music students filed through the house — ostensibly to boost her spirits, but in reality to say goodbye. Friends from church dropped by with casseroles and prayers. Renita was booked to enter palliative care in early February, but on the night of January 27th, she was very unsettled. She'd spent that day throwing up. Priya kept a steady supply of ginger ale in a plastic cup, slipping a straw into Renita's mouth to facilitate drinking. Cradling Renita's head in one arm, she would tip the cup toward her and coax her to drink.

"You're a good and patient granddaughter," Lottie observed after witnessing the myriad little things Priya did to make Renita more comfortable. Sponging her face, stroking her icy feet, and massaging her shoulders were just a few of the ways Priya could show Renita that, despite their rocky relationship, she genuinely loved her.

"No, I'm not," Priya mumbled, quietly feeling that she would be soundly paid back for wilfully making herself throw up when Renita could barely keep a teaspoon of water down to save her own life.

Priya was anxious for the following day until dawn. Daisy was finally coming. Ralph had been released from the hospital several days earlier and would be staying at his sister's place, allowing Daisy to be with Priya for a couple of weeks. Serena would pick up Daisy from the airport so Priya wouldn't have to leave Renita for even a short period of time. Priya felt certain that once her maternal grandmother arrived, life would improve for her. Despite the tension she perceived growing between Trent and herself, she was still looking forward to introducing him to Daisy. She was also excited about the prospect of reconnecting with Gabe.

"I don't think so, not yet anyway," Gabe duly informed her that night. He'd phoned as he often did to find out how Renita was doing and, more importantly, how Priya was coping.

"Why don't you want to meet Grandma?" Priya demanded.

"Because you have too much going on right now," he said reasonably. "If Daisy is staying for two weeks, there is more than enough time to reacquaint myself with her."

"Here we go again," Priya sighed with exasperation. "There's something you're not telling me."

"Possibly," Gabe admitted. "All in good time, Priya. Don't rush things."

Once she finished the call, Priya's thoughts drifted to her two grandmothers. Daisy, elderly and vibrant, possessed the energy and verve of a much younger woman. With medically-controlled high blood pressure as her only claim to ill health, she spent her days spreading cheer to others, be it through her baking, companionship, or keeping the minutes for the various community and church groups that dominated her life. Even though she'd lost her one and only daughter, faith sustained her in a way that Priya could not comprehend.

Renita, comparatively a much younger grandmother, was old before her time, sad and brooding. She, too, had lost her one and only child, but before reconciling herself to that death, was slowly losing the battle with cancer. Priya wondered which grandmother she more closely resembled. She felt she had more of Renita's temperament, but secretly strove to be like Daisy. She wondered what her Newfoundland grandmother would think of her very thin granddaughter.

After Priya settled Renita for the night, she drove back to her townhouse to make sure that everything was in order for her grandmother's arrival. The house was spotless, thanks to Priya's obsessions. Daisy would be sleeping in Jay and Delaney's room as Renita's room was to remain untouched. Priya wanted to keep the sick woman's room intact in the unlikely event that she went into remission and would be able to return home. Priya knew she was harbouring an unrealistic hope, but she felt disloyal if she attempted to erase Renita's presence from that room.

Priya wasn't sure why she awoke at 2:00 am that morning. After returning from the townhouse to Lottie's, she'd slept relatively soundly. She'd even treated herself to a half-cup of skim milk and one quarter of an energy bar, so for once it wasn't hunger pangs that made her sit up in bed. "Auntie?" Priya spoke into the stillness of the room.

Renita, cold and feverish, was bundled in several layers on the neighbouring bed. She was moaning softly to herself, hands pasted by her sides underneath the downy blanket."Priya," her hoarse voice penetrated the quiet grayness of a room illuminated by a streetlight outside the window.

"Auntie?" with her antennae at full power, Priya leaned to her right so that she was just inches away from Renita's ailing body. She could barely detect her eyes above the top of the blanket.

"You'll tell everyone ... in the eulogy," Renita spoke in slow measured tones.

"Tell what?" Priya asked, wrapping her own blanket tightly about her trembling shoulders.

"Tell ... them about Jay being my son and that dying now is the best thing that could happen to me because only in death, it would seem, I will not only be joining my son, but can acknowledge him as such."

"I can do that for you," Priya assured her, "but, Auntie, maybe we're being too hasty talking about your death. Things could turn around for you." Even to her own ears, her words sounded hollow and unconvincing.

Renita expelled a weak, bitter laugh that was followed by a violent fit of coughing. Priya was about to reach for the blue plastic bowl for the older woman to spit into, but Renita slid one hand out of the covers and waved her back to bed

"Even if what you say is true," Renita took a deep tremulous breath, "I wouldn't want it to happen that way. My time has come. In any case, Priya, I've been dying inside since the day I learned that I was pregnant with Jay. I knew that I would never be able to call him my son. No mother should have to face that."

"It must have been very hard," Priya said.

"Shall I tell you a small secret?" Renita asked.

"What is it, Auntie?" Priya thought there could be no secret on this planet that could be bigger than finding out that Renita was her grandmother and not her aunt. "When I first learned of the pregnancy, I began to act like you are now. But for a different reason. Priya, I thought if I starved myself, the baby would die quietly in the womb and life would go on as it should. Even when morning sickness was not to blame, I made myself purge. Of course, I not only wanted the baby gone, but I wanted to lose weight so nobody would ever suspect I was pregnant..." She finished with fit of coughing.

Priya wrapped her arms around her knees. It was ironic that Renita would reveal this to her as just hours earlier Priya had been thinking of how her own temperament resembled that of her paternal grandmother's.

"I've known about your anorexia for months," Renita went on quietly. "I didn't say anything because you and I treated each other like strangers..."

"Did Dr. Benson tell you?" Priya was surprised.

"He mentioned it to me when I saw him about my cough earlier in the fall," Renita admitted. "I know Jay was very critical of you, but I also know that he loved you very much. We were never allowed to show our emotions as children. We would level criticism and see that as a form of love."

"That type of upbringing does a lot of damage," Priya sighed.

"I know that," Renita cleared her throat.

"So when you say you purged, did you make yourself throw up? What happened to your pregnancy? Obviously the baby was unharmed," Priya commented.

"I didn't have to induce vomiting as I had terrible morning sickness. By purging, I meant that I ate a lot of prunes," Renita added with a slight smile. "Also, in our culture, there is this idea that if a woman eats pineapple or green mango within the first three months of pregnancy, she will miscarry. I tried it all, but as you now know, I gave birth to a healthy seven-and-a-half-pound son — your father."

"You must have felt so desperate," Priya said with compassion.

"I was young, healthy, and strong, and one day I woke up and told myself that it was wrong to punish the baby for my mistakes. Just like that, I stopped purging and allowed the pregnancy to take its natural course. Don't let it happen to you," Renita implored.

"Don't let what happen to me?" Priya asked.

"Don't let your eating disorder consume your life as I let the bitterness of not having Jay to raise as my son consume mine. You are young and bright. Let the doctors and your friends help you. Gabe and Trent seem like fine men. Accept their help."

"There is one huge difference in our circumstances," Priya said thoughtfully, "and that is I do have friends supporting me. Yes, you had Lottie, but if you had the nurturing and support that I am getting now, things might have turned out differently for you."

"As for Trent," Renita added, "take things slowly. Develop a true friendship first and then commit to each other if it feels right. You may think he is the right man for you. He comes from a good home, is well educated and kind. However, if the spark isn't there, if you feel you have to hide yourself from him, then you have to ask yourself: 'Is he really the one for me?'"

"How did you know about that?" Priya was startled.

"I overheard you discussing it with Serena on that night when she phoned before Trent visited the house for the first time."

"Seems so long ago," Priya mused. "It's as though a lifetime has elapsed since then."

"Follow your own heart, Priya. Take a stand for your happiness. I was a fool. I sacrificed my relationship with my son for the sake of what others might have thought. Don't do that to yourself. It's not worth it. I made too many mistakes in my life. If I had the guts and courage, I would have turned my back on propriety and raised Jay as my own, but I am a coward. Don't be a coward, Priya. Face up to your challenges with strength and fortitude." Then, as if she had said everything she needed to say, Renita closed her eyes and went back to sleep.

Priya perched on the edge of Renita's bed, placed her hands on Renita's dehydrated cheeks and recited prayers that came from the heart. No benedictions, no memorized scripture passages, just a message to God. She asked for Renita to have a quick and gentle passing so she didn't have to endure any more physical or emotional pain. Priya surprised herself by adding a footnote after her prayer. She asked for the strength to find a way out of anorexia. She wanted her life back. She knew that she couldn't reclaim the life that she knew before anorexia, because that life involved two parents and a home that actually felt like one. However, she could ask for a new life that would ease her out of anorexia and into a series of new beginnings with new people. She hoped that she'd find the courage to face that road.

Priya awoke for a second time later that night. She had the unshakable feeling that something was not right. She slid out of the cot and peered over at Renita's sleeping form. Her breathing was ragged and laboured.

"Auntie?" Priya touched her face. "Auntie ... wake up."

Since there was no response from the bed, Priya turned on the lamp on the bedside table so she could get a better look at her grandmother. "Auntie," she spoke louder. "Can you hear me?"

She was met with a vacant stare.

Priya's pulse raced. She went down the hall to Lottie's room and knocked on the partially open door.

"Auntie Lottie?" she called in a normal speaking voice. "I think Auntie Renita has slipped into unconsciousness ... I'm not sure though."

"Right ... right, I'm coming," Lottie called as she stumbled out of bed. She turned on the light and met Priya in the hallway, fumbling with the belt of her terry robe.

"How is her breathing?" Lottie demanded, hurrying past Priya to Renita's room.

"I don't like the sound of it," Priya said, following close behind.

Lottie called on her own nursing experience and snapped into professional mode. While saying Renita's name, she opened the bedside table drawer and whipped out a penlight. With a calm hand, she flicked the light into Renita's eyes, took her pulse, and shook her head. "She's unconscious. When did she last speak to you?"

"About 2:00." Priya glanced at the clock radio on the bedside table. It was now past 4:00 am.

"How did she sound?" Lottie asked.

"She was coughing a lot, but she was lucid. She asked me to mention that Jay was her son ... in the eulogy," Priya explained.

"Okay," Lottie nodded. "Call 911. Renita needs to get to the hospital immediately!"

Trembling with emotion, Priya hurried into the now familiar kitchen and grabbed the wall phone. As she punched in the numbers, she was overcome by a sense of déjà vu. Nearly two months ago, she was calling an ambulance for Renita from her cell phone in Trent's car — never dreaming that a few days later she'd be faced with a grim diagnosis. A lot had happened in that time. Renita had revealed herself to Priya in a way that she could never have anticipated. She'd had mere weeks to get to know the real Renita, a sad doleful woman who'd been dealt a rough hand by life, and who didn't know quite how to come out from under her unfortunate choices and even worse luck. It was one thing to fail to acknowledge her son as her own, but it was quite another to lose him in a plane crash and realize that they would never get a chance to set the relationship on the right footing. Renita's life was an unhappy malaise of betrayal, judgement, and lies. Nobody had loved her the way Priya was loved now. Even her own parents had judged and tried her. Renita had never been given a chance to fulfil her musical talent because she had conceived a child out of wedlock and the consequences of that action were thrown in her face over and over again. Her emotional life had been so bruised and battered by the harshness of her family that she had closed herself off from love.

Priya had just enough time to change into jeans and a shirt before the ambulance arrived. She accompanied Renita back to the same hospital she'd been taken to last time. Priya held her hand throughout the short ride. The paramedics gave her oxygen and checked her pulse, among a myriad of other things that Priya couldn't possibly understand. All she could do was sit beside the stretcher, praying for Renita's comfort. By the time Lottie and her husband met Priya in the emergency room lobby, Renita had been whisked behind double doors. Priya already knew that there would be no going in and out of that room to check on her as she had done during Renita's last hospitalization. She went to the bank of payphones and called the three people she had promised to contact when the end seemed imminent. Now it was as if the members of her tight little support system were all on stand-by. Trent answered on the first ring with the promise to be at the hospital as soon as he shovelled his car out of the driveway. Priya recalled how, earlier in the evening, it had been slow-going on the drive from the townhouse back to Lottie's due to a heavy snowfall. When Priya got Gabe on the phone, he told her that he would pick up Serena and they'd both meet her at the hospital as soon as possible.

A portly, blond night resident approached Priya as she hung up the phone. "Are you Priya De Souza?" he inquired.

"Yes? How is my ... Renita?"

"Things don't look good at this point," he said gently. "Her vital signs are slowing down and she hasn't regained consciousness. When she was diagnosed with cancer in early December, she'd indicated in writing to her medical team that she didn't want heroic measures. When the time comes, she wants to go peacefully."

Priya took a deep breath. "How much time does she have left?"

"Anywhere from a few hours to a day. It all depends on whether her vitals come back up. She could still rally and come around, but that's being optimistic."

"Can I be with her?" Priya asked.

"Of course," he responded. "She's being moved into a room in palliative care right now and all efforts are being made to ensure her comfort."

Priya followed the resident through the double doors and down the hallway to Renita's room. They'd connected her to an I.V. pump and heart monitor. The beeping sounds emanating from the latter machine were, at times, erratic, indicating a waning heartbeat. Without being told, Priya knew the time had come to say goodbye to her grandmother. She pulled a chair close to the bed and took the older woman's limp, warm hand in hers.

"Auntie," Priya's voice was hoarse with emotion. "I know you need to be with your son ... my father ... but I really will miss you. I'm sorry that we weren't as close as we might have been, but I am even sorrier for the misery you had to tolerate for so many years. I wish you had the kind of support system you truly needed and deserved." With tears choking her words, Priya got to her feet. She wanted to give Lottie a chance to say goodbye to her best friend. She stumbled down the hall, through the double doors, and back into the emergency lobby where Lottie and her husband were sipping cups of tea.

"Priya?" Lottie stood up. "May I see her?"

"I think you should say goodbye," Priya mumbled, wiping a stray tear from her cheek. "The resident who spoke to me said that her vital signs aren't good. She hasn't regained consciousness..."

"Right, child," Lottie nodded with understanding. "Are you coming back with me?"

Priya was about to say "yes," but was distracted by Gabe and Serena's arrival.

"How is Renita?" In a single stride, Gabe was at Priya's side, embracing her tightly. "How are you doing?"

"The end is coming," Priya rubbed her cheek against the snowy coldness of his jacket. She needed the chill to jolt her into the moment. Noticing that Lottie was still waiting for her, Priya gestured for her to go ahead. "It's okay, Auntie. Go to the first room on the left once you pass the double doors. I'll come in a minute."

"Right, right," Lottie told her husband to stay in the lobby and then disappeared behind the double doors.

Priya had just enough time to brief Gabe and Serena about

Renita's condition before Trent came blustering through the main doors, shaking snow off his boots. "My battery stalled," he gave Priya an apologetic kiss on the cheek. "I had to get my neighbour out of bed so he could give my car a boost. How is Renita?"

Once again, Priya recounted the events leading up to Renita being hospitalized. "It was eerie, Trent," she said. "I felt as if this was a repeat performance of last month when we called the ambulance that first time. But it's different now because she's unconscious and it looks like the end is near." Her words were cut short by an urgent summons on the public address system about a "Code 999 in room North 104."

"I think that message is for Auntie," Priya sucked in her breath and broke away from Trent's embrace. She charged through the double doors, back down the hallway towards Renita's room. There was a flood of medical personnel surrounding the bed. When Priya tried to enter, she was held back by a phalanx of nurses. She heard the guttural sounds of choking and coughing and the strident voices of authority.

"She needs oxygen," a doctor snapped.

"There's a 'do not resuscitate' order on her chart..." A nurse began.

"I ... need to go..." The unmistakable sound of Renita's rasping voice caused Priya's heart muscles to constrict with a combination of shock and hope. Was it possibly that Renita was rallying for the last time? Was there still a chance?

Once again, Priya made an attempt to push her way into the room, and a pair of strong arms held her back, but not before she witnessed Renita, writhing on the bed, eyeballs darting upwards, hands flexing violently out of control. Priya was gently steered back into the corridor. Lottie was also forced out behind her. The rhythmic beeping of the heart monitor, momentarily drowned out by the commotion, was now emitting a long, unending drone.

There was a moment of suspended silence when the hands of clocks froze the moment in eternity, when all activity ceased and the air hung still and heavy. It lasted barely a nanosecond, and then the voice of medicine prevailed once more. "Time of death ... 6:45am," a man spoke. Then, as if he were consulting a chart, he added "from diagnosis to death, seven weeks and three days."

As the doctor and nurses left the room, Priya was ushered back in. One by one they offered their condolences as Priya knelt by Renita's bed, eyes glistening with tears. Lottie returned and knelt quietly beside Priya. She finally broke the silence. "What happened, exactly? I heard Auntie's voice before the doctor told her to focus."

"Very briefly," Lottie said slowly, "Renita regained consciousness ... maybe for a few minutes. She said that she needed to go to the baby in the nursery."

"Baby in the nursery?" Priya was puzzled. "I don't get it."

"Jay."

"Oh, God," Priya whispered.

They lowered their heads in unspoken prayer. A few minutes elapsed. They heard footsteps approaching the room. Gabe, Serena, and Trent were gathered around the doorway.

"I'll go to the lobby and make calls for you," Lottie touched Priya's shoulder and got to her feet. "You're coming back to my place?"

"I'm not sure," Priya admitted as she walked her to the door. "I might go back to the townhouse. I'll let you know." Priya didn't mean to sound as ungracious, but her thoughts were in a jumble and she wasn't even sure she knew what she was saying.

Lottie squeezed her hand and left the room. Trent walked in and wordlessly took Priya into his arms and held her against him. "You've lost three loved ones in less than a year. That's too much," he whispered into her hair.

"I'm okay," Priya whispered. "Trent ... there's something you need to know," she slipped out of his arms and turned toward the bed. There was a relaxed expression on Renita's face — a look that suggested a level of contentment she might not have known during her adult life.

"What is it?" he asked, peering down at the lifeless body on the bed.

"Renita was not my aunt. She was my grandmother. It's a long story. I'm sorry I didn't tell you earlier, but I just found out a month ago." Priya rambled nervously.

"Look," Trent hugged her again, "you don't need to explain anything to me now. You need to grieve and make the necessary arrangements."

Priya nodded, realizing that the best thing to do was take him at face value. "Thank you for understanding."

"Would you like me to call Rachel?" Trent asked.

"I'd appreciate that," she said as she reached around her shoulder for her handbag. "Let me give you my address book. There are a few people…"

"I'll take care of it," Trent took the address book and kissed her cheek. "I think Serena and Gabe want to talk to you now."

"I'll meet you in the lobby when I'm ready," Priya said walking him to the door.

Serena stayed only briefly with Priya. "Girl, I think I'd be more useful in the chapel, lighting a candle for Renita's soul. There's nothing we can do for her on this earth now." She was philosophic as she looked down at the still form on the bed. Priya understood what Serena was really saying. She was uncomfortable being in the presence of death. If it was anybody outside of her own family, Priya might have felt the same way.

Gabe walked in as soon as Serena left. Like Trent, he gave Priya a powerful hug. "How are you doing?" he asked again, holding her close.

"I told Trent that Renita was my grandmother," Priya sighed deeply.

"That's okay," Gabe assured her. "What did he say?"

"He told me that I shouldn't even worry about any of that now. He's just concerned about my well-being."

"Smart man," Gabe nodded.

"I overheard a nurse saying that Dr. Benson is coming soon," Priya approached the bed. "I think, Gabe, I need to take in

Auntie Renita's physical appearance one more time. The next time I see her, she'll look different ... you know, the way they make people up at the funeral home. Right now, right here, this is the last time I will see her as she actually was in life. She looks like she's sleeping..." Priya couldn't stop rambling. Words, often meaningless, inarticulate phrases strung together, tumbled out of her mouth.

"Shhh," Gabe held her tightly and stroked her hair. "You don't need to say anything."

When she'd recovered herself, Priya spoke again, this time in a calmer, more tranquil manner. She told him about Renita's last moments with Lottie and how it seemed she was harking back to the birth of Jay.

"That was her special message for both of you," Gabe said thoughtfully. "In her own way, she was trying to tell you that she needed to be with her son. I know it's hard to hear now. But really, don't be sad. Just be glad that she's been delivered of her misery and reunited with her son. At least in the spiritual world she'll be able to acknowledge her connection to him. No more secrets, no more lies. That's a good thing, Priya."

As the winter sunrise coloured the morning sky a delicate shade of pink and the aroma of freshly brewed coffee permeated the halls, signalling the official start of another busy hospital day, Priya studied Gabe's face as if seeing him for the first time. He appeared much younger than his years. There was a quiet strength about him that she had not fully appreciated before. Filled with an unexpected sense of peace, the urge to cry and weep for her lost grandmother gradually dissipated. Grief-induced tears would come later, but for now, she could walk out of that room, knowing that Renita got exactly what she wanted, and in the quickest way possible.

Chapter 14

THE FIRST TWENTY-FOUR HOURS after Renita's death were a tableau of images and emotions too overwhelming for Priya to face all at once. Instead, she chose to compartmentalize her grief for later when she had time to sit and reflect upon her relationship with the grandmother she'd always believed to be her aunt. She functioned on automatic pilot, performing the necessary tasks at hand.

After spending the greater portion of the morning notifying friends and relatives from Ontario to Sri Lanka, and managing to down half an energy bar, she received a frustrated call from Serena who had borrowed her car to pick up Daisy from the airport. Daisy's flight was cancelled due to a raging snowstorm in St. John's. It was announced that no aircraft would fly for the balance of the day.

"Do you want me to call Daisy and tell her about Renita?" Serena inquired.

"I'll do it," Priya said. "You've done enough by going to the airport to pick her up. When did you find out the flight was cancelled?

"When I got here, I checked the computer screen. I should have phoned the flight arrivals and departure numbers before leaving home. Stupidness on my part!"

Priya grinned to herself. No matter what the circumstances, Serena's Guyanese accent never failed to make her smile. "First of all," she said, "you were only trying to help, and secondly, you're as much in shock as anybody else that Renita died so quickly. You can't expect to be on top of things all the time."

"Girl, you always say the right things," Serena said warmly.

"Here's what I'll do. I'll drive your car back to my place, pack up a few things, and spend the weekend with you."

"I'd love for you to do that, but it's not necessary," Priya protested.

Serena thought it was extremely necessary. Priya was dangerously thin now. She feared her young friend might collapse or experience heart trouble, especially with the stress of Renita's death. Knowing she couldn't tell her that directly, without risking a wall of denial, she simply stated she wanted to be of comfort and use to her. "Rachel is coming to spend the night at my place," Priya remarked. "It will be nice to have both of you here. Under happier circumstances I would have said it would be like a sleep-over."

"You got that right, girl," Serena chuckled. "Well, here, I'll head out on the 401 now before the rush hour gets in full gear."

"Drive carefully," Priya cautioned, knowing that Serena was a nervous driver, no matter what the situation.

Priya immediately phoned Daisy at home and told her of Renita's death.

"That sudden!" Daisy was aghast. "I would never have dreamt she'd go so quickly, tch, tch tch! Well listen, my Duckie, I think now that my flight has been cancelled, I'll see if I can get out in a few days ... perhaps after the funeral. I don't want to be in the way. If you'll recall there were tons of people milling around your townhouse after Delaney and Jay died, but once the funeral was over and things settled down, it was just your one or two close friends that stuck around to help. You'll need me more when things settle down."

"That makes sense, Grandma," she agreed. "As long as you don't get penalized for waiting a few days to take the flight."

"As a matter of fact, I won't be," Daisy assured her. "They offered a voucher to passengers willing to take a flight next week because all the seats are booked solid and they'd have to be bumping off other people to get seats for those of us scheduled to arrive in Toronto this afternoon."

"The hand of fate," Priya said.

"How are you managing, dear? I know you must be heart-broken. Three family members in less than a year. If that was me, now, I doubt if I'd get out of bed. Oh, I'm so depressed about Delaney as it is... tch, tch tch..." Despite her self-pitying words, there was a lightness in Daisy's tone that indicated her true strength of character.

"Grandma," Priya couldn't help but laugh a little. It would be so good to have Daisy with her for a few weeks. If anyone could ease Priya towards regaining her health it would be her.

"Are you staying over at Lottie's tonight?" Daisy inquired. "I don't want you at home by yourself. I'm afraid you'll cry yourself to sleep and there'd be no one to give you comfort. You need to be around people."

"Serena and Rachel are spending the night with me and people have been dropping by all afternoon. Trent and Gabe are here as well."

"Trent sounds like a lovely young fellow," Daisy said. "I can't wait to meet him."

"And Gabe..." Priya prodded. "He's been a tremendous source of strength for me."

"Oh yes, well, I'll phone you later this evening to see how you're making out," Daisy said briskly.

"How is Grandpa?" Priya asked.

"Well, now he's already settled in over at Gert's because I was supposed to leave today. He's good. I left him with a stack of books and papers. That'll keep him busy, along with the TV."

Once she was off the phone, Priya turned to the eulogy she was attempting to write. Because she had never considered herself much of a writer, she had no idea how to go about doing it. She'd been too distraught to pen the eulogies for her parents and left that in the capable hands of the principal of Delaney's ESL school and one of Jay's close friends.

Priya settled down at the computer and turned it on. She hoped that inspiration would strike. After ten minutes of impatient waiting that involved playing with the mouse, shuffling papers, and tapping a pencil against the desk, Priya grew frustrated and simply walked out of the room. However, one phrase kept popping into her mind: "What Love Is." She didn't know what relevance it had to the eulogy, but hoped that if she mulled over the words long enough, its significance would eventually reveal itself. It was still Thursday. The funeral was scheduled to take place on Sunday. Priya had less than three days to get her act together. It was now 9:30 pm. The townhouse had been full of people throughout the day. Renita's friends and students drifted in and out bearing gifts of food and condolences. Now the only people left were Serena, Gabe, and Rachel.

Even Trent had left a little while earlier. Tired and emotionally drained, he seemed to be struggling with his own unhappy memories of the passing of his sister. When she saw him brooding in the kitchen with a mug of hot chocolate, Priya wondered if she'd ever be able to have an honest discussion about her anorexia with him. She felt frustrated and angry that she was unable to share her deepest vulnerabilities with the man who professed to love her. "Trent," she'd approached him gently so as not to seem intrusive.

"How are you, Priya?" he asked, looking up from his mug.

"I'll get through this," she touched his cheek. "But I sense that you're preoccupied."

"Very much so." His candour startled her.

"Are you thinking about your sister?" she asked.

"I'm thinking about a lot of things ... including where you and I are going in our relationship." With those terse words, he drained his mug and went for his coat.

Priya wasn't tempted to go follow him. In time, he would share his thoughts and they would talk.

After he departed, she had returned to the den to work on the eulogy. She heard the sounds of people busy at work in various parts of the townhouse. Serena was running the vacuum cleaner in the living room, Gabe was loading the dishwasher, and Rachel was using her blow dryer in the downstairs washroom. Priya was comforted by the fact that her friends were making themselves at home. She felt so much at ease that when

Serena popped her head into the den and asked if she'd like a mug of hot chocolate, Priya readily agreed. For one brief, glorious moment she forgot about her bottle of chili powder and the calorie count of her drink.

"Honey, why don't you relax in a nice hot bath and then I'll have your hot chocolate ready for you in the kitchen ... or perhaps you'd be more comfortable having it in bed. You look so tired. I'm scared you'll trip over your feet when you stand up," Serena laughed to hide her fear for Priya's health.

"Oh God," Priya looked down at herself in disgust. She hadn't realized until that moment that she was dressed in the same jeans and denim shirt she'd put on after calling the ambulance to take Renita to the hospital. That had all transpired less than twenty-four hours ago, but it seemed as if an entire lifetime had elapsed since then. "It's been a long day, but I would just love the idea of a hot bath right now. I'll have my hot chocolate in the kitchen with you guys."

"Just now, dear, I'll run the tub for you," Serena gave her shoulder a gentle squeeze and left the den.

"Perfect excuse not to work on this thing," Priya muttered to herself as she turned off the computer and went up to her room to undress. Within minutes, she was soaking in a bubbly sea of lavender aromatherapy crystals, feeling more relaxed than she had in months. She was still numbed by Renita's death, just as she had been with her parents. However, with Renita she'd had time to prepare. She'd known for a month she was going to die. With Jay and Delaney, there had been no warning. One day Priya awoke to a morning that was no different than any other, but by the end of the day her life had been irrevocably changed.

After towelling off and applying a luxurious moisturizing lotion, part of a gift basket that Rachel had given her for Christmas, Priya looked forward to slipping into her favourite pink flannel pajamas. She hadn't worn them since her bout with the stomach virus in early December. It was one of three sets of pajamas that she had laundered and stuffed in the back of a dresser drawer because they reminded her of her very first real binge/purge episode. Now she really felt in the mood to put them on. Yet when she fished them out from way back in the far reaches of her bureau, she was disappointed to learn that her 84-pound body could not support them with grace. In fact, with the exception of her jeans, by virtue of tightening the belt on the furthest notch, and two or three size one skirts, there were few pieces in her closet that still fit her steadily shrinking frame.

Sighing with frustration, she settled on a short blue and white cotton nightie set that Renita gave her on her last birthday. How well Priya recalled smiling politely over the gift. However, when she was alone with Delaney, she grumbled about the choice of apparel.

"Oh, Ma, on any other woman this set would look good, but on me, forget about it!"

"Don't be so foolish," Delaney had scoffed. "You've got a cute little figure. I can bet, come summer, you'll be dying to wear that to bed."

This conversation took place just one week before the plane crash. Although Priya had not been anorexic at the time, she was overly conscious of her body. She was critical of her short legs and what she perceived to be heavy thighs. In her mighty opinion, little nighties with delicate embroidery belonged on catwalk models, not people like herself who needed to lose a pound or two. She'd promised herself that she would wear the set upon losing five pounds. Fortunately, Renita never inquired about the pretty nightgown and robe because Priya had never felt she was slim enough to wear it till now.

Once she put it on, she surveyed herself in the mirror. Her legs still look so big! How could that be, after all the weight she'd lost? Shivering with shame, Priya pulled on a pair of white socks and then her slippers. She hoped Rachel wouldn't say something snide about how chunky she looked. After securing her hair in a loose braid, she went into the kitchen for her hot chocolate.

"What!" a thunder-struck Rachel shrieked, nearly dropping her mug of hot chocolate when Priya approached the table. "What's happened to you!"

Priya picked up her own steaming mug and sat at the table, tucking her legs beneath her. She sipped the warm, soothing liquid and hoped that the urge to purge wouldn't spoil the tranquil mood that had enveloped her all evening. It was as though she hadn't heard a word that had come out of Rachel's mouth. She took another sip and smiled weakly.

"Once we're clear of the funeral, Priya's getting help for her condition," Gabe said point blank. He was leaning against the counter, skimming through a magazine while waiting for his tea to brew.

"Really, Priya, that's wonderful." Serena, bearing a plate of toast spread with basil pesto, joined the two women at the table.

"News to me," Priya shrugged. "Besides, even if I were going to see anyone about *my condition,* I doubt it would be Dr. Benson. He let me down."

"Oh, get off it, Priya!" Rachel said harshly. "He's an excellent doctor and you know it. You just don't like the fact that he shoved the truth in your face. It hurt your ego."

"Let's go a little easy on Priya," Gabe suggested mildly. "She's had a very rough time of it."

"Here," Serena cleared her throat. "I think what Rachel is trying to say is Dr. Benson never intended to hurt or insult Priya by suggesting that she couldn't look after Renita. Am I not right, dear?"

Rachel nodded, "Priya can't help anybody, least of all herself, 'til she faces up to her problem. What do you weigh now, anyway?"

"I don't have to answer that," Priya squirmed. "By the way, Serena, where did you get that pesto? I noticed the bottle on the counter earlier this afternoon..."

"Trent brought that from his uncle's place," Serena explained. "It's so good, it beat the record, man! Can I put some on toast for you?"

"No…" Priya began.

"Of course not," Rachel shook her head. "One teaspoon might have *ten* calories and that would really send Priya over the edge."

Priya didn't miss the scathing look Gabe levelled at Rachel.

"Stop judging me," Priya whined, taking a dainty sip of her drink.

"It's okay," Gabe interjected. "Nobody is judging you. We're just all concerned that you're losing control and we love you so much. It hurts us to see you this way."

Warmed by his kind words, Priya revealed that she was she was still losing weight.

"Are we aiming for 57 like Trent's sister?" Rachel inquired.

"No…" Priya stared into her mug. "Gabe is right, though. I am losing control and I want to stop … I just don't know how."

"Shells, girl, you need to eat. That's all there is to it," Serena said gently.

"I can't," Priya whispered, lacing her fingers together on top of the table. "If only it were that easy."

"She's right," Gabe affirmed. "Now, I've done a bit of reading on anorexia nervosa in recent weeks. According to my research, anorexia is a psychiatric illness with emotional and psychological roots. Food becomes the scapegoat for the anorexic. Priya is running away from other hurts in her life. I never knew Jay and I was acquainted with Delaney when she was a young girl, but I think that Priya must have suffered some sort of emotional upset that is at the root of her eating disorder. I hope I am not speaking out of place here."

"Oh, yes," Serena nodded in agreement. "Oh, yes. Jay was a good man in many ways, but he was always ridiculing poor Delaney and he was so very hard on Priya. I don't know, perhaps another girl wouldn't succumb to external pressure, but everybody is wired differently."

"For sure," an unexpected shadow crossed Gabe's tired face. He poured his tea and excused himself to the living room.

"What's wrong with him?" Rachel was puzzled.

"Men," Serena sniffed.

"I'll find out," Priya stood up.

"You know, Priya, I wish you were half as concerned about Trent's feelings," Rachel said.

"Excuse me," Priya stared at her.

"We had a chat this afternoon, while you were seeing to your visitors," she went on quietly.

"Oh, talking about me, nice!" Priya exclaimed with a sardonic laugh.

"He needed to vent, that's all," Rachel said. "Look, you might think I'm always coming down hard on you, but that's just my way. You're one of my best friends. I care about you a lot and I hate to see you destroying your life. Trent is very hurt. He feels you never trusted him enough to share your anorexia with him. He finds that whenever he tries to get close, you put up a big wall. Yet he observes that when you're with Gabe, that wall comes tumbling down..."

"Yeah, okay." Conscious of a slow warmth spreading across her cheeks, Priya strode into the living room where she found Gabe seated on the armchair with his magazine closed on his lap. His thoughts seemed far away.

"Are you all right?" Priya touched his shoulder.

"For sure," his bright tone belied the contemplative look on his face.

"You just seem upset," Priya observed.

"Don't be silly," he said. "Everything is fine. Don't worry too much about Rachel. She's a nice enough girl, but likes to shoot from the hip. I'm like that, too, but there's a time and place for all that."

"I guess," Priya agreed.

"Well, look, I should be going," he stood up abruptly. "I have to be into work early in the morning and I want to make it to one of the visitations tomorrow."

"Gabe," Priya said, walking him out of the room. "I don't know how I would have gotten through today without you."

He nodded. "No worries. You know I'm always here for you."

"If I never told you this before, I'm truly touched that you've taken the time to read about anorexia. Nobody has ever done something like that for me before. Thank you," her voice broke.

"Perhaps it's time people started doing things like that for you," he said gently.

As Priya reached into the closet for his brown jacket, she felt an intense urge to beg him to stay. Impulsively, Priya threw her arms around Gabe's neck and hugged him. "You've become my strength," she said quietly.

Gabe tried not to return the embrace too tightly, fearful that Priya's calcium-depleted bones would snap, but even more fearful that his troubled heart would break.

Priya had the best sleep she'd experienced in months. It felt good to lie in her own bed after nearly two weeks of drowsing in Lottie's camp cot, eyes and ears on alert for any crisis relating to Renita. Rachel was on the futon in the den and Serena was in Renita's room. When she woke up, Priya was surprised to find it was past 9:00 am. She'd slept for more than ten hours.

"Priya, honey," Serena's soft voice filtered through the partially open door.

"I'm awake," Priya blinked her eyes to another snowy overcast morning. "Did you have a good night?"

"Not bad," Serena floated in on a cloud of Japanese silk. She was wearing a floral satin kimono with bell sleeves. Even straight out of bed, Serena looked elegant and well put together. She felt fat and frumpy in Serena's presence.

"You know, girl," Serena went on, "those nasty old sinuses! I was up a few times but not too bad…" Her voice trailed into a silence of preoccupation.

"What's wrong?" Priya asked, pulling the covers snugly around her shoulders. Even though the townhouse was warm, she felt chilly.

"I was meaning to tell you this much earlier, but with Renita's health taking a turn for the worse these past few weeks, there didn't seem to be much opportunity," Serena said thoughtfully.

"What is it?" Priya asked.

"I know for a while there you might have thought that Gabe and I would be a thing. But I've been on my own too long to worry with a man. I was married for a few years and you know I had enough of that. I like my own little space to do my own thing. Oh, shells," Serena patted her hand. "Just so you know, we are just friends and nothing more."

"I don't know what to say," Priya replied, trying to keep her face and tone even.

"Gabe, he's tired of living alone. He wants a serious relationship in *his* life," Serena added.

"You think so?" Priya asked.

"Oh, shells, I know so," she threw her a mischievous smile. "I think since I met him his mind has been fixed on someone else. Don't you know who it is, eh girl?"

"Who?"

"He hasn't come right out and said anything to me, but haven't you noticed how he looks out for you?"

"You look out for me too," Priya pointed out.

"Never mind, dear," Serena said.

Priya shook her head; she couldn't comprehend what Serena was trying to tell her. "Well, I don't seem to be able to get the relationship thing right. It's not going that well with Trent and me," Priya sighed. "I guess the only relationship I'm capable of having is with my anorexia and not with a man."

"Don't say that," Serena chastised. "You have to get better. Remember what Gabe told you last night about seeing Dr. Benson again."

"How could I forget," Priya said dryly. "Rachel blasted me for my attitude. It's just that it's so hard, Serena. I've been mired in this disorder for nearly nine months. It's become my identity."

"Well, girl," Serena shook her head, "I think it's time for an identity makeover. And there's someone who cares waiting in the wings for you to take that step."

"I know you care about me, Serena, and I know you're right," Priya threw back the covers and stretched. "I feel like a creative mood is coming on. Maybe I'll see what I can do with that eulogy."

"Wouldn't you eat something first?" Serena asked gently.

"Maybe later," Priya grabbed her robe from the end of the bed and wandered down the hall to the den. Rachel was snoring away on the futon, so it wasn't likely she'd be disturbed by the sound of Priya tapping on the computer keyboard.

Wrapping her robe securely around her trembling body, Priya turned on the computer and typed the phrase: "What Love Is…" and then before she knew what was happening, words were tripping through her fingers like rain falling off an eavestrough. She opened the eulogy with this unplanned phrase, "The love between a parent and a child can provide intense and profound joy. However, that same bond can render heartbreak if it is denied of its rightful acknowledgement…" Then she launched into an impassioned testimonial about Renita's love for Jay as pitted against the demands of society's expectations. Priya went off on tangent after tangent, but always came back to the theme of love between parent and child, husband and wife, and finally among friends and relatives. She was shocked to discover that she had filled over twelves pages in just under an hour. She had no idea she was capable of writing like that. However, in true self-deprecating form, she convinced herself that people would find the eulogy longwinded and irrelevant. Although Priya had always received above-average marks for school compositions, she had to slog over them for hours and then have Delaney proofread them. She didn't often show Jay her literary efforts because he was so firmly steeped in Queen's English that he couldn't suffer the indignities that colloquial writing cast upon the reader.

"But, Dad," Priya protested on more than one occasion, "'one will find' and 'one did this' is very impersonal and stilted. People don't write like that anymore."

"Right, right," he'd shake his head in disgust. "You are the daughter of two highly educated teachers, but if you think you know more than we do, fine. Write what you want."

Priya tried not to dwell on those unhappy memories because she knew that if she did, her insecurity would cause her to delete the entire eulogy and start all over again. She decided to save the material and come back to it in the night. If it really was good, it could surely stand the test of twelve hours.

It rained on Sunday. The speed of the drops falling against the windowpanes rivalled the speed of Priya's typing ability when it came to the eulogy, which had subsequently been pruned into a succinct piece. Priya had showed it to Gabe and Lottie on Saturday during visitation at the funeral home. Upon reading it, they looked at Priya with surprise.

"Wow! This is amazing writing!" Gabe remarked.

"Renita didn't tell me that you were a writer," Lottie had sputtered.

"Who knew? Not even me," Priya blushed.

Gabe was impressed. "This is so touching. I don't think you'll have a dry eye in the congregation."

"I don't know how I did it," Priya admitted. "All I can say is that on Thursday night, I went to bed feeling incredibly at peace with myself. When I woke up the following morning, I felt as if the words had written themselves on the screen on my mind. How corny is that?"

Gabe shook his head. "It's really good, Priya."

Priya didn't know if the eulogy merited the positive response that Gabe and Lottie gave it and attributed their high praise to the fact that they were merely trying to boost her ego. She felt the people around her would do and say anything to help her.

"Priya, honey," there was a knock on the bedroom door which brought her back to the present moment.

"Come in, Serena," Priya called out.

It was past 9:00 am. She had a lot to do before the funeral and was grateful that Serena had sacrificed her entire weekend to stay with her.

"A few minutes ago, a delivery man arrived with a bouquet of champagne roses from Daisy and Ralph," Serena announced.

"I've arranged them on the dining room table for you."

"That was sweet of them and of you," Priya remarked, sliding out of the bed. "The only thing is that in the obituary, I specified that donations could be made in the name of cancer research in lieu of flowers."

"Oh yes, I know," Serena nodded, "but the flowers are specifically for you. Would you like to read the card?" she turned out of the room.

"I'll come now," Priya promised her. "Serena you've been so thoughtful and attentive to me these past few days. I don't know how I'll manage when you go home this evening."

"You'll be fine," Serena assured her. "Besides, your grandmother will be here on Tuesday afternoon, so it's really only two days you'll be on your own. I've laid your dress pants over a kitchen chair. You need to try them on before you take an iron to them."

"I'm sorry you had to go to all that trouble," Priya sighed.

"It was no trouble at all. I did it while watching late night TV so I didn't even notice the time passing. Besides I'm pretty handy with a needle and thread, although it's a pity that taking in your dress pants was even necessary," Serena said with resignation.

After returning from the funeral home on Saturday evening, Priya had combed through her closet in search of an appropriate outfit to wear for the funeral. The conservative black linen suit she'd worn for her parents' memorial service was far too big for her now and her only other black skirt was too short. Serena had Priya try on a pair of black dress pants. They too hung loosely around the waist but a nip and tuck here and there rendered them wearable. Priya paired them with her black velour jacket and a pale green blouse inside.

Satisfied with the fit of her altered pants, Priya ironed them and got dressed for the day. After sipping some green tea, she took her eulogy into the den and rehearsed it in front of her parents' wedding picture. She could imagine Delaney encouraging her on and Jay quietly critiquing her work. Her voice was bold and strong at home. She hoped her delivery would be equally powerful in church.

On completion of the service at the cemetery, everyone would return to the parish hall for refreshments provided by the women in the congregation. There was no issue of Priya using the townhouse to host this part of the proceedings, as she wasn't physically or emotionally well enough. Friends and co-workers of her own parents had met at the townhouse after Jay and Delaney died, but Priya was a different person then. She was physically able and mentally sound as well. She also had the support of Daisy, Ralph, and a host of Delaney's friends and co-workers.

How much had changed in the past nine months, she sighed as she slipped the eulogy in to her purse. Gabe would drive her and Serena to the church half an hour before the service. Trent had been aloof since the day Renita died and hadn't offered to escort her to the service. He'd shown up at the funeral home for visitation, but he hadn't made himself available to Priya. In the pit of her stomach, she sensed that things might be drawing to an end between them, but she wasn't as upset about this as she might have expected to be.

When Gabe arrived at the house, he warned them that his brakes were giving him a problem and he'd feel much more comfortable using Priya's car to get to the church.

"I'll shovel out the driveway a bit while the car is warming up," he said when Priya gave him her keys.

"You don't have to do all that," she protested. "I could just as easily drive."

"Of course you could," he agreed, "but Gabe Johanson never breaks a promise. If I said I'm driving you and Serena to the funeral, that's exactly what's going to happen."

Priya could do nothing but smile. Gabe was always so spirited and cheerful. She wondered if he ever had a down moment in his life.

While Serena made herself comfortable in the back seat, Priya settled into the front passenger seat and flicked on the

CD player. It was programmed to resume play, which meant the music picked up where it left off the last time Priya was in the car. Josh Groban's 'Broken Vow' was right on track. Priya blushed with embarrassment. Here she was listening to Trent's music with Gabe driving her car!

"You don't want to hear that," she blushed when Gabe tossed her a curious look.

"Why not?" he asked.

"Because ... because Trent gave me this CD for Christmas and the music makes me think of..." she was about to say 'Trent,' but realized that would be a lie. The music actually reminded her of Gabe, but she dare not admit it.

"Nothing," she sighed.

"Here I am, driving your mother's car," Gabe mused. "I can't think of a more fitting song."

"Why is that?" Priya inquired.

"Did I say something?" Gabe asked easily.

"Why is this song so fitting?" Priya demanded.

"Oh I don't know ... it just is," he shrugged.

"It's a haunting tune," Serena said from the back.

Priya stared straight ahead at the windshield. Focusing on the raindrops made more sense to her than trying to interpret Gabe's words. Gabe was a good driver. He'd get them there safely. Wrapping her gloved fingers around the strap of her handbag, Priya allowed herself to get lost in the music.

When she walked into the church, Priya felt as if she'd entered a time warp. At least half the people in attendance were the same ones who were there for Jay and Delaney's funeral. Jay's colleagues, family friends, and former classmates from Sri Lanka filled the seats on one side of the church. Renita's friends and Lottie's extended family occupied the other, as if they'd taken an unspoken vow to stand in as Renita's own relatives. Priya noticed a few unexpected faces in the back pews including Florence Marchand, Renita's hospital roommate for a scant few days. Priya was touched by her unexpected show of support. Florence had shared Renita's room just briefly, yet she cared enough to come.

Priya sat in the front row, with an empty spot saved for Trent. Serena, Gabe, Rachel, and Lottie's family took up the pews immediately behind her. Trent rushed in just before the service was about to start. "Sorry I'm late," he whispered apologetically in her ear, "but the roads are really bad out there and I had a couple of skids."

"You're here now, that's what counts," Priya squeezed his hand.

He gave her a grateful smile and scanned the bulletin inside his hymnbook. As the pallbearers carried the wooden coffin to the front of the church, the choir sang 'How Great Thou Art,' as especially requested by Renita in the days before she died. When it was finally time for Priya to speak, she walked with confidence to the pulpit, laid her notes out in front of her, and began to adjust the microphone to accommodate her short stature. She then began to read from the heart. "What love is ... the love between parent and a child can provide intense and profound joy. However, that same bond can render heartbreak if it is denied its rightful acknowledgement..." Her voice was as bold and powerful as it had been at home. As the words spilled from her lips, images and moments capturing the best of Renita's life flashed into her mind. She expanded on Renita's courage in raising Jay in a manner that would protect her family's reputation. She went on to say how brave Renita was in ultimately coping with his death and trying to carve a new life for herself in Canada.

While speaking, her gaze drifted toward the open coffin at her side. Renita, elegant and graceful in a marine blue sari, lay with her hands clasping a single rose. For one embarrassing moment, Priya thought she lost her place in her notes, but quickly recovered herself. "... And that, you see..." she concluded, "is what love is." As Gabe had predicted, there was hardly a dry eye left in the room when she finished.

All was silent except for the hum of electricity and the rain tapping against the window panes. Before Priya could step away from the pulpit, there was a thunderous burst of applause from one lone figure in the middle of the church. Shocked eyes turned toward the source of the noise. Sara, wearing a simple black dress was standing in her pew, clapping loudly.

"You are so cool!" she enthused, as if she were cheering on her favourite singer at a rock concert. "I wanna be just like you!"

Amidst the general murmur of disapproval that rumbled throughout the congregation, an elderly woman at the back hissed "I have never seen such disgraceful behaviour at a funeral."

"Sit down, Sara," her father pulled her down. "You're making a fool of yourself."

"No ... she isn't," Priya cleared her throat and returned to the microphone. "Sometimes an opportunity presents itself when least expected. Although we are here to pay our respects to Renita de Souza, I am going to digress for a moment because Sara's comments need to be addressed. Despite the present venue, it's vital that I do this for her now rather than later."

Nobody would have suspected how fast Priya's heart was beating and how clammy her hands had become. All they were aware of was how powerfully the emaciated speaker held their attention as she boldly shared her struggle with anorexia nervosa with one young girl in the congregation.

Chapter 15

ALTHOUGH PRIYA WAS ADDRESSING the congregation as a whole, she made exclusive eye contact with Sara, who was now comfortably seated between her parents, hands clasped in lap, an expectant look on her face.

"It would seem," Priya began slowly, "that in less than nine months I have come full circle back to this church, as have many of you who were with me at the double funeral of my parents Jay and Delaney. Today I found myself seated in the same pew as I was on that sunny Wednesday afternoon in early May of last year when I came here to say good-bye to my parents. At that time, I was a reasonably healthy twenty-five-year-old with a Bachelor's in Education and the promise of a good future. I had no idea that the stress and grief of losing my parents would steer me toward anorexia nervosa.

"Most women would like to lose a few pounds at some point in their lives. However, I carried my quest for thinness much further than I should have. By the middle of last fall I realized I had a problem because I didn't want to *stop* losing weight. The rush of adrenaline I felt as the numbers on the scale inched lower and lower intoxicated me. As of today, I am still on that downward spiral. My friends urge me to see my doctor about ways of putting a halt to my destructive need to keep losing even more weight. In front of all of you here this afternoon, I am committing myself to phone Dr. Benson's secretary to reschedule my appointment..." Priya paused for a moment. Daring to take her gaze off Sara's rapt face, she glanced around the room. All eyes were on her. There was no hint of disapproval now, just plain undivided attention.

"You see," she continued, "if I don't stop this train before it goes off the tracks, I might end up like the sister of a friend of mine. She died of anorexia at 57 pounds. She was thirty-one years old with an entire lifetime waiting to be experienced. She battled the disease for fifteen years, but to no avail. I do not want to *be* that person, Sara. So please, don't look up to me as your ideal. As a result of the anorexia that dominates my life and even my relationships with other people, I have developed obsessive/compulsive behaviours that have nothing at all to do with being fashionably thin, but have everything to do with plummeting self-esteem and feelings of worthlessness. Sara, do not go there. You are already beautiful."

Priya paused again, just long enough for this message to sink in, before she continued. "I know that a funeral is hardly the place to come out about my anorexia, but if Sara was so moved by my eulogy that she could not contain her admiration for me, a thin, emaciated woman, then her remarks have to be addressed. I don't want her to travel the road to ill health because of a warped perception of beauty that is ultimately unattainable."

Shaking visibly, Priya stepped away from the pulpit and took her place in the congregation. Even before she could meet Trent's horrified gaze, she was aware of the deepening chill between them. When she reached over to touch his hand, he stiffened and drew it back as if he were afraid of catching a virus.

"I'm sorry," she whispered during a hymn, "I should have discussed my anorexia with you a long time ago. As far as coming out in public, I felt I had no other option. I feel a compulsion to reach Sara anyway I possibly can, no matter what the price."

"We all have choices," Trent said bitterly, "You chose to lose control of your health and you chose to talk about my sister without first discussing it with me. You didn't pause to wonder how your remarks would affect me."

"I'm sorry you feel I offended you," Priya said "but I didn't mention names."

"How considerate," he shot her a look of cold resignation, folded his arms across his chest, and focused on the rest of the service."

Priya was left to wonder if Trent was simply angry about the fact that she had not told him personally about her condition, or if he was upset because she was anorexic. She knew they were long overdue for a serious talk, not only regarding her illness, but the future of their relationship as well.

At the end of the service, Priya realized that she was unable to look as the lid of the coffin was closed for the very last time. Shoulders shaking with silent sobs, Priya got down on her knees and used her hands to cover her eyes. She felt a gentle hand come to rest on her arm.

"Priya, are you all right?" Gabe asked tenderly.

She looked up through watery eyes to find him standing in the aisle, his eyes filled with compassion. The pallbearers were preparing to carry the casket down the aisle to the hearse that was parked by the front entrance of the church. "That's it," she whispered, "my third blood relative dead and gone in a matter of months,"

He gently placed his arm around her and murmuring soothing words into her ear, he led her into the aisle and out of the church. For the first time ever, Priya allowed herself to inhale the woodsy scent of Gabe's cologne and felt enormous comfort. In his formal gray suit, Gabe looked manly and distinguished, and much younger than his forty-four years. She cast her admiring eyes away from him and re-focused on Trent, who was a few steps ahead of them, his back stiffened with tension.

"He's so angry with me," she whispered as Gabe dabbed her eyes with a handkerchief.

"That's his problem," he responded curtly. "By the way, reaching out to Sara during the service the way you did was amazing."

"I'm sure I shocked a few people," Priya said.

"Not any that I know," Gabe retorted. "I am so proud of you." He hugged her again.

One by one, friends and parishioners came forward to offer her a comforting hug or a word of encouragement. When Trent finally approached, he turned to Priya, a look of profound sadness in his eyes. "Poor Renita. What a lot she had to endure, and what's worse she had no control over her cancer. It just took her away without any real warning... I'm sorry for your loss." With those words, he turned on his heel and strode from the church.

Priya made a move to go after him, but Gabe placed a restraining hand on her elbow. "Let him go, he'll be all right."

"He's so angry," she shuddered.

"I know that," Gabe agreed. "But the last thing I want is to see him take that rage out on you. Besides, you're needed at the cemetery."

"I was too bold," Priya announced as they walked down the aisle to the main doors.

"About what?" Gabe asked.

"That business with Sara. I know you're proud of me, but other people must have had their eyebrows practically scaling the ceiling with disapproval."

"You were just fine," Gabe slipped his arm protectively around her waist and led her out of the church and toward the car. It was still raining and the roads were slicker than ever, but Priya didn't mind. She felt safe and secure in Gabe's care.

An hour later they were back at the parish hall. Priya shook the raindrops off her coat and hung it in the foyer next to Serena and Gabe's. The timbre of the burial still clung to her. The priest's words, the lowering of the coffin into the ground, the prayers and hymns were all intense reminders of what she'd had to live through after her parents died.

Her thoughts were forced back into the moment as the taunting aroma of freshly brewed coffee seduced her nostrils. She followed the scent into the parish hall where trays and trays of sandwiches, squares, and cookies covered the paper-lined wooden tables that had been set up for the afternoon. Gabe had returned her car keys after parking her car at a convenient spot close to the main doors of the church and was now chatting to some of the other guests. Trent and Rachel were speaking in hushed tones by the window. Both were holding cups of coffee and munching on asparagus rolls.

One by one, people approached Priya to tell her what a wonderful job she had done with the eulogy, and some commended her for her impassioned words to Sara.

"I'm not at all surprised to learn that you have an eating disorder," Florence said warmly. "That day when we met in the hospital, I thought to myself, 'my, that girl is too thin.' I secretly wondered if you had cancer, but thank goodness you don't. Once you decide to eat, you'll be as good as new."

Priya thanked her politely and then approached a table heaped with platters of crudités and dip, asparagus rolls and a hollowed-out pumpernickel loaf bubbling with a warm spinach mixture and surrounded by chunks of bread. Overwhelmed with a light headedness induced by acute hunger, she wanted more than anything to take a plate and serve herself, but she dared not because she knew that once she started in on the food, she would be there all day. The whole world would realize the fraud that she actually was.

With her heart pounding out of control, she thought of hiding in the kitchen, away from temptation. She knew that, at least for the moment, it was empty as the coffee urns had been brought out to the various tables and the servers were there, filling cups and proffering bowls of sugar and jugs of cream. Hoping to seek refuge near the sink, Priya crept inside and then her face fell with dismay. There was even *more* food there! Foil-wrapped dishes graced the top of the stove, the counters, and inside the fridge.

"Mother of God," she groaned, closing her eyes. "Now what am I supposed to do?"

Suddenly, she caught sight of a stray plastic grocery bag lying by the fridge. She swooped down and snatched it between trembling fingers and began mindlessly hurling sandwiches and cookies inside until it was bulging obscenely. After poking and pressing down the bounty as deeply as it could go into the bag, she grasped the two handles and fashioned a knot. To any onlooker who happened to observe Priya making her way down the hall to the lady's washroom, it would appear that she was merely dispensing of some trash. Complacent over the fact that she had a good cover, just in case curiosity caused someone to stop and question her, she slipped through the door of the washroom and exhaled, relieved that all three cubicles were empty.

After entering the first one, she closed the door, latched it and dropped down the lid of the toilet. She flinched at the loud clatter it made as it crashed against the seat. After sitting down, she ripped an opening on the upper front side of the bag, without taking the time to untie the knot at the top. Before the first sandwich could fall onto her lap, she began to gorge. Her movements and mannerisms were almost manic in their intensity. Egg, tuna, crab, asparagus, and bits and pieces of bread virtually flew from the bag into her gaping mouth. Crumbs rained down the front of her top with the speed of paper scraps tumbling out of a shredding machine. She swallowed fifteen sandwiches, five chocolate-chip cookies, three white chocolate brownies, and an éclair. Mouth parched desert dry, she balled up the empty grocery bag, stuffed it into the mini trash dispenser next to the toilet and then unlatched the door. Breathing heavily, she trudged over to a sink, wrenched open a tap, and cupped her hands till they overflowed and then slurped icy water until she was thoroughly satiated. With sweat pouring down her forehead, she waited for the cramps to set in — the kind that made her feel like her stomach was a pop can being squeezed in the centre. She glanced at the door, praying that nobody would enter while she purged.

Taking a deep breath, she returned to the cubicle, stepped inside, latched the door and made herself throw up. When she finished, she slumped against the door of the stall, face and hair now drenched in more sweat than she could have imagined.

"When will this end?" she croaked to herself. "*When?*" Her chattering teeth were starting to show the signs of someone who purged regularly. The enamel was gradually peeling off. Even a rookie dentist would be able to detect the telltale signs of food being routinely regurgitated.

Feeling thoroughly deflated, not to mention hypocritical after her pleas to Sara, Priya stumbled back to the sink and proceeded to clean herself up. She ran cold water over her face, rinsed her mouth and sucked on a breath mint. After restyling her hair, she picked up a can of lilac scented deodorizer on the counter beside the sink and proceeded to spray the washroom. She then calmly rejoined the gathering in the parish hall.

"There you are," Sara rushed at her from some unseen corner. "I was looking for you all over," she exclaimed.

"I was in the washroom," Priya said innocently.

"Do you think we could get together and talk more," Sara asked, nibbling the edges of an egg sandwich. "I feel that maybe you could help me a little."

"I'd love to help you," Priya tried to sound sincere even though she knew she was a hypocrite. Here she was, Priya De Souza, trying to impart valuable advice regarding anorexia nervosa and yet lacking the will to curb her own obsessive need to keep food out of her body. If Sara really knew what went on in the church washroom, what on earth would she think?.

"Great," Sara watched as Priya unzipped her handbag, sought out a pen and an old dry cleaning receipt.

"Here's my number," Priya's hand shook as she turned over the slip of paper. She was suddenly confused. There were too many actions to perform at once. First she had to uncap the pen, then place that cap on the top of the pen so she wouldn't misplace it, then she needed to find a clear spot on the table on which to write. Overwhelmed, Priya fumbled and trembled, trying to prioritize the order of actions.

"Here," Sara led her over to a table that was relatively free of food. Priya, not realizing that she'd forgotten to zip up the handbag that was still slung over her shoulder, bent over and began to write her name, number, and address. "You're shaking," Sara observed.

"I think the shock of seeing Auntie Renita's coffin lowered into the ground has really gotten to me only now," Priya said evenly. She was actually revealing half the truth.

"You call me, anytime ... oh *man!*" Priya cried out as the handbag tipped to a side and some of the contents including her wallet, her cell phone and other sundry items rained to the floor.

"Let me get that for you," Sara insisted while a flustered Priya dropped the pen on the table, where it rolled toward the edge, while she whipped the strap of her handbag off her shoulder and tried to zip it up before any more items could spill out.

"Oh, oh," Trent appeared from somewhere. "What happened here? Let me help," he got down on his knees and joined Sara in collecting Priya's belongings. He gathered papers, credit cards and ... *what was this?* Trent's left hand froze in mid-air. Priya's mouth dropped open in shock. It was the back of a photograph.

"Oh my God!" Trent gasped as he turned it over to see what was on the opposite side. "This is a photograph of my sister."

"Oh, can I see that?" Sara popped up over his shoulder and peered closely at Lydia's shrunken body. "Hey is that the 57-pounder you were talking about?" she turned to Priya, who stood mortified by the table.

"I ... uh..." she stuttered.

"I don't believe this," Trent exhaled loudly as he got to his feet. "This picture was one of six in an envelope. Priya, don't tell me you took this home with you on Christmas night?"

"I'm sorry, Trent..." she mumbled, staring at the floor. "It was wrong, but yes, I stole that picture. I needed it for inspiration."

"For what?" he snorted incredulously. "Inspiration for what?"

Priya grew aware of some people openly staring at them. Rachel on her third cup of coffee tried to approach them, but Serena placed a restraining hand on her arm. Others looked on in that polite way of appearing to be doing something else, but were actually peering at the two of them from the corner of their eyes. Priya wondered where Gabe was. She'd seen him at the opposite end of the room talking to the priest, and then he'd disappeared down the hall. What would he think if he witnessed her shameful behaviour? She feared his compassionate view of her would be forever blunted, like the sharpest knife that could no longer cut through the heart of the matter for all the lies and deception that sprouted around it.

"I ... well, Trent, you see, when you have anorexia, you want be the thinnest person in the crowd. I wanted to be thinner than your sister, so I thought that if I ... if I..." Priya struggled to find the right words to continue, but realized that she was wasting her time. Even to her own ears, she sounded like a superficial idiot. *Thinnest of the crowd!* What kind of juvenile blathering was that?

"I've heard everything now," Trent slipped the photo into his suit pocket and approached her calmly. "Come with me." He encircled his tense fingers around her bony wrist. "Excuse us, Sara." He escorted her away from the table and out of the room.

"What's wrong?" Serena walked up to Trent. Having sensed the tension between the couple since they came together at the table, she could no longer stand back.

"Everything," Trent turned to Serena. "Right now, Priya and I need to be alone." He led the Priya into the hallway toward the narthex and asked her to sit with him on a wooden bench.

For her part, Priya was too emotionally and physically exhausted to resist. "Trent, I know you're angry..." Priya began, her voice shaking..

"The time to talk has come and gone, Priya," Trent's voice was tight. "We have been seeing each other for over two months and not once did you admit to me that you are an anorexic."

"I couldn't tell you," she whispered, clasping her hands around the strap of her handbag. "I thought that if I told you, you wouldn't be interested in me."

"Am I *that* shallow?" He demanded. "It wouldn't have occurred to you that just maybe because of what I went through with my sister, I would be in a position to help you somehow?"

"I just thought that you might have had enough of all that so I dediced to keep it quiet for a while."

"And you thought I'd never find out?" Trent laughed bitterly again.

Priya had never heard this laugh until now and didn't like it much. This was a darker side of Trent that she had not seen before.

"You're unbelievable." He shot to his feet and began pacing in front of the bench. "You didn't think I could see it for myself, Priya? Do you take me for a fool? You didn't think I saw you sectioning your food at the dinner theatre, or the fact that you took ages in the washroom that night? You think I was fooled when you didn't eat any of Renita's goodies that night you invited me to hear you play the piano? You think I didn't know something was up when later that same evening we went to that bagel place in the hospital and you refused to share a bagel with me? You think I needed Rachel to tell me what was as dark as the hair on your head? You thought I wouldn't notice these things?" The decibel level of his words rose with heightening emotion. "You think I couldn't see what was plainly in front my eyes?"

"Then why didn't you say something?" Priya was crying now.

"Because," Trent shouted, "I thought you'd have the decency, the courtesy, to be honest with me. I really believed you'd have enough trust in our relationship, in *me*, to say, 'Trent I am an anorexic.' But no, you chose to hide it the best way you could. It was fine for Gabe to know, and for Serena and for Rachel, but not for me! Why, Priya, why? I am asking you *why?*" he thundered.

"Because I am not really sure where we are going with this relationship. Sometimes I think we're moving too fast and other times … I don't know, I'm just so confused," Priya spoke in a broken voice. She fumbled in her handbag for tissues.

"Oh, I see. Here I thought we were developing a serious relationship but I should have known better, You've been pulling away from me for some time now. Is it because of Gabe?" Trent grasped her shoulders with unexpected force. Priya flinched with alarm and even a bit of pain.

"You're hurting me," she whimpered, wrenching herself free.

"Well, you hurt me," he roared. "Maybe I might have said we should cool things off for a while so you could concentrate on getting better. However, I would *never* have turned my back on you."

"You were so judgmental about your own sister. You refused to understand what having anorexia means to people like us," Priya shrieked, her voice bordering on hysteria. "I was so enamoured with you, Trent, I didn't want to rock the boat."

"Rock the boat," he laughed again, "Priya, you *capsized* the boat. You had the nerve to walk into my parents' home and steal a photograph that my mother considers almost sacred. When they came back from Italy, the first thing she did was look for that envelope. Right away she noticed that one of the photographs was missing. We searched all over for it, but it didn't turn up. You know the reason why, Priya? You know why it couldn't be found?" Trent's face was almost purple with rage.

"Trent, stop," Priya implored. "You're scaring me."

His temper reminded her of the raw, untapped emotion that Jay was capable of when life didn't go his way, when Priya's report card didn't sport enough As, when Delaney forgot to put enough *goroka* into the fish curry and the fish began to crumble into little pieces. This was the kind of rage that Jay unleashed upon his family when the good money he spent on king fish was dissolving in a red sea of tomato paste and chili powder. It was the kind of temper he showed when he thought Delaney got ripped off by the dishwasher repair man.

Trent's fury called back a memory that Priya had buried years ago. As a young child, she would seek refuge in the washroom when her parents began to fight. After brushing her teeth and washing her face umpteen times, too fearful to leave the solace of the enclosed room, she would use her toothbrush to clean the grout out of the ceramic tiles. It was a nervous activity, but it served the purpose. She'd run contests with herself. How many tiles could she clean before the fighting ceased?

"You're scaring *me*," Trent said and buried his hands in his head. "You just watched your poor aunt or grandmother, whoever the hell she was to you, waste away with cancer, but you went on doing things to your healthy body in a vain attempt to be skinny. I saw you stuff a grocery bag with sandwiches and creep into the kitchen a little while ago. Where are they now, Priya? Are you sharing them with Gabe over a romantic candlelight dinner this evening, or will you eat them all by yourself and then purge them out of your system?"

"That is so cruel," Priya's face burned with guilt. "Why are you saying those things to me? Or, no, wait, maybe it's not me you're talking to? Maybe it's your sister's face you see, instead of mine. Is that it Trent?"

"I don't know who I see," Trent placed his cold hands on Priya's pale cheeks and drew her close as if to kiss her. "You are a woman who plays games. I don't know who the real Priya De Souza is because I never got a chance to meet her. The woman I know is a chameleon. You change your colours to suit the man! I'm still at a loss to understand why you confided in Gabe about your illness and not in me."

"For one thing," Priya pushed Trent's hands away from her face and backed up against the bench, nearly catching the heel of her left boot in one of its legs. "One reason I can talk to Gabe about my anorexia is because he is far removed from it. Unlike you, he didn't lose a loved one to the disease. I always feel I have to be very careful of what I say and do around you because I don't want to cause more pain in your life. I know more than anyone what it is to lose a loved one. I've lost three in less than a year, remember? Secondly," she hurried on, "Gabe has taken the time and trouble to understand me. I think you just fell in love with an illusion of who you think I am. Or maybe, now that I think about this, maybe you thought you could rescue me because you couldn't rescue your sister. "

"How dare you? Don't mention my sister," Trent said through gritted teeth. "I can see now that you've got more baggage than an overbooked flight, so let's just leave it at that."

"You're breaking up with me?" Priya asked.

"It's been coming for a while Priya. Don't worry," Trent spoke in a cold, simpering tone, "Gabe will comfort you. He's very good at that."

"Okay, whatever. I need to get out of here." Choking on her sobs, she raced towards the wooden doors and flung them open.

"That's right, Priya, run away from yourself," Trent yelled after her.

Priya did a visual sweep of the parking lot, spotted her car, and ran blindly toward it, not knowing where she was going or why.

Gabe didn't like that rumble-in-the-gut feeling he got when he felt trouble was brewing. Initially, he enjoyed chatting to the Reverend about his personal quest for spiritual enlightenment during the months he traveled throughout the Orient and India. While speaking, he observed Trent and a teenage girl scrambling on the floor for some objects that had fallen out of Priya's handbag. He had no idea what was going on, but sensed it would be unwise to interfere. He had turned the ringer of his cell phone back on after turning it off for the duration of the funeral and burial as his business required him to be available by phone. Not surprisingly, a call interrupted his conversation with the Reverend. He excused himself and slipped into the corridor to take the call. One of his drivers was ill and a replacement needed to be found. When Gabe finished sorting out the problem, he returned to the main hall and to look for Priya. There was no sign of her anywhere.

He hunted down Serena who was making herself useful in the kitchen. She was scouring a stainless steel coffee urn at the double sink when Gabe approached her.

"Have you seen Priya?" he asked.

"No," she responded to Gabe in her usual sweet manner. "Why?"

"I saw her with Trent over by the sandwich table and she didn't look very happy. Now they've disappeared," Gabe explained.

"Just now, love," she thrust a dishtowel into his unsuspecting hand. "Dry this off for me while I load these cups into the suds." She turned to a tray of about thirty empty coffee cups and deftly transferred ten into the soapy water in the second sink. "Now, what is it you'd like me to do?"

"I'm thinking we should find those two and see what's going on," Gabe said.

"What two, dear?" she asked distractedly as a woman laden with a stack of dirty plates passed them over to her.

"Trent and Priya." Gabe was growing impatient. .

"Oh, yes ... why should we find them?" Serena plunged her hands into the warm water. "Now, Gabe, just lay that urn over by the stove so we don't wet it up with dish water."

"Trent looked angry ... and... wait, what is that? Do you hear shouting?" Gabe deposited the urn on the stovetop and hurried into the hallway. Sure enough, Trent's voice could be heard bouncing off the walls yards away.

"Serena, they're in the narthex. Let's go," he ordered.

"No!" Hands on hips, Serena regarded him sharply. "Hear, now, Gabe Johanson, I never allowed a man to tell me what to do before and I won't start now. So don't make sport with me on that!" Her tone softened when she saw the disappointed look in his gentle eyes. "You can't take this on. Priya and Trent need to work out whatever it is they're arguing about."

"Fine," he cleared his throat. "I'll go by myself."

When he arrived at the narthex, Gabe found Trent sitting on the wooden bench, head buried in his hands. There was no sign of Priya.

"What's going on, buddy?" Gabe tried not to sound confrontational, but deep down, he was fighting the urge to throttle him. Who was the brute that could confront a woman who had just buried her grandmother?

"Can I help you with something?" Trent straightened up and met Gabe with a chilly stare.

"I want to know where Priya is," Gabe said calmly.

"She stepped out," Trent said. "We had words."

"I gather that," Gabe said wryly. "I could hear your 'words' all the way into the parish hall. You were pretty harsh, don't you think?"

"Is it really any of your business?" Trent asked, getting to his feet.

"Priya has been my business from the time I first met her," Gabe said evenly. "That young woman has gone through hell, physically and emotionally. The last thing she needs is to stand on judgement in your pristine eyes. God knows you never made a mistake in your life."

"Not that it *is* any of your business," Trent said "But the fact of the matter is that Priya has lied consistently to me since the day we met. However, I said what I had to say to her and, if you like, you can pick up the slack because I'm finished with her."

"You give up on her so easily," Gabe shook his head. "What kind of man are you?" he muttered under his breath.

Trent's eyes flashed with rage, but before he could offer a response, Serena came rushing down the hall, a black woolen pea coat draped over her arm. "She must still be in the building," she addressed both men. "Her coat is still here."

Gabe took the coat from Serena and held it up. "It's Priya's all right. It has a her distinctive vanilla scent."

"Let me solve the mystery for you," Trent said wearily. "The reason you're standing there with Priya's coat is because she rushed out in hysterics. "

"Good God!" Gabe shot him a look of ill-concealed contempt. "It is below freezing outside and Priya has barely enough fat on her body to keep a bird alive, and you just let her go?"

"Yes, apparently I did," Trent nodded.

Gabe pushed past him, opened the doors to the parking lot, and scanned the cars for Priya's Toyota Corolla, only to discover that it was gone.

"She's taken the car and gone," he turned back to the others. "Well, there's a recipe for disaster. Between the lousy weather and her present state, who knows what might happen?"

"Well, if you're that worried about her, why don't you go after her?" Trent suggested tersely.

"I would," Gabe responded, "but my car is at her place. The brakes are giving me trouble so I left it there and drove Priya's car today. Would it be asking too much for us to take your car and for you to help us search for her?"

"I guess it's the least I can do," Trent said, pulling his keys out of his pocket. "My car is across the street."

"Thank you," Gabe said. "Serena, are you coming?"

She nodded.

Gabe hurried back to the parish hall to retrieve their coats. He decided there was no need for visitors to know that Priya had left. Lottie and the other women at the church were already clearing off the tables. In due time they'd realize that Priya and her closest friends had departed. It was best to leave it at that — for now.

Priya was lulled into quiet contentment as the windshield wipers tapped rhythm against the glass. Coupled with the sound of the raindrops and the warmth generated by the heat turned to the highest setting, she felt as secure as she imagined she might have felt in utero. She was surrounded by warmth, water, and a rhythmic beat, what could be more conducive to a soothing womb-like setting than that? With the car heated so comfortably, she no longer cared that she'd left her coat back at the parish hall. She could always return for it later. With her stomach cramps diminishing, she was confronted with an overwhelming urge to sleep. She thought she'd drive home, undress, and go to bed.

She'd let her voicemail pick up her messages and then tomorrow she would definitely phone Ruby to set up appointments with Dr. Benson and even Dr. Farrel. Priya felt she had to do this, not so much for herself, but as an example to Sara. If she had the nerve to get up in front of that pulpit and proselytize about the anorexic experience, then she had to follow through on her words. She chose to blank out her fight with Trent. She knew dwelling on it would drive her crazy. It was better to tuck that fight and that relationship into a special compartment in the back of her mind to be dealt with later.

She slipped the car into reverse, looked in all directions, and quietly eased out of the convenient parking spot Gabe had found for her. Gabe would worry when he discovered that Priya had disappeared from the parish hall, but on getting home, she'd leave a reassuring message on his machine that she was all right and just needed some time to herself.

She pulled into a thin stream of traffic and kept her eye on the road. The streets were icy and very slippery. Priya's main goal was stay as focused as possible, so she kept the music off. She stopped for first one red light and then another. Things were going well. She watched with mild anxiety as the car directly in front of her went into a scary skid, but managed to recover traction and carry on. She turned right and approached a street that was actually traffic free. She wasn't far from home now and, it being a Sunday evening, she had the run of the road.

As thin as she was, even without the benefit of her wool pea coat, the intense heat in the car overcame Priya. Her eyelids were heavy with fatigue. She fumbled for the temperature controls but couldn't remember which knob to turn. Blinking back the sleepiness that was encroaching upon her tired, wasted body, she startled with alarm when she discovered that she herself was sliding into a terrifying skid. With a jolt, she realized that she'd forgotten to put on her seatbelt. Fortunately, there were no cars in front of her, just a slushy snow-bank looming toward her right side. Priya's heart froze as the car began swerving from side to side. Digging her nails into the padded steering wheel, she screamed with mounting terror. She tried to apply the brakes but she was too far into the skid for the car to stop effectively and safely. Bearing down on the horn, she felt her heart leap into her throat as the front end of the vehicle hurtled into the snowbank, her head crashing against the steering wheel. Warm blood coursed down her forehead, bathing her hands in crimson. Numb with shock, Priya's world turned black as she slumped against the dash, her bony shoulder bearing down on the horn — a loud blaring sound that pierced the blackness.

Chapter 16

RAINDROPS STREAKED THE WINDOWPANES, forming a silvery design on a dusky palette of winter gray. Dr. Mark Benson leaned back in his chair, enjoying the quiet moment as he sipped his freshly brewed coffee amidst a sea of paperwork on his desk.

It was just after 5:00 pm. Although he'd been on call throughout the weekend, he wasn't required to be at the hospital now. He could have easily stayed at home and caught up on his correspondences or surprised his youngest daughter, Lauren, by setting up her new DVD player — a sixteenth birthday gift from her parents. It had sat, unopened in its cardboard box, for the past week as Lauren had been too busy preparing for her mid-term exams to think about it. But, one of his favourite patients was due to give birth to her first child at any moment, so he really didn't mind being in his office at the hospital. Later in the week, he would be stationed at his mall clinic, which offered him a slower pace and allowed him the chance to catch up on the lives of his regular walk-in patients.

One of them in particular shouldn't even *be* a walk-in but rather an inpatient, right here in this hospital. There was only so much calling, coaxing, and cajoling Ruby could do to get Priya De Souza back in to see him. They both knew she was declining, but there was very little they could do about it. Priya was a twenty-five-year-old adult. Unless she was declared incompetent, it was her right to refuse medical treatment and to allow her eating disorder to destroy her, if that was what she wished. Dr. Benson was hoping that when her maternal grandmother, Daisy Saunders, flew into town on Tuesday, she might be able to exert some influence over Priya's choices. He had been quite disturbed over Priya's appearance when he last saw her. He estimated she'd lost over twenty pounds since her parents died, and ten of them in the past few months. Gaunt and lifeless, her shrunken body was clearly pleading for help — help she was refusing to accept. Dr. Benson had always harboured a special interest in the young woman because he'd helped bring her into the world. He didn't want to help her leave the world by watching while she destroyed herself.

After diagnosing her with anorexia nervosa in November, he didn't think the problem would escalate to this level. He had naively hoped that, over time, she would realize she was endangering herself and turn things around. As he pushed back his chair and stood up, he heard his name crackling on the intercom. "Dr. Benson to Emerge, Dr. Benson to Emerg..."

Priya had demanded to see Dr. Benson as soon as the paramedics brought her to the hospital. In her confused and agitated state, it hadn't even occurred to her that he might be off duty. But her wish was to be granted because he was there by her side, seemingly seconds after she'd asked for him. He gazed down at her with fatherly concern. Priya knew she looked and felt like a mess. Her head ached mercilessly and her blood-splattered face and neck probably made her look more severely injured than she actually was. The fact that the snowbank had buffered the crash to some degree was a miracle in itself. If not for that cushion of compacted white powder, she would have veered toward a nearby telephone pole, and that might well have been the end of her.

She'd regained consciousness a minute or two after the accident. Extricating her aching body from the driver's seat was tricky as she was weak and in shock. Shivering in a way she never experienced before, she managed to grasp the lock, slide it back, and open the driver's side door. Struggling to keep hysteria at bay, she had stumbled out of the car and tumbled into the snow, in a vain hope that the ice-pack sensation of cold would be physically soothing. It seemed that almost immediately the flashing lights of what she thought was a snowplow, but was actually a police cruiser, came screeching to a halt several yards away from her. She was relieved. Maybe another motorist had alerted the police. The police team that questioned and assisted her might have been alarmed by the amount of blood they saw because an ambulance was promptly dispatched to the scene. Priya was gently loaded onto a stretcher after she proved that she was able to move her arms and legs.

"Priya," Dr. Benson said gently, "I'm actually very glad to see you here."

"Why is that?" she asked tentatively as a nurse approached her with a blood pressure cuff.

"Because just moments ago, I was in my office thinking to myself, *how in the world can we get Priya into the hospital?*"

"It must be destiny, then, because as far as the accident is concerned, I don't think I'm seriously hurt," she remarked. "Just patch me up and send me home."

"You've got a pretty angry gash on your forehead and, according to what you told the police about the dent in your dashboard, you got one nasty jolt to your head. I'm going to keep you here at least for a day or two in case you sustained a concussion."

"If I don't, I can go home?" Priya asked weakly.

Dr. Benson decided not to answer the question, partially to encourage Priya's silence while the nurse took her blood pressure and also because he already knew that he was not going to discharge her until her anorexia nervosa was confronted. If a minor auto accident was the ticket to get her admitted, then he was going to run with the opportunity to use it as a pretext for keeping Priya in the hospital as long as it would take to get her the treatment she needed.

Priya was so consumed with panic at the thought of being in hospital that she that she was barely aware of being wheeled into room after room for various tests, including a CAT scan and an MRI on her brain. The only thing she was able to focus on was the fact that while she was here, her food intake would be controlled and, short of refusing to eat, there was very little she could do about it.

While she waited for test results, one of the policemen who'd been at the scene of the accident told her that her car would be towed to a body shop and the damage would be assessed. "Looks like that snowbank saved you from something more serious," the constable shook his head in wonderment. "Seems like you're pretty lucky."

The tests revealed that she was suffering from a minor brain concussion and several mild contusions to her left shoulder and forehead. She was given painkillers and admitted to a general ward on the third floor. Once the kindly Jamaican nurse had settled her in a private room, Dr. Benson appeared in the doorway.

"There's a bunch of your friends waiting to see you," he said brightly, "but before I let anyone in, you and I will have a chat."

"Sure," Priya clasped her hands on her stomach and gazed at the ceiling tiles. The overhead light above her bed was the only source of illumination, as the main fluorescent had been switched off at Priya's request. The glare was a strain on her tired eyes. Since the window on her left side overlooked the front parking lot, Priya could see the reflection of a flashing neon fast food sign against her right-hand wall.

"You're feeling headachy and ill tonight, so I'm not going to push the idea of food on you," Dr. Benson said gently as he drew up a chair to her bedside, "but from tomorrow morning onward, things are going to change."

"How?" Priya asked.

"You are going to start your official treatment for anorexia. Now, before you panic and tell me that you're too frightened to co-operate with me, I will lay out the rules. If you don't agree, I'll have to speak to Dr. Farrel and have him recommend a nasogastric tube because, frankly, Priya, your weight loss is putting you in the danger zone, and I am far more concerned about that than the injuries you sustained this evening."

"I went into a skid," Priya protested. "It can happen to anyone. You know how bad the roads are."

"I realize that," Dr. Benson said, "but at the risk of sounding unintentionally cruel, I am glad it happened to you, because it forced you into the hospital."

"You know yourself that my gaining weight while I'm here is no solution to the problem," Priya said reasonably, "because once I get out, I can lose it again."

"Deep down inside, I know you don't want to," Dr. Benson remarked. "You told me yourself that you felt you were out of control and you wished you could stop. Priya, nobody is blaming you for having anorexia. Your disease is simply a destructive way of coping with a difficult situation."

"I'm losing everything," Priya said softly. "First it was my parents, then my aunt, and now my boyfriend. We had this big blow up at the parish hall after the funeral."

"It's going to be hard, I know," Dr. Benson stroked her hand, "but I can promise you that I am here to help you. I won't let you down. However, you need to trust me. You are not alone. You still have Serena and Gabe. I met them at the hospital over the course of Renita's illness. They're nice people. And then your grandmother is flying in from St. John's. You will have the support you need, but first, you have to tell me that you want to get better, then half the battle is over."

"Before the accident I promised myself," Priya's voice shook, "that tomorrow I would call Ruby to set up new appointments. I even told a teenager today that anorexia is no way to go..." Then suddenly overcome by fatigue, Priya's words spilled out in a confused garble, but somehow she was able to convey to the doctor the crux of her message to Sara at the funeral.

"Priya, we'll talk later. You are very, very tired and need a tremendous amount of rest. In fact," Dr. Benson stood up, "I'm going to request that your friends come by in the morning." Dr. Benson surveyed his frail patient with bandages that were almost broader than she was and her brittle hair matted with sweat and dried blood, "I must warn you that as much as you want and crave sleep, the nurses will wake you up from time to time. That's customary with a concussion, no matter how minor it appears to be."

"When will they help me wash my hair?" Priya asked. "I'm not even sure I want my friends to see me looking this bad."

Dr. Benson chuckled. "Well, in my opinion, your skeletal appearance is far scarier than a bunch of bandages As far as your hair is concerned, let's make sure that you're recovering well from the concussion before we worry about that, okay?" He gave her good right shoulder a gentle squeeze.

"How long are you keeping me here?" Priya asked.

"If you were in good health, I'd send you home tomorrow morning. But as I said before, I'm not discharging you until we get a handle on your anorexia. I'm not saying that you have to stay here until you are fully recovered. It took you nine months to get to this point. It will take you that much longer to heal. What I want to do now is to jump-start that process through different kinds of therapy."

Priya fixed her gaze on the portable I.V. pump that was connected to her left arm. "What are they putting in me?" There was panic in her voice.

"Right now, just saline," Dr. Benson explained.

"That means I'll become bloated and my weight will sky-rocket."

"Water weight is no big deal," Dr. Benson assured her. "You'll get that off once you start moving around. Anyway, you won't even know your weight for the time being because we'll weigh you standing backwards on the scale."

"Forget that," Priya protested weakly. "I weigh myself several times a day. I can't cope with a rapid weight gain. I'd rather be dead."

"I won't let you gain rapidly," Dr. Benson walked to the door. "Look, tomorrow, when you're feeling better, we'll talk further. Right now, you need to rest. Do you think you could handle some light soup, or do you feel it will induce panic?"

"Why do you care if I panic?" Priya asked.

"I care. You were in a car accident tonight and you are suffering from a brain concussion. Your mind has to be at rest so that your body can rest. You won't dehydrate because of the saline solution, but if you think you're able to eat..."

"Not if I can't exercise," Priya said stubbornly. "Look, Dr. Benson, I know you think I'm in bad shape right now, but to me, it's a basic: calories-in/calories-out. You put calories into your body with food and then you burn them out them with exercise, or any other way that becomes necessary.

"You're feeling bold now because of the pain killers, but by tomorrow morning, you will feel so sore and so uncomfortable, as the true impact of your injuries set in, that you'll be begging us to let you rest," Dr. Benson said lightly. "I'm going down to the lobby to kick your friends out of here. Tomorrow you can see whomever you wish."

His words were lost on Priya as she'd already drifted into a murky slumber punctuated with discordant fragments of dreams that, at times, seemed like virtual reality.

It was only in the wee hours of the following morning that Priya began to feel the full extent of her injuries. Her bruised left shoulder, her forehead, and the top of her head ached more than she could ever have imagined. No matter which way she turned, discomfort followed her like a plume of smoke from a burning building. Sleep seemed to offer her the only escape from a body humbled by grief, anorexia, and now finally an auto accident.

Bed rest was the panacea for what ailed Priya. Although the night had started off with fragmented dreams that made no sense to her whatsoever, there was a pristine moment of respite when she felt physically and spiritually enveloped by an all-consuming love she had never before experienced. The dream was stark in its simplicity. Gabe, seated by her bedside, was stroking her hand. His words were so utterly tender and distinct, Priya actually questioned herself as to whether she was, indeed, dreaming at all.

"I don't know how or when it happened, but I now realize I love you as a man loves a woman. I don't know if it's the right way to feel, but that's just how it is. I don't care about the anorexia or the fact that you are much younger than I am. Love can solve all of those problems..."

When Priya emerged from sleep, she actually blushed with embarrassment. What would Gabe think if he knew about this? Up to now, he had treated her with the benevolence and tolerance of a doting brother. He'd be surprised and shocked that this dream had stirred undeniable feelings in Priya's heart. With a jolt, she suddenly got it. Ever since he'd held her that Sunday afternoon as she tearfully told him about Renita's secret, her heart had been warming toward him. She felt his absence keenly when he wasn't around. No wonder, she couldn't connect with Trent the way she thought she should have been able to. *Oh God, now what?*

She sighed and then shifted her position in a vain attempt to get comfortable. When she awoke again, she glanced at her left wrist but her watch was gone. Disoriented and confused, she peered up at the clock on the wall opposite her bed. It was 11:00 am. A quick glance out the window told her that it was another rainy, drizzly day. Frightened and shivering in a powder blue hospital gown, she fantasized about being kept forever warm in her slate blue fleece jogging pants and top. She wished someone would go to her townhouse and get her some decent clothes to wear. Yet a mental roll-call of her friends told her that there really was nobody who could fulfill that wish today. Rachel couldn't drive. Serena might have willingly complied if Gabe was able to drive her to the townhouse, but Gabe's own car was giving him trouble. She couldn't very well have Trent going into her drawers searching for clothes. Besides, they had broken up, hadn't they?

Priya's thoughts turned to her handbag. Where was it? What about her wallet, driver's license, and keys? She was about to ring for the nurse in a panic when Trent appeared in the doorway. He was dressed for work in a crisp pair of grey slacks, a pale blue shirt and tie, and a navy blazer. Tired eyes peered above a bouquet of foil-wrapped flowers in his arms.

"Priya," he edged slowly into the room.

"Hi, Trent," she forced herself to smile.

"How are you doing there?" He laid the flowers on the bedside table.

"I don't think I'm as badly injured as I look," she tried to put him at ease with her choice of words, but knew she sounded hoarse with fatigue.

He pulled up a chair and sat next to her. "I don't know what to say. I feel so responsible for the accident."

"Were you driving?" she asked.

"Well…" Trent shrugged, "I practically drove you out of the parish hall with my temper on full throttle. I really lost control of myself. It wasn't the time or place."

"I had it coming," Priya said. "I lied to you about your sister's picture. Our whole relationship was an illusion. I'm sorry I hurt you, Trent," she began to cry.

"I said some very hurtful things to you," he reached to the bedside table and plucked a tissue from a box and gently dabbed her swollen eyes. "In fact, soon after you tore out of there, Gabe laid into me like a lightening rod. He told me that only a brute would have acted as I did and he was right."

"I don't think he's too impressed with me, either," Priya sighed.

"Why is that?" Trent was surprised.

"Not that I'm expecting attention from all my friends, it's just that I thought he might drop by to see me," Priya tried to hide the hurt from showing in her voice, but it was hard.

"That's strange," Trent shook his head. "Once he realized that you had taken off, he practically ordered me to take him and Serena in my car to find you."

"How did you?" Priya asked.

"We were on our way to your townhouse when Serena's cell phone rang. It was a nurse from the hospital calling to inform us about the accident. So we headed over here and Serena and I stayed until about 8:00, until Dr. Benson advised us that you were in stable condition, and that you were sleeping. He requested that we come back in the morning. I offered to drop Gabe at his place, but he refused, reminding me about his car needing attention in your driveway. He said he'd call a cab when he was ready. We left and that was the last we heard of him."

"I'm sorry, Trent," Priya tried to hide the disappointment from her voice. "It's insensitive of me to talk about Gabe to you…"

"Don't worry about that," Trent was quick to assure her. "Our problems, yours and mine, had very little to do with him. They had more to do with us … you and me."

"We're just not meant to be," Priya whispered.

"We can be friends," he pointed out.

"You said you didn't think men and women could be friends," Priya reminded.

"I was wrong," Trent admitted. "Last night, after Dr. Benson assured me that you were going to be all right, I blew off steam at the gym. I thought about us and how the most fun we have is when we sit and chat like a couple of friends. Remember that first night your aunt was admitted to the hospital? You and I were at that bagel place. We talked and talked and talked! It's funny when I think back, but I think I *was* treating you like a sister. And maybe, meeting you made me think I could have her back."

"I never wanted to hurt you, *ever*," Priya spoke in a choked voice.

"I think under different circumstances, you and I might have had a chance," Trent said. "You need professional help and physical healing. I went through all of this with my sister over a year ago, and I realize now that after fifteen years of hell with her, I need a break."

"I know that," Priya responded sincerely because she really *did* know it. "Trent, thank you for giving us a chance."

"Well, look, I got strict orders from Dr. Benson last night about not overstaying my welcome. He says you need a lot of rest." Trent got up to leave.

"I'm really glad you came," Priya squeezed his hand. "Before you go, can you tell me what happened to my handbag and other belongings?"

"Serena is holding everything for you," he assured her. "She even has your house keys and will take a cab tomorrow to pick up your grandmother from the airport."

"Good," Priya said quietly.

"May I do anything for you before I leave?" he asked, a slight catch in his throat.

"You did everything you possibly could by being my friend," she said. "Thank you, Trent, and good luck."

Trent turned back to the bed and gingerly gave Priya a final kiss before he departed. There were tears in his eyes.

Priya suffered in silent anguish for the rest of the day. Though Serena and Rachel came by in the evening to visit her, though Dr. Benson was on hand with another lecture at 7:00 pm, though a plethora of nurses, nutritionists, and psychology majors dropped by her room, there was one person who didn't come, and that was Gabe.

Priya felt silly about the dream she'd had about him. When she'd asked Serena if Gabe had mentioned coming up to see her, Serena's response had been circumspect. "No, dear," Serena had shaken her head. "He just said something about grabbing a cab back to your place to see about his car. That's as far as I know."

"He didn't come up to see me," Priya said plaintively.

"Well," Serena sighed, "I don't know why, because he was very concerned about you. Perhaps he's not too good with bedside scenes. I don't know. Here, don't take this on. I'm sure you'll hear from him soon."

Priya didn't hear from him, not at 7:00, 8:00, 9:00 or even 10:00 pm, the official end of visiting hours. She toyed with the glass of skim milk she'd been ordered to drink. Dr. Benson had promised her that if she co-operated and agreed to the small amounts of calories he was prescribing for her, she could leave the hospital sooner than expected. During their bedside chat that evening, they had agreed that if Priya could reach and maintain a goal weight of 105 pounds, he would consider her recovered. With that goal in mind, intensive psychotherapy, group and individual therapy could be carried out with Priya as an outpatient.

But all Priya could think about was Gabe. In the back of her mind, she feared that he had washed his hands of her. How else could she explain his silence? That night, she cried herself to sleep, heart-broken. She felt utterly abandoned. A caring phone call from Auntie Lottie hadn't done much to buoy her spirits during the day. Just one day after burying Renita and running her car into a snow bank, she and Trent had sounded the death knell for their relationship. She knew she would have to pull herself together when Grandma Daisy arrived the following day, but for now, she was completely and utterly alone.

When she awoke that snowy Tuesday morning, a nurse was standing at the foot of her bed, bearing a breakfast tray. "Good morning, Priya. I'm Shelly and I'll be your nurse for this shift. How are you feeling?"

Priya looked at the youngish woman with the bouncing blonde curls and open face that stood before her. Shelly was of average size and build, but judging from the sparkle in her eye, it was unlikely that she spent much time worrying about how thin or fat she might be.

"I'm all right," she finally said. "What are they making me eat for breakfast today?"

"*Making* you eat," Shelly shook her head, a bemused expression on her face. "I'd pay to eat this meal at a restaurant. It smells so good!" Shelly said. "You're getting one poached egg, one slice of whole wheat bread, and a glass of orange juice."

"How many calories do you think is in all of that?" Priya asked, calculating a spreadsheet in her mind.

"Not enough for a bird!" Shelly clapped a hand across her mouth. "Oops. I'm not supposed to render personal judgements. That's not in my job description, but I do it anyway. It's not the first time my mouth has gotten me in trouble."

Priya couldn't help but smile.

"Your chart says you are suffering from an eating disorder," Shelly continued, "but I can tell you one thing: Dr. Benson is the most sensitive, empathic doctor that I have ever worked with. Other doctors would be ramming calories down your throat, but he's different. He wants you to regain your weight in a slow, methodical manner. You're in good hands."

Priya nodded.

"Now, like it or not, I'm required to sit beside you till you finish at least three quarters of this meal, and then I have to wait another twenty minutes or so till your food starts to digest. I can't have you running to the washroom to purge."

"Do I really look like I'm strong enough to pull that off?" Priya asked wearily. "Look at me, Shelly. I'm a huge mess. I've got an I.V. and bandages coming out of me like a science experiment gone wrong. I'm not going anywhere."

"You're funny," Shelly chuckled.

"Seriously," Priya studied the kindly woman in front of her and estimated that they were about the same age. Shelly was wearing a wedding ring. "Do you think I can have some sort of bath this morning? My hair needs washing."

"If you finish your meal fast enough, I think we could squeeze in a shampoo and set," Shelly teased, "but what about clothes? You can't go to the ball in hospital couture, or can you?"

Priya giggled. "Well, hopefully now I can talk my grandmother into bringing in my own clothes this afternoon. Until then, hospital chic will have to do."

"You're going to be all right," Shelly tossed her an approving smile and then proceeded to supervise the meal.

Priya managed to swallow a few bites of egg, half of the toast, and all of the juice. She was being fed electrolytes on the hour now to replenish her depleted potassium levels and hydrate her weakened body.

A member of the housekeeping unit entered just as Priya had pushed her plate away. It was time to change the bed linen and also time for Priya to have her first weigh-in of her stay.

Shelly helped her out of bed and led her to the weighing scale by the nurses' station.

"Can I see?" Priya asked eagerly.

"I'm sorry, but no." Gently grasping Priya's bony shoulders in her strong hands, Shelly turned her backwards on the scale and adjusted the balances. Priya tried to read the nurse's expression, but Shelly revealed nothing.

"How fat am I now?" she demanded. "My fingers and ankles feel swollen and my stomach is positively bloated, as if I scarfed down two turkey dinners."

"It's all water, my dear," Shelly shook her head. "Remember, too, that your stomach is no longer used to holding large amounts of food. Although the amount of food you consumed was scant, to your starved, deprived body it was a smorgasbord because you are no longer used to eating normally."

Once they returned to her room, Shelly settled Priya back into bed, changed her dressings, and with the aid of shampoo and a bowl, gingerly washed the dried blood and tangles out of her brittle hair. After helping her change into a fresh gown, Shelly announced that she would return in three hours with Priya's lunch.

"And remember," Priya reminded her, "I ticked off skim milk as my beverage of choice. Dr. Benson assured me that I didn't have to drink two-percent milk."

"It's on your chart as well as ticked off on your menu, so don't worry about it," Shelly assured her.

Once she was alone, Priya realized that there wasn't much to do but rest. Still tied down by her I.V. unit, she wasn't free to run laps in the hallway or even do crunches on the floor. She had no TV in her room because it hadn't occurred to her to order one. She could sit and worry about the fate of her car, but that would cause more stress than she could cope with at that moment. Instead, she huddled under her blankets, fantasizing about owning polar fleece jogging sets in every shade of the rainbow. Even then, she doubted if she'd ever be warm enough. She dozed intermittently, her thoughts flitting between polar fleece and Gabe. There had to be a connection somewhere. Then it came to her: One kept her body warm and the other — her heart.

A sudden knock on her partially opened door made her think that a nurse had come by to draw blood, but when Priya saw Gabe peering at her, she broke into a self-conscious blush and turned her face away.

"And how is Priya doing on this morning?" His tone was cheerful, as if nothing had happened.

"I'm all right," she said. She wanted to ask him why she hadn't heard from him since the accident, but she didn't have the courage. She remembered her dream and felt a flush creeping up her neck and face.

Gabe was carrying a load. In one hand he swung the handle of a large pink gift basket and in the other he held a molded plastic case that looked it might have a laptop inside.

He placed both items at the foot of the bed and approached Priya, almost shyly. Though his eyes were warm, his face was solemn, as if he had come to deliver unsettling news. "How are you feeling?" He dropped a tender kiss on her cheek and sat down.

"Strange," she confessed as she looked down at her hospital ID bracelet. She began to twist it nervously with her other hand, much the same way she might have twisted her watch band had she been wearing it. "I had this really strange dream about you the night of the accident ... but first, where were you yesterday? I thought you might have come to see me," her words caught in her throat. She was surprised at how close to tears she actually was.

"Hold on now," he said. "I want to hear about this dream first."

Still unable to match his gaze, she turned her attention to the window. Large snowflakes drifted like petals onto the outside of the windowsill.

"Look at me," he cupped her chin in his palm. "Look at me and tell me your dream."

"It was…" She was disgusted with herself for blushing so much. Why had she mentioned it in the first place?

"Tell me," he urged.

"I dreamt…" she took a tremulous breath, "that you … oh, this is so hard!"

"I'm listening," he prodded gently.

"You said that you loved me the way a man loves a woman and…"

"I don't know how and when it happened," he finished softly. She blinked in surprise. "Excuse me!"

"Priya, darling, that was no dream. That actually happened," Gabe leaned forward in his chair and took her frail hands in his. "At 6:00 am yesterday morning, I sat here as I am right now and poured out my heart to you."

"I thought it was a dream," Priya whispered. "Why … Gabe? Why did you say those things?"

"Because they're true," he said simply. "I don't know when the realization came to me. Perhaps it was the day Serena and I came to see you after you had that virus. Who knows? Anyway, not only do I love you with all my heart, you and I are destined to be together."

"But…"

"No buts," he placed a finger on his lips. "I was thinking to myself that under that delicate exterior, you are a strong, independent woman … a survivor. I love that about you."

"Then where did you go?" Priya asked, her voice breaking. "Where were you? I waited and waited for you to come yesterday."

"I couldn't come," Gabe said slowly, "because I had to exercise some degree of self-control. I knew that if I stayed on yesterday, I would have told you what I've been holding back for months … a piece of the past that you really need to know. It would have been selfish of me to tell you, just hours after your accident, with you being so weak and unwell. Besides, Dr. Benson had made himself more than clear when he said you needed a lot of bed rest. So I busied myself as much as I could and stayed as far away from the hospital as I could. One of the things I did yesterday was visit a gift shop and have a kind lady put together a basket of goodies for you."

"Oh, Gabe," Priya's gaze drifted towards the basket where layers of iridescent cellophane reflected the white of the overcast sky.

"Vanilla bubble-bath, lavender-scented candles, chamomile tea ... feel-good things for when you're ready," Gabe continued softly.

"That was really kind of you, thank you," Priya squeezed his hand.

"After I left the gift shop, I thought I'd give myself the rest of the day to clear my head and come back here and tell you everything you need to know about your mother, me, the past."

"Nothing you say will change how I feel about you," Priya shifted her I.V. pole aside and drew toward Gabe so he was now partially holding her against his chest.

"I have wanted to hold you for so long," he buried his face in her freshly washed dark hair. "As I said yesterday, I don't care about the anorexia or the fact that you are a lot younger than me. I see a beautiful young woman, confident and strong, who is struggling to get past a very tough year, and you will do it, my darling, you will do it!"

"Now I know why I could never commit myself to Trent," Priya whispered against Gabe's shoulder. "I fell in love with you and didn't have the courage to face it."

"Hello..." There was a subtle knock on the door.

They sprang apart like a pair of guilty teenagers. Shelly popped her head in. "Soup's on."

"That's good, I'm hungry. What are we having?" Gabe winked at the nurse.

Chuckling, Shelly pulled out Priya's bed table and arranged her tray. "Cream of spinach soup, two carrot sticks, a chocolate brownie, and..."

"What's that!" Priya stared in alarm at a small carton of two-percent milk.

"Your milk. What's wrong with it?" Shelly was perplexed over Priya's strong reaction.

"I'm not having *that*." The warm feelings Priya had enjoyed with Gabe were eclipsed by hard-edged panic.

"What's wrong with the milk?" Shelly who'd been so cheerful and affable all morning was now growing impatient.

"Dr. Benson promised that I could have skim milk. I haven't had two-percent in over five years," Priya protested.

"Oh, yes. You are right. Well, there must have been a mix up in the kitchen. Drink it for now. It won't kill you. Actually, if it were up to me, you'd be chugging down a carton of *whole* milk." Shelly said briskly.

"That's not going to happen!" Priya screamed, surprising herself as much as anybody else.

"Okay, well look, this has gotten out of hand…" Shelly began.

"I don't think so," Gabe having stayed quiet long enough interceded on Priya's behalf. "If Dr. Benson told Priya she could have skim milk, then skim milk is what she will get."

"Well, I just don't have the time to run back to that kitchen to get the milk. This isn't a drive-through take-out."

"I respect that," Gabe stood up. "Tell me where to go and I'll get the skim milk."

Grudgingly Shelly gave him directions to the kitchen and then took up her post on the chair. "I need to monitor her intake anyway."

Shelly, clearly irked by Priya's outburst, said nothing while her patient struggled through the cream of spinach soup. As at breakfast, Priya did a mental tally of her calorie intake. According to her calorie counter at home, the bowl of soup would run about 185 calories if it was prepared with skim milk.

There was another knock on the door.

"Yoohoo," Grandma Daisy's unmistakably cheerful voice filled the room. "Priya, I am finally here."

"Grandma!" Grateful for the excuse to put down her spoon, she pushed her tray aside and extended her arms to her grandmother who caught her up in a warm embrace. Dressed in a cherry red skirt and matching red sweater, the ebullient senior covered Priya's wan face with kisses, ever mindful not to disturb the bandage that stretched across her forehead. It seemed that Daisy had been thoroughly briefed by Serena about Priya's condition. If she was surprised or even shocked by her appearance, she didn't show it.

"We were a bit late getting here," she explained breathlessly. "Serena was kind enough to bring me back to the townhouse so I could drop off my bags and pack some things for you." She pointed to a colourful gift bag brimming with the longed-for polar fleece pants and tops. Matching socks and underwear were buried at the bottom of the bag.

"As soon as Priya finishes her lunch, we'll help her change," Shelly said approvingly as Daisy held up the different outfits. "I brought three. I was going to bring your jeans, but thought they'd be uncomfortable when you're in bed."

"Bed," Priya rolled her eyes. "So much the better to wear when I start my jogging regiment in the halls." Priya regarded her nurse without a trace of irony. "Do they have gym facilities here?"

"What do you think this is, the Ritz Carlton?" Shelly snorted.

Daisy hustled around the room, tidying up and prattling. "How is your head feeling, my Duckie? I know you had a pretty nasty accident. Oh, girl, if it isn't one thing it's the other! Grandapa falling and hurting his hip, Renita dying, and now you ... goodness, gracious me!"

"I'm much better," Priya assured her.

"Heavens above, I need to sit." Daisy flapped her wrist impatiently at Shelly who was still seated in a supervisory capacity on the chair. "Give an old lady a chance to sit."

Shelly sprang to her feet as if stung by a bee.

"Now..." Daisy's face grew hard as she sat down in the vacated chair. "What is this not-eating thing? Imagine an old lady such as myself having to hear about this crazy condition from Serena. You people have been hiding it from me for months. Shocking!"

"I didn't tell you about the anorexia because I didn't want you to worry," Priya insisted.

"Well you look too thin to be alive, but I guess that's why you're still here," Daisy observed. "Now, when am I going to meet that gorgeous man I've been hearing about since the fall?"

"Oh, you mean me," Gabe said, showing up at Priya's bedside with the carton of skim milk.

"Oh, my word!" Daisy sighed. "A ghost from the past!"

"Hello, Daisy, it *has* been a long time," Gabe extended a welcoming hand.

She levelled an accusing finger at Gabe. "What are you doing here with my granddaughter?"

"Grandma," Priya began. "Gabe and I are..."

"Where's the young man you're involved with?" Daisy demanded. "He's the one I want to see."

"Trent and I broke up," Priya said calmly.

"What happened?" Daisy glanced at Gabe.

"Life happened, Daisy," he said evenly.

Daisy turned to face Gabe directly. "After not having seen you in years, please tell me why you are here and in my granddaughter's life?"

"Whatever is going on here should be taken out into the hallway because Priya is not up to this," Shelly said as she placed the soup spoon back in her patient's hand.

"She needs to hear the truth and then maybe she'll heal," Daisy said harshly. "Does Priya know the real story with you?"

"Actually, I was about to tell her," Gabe was still calm and relaxed.

"Never mind," Daisy grunted. "You'll just give her your sugar-coated version of events from twenty-five years ago. Priya, my Duckie, let me tell you the kind of man Gabe Johanson is."

"I know who he is," Priya protested.

"No you don't," Daisy snapped. "Thank heavens your grandfather is home because if he were to walk into this room and find Gabe here, he'd have heart failure for sure!"

Chapter 17

PRIYA TOOK ANOTHER TENTATIVE SIP of the lukewarm spinach soup and laid the spoon back in the bowl. "Shelly," she spoke in an even voice. "I'll tell you what. You give me a few minutes alone with these two, and I will eat not just three quarters of the contents on my tray, but *all* of it!"

"I'm not allowed to leave you until twenty minutes after the meal," Shelly reminded wearily.

"Look," Priya said, "Between Grandma and Gabe, I'm not about to pull any stunts. They can document everything in my chart, but right now I am asking for some privacy."

"Oh, let her have that," Daisy cajoled. "If she tries to bolt to the bathroom, I'll sit on her."

"*Grandma,*" Priya was mortified that Daisy would speak that way in front of Gabe.

"Well," Shelly reached into the pocket of her flowered jacket, retrieved a pen, and handed it to Gabe. "You seem to be the sanest of the lot, so you write it down here," she indicated the chart at the foot of the bed. "I mean *everything* ... just follow the headings."

"No problem," Gabe said easily.

"I'll be back later," Shelly tossed over her shoulder before departing from the room.

"Now then," sighing lugubriously, Daisy settled back in her chair and closed her eyes. "My, oh my, this day will be longer than I ever thought possible."

"Okay, Grandma. Tell me what you have to say about Gabe," Priya urged. "But just be forewarned, nothing you tell me will change my mind about how I feel about him. Gabe?"

"Yes, Priya," he regarded her with tenderness.

"Stay close to me," she was seated on the side of the bed.

With pen and chart firmly anchored in his hand, Gabe moved silently to the bed and sat beside her, taking care not to disturb the contents of the bed table suspended over Priya's lap.

"I'll put these aside," Gabe removed the laptop and gift basket that were still on the bed and placed them on the floor.

"Priya," Daisy fixed her gaze on her granddaughter and cleared her throat. "Did your mother ever mention Gabe before she died?"

"No," she shook her head.

"Why do you suppose that is?" Daisy asked, not unkindly.

"I don't know," Priya reached for Gabe's hand and laid it on her lap. His touch was strong and warm against her shivering body. She felt better just by having him near her.

"Come on, now, you've got to eat," Gabe prodded gently.

"I will once Grandma decides to get going with the story," Priya tossed an impatient look at the senior.

"Gabe, I don't know what fairytales and lies you're planning to share with Priya, but what she will get from me is the un-adulterated truth," Daisy cleared her throat again. "Now then, as I was saying. Delaney and Gabe grew up together. We were neighbours with the Johansons. Delaney was friendly with all the kids on the street, but she had a particular fondness for Gabe. As they got older they became attracted to each other. I thought Gabe was a fine young man, at one time. He wasn't a great student, but it wasn't for a lack of potential. He was just bored. Too bright for his boots, if you ask me. He was itching to be out there in the working world, making money. Just couldn't focus on his studies. Anyway, by the time they were eighteen years old, their friendship had blossomed into what they thought was love. Or, to say the very least, Delaney was head over heels for Gabe. Am I right so far?" She shot a meaningful glance at Gabe.

"Indeed, you are," Gabe nodded respectfully as Priya took a tentative bite of her carrot stick.

Priya shot Gabe a startled look. "You were my mother's *boyfriend?*"

"Yes, he was, Duckie," Daisy retorted emphatically. "Well, Grandpa and I were fairly excited about Delaney and Gabe getting together. We figured that after university or whatever, the two of them would get married, settle down, have a couple of kids, and live near-by. The picture was fairly idealistic."

"Perfect, if it had worked out that way," Gabe scribbled a note about the carrot stick in the chart.

"Due to their youth, we anticipated a long engagement, maybe a couple of years," Daisy went on reflectively. "They were both still very young, remember,? Both needed time to mature and get a bit established in the world first."

"And?" Priya had another spoonful of soup, unaware that her interest in Daisy's story had temporarily usurped her interest in calorie-consumption. She was almost down to the bottom of the bowl.

"She's right," Gabe said as he kept on entering information in the chart. "We were teenagers in love and somehow managed to convince our parents that we could handle a long engagement and marry in our early twenties."

"But Mr. Johanson here," Daisy interrupted curtly, "suddenly developed eyes for Angela, a co-worker of his at the insurance company where he had found a job as a junior sales trainee. This Angela was very tall, very blonde, and had Wedgewood blue eyes. The exact opposite of my Delaney, who as you know, was small, and dark, and round. Gabe was smitten by Angela's looks. When you mother found out, she was devastated. That man over there dropped your mother like a hot potato! Within six months, he married Angela. Your poor mother was heartbroken and cried herself to sleep every night for months! Deny that, Gabe! I challenge you."

Gabe turned towards Priya. "What your grandmother said is the truth."

"You were engaged to my *mother?*" Priya stared down at her nearly empty tray. "Now you say you love *me?* Gabe, I am not naive. You're forty-four years old. I know you have had a past, but *this*!" Tears sprang into her eyes.

"Hold on now, before you get upset." He grasped Priya's hands and gazed directly into her eyes. "Please know this. I love you more than anything else in this world, but, yes, I have made mistakes in this life. If Daisy will allow me, I'd like to continue on with the story."

"By all means." There was a sarcastic edge in Daisy's voice. "I'd love to hear you defend yourself ... after all, it's men like you that cause women to develop anorexia. Delaney's self-esteem plummeted after you left her!"

"But Ma didn't have an eating disorder," Priya pointed out. "She took pleasure in preparing and eating food. The only person who had a hang-up over Ma's weight was Dad."

"That's because he was feeding into his own insecurities," Gabe explained, "but I'll get to that later. Priya, your grandmother is right. At the age of nineteen, I was as superficial and directionless as a wayward summer breeze. I broke up with your mother because Angela just knocked me over. Angela was also much freer with me than Delaney had been. She was a couple of years older and she was seductive. I was young and brash, impulsive. I confused sex with love. And yes, we were married within six months." He paused for a moment, "I think it was just after we married, that your mother left for Sri Lanka, where she met your father."

Daisy was nodding, listening intently.

"Well, let me tell you, Priya," Gabe continued, his eyes fixed on hers, "my life was never the same after Angela and I got married."

"Why do you say that?" she asked.

"In the beginning, our relationship seemed idyllic," Gabe, speaking from the heart turned to look at Daisy. "We rented a nice house close to my parents' place. We worked, paid the bills and had fun. Within a year of our getting married, Angela got pregnant. We had the most beautiful baby girl you could imagine. She was born with a halo of golden hair. She looked like an angel, and that's what we called her — Angel Nicole Johansen." A light entered Gabe's eyes. "She was a delicate child, just under six pounds. Just as if it were the other day, I recall the doctor saying 'she'll be a heartbreaker one day,' and, oh, Priya, that doctor was just a bit too accurate," Gabe's voice broke.

"Why? What happened?" Priya asked, a note of alarm in her voice.

"Angel was just that," Gabe nodded. "She was an angel come from heaven, but you know what? Despite her healthy appearance, I had a bad feeling in my gut."

"What do you mean?" Now even Daisy was drawn into the story. She leaned back in her chair and relaxed.

"Each time I looked into her tranquil blue eyes, I thought 'this child is not for this world. She's too gentle, too tender to withstand its rigours.' She was sitting up at six months old, walking at nine. She was a happy baby. If she cried, it was for a reason, and then her smile was back."

"Where's Angel now?" Daisy asked, a hint of suspicion in her tone.

"Well, now," Gabe cleared his throat. "When she was was eleven months old, she developed a low-grade temperature that just wouldn't go away. Initially, our doctor tried to put it down to teething difficulties, the flu ... but when she started losing weight, despite the breast milk and bottled baby food she usually enjoyed, we began to panic. Routine blood tests came back positive for childhood leukemia. They tried everything to save her, but she was only with us for a year from the day of her diagnosis. She underwent the best cancer fighting therapies of that time, but ultimately she was in and out of the hospital the way other kids are in and out of the sandbox. In fact, she became such a fixture there that the staff grew to love her as their own. She learned to walk, talk, and throw her milk bottle right there in the hospital. She'd follow nurses around her room, charming them with baby giggles one minute and breaking their hearts the next. She screamed because of the needles that she was forced to have, one after the other. Angela and I couldn't cope with the grief of losing her. We were too young and too immature. Our relationship fell apart about six months after Angel died. Even back then I thought that this suffering had to have come upon me because of the shabby way I'd treated Delaney who, by this time, I'd heard, was happily married to Jay and living in Toronto."

"Oh, Gabe," Priya pushed her bed table aside and turned towards him. "I am so truly sorry about the baby. I don't know how you'd get over something like that."

Gabe brushed the hair out of her eyes and stroked her cheek. "It's almost as if you have no choice. You grieve, cope the best way you can, and then get on with the rest of your life."

"What happened then?" Daisy asked.

"Well, I threw myself into my work and made it into senior sales," Gabe said. "I wasn't very happy and, to top it off, I'd started to drink. Here I was, this young executive going to work in a suit and tie every morning, winning all kinds of awards for highest sales for this year and that, and then on the weekends, I'd go drinking with my buddies. It was an empty way of life. I met other women, but none of my attempts at other relationships worked out. I was young and foolish and had a lot of baggage. Well, as I started to approach my forties, I sobered up a little and then, while on a fishing expedition in British Columbia, I realized I had to turn my life around. I think that part of the story you know."

"Gabe…" Priya's voice broke. "As horrible as it is for me to have lost my parents you accept that you outlive your parents, regardless how old they are when they die. However to outlive your child…" She hugged him tightly. "I'm so sorry. All these months, you've had to deal with my problems, my pain, my this and my that, and look at you … and your heartbreaking past." Unable to contain herself any longer, she began to weep quietly in his arms.

Gabe stroked her hair. "There's no need for all those tears. I'm fine now. In fact, the reason I was able to help you through

these last few months is because of what I went through and
had to learn to deal with."

Emotionally drained, all Priya wanted was to sleep. She
needed to numb the encroaching sadness that made her heart
feel heavy.

"Gabe," she regarded him through watery eyes. "Do you
think I can be alone for a while? I just need some time to myself
… to process everything you've told me."

"Too much information?" he questioned gently.

Before Priya could respond, Shelly appeared in the doorway.

"How are we doing in here?" she asked.

"Perfect," Gabe called out cheerfully. "Priya ate everything
on her tray, but I think she's tired. Daisy, what say we head
out and I'll buy you a coffee on the way home?"

"I don't know…" Daisy was torn. She was tempted to stay
on and sit with Priya while she rested, but compassion for
Gabe was setting into her heart.

"Oh, come on," he urged., "Give me a chance to prove that
I am a different man from who I was years ago."

"I think you should go, Grandma," Priya said thoughtfully."Get to know the only Gabe Johanson that I know."

Gabe turned back to the bed and relieved Priya of the tray.
He then slipped his arm around her waist and gently lowered
her onto a nest of pillows. After tucking the covers around her
shoulders, he planted a gentle kiss on her parted lips.

"I'll come back after supper, perhaps 7:00 or so, hmmm?"
he said.

"I'll look forward to that," she gave his hand a tight squeeze
and closed her eyes.

Gabe was pensive as he stirred his coffee. Daisy, seated across
from him at the bagel shop, was the same woman he'd known
in his youth. The years hadn't diminished her warm spirit and
cheerful demeanor. Yet there was a wisdom and maturity in
her eyes now. Daisy, who didn't like coffee much, had ordered
tea and a raisin scone. She gazed across the table at the man

her daughter had once loved and tried to reconcile herself to the far-fetched notion that now it was her *granddaughter* who loved him.

"Well, I suppose nothing should surprise me anymore," she said at length. "I'm in my seventies and thought I'd seen everything, but I guess I was wrong."

"Daisy," Gabe said slowly, "I don't expect you to understand any of this ... not yet. It's far too soon. You have a lot of information to sift through — Priya's eating disorder, and now this. It must be a shock to you."

"Well, yes," Daisy cleared her throat. "First of all, why wasn't I told about the girl's eating disorder? I love Priya more than anything in the world. She is all I have left of my daughter. Why did she hide it from me?"

"She didn't want to burden you," Gabe said. "She thought you'd gone through enough losing Delaney and, honestly, I don't think she saw her anorexia as a problem. She thought that by getting thinner and thinner she could maintain some control over her life."

"But why?" Daisy was perplexed. "She was always a lovely looking girl."

"She most definitely was. Now, I don't know all the details," Gabe admitted, "but from what Serena told me, I gather that Priya had a tough line to tow with her dad. From what I've heard, Jay was a difficult man to live with and had very high expectations for his wife and daughter."

"Jay was a fine man," Daisy said defensively. "He made a good home for Delaney and Priya. Granted, at first, when I found out that Delaney had eloped, I was out of my mind with worry. I thought for sure that he was making use of her to get sponsorship into Canada, and that she had fallen for him on the rebound from you. Once we got the cable about the marriage, her father was ready to hop a plane to Sri Lanka to bring her back. Later, when we got to know Jay, we saw that the young couple was in love. But, let's face it, Gabe," she looked at him sharply. "Delaney running off to Sri Lanka on that teaching mission was strictly an escape. She needed to get over you."

"I know that," Gabe stared into his cup as if the remaining coffee could furnish him with explanations and answers for his youthful, misguided behaviour.

"I know that Jay wasn't an easy man," Daisy conceded. "But, then, he had a lot to cope with. Delaney was in tears when she told me about what the young man had to endure — being raised by a mother who made him believe that she was his sister."

"You know all about that," Gabe was surprised.

"I'm sure Jay didn't want me to know, but Delaney and I could never keep secrets from each other. She made me promise not to breathe a word to Priya because Jay had chosen to take on the secret as his own personal shame."

"Renita told Priya the truth just before she was diagnosed with cancer," Gabe said, "and that in turn devastated Priya. She was in tears when she told Serena and me the story."

"Well, there you have it," Daisy popped the last of the scone into her mouth. "I know that Jay could be a bit of a tyrant at times, but he meant no harm. He was a good and moral man. He provided well for his family. I know that he could be very strict and demanding with Priya, but he loved her."

"He used to harass Delaney about her weight," Gabe said casually.

"Priya told me," Daisy shook her head, "but, now, that didn't bother Delaney at all. Anyone could say anything to her and she'd just go on. Gabe, the fact is that nothing Jay ever did could hurt Delaney as much as you leaving her for another woman."

"I can never undo the hurt I caused Delaney," Gabe said thoughtfully. "But I believe I paid the price for my superficial ways. Then, about five years ago, I had an epiphany."

"Oh?" Daisy looked at him.

"I was ice fishing one sunny February morning. I was out alone. The fish weren't biting that well and my thoughts were straying all over the place. As I sat in my ice hut, surrounded by snowcovered ice and a gentle winter breeze, I was inclined to pray in a way I had never done before. Guidance came in the most unexpected way."

"I'm listening," Daisy prodded.

Gabe told Daisy how he ended up travelling through South Asia in search of his own personal truth. "After a tremendous amount of soul searching, I realized the only way I could put my life in order was to help others. Once I returned to Canada, I discovered a business opportunity here in Mississauga for someone to organize transportation for the disabled as well as seniors to get to their medical appointments and run errands. So I established a company that could do that and I now have a fleet of six mini-vans and several drivers."

"That's good," Daisy nodded approvingly.

"And," he added, "the big thing for me is when I realized that Priya was anorexic, I made it my business to read and research every aspect of the disease that I could find."

"Why?" Daisy was taken aback at the earnestness of his admission.

"Because from the moment I'd heard that Delaney died, I wanted to do something for her daughter. I thought to myself, 'I hurt her mother years ago. If I ever meet up with her daughter, I am going to try to help her in whatever way I can.' In a sense, I was connected to Priya long before I laid eyes on her in person."

"Of course, 'in person.' How else could you lay eyes on her?" Daisy was impatient.

"Here, look," Gabe reached into his coat pocket and took out a thick brown envelope. It was bulging with a mix of photographs along with a hand-written note.

"I knew we would meet at the hospital today, so I brought these along." Gabe slid the packet across the table toward Daisy.

"Oh my!" Daisy opened the envelope and took out several photographs at once. She laid them on the table. She observed that each one showed family scenes featuring Priya and her parents during various stages of their lives. There were shots of Priya as a baby, Priya at the beach in Sri Lanka, and Priya dressed in her uniform, posing with her parents in front of her high school. There were at least thirty photos, including some taken the Christmas before last — Priya's last with her parents.

"Did Delaney send you these?" Daisy was positively flummoxed.

"No," Gabe shook his head. "Jay did. There's a note buried in that envelope. Read it and you'll find out why."

Daisy unfolded the yellowed sheet of paper and gasped in surprise when she saw the date — May 10, 1978. "What in the name...?"

"Read what it says," Gabe prodded.

Daisy cleared her throat and assumed a professional reading voice.

Dear Mr. Gabriel Johanson,
Thank you for your card, wishing us well on the birth of our beloved daughter, Priya, who is now well over two weeks old. Mr. Johanson, let me get to the point. I know that you and Delaney had a powerful past, but make no mistake, you walked away from her. Now, she is mine. Just to remind you of this pertinent detail, I will occasionally be sending you photographs of the three of us at various stages of our lives.
Yours sincerely, Jay De Souza

"My, oh my," Daisy shook her head in confusion. "Why in the world would he send you that letter and follow through with those pictures?"

"At the time it made no sense to me whatsoever," Gabe admitted. "But then, after Priya told me about Jay's background, it all came together. I think that he was so insecure about his place in life because he'd been raised as his mother's brother. And by the time he found out the truth, it was too late to forge a real relationship with Renita. I think he wanted the world to know that he was Priya's father and that there were no secrets."

"Of course he was Priya's father," Daisy was nonplussed.

"Why would there be any doubt? You and Delaney had no contact with each other once you broke up with her."

"I know. Delaney was so hurt, she'd have nothing to do with me. My sending a card of congratulations on Priya's birth was a goodwill gesture and nothing more. Maybe Jay felt threatened by that, and feared that I might try to become a part of her life again. But what we had was over and that was that. Jay was too insecure to realize that. Later, of course, Delaney forgave me. I suppose Jay perceived her forgiving me as another threat and that she wanted me back in her life, but this was far from the truth. "

"What did Delaney say to make you think she'd forgiven you?" Daisy asked.

"Several years ago, when Delaney and her family came back to St. John's for a visit, we ran into each other at the post office. We chatted briefly and wished each other well. It was as simple as that. She was friendly and warm, and very obviously happy with her life and with Jay."

"That's your version of events," Daisy was doubtful. "Delaney isn't here to substantiate the story."

"Maybe this will help," Gabe reached into his pocket and removed a simple white envelope. He removed a card featuring a nativity scene.

"You really did come prepared to meet me," Daisy smiled.

She opened the card and peered at her daughter's distinctive teacher's script.

Dear Gabe,

It was great to run into you after all this time. I'm so glad that we have both found our way in this life. I am sorry about the loss of your child, and the end of your marriage, but I am sure you will find happiness again. All the best to you and yours in the years to come. Delaney

"Are you planning to show this, along with the pictures, to Priya?" Daisy handed the card back to Gabe.

"I think the time is right to share this with her," he said quietly.

"As innocent as your communication with Delany was, I'm sure Jay wasn't happy," Daisy said.

"Maybe," Gabe agreed. "She must have told him she ran into me, because after that I started receiving another spate of photographs. Anyway, getting those pictures in the mail didn't bother me at all. In fact, I looked forward to them. Daisy, I have become a very strong man. What I did to Delaney was wrong, and if Jay needed their successes rubbed in my face, then so be it. I could take it."

"I always knew that Jay was a troubled man," Daisy admitted, "but I overlooked his moodiness and sullen ways because he was a devoted husband and father. He sacrificed everything for his wife and child. Nobody is perfect, Gabe."

"Agreed," he nodded.

"So Jay sent you these pictures and you carried on with your life."

"Yes, until I read about the plane crash in the papers and thought that I might be able to help Priya in some way."

"What if the plane crash had never happened?" Daisy challenged. "Would you still have located Priya? I imagine Jay would have had you drawn and quartered if he knew you were after his daughter."

Gabe couldn't help but laugh. "I'm not 'after' his daughter. I simply love her. I never intended for that to happen. I just assumed that I would play a peripheral role in her life as a friend, an advisor. I don't know ... anything but a romantic partner! Believe me, it's taken me by surprise as much as anybody else. If we had fallen in love with each other under other circumstances, well then, we would have dealt with them."

"Oh my," Daisy sighed.

"Daisy, the truth is, I might have fallen in love with Priya the moment I laid eyes on her, but I didn't realize it until much later. I told myself, 'she's just a young girl. Forget about it! As I got to know Serena, she sensed my growing attraction to Priya, and let me know that she would be supportive."

"But Priya's almost twenty years younger than you," Daisy frowned.

"I know that," he nodded. "So what? We are spiritually in tune with each other. We could be just two years apart in age and one of us could get cancer and the other would be left alone for years to come. There are no guarantees, no matter what the age difference."

"What now, Gabe? Why do you love her?" Daisy pressed.

"I love her because she has given me a reason to believe in myself again. I see beyond the woman with the difficult past who lies in that hospital bed. Priya, it would seem, never fit into the mainstream. She's not your conventional twenty-five year old."

"She never was — at any age," Daisy conceded. "With her, we didn't have to worry much about anything. She was on the straight-and-narrow. But, yes, Jay was always critical and exacting. He was down on her about not excelling in music, or not getting the highest marks in school. He killed her zeal for competition when she tried to participate in a charity run for school. He coached her like a drill sergeant, but was so verbally abusive, she dropped out in tears."

Gabe merely sighed.

"I was so happy when she met Trent," Daisy went on. "I was thinking he would be a fine young man from the right background, only a few years older, what better?'"

"I knew right away though that Trent was not the man for Priya," Gabe said. "Priya couldn't even bring herself to admit to Trent that she was anorexic. She went to all lengths to hide it from him. Part of the reason being that Trent lost his sister to anorexia."

"And with you she could be open?" Daisy's eyebrows arched.

"She was far more trusting toward me," Gabe admitted. "I made sure she knows I will never judge her, no matter what."

"And you love her," Daisy reiterated. "What does that mean for the two of you?"

"The first order of business is for Priya to get well," Gabe said. "After that, she needs to pursue her career."

"No luck on the job front yet?" Daisy mused.

"To be honest, I don't think she's been trying," Gabe admitted, "and that's partly because of her illness and partly because I sense she's not really interested in teaching."

"What does she want to do then?" Daisy asked.

"We talked about this only once, but I feel that Priya would make an excellent motivational speaker. She could go into the schools and address students about the perils of having an eating disorder." He related to Daisy how impressed he was with the way Priya reached out to Sara at the funeral. "That took tremendous courage to do," he said. "I feel she has a real gift for reaching out to youngsters."

"You have it all figured out, don't you?" Daisy said.

"Daisy, I want to spend the rest of my life with her," Gabe said. "I will never hurt Priya because deep in my heart I know that I was given a last chance to straighten out my life. I want to look after her, love her, protect her, and watch her blossom into her full potential. Down the road, when she's ready, we'll explore the possibility of marriage."

"Well, that's still in the future," Daisy glanced at her watch. "Goodness, I had no idea it was getting so late! I should get back to the townhouse and unpack."

"Would you like me to bring you back to the hospital in the evening?" Gabe asked.

"I don't think so," Daisy said after a moment's pause. "It's been a long day ... an overwhelming day, what with getting up early to catch the flight out of St. John's, then coming here to find out that Priya is suffering from anorexia and that you're the new man in her life. It's all too much to take in. I'll go to Priya's, rest, and straighten up the place for her return. When I dropped my bags off, I noticed that her fridge is crammed with casseroles. I need to do an inventory of what's worth keeping."

Gabe nodded. "People from Renita's church dropped by right throughout the weekend with food, but, you know, Priya didn't touch any of it."

"I hope she gets better," Daisy murmured.

"For sure," Gabe said. "Priya will be just fine."

Priya felt refreshed and relaxed after resting throughout the afternoon. Dressed in her polar fleece pants and top, her hair brushed and falling in loose curls around her wan face, she watched as Gabe approached the bed.

"How is my girl doing?" he asked, extending his arms to her. She climbed off the bed and walked into his waiting embrace.

"You have no idea how long I've waited for this moment," she whispered rubbing her cheek against the icy chill of his beige winter jacket. "Not just this afternoon, but for months … but I didn't realize it until now."

"I know, sweetheart, I know." He walked her back to the bed.

"Gabe," Priya took his strong hands in hers and squeezed them as tightly as she could, in a vain hope that some of his strength would transfer to her. "You have suffered so much. For months, we've been focusing on my pain, but what about you? You loved a daughter for twenty months and then had to lose her."

"It happens," Gabe said. "But then you accept that life has its share of suffering and after that joy will follow, if you open your heart and allow yourself to trust again. Of course it took me years to discover that joy …with you."

"I lost my mother and father at the same time," she said as he helped her back under the covers. "But how can you accept the loss of your child?"

"You mentioned that earlier today and as much as time heals, it's still a shock to the soul. You make the best of it and be grateful for what you *do* have in this life." Gabe said philosophically as he drew the chair up to the bedside. "Look at your grandparents. They're going through that right now."

"I know, and Delaney was their only child as well," Priya murmured. "And then there's Renita who lost a son that she could never acknowledge as her own. How sad is that?"

"We've all grieved for loved ones at some point in our lives."

Gabe took Priya's hands in his and rubbed them gently. "But it's how we choose to deal with that grief that matters. I buried my pain with work and drinking. You chose to cope with grief by not eating. In your case, the anorexia was a symptom of a deeper problem in your life. But, Priya, don't underestimate yourself. Right now you may be as physically fragile as a buttercup, but I know under that delicate exterior lurks a woman as fierce as a pit bull."

"How was Grandma on the way home from the hospital?" Priya suddenly asked.

"We went to the bagel shop downstairs on our way out," Gabe explained. "I told her everything that had to be said, and then I showed her this," he reached into his coat pocket and took out the envelope of pictures he'd shown Daisy earlier in the day.

Priya riffled through the pictures and then read Jay's letter. After studying the familiar script of her father's hand, she frowned. "With a father as insecure as that, no wonder I have problems," she said, handing the letter back to Gabe.

"As far as his relationship with your mother was concerned, he had no reason to be insecure," Gabe admitted. "What Delaney and I had ended long before you were born."

"How did you know about me, then?" Priya wanted to know.

"I saw the birth announcement in the paper, so as a goodwill gesture I sent a card to your mother. I don't know if Delaney ever got to read it. I suspect now that the card made your father angry enough to write me this letter and keep sending me photographs"

"So you watched me grow up," Priya mused. "That feels so strange."

"How do you feel about your mother and me?" Gabe asked.

"I was thinking about that after you left," Priya admitted. "It's just as well you didn't tell me when we first met. I might have just walked away."

"And now?" Gabe asked.

"And now, I can't imagine my life without you," Priya leaned up and kissed his cheek. "Everything happens for the best."

"I am convinced that you and I were meant to be together," Gabe said quietly. "If it wasn't one way, then it would be the other. Your mother was the connection."

"I guess you and I have been connected in a very profound way," Priya said. "Now when I look back, I find that idea comforting." Priya chuckled. "I can't imagine what people will think."

"You mean people like Trent and Rachel?"

"I guess so," Priya sighed. "But then again, I don't believe I really care. Auntie Renita spent her entire life worrying what others would think of her. Ultimately, she sacrificed her relationship with her son because of that."

"Now look, enough of the past. There is something I want you to start doing for me and ultimately for yourself."

"What is it?" she asked.

Gabe walked over to the opposite end of the room and picked up the briefcase. Priya had forgotten about its existence until now. "I brought in a laptop for you to get started," he explained, popping it open on the bed.

"Start what?" Priya was intrigued.

"Start writing. Write your heart out, whatever comes to mind. Maybe an account of your eating disorder and how you feel you developed it. I truly believe you have a story to tell, and in writing it down, it will help you heal."

"I'm not a writer," Priya protested.

"Listen to me, Priya De Souza," he cupped her chin in his palm. "I believe in you. I don't know if anyone has ever told you that before, but I am telling you, right here, right now, that I, Gabe Johanson, am committing myself to helping you achieve your goals because I love you with all my heart."

Chapter 18

PALLID RAYS FROM A WATERY SUN trickled across the blue-gray sky with the fluidity of a half-boiled egg yolk streaming across a plate. The hollow sound of wind rushing through leafless branches and rippling the shimmering surface of a narrow stream provided just the right degree of calm Priya needed to free her mind of her week-long hospital stay and focus on the arduous journey back to good health.

Although only seven days had elapsed since the accident and Priya's forced hospitalization, it seemed that an entire lifetime had transpired since then. From one Sunday to the next, Priya went from a troubled life, sickened body, and broken spirit to a renewed life, a healing body, and a trusting heart.

She was discharged the following Sunday, exactly one week after the accident, with a schedule heavy with appointments and meetings, all intended to aid her recovery. Therapy with Dr. Farrel actually commenced while she was still an inpatient. Priya was now expected to follow a regimen of individual behavioural therapy, group therapy, and psychotherapy with an eating disorder counsellor. She would also meet with a nutritionist and a dietician who would help establish a healthy eating plan that Priya could use to guide her back to health. Priya would also have regular contact with Dot Carmichael, a cheerful blonde in her early fifties who'd spent years overcoming her dance with bulimia.

Dot met Priya at the hospital a few days before she was released. A tall woman with an open face, a bold sense of fashion, and a startling air of confidence, Dot's bubbly personality filled Priya with a badly-needed infusion of positive energy. When they met, she was wearing a white fur vest over a powder blue sweater and tight acid-wash jeans. The outfit was completed with a pair of tan suede boots. Her bottle blonde hair was short and fluffy. With bold make-up and chunky bracelets, she looked as if she'd be equally at home in a Hollywood production studio or reading fortunes at the local psychic fair. Image aside, she worked as an executive assistant in a digital photography and video company. Her first suggestion was for Priya to trade her standard toothbrush for an electric model, thus easing the temptation for Priya to descend into one of her manic cleaning frenzies when overwhelmed by anxiety.

Priya had made an encouraging start by gaining three pounds while in the hospital. But there was a lot more work to be done before she not only regained an acceptable amount of weight, but also was able to maintain it with confidence and, more importantly, without fear. With the weekend day-nurse supervising her, Priya had enjoyed a wholesome lunch of pita bread and humus, but refused dessert because Gabe was taking her to Starbucks to honour their usual Sunday afternoon ritual before driving her home.

Priya had amassed quite a few plants and fruit baskets while in the hospital. The gift she treasured the most was Gabe's pink gift basket. She'd tried the soothing chamomile tea her last night in hospital. She was taking home all the plants and flowers, but she requested that the fruit baskets be donated to the staff for their kind and patient treatment toward her — especially warm-hearted Shelly.

While Gabe loaded the back of his car with Priya's belongings, Priya sat in the front passenger seat and decided that she wanted to make a special stop before heading to Starbucks. "I want to walk in your world for a few minutes," she said once Gabe was behind the wheel.

"My world?" he fastened his seatbelt, somewhat puzzled by her request.

"Yes," she nodded. "You love the great outdoors. I would like you to take me to one of your favourite places so I can relax my mind enough to face the rest of the day.

"You have nothing to worry about," Gabe said as he slipped the key into the ignition. "Your grandmother, Serena, and I will be there to get you through your first day at home." He already understood that Priya was frightened that without the cosseting effect of the hospital around her, she might regress into her anorexic ways.

"What time did you tell Serena you'd pick her up?" Priya asked.

"I said we'd come after leaving Starbucks," he explained. "So we have the time to go into the country a little ways, but..."

"I get it," Priya sighed. "You think I want to walk for the sake of burning as many calories as I can to mitigate my lunch, not to mention the roast chicken Grandma is serving this evening."

Gabe was silent. This was exactly what was on his mind, but he hadn't the heart to admit it. He wanted to be a source of ongoing encouragement to Priya, but at times he wasn't sure if she was really committed to getting better. He saw the fear in her eyes when she commented about the roast chicken.

"I don't think you're ready for walks in the great outdoors yet," he said carefully.

"Why?" she challenged.

"Because you are still very weak and, from all appearances, no matter what you do, what you wear, you are still so cold," he said. "You told me that yourself this morning."

Priya couldn't deny it. Under her black pea coat, she wore a polar fleece sweater, long sleeve blouse and jeans. Even the white tights underneath did little to chase the chill away. It was almost as if her body had finally woken up to the realization that it had been deprived for months and now, under the nurturing guidance of the medical establishment, was starting to rebel.

Dr. Benson had warned that she might notice the cold more now than before the accident because her activity level had been drastically reduced. Gone were the days of frenzied cleanings and manic jogging. These were pursuits that kept her metabolism revved and her body in a state of thermogenic climate control.

Because she lacked the energy to move around as quickly and efficiently as she had just a week earlier, she felt far less tolerant of the cold. She knew that once she regained weight and strength, her body's internal thermostat would normalize itself and she could gradually re-introduce an appropriate level of exercise and weight management into her lifestyle.

"Gabe," Priya placed her gloved hand on his elbow, "I've trusted you for the longest time, now you in turn need to trust me. Yes, the temptation to burn as many calories as I can in the shortest possible time between meals is still very real in my present state, *but* I'm not about to give into it. I have followed doctor's orders throughout the week and am so looking forward to a future with you; I wouldn't do anything to jeopardize it by risking my life any more than I already have. Do you believe me?"

"Of course I do," Gabe's manner softened. "But I know you're on a difficult road and at times you'll be scared."

"Does that mean I can't go for a walk ... just to be alone with you?" she asked coyly.

"We have a lifetime to be alone," Gabe assured her. "Right now our priority is to get you well."

"I just want to hold your hand and feel the wind on my face and then hopefully warm up with a nice latte at Starbucks before we pick up Serena and get back to the townhouse," Priya explained.

Gabe leaned over and dropped a tender kiss on her waiting cheek. "Okay then, let's get going."

Gabe took her to an out-of-the-way walking trail in Milton, just outside Mississauga. After parking at the entrance of the park, they strolled hand in hand beside a narrow brook. They didn't say much as words weren't necessary. They simply basked in the joy of being together. Priya was as good as her word and made no attempt to pick up her speed or sprint into a jog. She merely snuggled into Gabe's side, enjoying the comfort and security of his arm around her shoulder. Dr. Benson had encouraged Priya to practice deep breathing to help her relax. She flooded her lungs with fresh air and exhaled slowly, meaningfully, releasing months of pent-up stress and misplaced energy. After just ten or twelve minutes in utter quietude and tranquility, she told Gabe that she was ready to leave. They drove to the Starbucks where their friendship had officially begun, and ordered lattes. As a nod to her anorexic past and health-conscious future, Priya still insisted on having her drink prepared with skim milk.

"Some things, Gabe, will never change," she said as she bravely placed a slice of low-fat cinnamon swirl coffeecake next to her drink.

"What do you mean?" he asked as they carried their order to a table.

"I will probably count calories for the rest of my life," she explained, "and hazarding a guess, I'd say we're looking at 200 calories for this piece of coffee cake alone. Rather than sectioning it into fifty micro pieces as I might have done up to a week ago, I will divide it in half and, if you like, you can have one half, or I'll take the balance home for later."

"I would love to share that with you," Gabe smiled at her.

Priya took a long look at the man sitting across from her. His light brown hair was thinning, but he had large soulful eyes and kind face and smile that right now was beaming at her. "What's on your mind?" he asked.

"Remember the day we first met, at Walmart?" she asked.

"How could I forget?" he laughed.

"I ordered a muffin, but sectioned it into several pieces and ate virtually none. I was just too scared, but I didn't want you to know."

"I knew," Gabe said, "but I couldn't say anything, fearing you'd get up and leave."

"I've come a long way since then, haven't I, Gabe?" she pressed.

It was 5:30 pm. The late afternoon sun had dissolved into a pale blue dusk. The reassuring sounds and smells of domesticity filled the townhouse with a long forgotten ambience of comfort and stability. A springtime scent of fabric softener wafted from the dryer in the main floor laundry room while the aroma of roast chicken and baked potatoes filled the air. There was a general feeling of well-being and contentment as a smiling Daisy folded freshly laundered sheets in the living room and then stacked them neatly atop the coffee table. Serena sipped tea at the dining table while alternately flipping through the pages of a magazine. Meanwhile, Gabe and Priya, comfortably settled on the chesterfield, sorted through the get-well cards and notes she'd received at the hospital. Priya wasn't sure if she'd read them all now.

"Here's one from Sara," Gabe remarked as he handed her a pink envelope.

"Let me see what she has to say." She took out a single sheet of computer paper, bordered with graphics, and read it out loud.

Dear Priya,
Sooo sorry about the accident. Glad it wasn't serious though. It was so cool the way you spoke at Renita's funeral. I don't know how you had the guts to get up there and speak to me the way you did, but it made a big impression. In fact, the very next day at school I saw my guidance counsellor and confessed that I had been playing with the idea of making myself throw-up because it seemed like a perfect way to eat what I want and not gain weight. She set me up with an eating disorder specialist who'll be visiting our school next week.
Well, I've got to go. Mid-terms are coming up. It's a drag, but if I don't get my act together I'll flunk geometry.
Love, Sara

Gabe beamed at Priya. "That's a testimonial and a half."

She skimmed over the letter one more time and slipped it back into the envelope.

"The impact you had on one young girl..." Gabe shook his head in wonderment. "You have a real gift."

"I'm not surprised." Serena, overhearing the conversation, ventured over to the chesterfield. "Girl, you got a lot of cards and letters. I think you should think about going into the schools and talking to kids like Sara ... oh, yes, and piano lessons too."

"Piano lessons?" Priya was puzzled.

"I didn't get a chance to tell you this earlier," she shifted the pile of correspondence aside and sat between her two friends. "At the parish hall, before your accident, I chatted with some of the visitors — a lady called Florence, for one, and a couple of others..."

"And?" Priya interjected.

"Well, Florence was telling me how she enjoyed having Renita as a roommate, even for a few short hours. It turns out that Florence always wanted to play the piano, but felt too old and embarrassed to inquire about it. Renita had assured her that nobody was ever too old to learn the piano. So anyway, I told her that you were an excellent pianist."

"Serena..." Priya groaned, passing a hand over her forehead.

"Oh shells, you're being silly," Serena cuffed her playfully on the arm. "You play beautifully. Just then, girl, another parishioner joined in the discussion, and it turns out that she, too, wants to learn to play. They aren't too interested in qualifying with exams or anything. They simply want to learn for their own enjoyment."

"And you suggested I might be able to teach them?" Priya frowned.

"Sounds like a great idea," Gabe said. "Make a little money and have some fun."

"I can't get into classical music again," Priya shuddered. "I have too many dark memories of my childhood, being forced to practice for hours. Then, of course, there was Dad with what he called his 'early morning infusion of baroque while breakfasting'..." Priya rolled her eyes and began to laugh.

"Did he really talk like that?" Gabe was chuckling.

"Oh my guy, he did," Serena nodded. "Gabe, you don't know our Jay. He was a case and a half." Long forgotten memories must have surfaced in her mind because she dissolved into a fit of giggles. When she finally recovered, she gave Priya a quick hug. "Don't mind old Serenie here, girl. The smell of that chicken will send me into an institution if we don't eat soon. Besides, the fact that we can laugh this way proves that your relationship with classical music couldn't be that badly damaged."

"Well now, Duckie, that does sound interesting," Daisy said. "Honey, I think it's something to think about."

"We'll see what happens," Priya agreed. "I've barely been out of the hospital five hours. It's too soon to think about anything like that."

A reflective look settled over Serena's face.

"What are you thinking about?" Gabe asked, picking up on her pensive expression.

"Life is so different for everyone," she mused. "My mother died when I was a mere infant, but my father ... now *there* was a man!"

"What do you mean?" Priya asked curiously.

"I have the opposite attitude toward classical music than you have," Serena explained. "You see, on Sundays after a hearty lunch of dhal puri, curried goat, and okra, we would sit out in the veranda and listen to the classics while sipping iced coffee. It was a treat. I loved Bach's *Jesu, Joy of Man's Desiring* and Pachelbel's *Canon* ... all the great masters. We'd sit and chat as a family for about an hour, allowing our food and young ones to settle before we would go out to play field hockey or soccer. My, oh my, those were the days..."

"Sounds idyllic," Gabe nodded. "Warm weather, great food, and fun with your family and friends. Ah, now that's the way to enjoy life!"

Daisy tossed a smile in Serena's direction and headed for the kitchen. "I think that chicken is ready to come out of the oven. Let me get this laundry out of here and we can eat."

Before long, the four were gathered around the dining table with plates ready to be served. "Help yourself, there's lots here." Daisy made a sweeping gesture with her hand to indicate the bounty on the table: Roast chicken, baked potatoes, rolls, steamed root vegetables, and an assortment of Daisy's home-made bread-and-butter pickles. "I wanted to make a special meal for Priya's first day at home," Daisy beamed at the group.

"Glad I showed up," Gabe chuckled as he took a seat beside Priya.

All eyes turned toward the young woman at his left. By unspoken agreement, it was understood that she would serve herself first and others would follow. Nodding, Priya placed two slivers of white breast meat on her plate. This was followed by a modest serving of steamed vegetables and a tablespoon of gravy. She began to eat.

"And?" Daisy stared at her.

"And what?" Priya was perplexed.

"Well, girl, you've only got what a three-year-old would eat. Have some potatoes now, a roll? The pickles I brought up from home especially for you." While speaking, she leaned across the table, grabbed Priya's plate, and began piling on the food.

"Grandma!" she protested. "What are you doing?"

"Well, now, look at yourself, my child," Daisy's hands shook with emotion as she replaced the plate in front of her granddaughter. "You look like the walking dead. You need to plump up as fast as you can. I'm scared you'll just collapse and that'll be the end."

"Daisy," Serena shot the older woman a warning glance but it was too late. Highly stressed and trembling with emotion, Priya threw down her cutlery and pushed back her chair.

"This is a bit much," she whispered.

"I think we need to go easy on Priya," Gabe began.

"Easy on her!" Daisy sounded exasperated. "So she can wither to death? I know you like 'em thin, Gabe, but surely not like this!"

"Oh, just give it up!" Priya cried out and raced from the room, down the hall, and into the den where she hurled herself on the futon. Gut-wrenching sobs erupted from her narrow chest. Pent-up fears rained upon her like a barrage of headlines portending the worst in world news.

"Priya, sweetheart," Gabe was bending over her. "It's all right. Daisy doesn't quite understand how your eating disorder works. Give her time."

"Oh, Gabe, I can't do this," Priya sobbed, burying her face in his navy sweater. "It's pointless."

"Shhh, it's all right, sweetheart, it's all right. I'm here." He sat down and gathered her into his arms. Cradling her head against his chest, he began to rub her back, gently slipping his large fingers under her sweater and blouse to caress the fragile skin that covered bone made vulnerable by an obvious lack of flesh. He held her in silence till Priya's tears subsided.

"Daisy has no patience with me and neither will you," she choked. "Gabe, I'm overwhelmed by the thought of making this recovery. I have a full schedule of meetings and therapy sessions to attend this week — some with Grandma and you. After a while, you'll both get tired of helping me."

"That's not going to happen." Gabe kissed the back of her neck. "We love you and want to see you heal."

"Gabe," Priya raised her tear-stained face towards him, "You have been through so much pain in your own life. One of these days you'll say 'enough of all this sadness,' and walk away."

"I'll never walk away from you, Priya," he assured her. "If you have any fears about me based on how I treated your mother, please understand I was a different man then. I will never do anything to abuse your trust."

Priya wiped her eyes. "I feel that until you came into my life I was completely alone. Yes, I had my friends, but even before that, when my parents were alive, I felt I had absolutely nobody who really understood me — until you."

"You have me," Gabe said solemnly. "I already told you this at the hospital, but I will tell you again: Priya, you will get better. You can do it!"

"Perhaps I can manage a little dinner after all," Priya took a shaky breath.

"You tell me exactly what you can eat and I'll take it up for you," Gabe said.

"Grandma won't be happy..."

"She'll come around," Gabe assured as they got to their feet. "Now let's hurry before that Serena puts everything away for the night."

Priya chuckled. "She and Grandma are alike in that way. They both like to keep things super organized and moving efficiently."

"All that's fine as long as they understand that you need lots of time to recover," he said, then kissed her tenderly.

Priya's recovery was a long, frustrating process that began with micro steps. There were days when she felt she would never shake her anorexic mindset, and yet there were others when she felt she could rise above the universe — so temperamental were her moods. The one constant in her life was Gabe's nurturing guidance. In his quiet, unobtrusive way, he helped Priya reclaim her self-esteem. "I'm like the wilted flower you tended back to life," she told him on more than one occasion.

"What you say I do for you," he would respond, "is pure and simple love. True love isn't lust or good looks. It is the ability to bring out the best in the one dearest to your heart."

Despite their age difference, Priya and Gabe were a perfect match. Beyond conventional commonalties and values, theirs seemed to be a relationship based on two old souls coming together.

Serena was thrilled for Priya. "Girl, you've lost so much," she told her on the phone one day, "I'm glad that Gabe can give you the stability and love you deserve."

Even Rachel's critical eyebrows were lowered when she saw the positive impact Gabe had on Priya's life. For the time being, however, Priya's immediate goal of achieving good physical and mental health and going on to carve a rewarding life for herself was the main focus of her recovery.

On the Monday following her discharge from hospital, Priya

attended the first of many therapy sessions. She met Dr. Farrel in his spacious, well-lit clinic where they delved deep into the neuroses stemming from her childhood. Their exploration took them back to the days when Priya took refuge from her parents' arguments by hiding in the bathroom and using toothbrushes to scrub away the grout between the tiles. Priya discussed Jay's preoccupation with her mother's weight and the constant pressure Priya found herself under to achieve and excel. She opened up about her uneventful years in a private Christian school that coupled moral law with a solid work ethic. They talked about Jay being raised as his mother's brother and how it manifested itself in a profound insecurity that was probably far greater than Priya's own. The very fact that in adulthood Jay needed to prove to Gabe time and time again that Delaney was his, indicated a severe lack of self-esteem, which he directed towards easy-going Delaney by harping on her weight and other areas where he felt her to be weak.

Family therapy with Daisy wasn't very successful, as she couldn't grasp the concept of someone starving for the sake of being thin. She simply didn't *get* the psychological implications of the disease. As a child of the Depression, she argued it was nearly impossible for her to grasp how anyone could not eat when food was plentiful and available. She spoke of how her parents rationed food to make it last and how simply entering a store was no guarantee that there would be any groceries there to purchase. She didn't mean to sound judgmental or accusatory, but the fact was that Daisy came of age in a different time than Priya and it showed. A willful refusal to eat made no sense to Daisy, even after Dr. Farrel explained that eating disorders and women had been linked for centuries, but it was only now that universal awareness was thrusting it into the limelight. He recommended a comprehensive reading list to Daisy on the subject, but she shook her head.

"I could be more use to Priya if I made her some good, nourishing meals and kept the house up for her while she gains some weight and resumes her job search."

As far as the group therapy experience was concerned, Priya didn't enjoy it — at first. She felt at odds with patients so much younger than herself. Yet, after attending a few sessions, she noticed the teens in the group were starting to view her as a role model. Like Sara, they were trying to take their cues from her. Priya thought that once she recovered, she might take Gabe's advice and enrol in motivational speaking classes, as they would help her fine-tune her speaking skills and sharpen her delivery as she shared her message with others afflicted with eating disorders.

One snowy Thursday evening, not long after Priya was released from the hospital, she found herself seated on the chesterfield facing the LCD screen of the laptop Gabe had given her. Daisy, who at seventy years of age was still incapable of staying still for five minutes, was in the kitchen baking oatmeal raisin muffins while the dishwasher hummed in the background. Priya was pleased over the fact that she'd been able to enjoy a slice of meatloaf and five baby carrots without stressing over the number of calories consumed. She'd gained another pound since leaving the hospital and wanted to keep the rate of weight gain at a very slow pace. If she could reach 100 pounds by the summer, she was not only fairly certain she could maintain it, but felt that she could stave off the panic of uncontrollable weight gain.

Gabe had been over for dinner that evening but left a little while ago as he had to prepare for a two-day ice-fishing trip. Priya recognized that Gabe, who'd lived alone for much of adult his life, was an insatiable adventurer and would need to do his own thing from time to time. Priya, in turn, would be left to focus on her new projects and her old friendships. She was to see a movie with Rachel on Friday night.

Growing restless with the lack of inspiration, Priya had a sudden impulse to put on the Josh Groban CD Trent had given her for Christmas. After turning on the music, she returned to the chesterfield and waited for ideas to hit. Track one came and went, followed by track two. Priya's mind remained as blank as the computer screen. Sighing with frustration, she was about to put her literary efforts aside for the night when suddenly the cello stylings on the third track — "Il Postino" — seized her with a forceful need to write. She closed her eyes to accommodate a picture developing in her mind. She was actually seeing herself the way others did, skeletal and desperate. She wouldn't qualify as it as an out-of-body experience, but she could definitely see herself sitting on the edge of her bed, studying her emaciated face and delicate neck bones in her mirror. The feelings of helplessness and fear that had gripped her during the many mornings she'd awoken to this real-life image of herself compelled her to place her fingers on the keys and start typing with furious urgency. After several frenzied minutes of mad typing, she stared at the screen to find out that she had poured out her heart and soul about her experience with anorexia nervosa, and how love was ultimately saving her life.

Although she didn't know it at the time, those words were a catalyst for the turning point that Priya was about to make. The only thought she had at that moment was that the music had stopped. The room was filled with an unexpected silence. Wondering why the CD had stopped playing, she walked over to the stereo and gazed at the readout on the player. Sure enough number thirteen flashed at her attention. There were thirteen tracks on this album. How did she come to the end that quickly? She glanced at her watch. She was stunned to discover over forty-five minutes had passed since she started writing. So quickly! The best part was that it all made perfect sense. Clean, crisp prose, good choices of words, and most importantly a powerful message conveyed. She decided to save the material and expand upon it later.

"Honey, why don't we have a muffin and a cup of tea," Daisy suggested, peering into the living room. "There's a good mystery on TV tonight we could watch..."

The reference to the mystery brought back cozy memories of Priya and Delaney back in St. John's on holiday, watching a late night murder mystery with Daisy. They'd all speculate over who the killer actually was, but generally Daisy was the first to figure it out. Priya smiled over the warm recollection.

"Sure, I'll watch the movie with you, Grandma," she said. "But I'll pass on the muffin. I'm just not ready for that yet."

Daisy nodded with resignation. She had learned a little since the debacle with the chicken and potatoes the previous Sunday. Priya glanced at her watch. The movie wouldn't start for another half an hour, giving her time to skim through some of the health and nutrition books she'd acquired from the eating disorder clinic. She'd been studying them over the past few days, trying to discover ways to achieve and maintain a healthy weight without fear. She already knew that she would introduce low-carb specialty breads into her diet, along with more foods containing omega-3 fatty acids. She'd increase her fibre intake with bran and bran-based products. She would continue to drink lots of skim milk and choose brightly co-loured vegetables to fill her plate. Once she was ready, she would re-introduce sweets and chocolates into her diet; but, for that, she would maintain her old anorexic standard of sectioning them and eating the minimal amount with coffee or milk. She would implement a new rule into her life: When she was stronger, Priya hoped to resume a new form of exercise. She'd been reading about a new style of walking that was in-terspersed with brief bursts of running. All of those changes would take time and determination. She had a full supply of both and that's what counted.

Chapter 19

THE WARM, HUMID WEATHER was a sure harbinger of summer's imminent arrival. It was the end of May, well over a year since Priya's descent into anorexia nervosa. She stood slim and pretty in a short pastel pink sundress topped with a delicate bolero of the same fabric. She no longer displayed the telltale signs of undernourishment. The skin folds behind her bare legs had disappeared. Her soft café-au-lait complexion contrasted prettily with her pearl necklace and off-white sandals. The bounce and curl had returned to her formerly lackluster hair, and her face, once wan and skeletal, had reclaimed some of its former fullness.

Priya had gained eighteen pounds since her release from the hospital. She had a few more to go before Dr. Benson declared her recovered. Yet the last five or six pounds were to be gained as slowly as Priya could manage because the fear of gaining too quickly still loomed in the background of her healing mind.

On this bright sunny Wednesday afternoon Priya found herself addressing a packed assembly at Sara's high school where a variety of guests had been invited to speak on the addictions and disorders that could plague the teenage years. The program included a former alcoholic, a drug addiction counsellor, a compulsive overeater, and then Priya's heartfelt testimonial about coping with *her* illness.

While standing at the podium, Priya was relieved to see that her flamboyant sponsor, Dot, had assumed a proud position in the front row next to the guest speakers. Wearing a marine blue sundress, her skin already richly tanned, her face heavily made-up, and diamond-studded sunglasses perched on the top of her head, she beamed a high voltage smile at Priya and urged her on with her eyes.

Gabe, assuming a self-effacing but nevertheless proud stance, was more than content with his back row spot. He watched Priya with a mix of pride and tenderness as she shared her message with her audience. He was dressed smartly in gray cotton slacks and a blue short-sleeve polo shirt. He balanced a gray summer cap on one knee while listening to what Priya had to say.

She explained how she restricted her food intake as a means of coping with her parents' deaths, and walked her audience through a week-by-week, pound-by-pound epistle of her mental and physical deterioration, climaxing with the car accident that forced her to seek treatment.

"Let me tell you this," she said warmly. "There is no glamour in being seventy-nine pounds, hooked up to an I.V., your body looking as if it has been through the deprivation of famine … which, in essence, anorexia mimics. We look half-starved and pitiful, but in our skewed perception we still look fat. The idea is to recognize that developing an eating disorder has little to do with outward appearances. It might start out that way but that's just a superficial pretext. Most of us wouldn't mind losing five or ten pounds at some point in our lives, but when those five or ten morph into twenty or thirty and we were never overweight to begin with, then we are in major trouble. So please," Priya appealed to the eager young faces before her, "recognize that there is nothing wrong with aspiring to be slim as long as remaining healthy is your number one priority. You girls out there who think it's attractive, take a look at this!" Priya took out a photograph from the pocket of her dress and held it up for scrutiny. "I hadn't even reached my thinnest yet, but here I am last Christmas at a friend's place." She gestured for anyone in the front row to step forward to take the picture and pass it around the auditorium. Dot walked up to the stage and plucked it out of her hand.

"I look at that photo now and feel pain," Priya continued,

"and then the sorrow comes. How did I let myself get that way and why didn't someone just shove a burger in my mouth? Of course, in retrospect, it's easy to say that, but at the time, I wouldn't have let anyone come near me with food. I was so distressed, I would have probably thrown it at them." This last remark was met with a ripple of amusement.

"Are you happy with your appearance now?" a girl seated next to Dot inquired.

"Technically, yes," Priya admitted. "I know I'm still on the thinner side of slim, but I'll try to gain just a few more pounds because in my heart I feel I'd be less tempted to start losing again if I'm a little closer to what I weighed a year ago."

"But that's when you started losing weight?" somebody in a back row pointed out. "If you go back up to your original size, you might start to flounder again."

"I won't go all the way back to my original weight," Priya explained. "I'll fall about five pounds shy of that ... just to give myself a bit of flexibility. Besides, now I have something to help me that I didn't have a year ago."

"What is that?" a male student inquired.

"I have an amazing support team behind me," Priya explained. "Half way through my illness, a wonderful man entered my life and gave me unconditional support and encouragement. In that way, I was extremely lucky." Priya's gaze swept the audience till it rested squarely on Gabe's glowing face. "I've had an excellent team of doctors to look after me, good friends, and now a fine sponsor whom I call at all hours of the night, driving her crazy, I'm sure," she added with a chuckle.

Another wave of laughter resounded through the room as Dot partially rose in her seat and waved enthusiastically towards the stage. "She's teaching me the piano in return." The audience clapped.

"So, to gain all this weight, you could pretty well eat all the junk you want," a boy with fiery red hair observed.

"As tempting as that is," Priya smiled, "I never allow myself to go there. When I was at my lowest weight, I had a tremendous fear that everything that went into my mouth would make me fat. I decided that the only way I would allow myself to regain the weight was to do it slowly and gradually. Fortunately, I have an excellent doctor who supports my way of doing things. Unfortunately, you get many situations where people are so grossly emaciated that their lives are at stake, causing the medical establishment to force-feed them as a temporary life-saving measure. What this sometimes does is set the patient up for future anorexic behaviour. We've all read of cases where a patient was discharged after regaining an appropriate amount of weight, only to lose it all over again. The physical problem is met but not the emotional one that caused it in the first place.

"How come you were able to figure that out for yourself and most people can't?" somebody asked.

"I think," Priya chose her words carefully, "it's because I was older than average when I developed the disease. The majority of anorexic patients present symptoms in their early to mid-teens. I have age and hopefully a bit of wisdom on my side," she paused long enough for her playful words to incite the inevitable laughter that followed.

The question and answer period continued for some time. At the end of the session, Priya was treated to a hearty round of applause from teachers and students alike. As she left the podium, people clamoured up the steps of the stage to shake her hand and a few even hugged her. She stayed on to answer a few more questions until the sound of the school bell signaled a change of period. Collective groans and sighs filled the air as the students dispersed, making their way toward their last class of the day.

"You were fantastic!" Dot rushed toward her as Priya made her way toward a beaming Gabe.

"Wasn't she just amazing?" Dot continued to squeal with delight, her chunky jewelry jangling with affirmation.

"Definitely," Gabe nodded.

"Look," Dot said breathlessly as she glanced at her rhinestone-studded watch. "I have to be at a photo shoot within the hour, so I'm going to rush on. But look, you two ... what about dinner at my place on Saturday evening? Priya, I'll call later in the week with details.

"Sounds great," Gabe said.

"Well, yes..." Priya hesitated. Although she'd accepted dinner invitations throughout her recovery, the initial thought of eating with others filled her with trepidation. But, she'd learned to control the fear to some degree.

Dot gave her a quick hug. "I know where you're coming from Priya. I've been there, remember? I'll make something low calorie and healthy. Gabe, you can handle something light and low calorie, can't you?"

"Actually it wouldn't do me any harm," he patted his stomach. "We can all stand to get a little trim."

"You know what," Priya broke into a big smile, "I can't wait to have dinner at your place on Saturday. Everything will be fine."

Later, when they were walking out of the school together, Gabe turned towards Priya and gave her an unexpected embrace. "I am so proud of you," he said, drawing her into the crook of his arm.

"Thank you," she smiled at him. "But to tell you the truth, I don't think I would have come this far without your love and encouragement."

"You're the one doing all the work," he reminded. "I'm just cheering you on. That's all."

"That's a lot," Priya responded. "Let's do our Starbucks thing before you drop me back at the townhouse and head back to work," she urged.

"I knew you were going to suggest that," Gabe said slipping his arm around her shoulder. "That's fine for now, but this evening I want to take you out to dinner."

"I'd like that, Gabe," Priya smiled, though a shudder went through her when she thought back to her former diet of green tea and grapes. How had she done that? The drive was slow as they were on the cusp of rush hour traffic. Priya didn't mind as it gave her an opportunity to reflect on the last four months. Her life had changed remarkably since January. In late February, she secured a permanent part-time teaching position with an alternate day junior/senior kindergarten in a school just blocks away from her neighbourhood. Working part-time was ideal for Priya while focusing on her recovery.

Gabe had also set up a website promoting her availability to speak to schools and social groups about her condition. And Priya had enrolled in a bi-weekly night class that would go toward a diploma in oral communication and motivational speaking.

On Tuesdays and Thursdays, Priya had several students wanting to learn to play the piano. She bought books on teaching piano to adults and told her students that she would teach them to play the kind of music that made them happy. Very often, Gabe would drop in as her last student was preparing to leave. He would stay for dinner or they would go out. Either way, they were happy just being together.

"You're in a pensive mood," Gabe observed, resting his hand on Priya's knee. They were stalled at a traffic light. Road work and a minor accident three cars ahead had slowed traffic to a crawl.

"I was just thinking," she said, "that in the last six months I've come from being a directionless kindergarten teacher with full blown anorexia to a recovering anorexic with defined goals and purposes in life. Gabe, I have to place some of the credit for that on you."

"I just saw your potential and then helped point it out to you," he said modestly.

"No, dearest Gabe," she smiled at him. "You brought me out of an emotional abyss and helped me find my way. That is the greatest thing anyone ever did for me."

The light turned to green. Gabe proceeded in silence. "That's what love is," he said finally.

Acknowledgements

I'd like to thank my editor, Luciana Ricciutelli, at Inanna Publications for making the editing process so easy and enjoyable, and Paul Butler, my St. John's editor, who believed in this book, and the friends and family who encouraged me to write: like Lexie, who told me I should really "do something with that book," and Minnat, who reminds me to get writing because it's my "job."

Many thanks to the friends, family, and literary professionals who inspire me to do my best and a special thank you to my mother, Marcia "Amma," who was my very first editor, and to my two wonderful children, Leah and Tristan, for reminding me to "have faith."

Tara Nanayakkara was born in Sri Lanka and immigrated to Canada with her family when she was three. She is the author of two novels, To *Wish Upon A Rainbow* (1989) and *Picture Perfect* (2007). A professional writer for the past thirty years, her writing has appeared in the *Toronto Star, The Telegram* and *Canadian Living* magazine, among others. A mother of two, she divides her time between Toronto and St. John's, Newfoundland.